Scare
the Light
Away

Scare
the Light
Away

Vicki Delany

Poisoned Pen Press

Poisoned Pen Press
6962 E. First Ave., Ste. 103
Scottsdale, AZ 85251
www.poisonedpenpress.com
info@poisonedpenpress.com

Printed in the United States of America

For Carol May Lem
(1953-2004)
dear sister-in-law and
enthusiastic supporter of my writing

and Doug Cargo
a good brother and
an excellent unofficial publicist

Many thanks to Wendy Solway, Karen Mitchell, Julia Vryheid, and Gail Cargo, good friends, beloved mother, and unofficial editors.

Chapter 1

I stood outside the hardware store at the unmarked intersection. Not because I was curious but merely as an excuse to delay the inevitable, I had pulled into the far corner of the dusty, deserted parking lot. Reaching into the back seat, I snapped the leash onto Sampson's collar. She hadn't liked the flight in the least, but in true doggie fashion all was forgotten and forgiven and she bounced from one side of the car to the other with enthusiasm, eager for a stretch, a long satisfying pee and a good sniff.

It was three o'clock on a Saturday afternoon in early May. Surely someone should be around. After letting Sampson sniff to her heart's content, I filled her water bowl, put her back into the SUV, and walked over to the hardware store. The sign above the door still said *Fawcett's Hardware*, exactly as it had when I stood outside in the dust clutching my purse, my single suitcase and my ticket, waiting for the bus that would take me away from Hope River to a new life. But the store itself had been painted recently so that it was bright, cheerful, welcoming in a way that the old Fawcett's had never been. A row of neatly trimmed shrubs lined either side of the front door. Coming closer I could see that the door with its bright new wood and clear varnish bore a hand-printed sign: *Closed for family emergency*.

A couple of bunches of wilted carnations tied in thin red ribbons lay across the step. It was the sort of thing you increasingly see these days on roadsides, marking places of accident and death. I've never thought that rotting flowers make a very nice memorial. A greeting card missing its envelope had been tucked into the doorframe. I wasn't interested enough to read it.

Sampson's massive head hung out the window of the SUV and she started to whine, using all of her formidable powers of persuasion to lure me back into the driver's seat.

I started up the SUV and slipped a Bruce Springsteen CD into the player. I love to drive to the sounds of The Boss and as I got closer to my family home I'd need something to keep my courage up.

I pulled out onto the dirt road.

It wasn't far from the hardware store at the intersection of the highway on down the old road to my family home, but I drove slowly. You never know when you might meet an oncoming car traveling much too fast for these narrow country lanes.

Never is a long time. Much longer than it appears to a young girl standing on the cusp of womanhood and the wide world that lies beyond her front door. I hadn't driven down these roads for nearly thirty years. Since the day I stared out of the filthy, bug splattered window of the bus bound for Toronto, and swore that I would never return. A promise I have kept—until today.

All too soon, I arrived. I sat in the car for a few minutes, looking around and gathering a bit of strength. This was the same house that lived in my memories, although the paint was fresher and a different color, a nice natural gray. The trees were taller and the shrubs bushier. Masses of early-blooming crocuses flowered in neat beds under the living room window, and the tulips around the ancient white pine in the center of the yard poked the tips of their eager green heads out of the warming soil.

It had been a small house when I was growing up, and seen through my adult eyes it appeared smaller still. Tiny, nondescript, clinging to a rough patch of the Canadian Shield as if it would give up the struggle and slide across the road and into the lake given half a chance. As a child, I'd read about a village swallowed up by a mudslide—the whole town sinking downward to disappear from view forever. I'd half hoped the same thing would happen to my house.

I looked at the property with my big-city eyes, but those same eyes that dismissed the old building surveyed the grounds: thick stands of white and jack pine and maple trees as big as they could possibly grow in the temperate climate they loved. All of them strong and healthy, their thick roots burrowing into the underworld of rocks and soil, tendrils reaching for every bit of good, dark earth they could find. On the other side of the private road that ran in front of the house and continued on up the hill lay a wide panorama of blue lake. The light danced on tiny waves to reflect the yellow sun, as large and bright as in a finger painting carried proudly home from nursery school by a truly happy child.

Finally I opened the car door and climbed out. Sampson disappeared into the woods in an instant. The poor squirrels and chipmunks didn't know what was coming.

I don't know what sort of welcome I was expecting—but certainly not that I was going to be ignored.

The phone in my parents' house hadn't been answered by human or machine, so I'd left a message on my sister's voice mail with my flight information and time of arrival. Yet no one came out to greet me.

In the recesses of my mind I heard frantic barking and was aware that Sampson had found some tiny animal with which to play hunter.

A new brick walkway led from the drive to the house. I placed my feet carefully on the bricks and remembered the rhyme we would chant when we were children: *Step on a crack, break your mother's back.* Did the rhyme apply to brick? Probably not. But no need to worry now, my mother's back was beyond breaking. Terracotta pots lined the pathway, standing abandoned in the spring sunshine with only a few cracked, dead, brown branches stretching up out of the dry soil as if reaching for a last desperate chance at life.

A deck had been added to the front of the building, a wide wrap-around deck made of blond wood and Plexiglas siding. It was lovely, but this early in the year it stood empty. No deck chairs or sun umbrellas or low tables or pitchers of colorful cocktails or glass bowls full of peanuts and pretzels.

I brushed a touch of moisture from my eye. Spray off of the lake, perhaps, although it was not a windy day.

"Becky." The voice cracked with age.

My father stood by the open door, unmistakable even after the wear of thirty long years. Of course his jet-black hair was now solid gray, his handsome face sunken and lined, his body stooped with age. His blue eyes burned with more intensity than I remembered.

"Becky. You're here."

"Yes, Dad. I'm here. Didn't Shirley tell you to expect me?"

"Don't think so. But I'm glad, so glad, that you're here."

We looked at each other for a few seconds. I simply didn't know whether or not to hug him. The moment passed as Sampson burst out of the undergrowth and bounded up the steps of the deck. She bared her formidable teeth and the hairs on the back of her neck rose in a stiff row.

"Sampson. Stop it. Back off." I snapped my fingers and growled low in my own throat. She sunk to her quivering haunches and slithered back down the steps to stand at my side.

"Sorry about that," I said to my father. "This is Sampson. She'll be friendly once she gets to know you."

He almost smiled. Almost, but not quite. "No need to apologize, Becky. It feels rather nice—been a long time since anything or anyone considered me to be a threat. But you must have luggage, let me help you bring it in. You can have your old room. Won't take me a minute to make it up."

"My name is Rebecca, Dad. No one calls me Becky anymore." I walked up the steps, my heart pounding in my chest. Sampson sniffed at my father's outstretched hand and wagged her bushy tail in friendship.

"You didn't know I was coming?"

"No."

"I called Shirley, left a message."

"Maybe she told Jimmy and he forgot to tell me."

"Sounds like Jimmy."

"Why's your dog got a boy's name? If it's a female?"

"Ray named her. I don't remember why."

"Real sorry to hear about his death."

"Thanks, Dad."

I shouldn't have been surprised that my family home had changed. But I was. The furniture was not only more modern, but nicer, more expensive than the junk sale rejects that filled it in my childhood. A giant-screen TV and facing leather lounge chair dominated the room. The formerly dark, pokey kitchen was bigger and full of light. The back wall had been pushed out a few feet and wide windows installed. The wallpaper was bright and cheerful, the new backsplash crisp and white. But the same old fridge and stove. Avocado green.

"You made some changes," I said. "Looks nice."

"But we've kept your room the same."

If I hadn't taken a firm hold of Sampson's collar and held her close I would have fainted as my father pushed open the door and stood back to let me go first. For the room was the same, the very same. As if they'd kept it as a shrine to me all these years. The few ribbons I'd won in track and field at school were still pinned to the corkboard. My academic awards, now tattered and fading to yellow in cheap frames. The posters of rock and roll bands whose names I could no longer remember.

Sampson whimpered and nuzzled my thigh. She had been Ray's dog, no doubt about that. But when he died, she and I (the human full of rage, the dog merely grief-stricken) sought solace in each other and she was now attuned to my every emotion.

I dug my fingers into her thick ruff. "Jesus, Dad."

"You must want to wash up after your long trip. Is your luggage in your car? I'll bring it in."

"I can't stay here, Dad," I said. "I'll take a room at a motel or something. I passed a place on the highway, not far back."

"A motel? You can't, Becky, ah, Rebecca. Goodness. I can't expect my daughter to stay in a motel."

"I'd rather not sleep in this room, Dad. Maybe I shouldn't have come."

"You can have our old room—what was your mother's and mine."

"I can't kick you out of your own bed."

He laughed. My dad's laugh was always the best—deep and hearty and full of fun. If only we children had heard it more. "It's not my bed any longer. We expanded Jimmy's old room years ago. When we put on the addition at the back. Your mom and I bought a big new bed and moved in there. I haven't slept in the front room in years. Your mother calls it the guest room."

"I don't know. I don't want to impose..."

"Rebecca. You're my daughter. It's no imposition. I'm glad you're here." He looked at me, wide-eyed, asking me to stay.

Sampson whimpered and wiggled out of my grip. "Okay, Dad. I'll take the room."

He beamed.

Together we went to get my things out of the car. Human tensions passed, for now, Sampson scurried around the property, trying her best to sniff every bush and every tree, stopping now and again to pee at a spot of particular interest. Dad exclaimed over the size of the vehicle while I pulled out my single traveling bag. I fly a great deal on business, and if I have managed to accumulate one skill in this life, it's that of avoiding the perils of checked luggage by packing light.

"Where's... Mom?" I asked, choking on the words.

"Watson's."

"The place in North Ridge? Are they still in business?"

"Old man Watson's grandson took over when he retired. People round here trust what they know."

"I stopped at Fawcett's on the way up. To give the dog a stretch. Does the family still own the store?"

"Nope. Bought by the Taylor family." He clicked his tongue against his teeth and made a tisk-tisk sort of sound. "Terrible business that Taylor girl."

I wasn't the least bit interested in the juvenile antics of the daughter of some small town hardware store owner.

But I should have been.

Chapter 2

The Diary of Miss Janet Green. July 17, 1943

Today, I met HIM. HE is the most wonderful, perfect, handsomest, smartest man in the entire world. I am IN LOVE. Is it mere happenstance that only last week I received this diary from Aunt Joan for my 17th birthday? It can't be. I am sure that I was meant to start the rest of my life in the pages of this very book.

I went with Jenny; she practically had to drag me there. To the dance they put on in Woking for the Canadians. I had nothing at all suitable to wear. Aunt Betty fussed; she even dragged out one of her old hats for me. Horrid thing. I'm sure she has owned it since the <u>last</u> war. I stuffed it inside the Robinsons' hedge and fetched it again on my way home. I didn't want to go to the dance. I always feel so awkward and uncomfortable—so <u>tall</u>—at those things: all the girls lined up against one wall, drinking tea or lemonade, the soldiers watching us, most of them as shy as we are, some of them nipping outside regularly for something stronger than lemonade. Everything made worse of course, by the simple fact that Jenny, of the long golden hair, the huge green eyes and figure I once heard called 'ripe' was the prettiest girl within twenty miles.

I might not have gone had Jenny not begged me. She might be pretty, but even she couldn't go to a dance alone. And poor Mary Jones is confined to bed with the flu.

I might not have gone!!!!! It doesn't bear thinking about.

I promise that I will write in this diary as often as I can for the rest of my life.

Wednesday, August 4, 1943

Bob called on us today. He came for tea and to meet Aunt Betty and Dad. Dad even closed up the shop for a while so as to be home at tea time.

Nancy Young, who always helped out at the shop, has turned 18 and it's time for her to be conscripted. Her mother wanted her to join the Women's Land Army and stay close to home, but she didn't want to do that (neither would I, if I had HER mother!) so she went up to London for a factory job, Dad said. I heard him tell Aunt Betty later, when they didn't know I was listening, that to his mind Nancy was looking for trouble. Mary Black joined the Land Army. She's gone off to Yorkshire to work on a farm. I will have to do something when I turn 18, although they might let me stay on at the factory if they think that what Barnum and Son is making is important for the war effort. I'm just the junior secretary, but only last week Mrs. Bradley told Mr. Barnum what a big help I am. I have been thinking I might like to join the Land Army too. It must be a lot more fun than stodgy old Barnum and Son and it's important work. Very important, Mary told me. If we all starve then the Germans can take over England without firing a shot.

But now I don't want to go. I want to stay here with Dad. Near Bob.

Aunt Betty did a nice bit of a cake with some of the sugar rations she's been saving up. There were only a few tiny currants, but it was so nice to have a proper cake. Bob ate every bit on his plate and then accepted more when Aunt Betty offered.

He is so wonderfully handsome. I love his accent. It's ever so smart and sophisticated. He told Dad and Aunt Betty all about his family farm in Ontario (it sounds just huge, with lots of cattle and miles and miles of wheat fields). Dad enjoyed having him here. They went for a walk out to the yard after tea with their cigarettes and to look at the coop Dad built for the chickens Aunt Betty has taken to raising for the eggs. It must be so nice for Dad, to have a young man to talk to, again.

And it's so nice for me!!!! Bob asked me if I would go with him to the dance next Saturday. I pretended to think very hard as if I had something else planned. Then of course, I said 'Yes'. It will be wonderful. He is so handsome, and it isn't just the uniform either. He is much more handsome than any of the other soldiers that were at the dance, or the ones that I see around the village. I only wish he wasn't quite so short. The man should always be the taller in any couple. But at least he's strong. He looks to be very big underneath his uniform shirt. That makes him look taller, so it's perfectly all right.

Chapter 3

"You're back."

"Indeed I am."

My sister blocked the entrance to her house, hands resting firmly on her flat, bony hips. Her bitter, pinched face was as familiar to me as if I'd last seen it this morning. But the combined effects of weather and hard work had beaten the skin into leather, and the brittle brown eyes were collapsing into bags on her cheeks. Her hair was the same shade of fake blond as always, but the lush, thick locks were now only a memory, and patches of pink scalp shone through the thin, bleached hair.

Underneath the stiffly ironed apron, she wore a proper suit with pantyhose and pumps. A tiny string of cheap, fake pearls was wrapped around her crepe-paper neck. She was eleven years older than I.

"Why didn't you tell Dad I was coming?"

"I did. He must have forgotten."

"Right."

I was afraid I was going to have to push her aside and elbow my way into her house, but then my father bustled up, brimming with platitudes about how wonderful to have his two daughters together again, and Shirley stepped aside to allow me entry.

I hadn't been to this house before. It wasn't the hovel she and Al lived in when they had finally moved out of his parents' place, but a neat, although tiny, modern bungalow not far from the center of Hope River.

The screen door leading off the living room opened and Al stepped through, carrying a vicious-looking barbecue fork. The scent of burning flesh drifted in behind him. He smiled broadly and wrapped me in a fierce hug.

"Rebecca. Look at you now. Still the beauty of the family after all these years. Doesn't she look great, Shirl? Just great."

"I'll finish setting the table," my sister said.

"It's nice to see you, Al."

In our youth he'd been painfully thin and cursed with the greasiest hair any of us had ever seen. Everyone knows an Al Smithers. So nerdy that even the mention of his last name would instantly have the "in" crowd in giggles. Every small town has a loser, and Al personified it for Hope River. But nerdy Al Smithers managed to knock up my sister (not that a McKenzie amounted to any great catch), and thus here he was, all these years later, the scrawny frame replaced by a substantial beer belly, bowing and scraping in his tiny living room.

"Let me get you a drink? What'll you have?"

"A glass of white wine?"

"Sure, sure. And a beer for you, Bob?"

We settled into sagging chairs while Al fetched the drinks.

"To family." My dad offered a toast. Mom had told me that Dad now had "control over" his drinking. I could slap Al for offering him a beer. But it wasn't my business—I was only here for a couple of days, and then I'd be well out of it.

Al and I nodded and raised our glasses. "To family," he said. I swallowed heavily.

"Our first barbecue of the year," Al announced proudly, hurrying back to attend to his duties. "With the weather being so nice after all that rain we've been having."

Living on the West Coast, making rivers of money and having no children, my husband Ray and I had become accustomed to eating only the freshest of foods usually prepared in one of the city's best restaurants. I have become quite the "foodie." So much so that I had forgotten what bad food tasted like. Al's steak was thin, cooked to the consistency of shoe leather, and drowned in commercial barbecue sauce, the potato salad slimy with bottled mayonnaise. Shirley stared sullenly into her lap, merely pushing her food around her plate although Al chowed down enough for the both of them. I forced myself to keep on eating although the food stuck in my throat. Dad babbled on as cheerfully as he always did, even in far tenser situations than this.

But one thing was certainly different from the old days: Although Al offered another round, Dad refused and made that one drink last right through the meal.

And my mother was missing. Her calm, caring presence wasn't here to cast a loving blanket over the troubled undercurrents.

But no torment lasts forever and dinner finally ended.

To make way for the worst torment of them all.

We traveled together in the SUV. It being the largest, by far, and Dad eager as a schoolboy to show it off. He was a strange man, my father. As a child and then a teenager I never knew whether he really didn't understand the hurricanes of emotion that were constantly rolling through his family or whether he simply didn't care. Here he was leading us all out the door, chattering on about the speed and horsepower of my rental. What Dad doesn't know, he makes up.

Watson's had undergone quite a transformation since I'd seen it last. Perfect rows of carefully pruned tea roses were stirring themselves back to life, and crisply pruned hedges lined the neat brick path. Not only Watson's, but the entire downtown of North Ridge, the larger town to the north of our own Hope River, was light-years from the town I left so long ago. Someone, or something, had brought money into this once almost abandoned Near-North Ontario town.

A smiling woman in a severe gray, pinstriped suit, long dark hair pulled back into a skin-stretching bun, stood at the door to greet us. "This way, please," she said, her young voice forced into deep and somber tones. "I am so sorry for your loss."

I followed my family into Watson's Funeral Home.

Chapter 4

Diary of Miss Janet Green. January 14, 1944

Mrs. Robert McKenzie. Mrs. Robert McKenzie. That sounds so perfectly wonderful. Last night we went to a dance in town with Bob's best mate Charlie and Charlie's date Louise, who is Mrs. Bridges' niece, come up from London to stay with her grandparents for the duration of the war. It's safer, they say, out here in the countryside. Charlie and Bob were walking us to the bus when Bob took my arm and we dropped back a bit. Then he asked me if I would marry him. I said "Yes" so loudly, I was sure that the whole of Surrey would hear me. I am to be married! Mrs. Robert McKenzie. I can't wait to tell Dad and Aunt Betty. She has gone to London for a fortnight's visit to her and Dad's sister Joan, who got word that her second son, Raymond, has been killed in Italy. And that after losing her Arthur, named in honor of my own dad, in North Africa last year. Two of my cousins, gone. I remember when we traveled on the train to London that Christmas before Mum left. They were horrid boys, Raymond and Arthur. I cried and told Mum and Dad I wanted to go home. Mum hit me and told me I was a foolish girl and I would never get a husband if I didn't learn how to be nice to boys. Things have changed so quickly. Is it the war, I wonder? Or do things always change? Must be the war. Dad has lived in this village for his whole life, and his parents before him. Aunt Betty escaped for a while. She went up to London. I was only little then, but I remember Granny saying she would never speak to Betty again. And she never did.

Granny died the next winter—as if the devil was getting back at her for making such an evil promise. But Aunt Betty came back, and now she keeps house for my dad and me.

What was I saying? Oh yes. I'm not that plain little girl any more. I'm seventeen years old and engaged to be married and Raymond and Arthur are dead. I wish I could tell Mum, tell her I am going to be married.

I told Bob that I don't want to tell Dad before Aunt Betty. So we will wait until next Tuesday, when she comes home. They will be so happy for me! In the meanwhile Bob will start whatever it is that he has to do to get us married. It is such a dreadfully complicated process. I would love to just skip down to the rectory one sunny Sunday and ask the Vicar to marry us. But Bob has to fill out all sorts of papers, and talk to his commanding officer, who I hear is a perfectly horrid brute. Bob said he might even want to meet me before he gives us permission. I hope not! I would be simply terrified!

I want to get married today!

Chapter 5

"Reverend Wyatt's come home a day early from his conference to take the funeral," my father said, slathering strawberry jam onto his toast. "We coulda had the visiting Reverend, but your mom, she and Mr. Wyatt were real close these past few years. He knows she'd want him to be there."

I poured hot water into the old brown betty. The handle was cracked, the lid broken into several pieces and badly glued back together. It wasn't one of the procession of traditional brown teapots I remembered from my youth, but it seemed like an old friend nonetheless. My mom, English to her core, loved her teapots. Earlier, scrounging through the unfamiliar cupboards searching for breakfast ingredients and utensils, I had uncovered the gift I sent her for her birthday a few years ago: a replica of an English cottage, cast in the mould of a teapot. Unwrapped, it lay abandoned in the dark recesses of the cupboard. In other circumstances my feelings might have been hurt, but they weren't. I should have known that she would discard it as a modern frivolity. I smiled as I imagined her steeping her afternoon cup of tea in the chipped brown betty while she contemplated what she would do with this monstrosity of a gift.

If she had known I was coming, it would have been laid out in pride of place.

I haven't eaten bacon and fried eggs for more years than I can count, but there was no granola, yogurt, or even bagels in my mother's kitchen. I like a big breakfast, so along with Dad's meal I prepared a serving for myself. I tentatively lifted a slice of crispy bacon to my lips, telling my inner diet cop to ignore the fat and calorie content. It tasted rather good. I took another bite.

"I'm so glad you're home, Rebecca." Dad smiled at me through a mouthful of fried egg. "I trust you can stay a while."

"I've taken time off work, Dad." An extended leave of absence, in fact. After the hours I'd put in since Ray's death, they owed me something. (Of course, I'd left my father's phone number with my secretary and brought my laptop computer so that I could dial into the office every day.)

"Good." He turned his attention to his breakfast, scooping up a bit of runny egg yolk with a thin slice of toast. What my mother called a "soldier." Sampson thumped her tail on the floor and watched the food with wide eyes.

"Always liked a cup of coffee in the morning," he said finally, placing his knife and fork neatly in the center of the scraped-clean plate. "When I was a young man. But your mother wouldn't hear of it. Insisted on making tea. Every day of her life, 'cepting when she were in hospital having you kids."

"You could have made your own coffee."

He looked genuinely astonished. "Now why would I have done that?"

I shrugged and tossed Sampson a piece of toast. She would have preferred bacon, but she accepted the toast with an air of offended grace.

"She didn't much cling to her English ways, your mom. She tried to fit in real well to how we do things here. But she wouldn't give up that tea." His old eyes clouded over with sorrow. I walked over to him and placed one hand on his shoulder. It was all I had in me to give him.

He gripped my hand with his own, worn by work and lined by age. "Don't know how I'm gonna manage without her, girl."

"I know, Dad. I know. I'll make coffee tomorrow. More bacon?"

"Don't mind if I do." Embarrassed, he rubbed his hand across his eyes, trying to wipe away the traces of emotion. My dad had certainly not been raised to show his feelings. Exactly the opposite. "Too bad Jimmy didn't make it to Watson's last night. He should be by this morning."

I sat back down and the cracked vinyl squeaked under my weight. I stirred milk into my tea. "Where's Jimmy living?"

"In the big house."

"Mom didn't tell me that. I assumed you sold it years ago. It's bigger than this place. If you didn't sell it, why didn't you move in there when Grandpa died?"

"Not mine to sell. Dad left it to Jimmy."

"And you didn't object to that?"

"Nothing to object to, girl. It was his home. He could do with it as he wanted."

"Even after he's dead?"

"Specially then."

We finished our breakfast, the silence broken only by the patter of Sampson's toenails on the linoleum and the thumping of her tail as she snuggled up to her new friend's legs.

"Got any plans for today?" I rose to clear the table.

"Thought I'd drop in at the Legion after lunch. Play a bit of snooker."

"Okay. I have some work to do. Do you mind if I plug my computer into the phone line in the living room?"

"Sure," Dad said. "You got that Internet on your computer?"

"Yes."

"Can you show me how it works sometime?"

"You've never been on the Internet?" In my world that was like saying you'd never driven in a car, nor seen a television.

"Woulda liked to give it a try. But your mom, she said we didn't need it."

"That's too bad. She could have kept in touch with some of her family in England or her old war bride friends. E-mail makes it so easy."

"She didn't want much to do with any outsiders," Dad mumbled. "Said we were her family now."

Too ashamed, more likely. I bit back the words. I hadn't come here to fight ancient battles.

He pulled his cap down from the hook by the back door. "Going for a walk. Up to the big house. Talk to Jimmy. You wanna come?"

"No."

"Your dog would like a walk."

Sampson was already in position in front of the door, her expressive brown eyes wide and expectant, a happy smile on her face. It would take a bulldozer to move her out of the way.

"Take the leash, but you won't need it. She'll be good."

"Maybe we can have Shirley and Al, Jimmy and Aileen over for dinner tomorrow?"

I stared at him.

"Give Shirley a treat. Not to have to cook after work. You and Jimmy can have a visit."

"Shirley has to work? The day before her mother's funeral?" I was horrified.

His turn to stare, as he might at a creature from another planet. As perhaps I'd become. I certainly hoped so: I'd spent thirty years trying to. "Don't work, she don't get paid. It's been hard for them, with Al out of work all this winter."

"Oh, all right. Do I have to cook?"

"If'n you don't want peanut butter on toast."

I finished loading the breakfast dishes into the dishwasher and tidied up the kitchen. My dad was going to have a very hard time indeed coping without my mother. I'd never seen him wash a dish or boil an egg in his life. Apparently nothing much had changed while I was away, if peanut butter on toast made up the extent of his culinary repertoire. He'd probably end up moving in with Shirley and Al. They must have the room, now that their daughters were long married and out of the house. Poor Shirley.

Poor Dad.

I quickly cleared space on the coffee table in the living room to make room for my computer and papers. My parents had modernized the house nicely, but they hadn't stretched quite as far as a CD player. The music center consisted of a tape deck and that relic of a bygone era, a turntable. I popped the Indigo Girls into my Discman and settled the headphones over my ears. A copy of the local newspaper, still the *Gazette*, several days old, caught my eye. I settled back to read and listen to the music while the laptop booted up and dialed my company's Internet connection. Poor Shirley, going to work tomorrow—the day before her mother's funeral. But on the other hand Shirley wasn't spending her Sunday morning dialing into the office to pick up whatever mail had accumulated since Friday afternoon.

Old economy versus new economy.

Pick your poison.

The paper lay open to the sports page. The senior baseball team of Wilfred Laurier High School, my *alma mater*, had been thoroughly trounced by the team from North Bay. It was a good while later, after getting through all my e-mail, that I finally flipped to the front page. A girl, pretty in a generic, modern teenage way, stared out at me from what could be nothing other than her school photo. A breathless, screaming headline reported STILL NO TRACE OF JENNIFER. SEARCH CONTINUES.

Jennifer Taylor, a grade twelve student at the same school as the losing baseball team, had not been seen since leaving the house of a friend last Thursday evening. The friend had stood on the front porch watching as Jennifer took a shortcut through the woods for home. She was described as last seen wearing a blue wool coat with matching cap and scarf. In Vancouver I wouldn't have given the article more than a cursory glance. Common enough, unfortunately. But up here, in small-town Ontario? I stared into her eyes, reduced to no more than dots of black and white in the poor photograph, and then read on. There was no sign that the girl had run away. The paper described her as a good student who never gave her parents "a minute of trouble." The friend didn't notice anything amiss with Jennifer that day, and the girl gave no indication of being unhappy at home or school. That meant nothing—what do friends know? Or teachers? Of what really goes on in families? And certainly not police officers, nor newspaper reporters. How could they know to what lengths a young girl would go to hide the depth of her pain? I looked at Jennifer's eyes one more time, as if I could find a clue hidden in the grainy newspaper photograph. Not that she would tell me anything, had she anything to tell. I was an adult now. One of "them."

Sampson barked once at the back door, and my father's heavy footsteps sounded on the wooden stairs. I slipped the paper under a pile of sports magazines, shut down the Internet connection, and removed the headphones.

"Get down, Sampson. You're a mess." I leapt up to hustle the mud-encrusted dog back into the kitchen. "Wipe her paws off with a towel, Dad, before letting her in. Look at the mess she's made."

"Nothing but a bit of mud." He pulled his own rubber boots off and placed them neatly on the back step. "Won't hurt nothing."

Not if you don't have to clean it up.

Sampson sat politely and offered one paw after another for attention. "Have a nice walk?" I asked.

"Yup. Good dog you got there. Smart."

"She gets it from me."

"Eh?"

"Never mind."

"Really muddy out there. Lots of rain this past week. Warm. Must be this global warming I been hearing about. If it gives us summer sooner, I say bring it on."

"Do you want something for lunch?"

"No thanks. Ate lunch at the big house. Aileen says she and Jimmy'll be happy to come for supper tomorrow."

"Was Jimmy there?"

"Nope. Just Aileen. Jimmy was off at work."

"That must make a change."

For once he picked up on my tone and looked at me sharply. "Jimmy's doing well these days, Becky. He made a few mistakes when he was young but he's had a hard life."

I turned my attention to my dog and gave the thick fur under her chin an extra deep rubbing. "And maybe he's just plain lazy."

"Now Becky, that's no way to talk about your brother." He changed the subject; my dad was always good at changing the subject. "Aileen phoned Shirley about dinner tomorrow. They're going to come, and she'll ask the girls. It would be nice if we could all get together."

Yeah, swell.

"I'm going to the Legion now. Play a bit of snooker, hang out with the boys. I'll take the car. Too far to walk into town on these old bones." He stretched up on tiptoe and kissed me on the cheek. "It's nice having you here, Rebecca. I'll be back in time for dinner."

My dad was shorter than Mom, something they were always embarrassed about, although they pretended not to be. My grandpa had been even shorter than his son and when feeling particularly mean he usually had something to say about Mom's height. And then he would throw in a dig at my dad, something along the lines of not looking like he wore the pants in his family. Which was sort of funny, as the old man made sure that my dad didn't wear the proverbial pants. Shirley and Jimmy took after Dad, short and scrawny. I'm a tall woman, like my mother. Tall and thin. Thin but filled out in all the right places. Lucky in the gene pool, me. Just another reason for my sister to resent me.

I remembered when I was twelve years old, sprouting like one of the beans in my mother's garden in springtime, and deeply embarrassed about it. Already taller than my older sister and gaining on my brother, eight years my senior. I towered over my grandparents. And to make matters worse, my chest had been swelling with matching speed. I tried to hide it with baggy sweaters and stooped posture, hard in a mid-summer heat spell. My brother (twenty years old!) had taken to hiding behind doorways and leaping out to grab a handful whenever Mom wasn't looking.

My mother didn't often leave me alone at my grandparents'. Practically never. In her own quiet way she tried to protect me from the venom from which she couldn't protect herself. I don't know why I was there that day, with her not around to deflect the verbal blows onto her own shoulders.

My grandmother had smiled vacantly and bustled off into the kitchen for lemonade and cookies. Grandma always bustled. She also spent a lot of time in the kitchen.

I made to follow, but my brother Jimmy blocked my way. And then he grabbed my shirt and pulled it up, twirling me around at the same time so I faced the hated old man. Grandpa chuckled. I still dream about that chuckle.

I swallowed hard and hugged Sampson. She whimpered and I rubbed her ruff. "Wish I had you then, dog. No one would have messed with me if you'd been around." She licked my face, at the tears that I refused to shed. I had cried the day I left home, and I vowed that I would never cry again. And I hadn't. Not until I stood over Ray's coffin, when it seemed that the tears would never stop. On that day I gave myself permission to cry for Ray and all that we had lost.

"You and me and Ray, eh?" I smiled at Sampson. "What a team we were. God, I miss him. I need him to get me through this."

She barked once in agreement.

Dad had said that he would be back for dinner. Presumably that meant he didn't plan on preparing the meal himself. Thus the only one left appeared to be me. Ray always said that the best thing I made in the kitchen was reservations. But he was a great cook, and I'm pretty smart, if I do say so myself. I must have learned something by watching him.

I opened the door of the avocado-colored fridge. The only food in sight was milk, eggs, and bacon, along with a scrap end of butter and a shelf full of jars of preserves. That seemed odd; I would have expected that all the ladies of the town had descended on Dad bearing fragrant casseroles and homemade pies. Nothing for it but I'd have to go shopping.

"Car ride." I said the magic words and Sampson leapt up to bounce eagerly at the back door.

I hadn't been taught to drive as a girl. If Dad or Grandpa weren't using it, the family car was reserved for Jimmy. Jimmy would take me, they told me, wherever I had to go. Which meant that I went nowhere, except to school and back on the big yellow bus that picked me up at the end of the road.

I revved the engine of the SUV to feel its power throbbing under my feet.

At the top of the driveway, I impulsively swung the car right, instead of turning left to the public road. A lead weight settled into my stomach as we drove down the private road that ran parallel to the lake and up a small hill. In my youth it was always pitted badly in the spring, the effect of ice and snow. Dad and Jimmy were always filling it in and trying to level it off. Since then it had been paved. A more comfortable drive, but the butterflies fluttered in my stomach as if there was a hurricane going on in there.

There it sat. The old farmhouse. Solid gray stone, thick, sturdy and unyielding. Like the people who had lived in it. The house we always called the big house. (My parents' house was, of course, the little house.) Built for huge families with farm hands to feed and work to do around the clock and through the seasons. In this country of rock and dense bush it was one of the few farmhouses around. It had once sat on one of the few decent patches of farmland for miles in any direction. My family sold the property after World War One, keeping only enough land on which to build a smaller house. And it was there that my grandparents lived when their only son came home from the war with his English wife and baby. But they made some money, somehow, shortly after I was born. Enough to buy the big farmhouse back, and my grandparents moved into it. They didn't buy the farmland, though, and now most of the surrounding land was owned by the government.

I pulled to a stop near the top of the hill. On this perfect spring day the yellow sun hung in the sky full of the promise of summer soon to come. The house was perfectly located, high over the lake with its blue waters sparkling in the sunshine. A modern deck of good wood and glass wrapped around the front, looking as out of place as if Mrs. Rochester were to descend from the attic dressed in low-rise jeans and a crop top.

I stared at the house. To me, hell was this house. It had loomed in my imagination as such for more than thirty years. But I sensed no whiff of brimstone in the air. No cauldrons boiling in the kitchen, no thunder or lightning overhead, no screams emanating from the dungeon—only the sparkle of the spring sunshine and the heady scent of good lake water and freshly turned garden earth.

A woman came around the corner of the house just as I was about to put the car into reverse and back down the hill. She carried a basket of gardening tools and waved cheerfully at me. I could do nothing but wait while she walked along the driveway and up to the car.

She was middle aged, dressed in a lovely flowing dress containing all the colors of the rainbow. She wore thick Birkenstocks on her feet, and strands of gray streaked through her abundant black hair. Wild curls were pulled, without much success, into a casual knot at the back of her head. She rounded the front of the SUV and approached the driver's door, hand held out in greeting.

"You can only be Rebecca. Welcome. What a lovely dog. Can I pat him?"

"Her. She won't bite." Of all the types of people I expected to encounter at this house of bad memories, she was just about the last.

Of course in the old stories, horrid monsters can, and often do, disguise themselves as lovely maidens. But in the same old stories, dogs always see beneath the pretence, yet Sampson appeared to be experiencing something like love at first sight.

"I'm Aileen. Aileen O'Connor. I was going around back to pick a few of the early flowers to take down to the house to welcome you. But you're ahead of me." She smiled. A lovely, warm smile full of good teeth and welcome. Her brown eyes reflected the smile.

Aileen. My mother told me that Jimmy had married for the fourth time. I paid as much attention as I had on the other three occasions.

"I must apologize for not being here last night to go to the funeral home with you and Bob. But my mother is in a nursing home and they called to say that she was having a bad spell. Jim and I thought we should be there. We knew we'd see you today. Heavens, where are my manners! Please don't sit there in the car. Come on in. I have tea, or something a bit stronger if you would prefer. I do believe the sun is over the yardarm."

I turned into the driveway, switched off the engine and clambered out. Sampson sniffed once at Aileen in order to be polite, and then dashed off to explore.

"I've never really known what a yardarm is," Jimmy's wife said. "But I'd just as soon not find out. Ignorance is sometimes bliss. That way the sun is always over it, right?"

"Uh. Right."

I hesitated at the bottom of the steps leading to the deck, but Aileen scurried on ahead, still talking. The deck didn't suit the age or the dignity of the house, but I, who knew that beneath its façade this house didn't have a shred of dignity, thought the effect was perfect. Wide and open to the elements of water and wood and sky, this deck would conceal no secrets.

Aileen looked back. "Why don't we have our drinks out here? It's a lovely day. I'll pull the seat covers out of storage. Would you like a glass of wine? White or red?"

"White, please." I sank onto an uncushioned lounge chair. Someday I might venture into this house. But not today.

Since Ray's death, I'd grown accustomed to Sampson being in tune with me. If I was unhappy, she was unhappy. If I was euphoric, which was exceedingly rare, she was euphoric. But today she didn't match my mood in the slightest. She charged back from the woods, burrs clinging to her tail and belly, and danced about the deck, ears up and tail swishing, sniffing at the empty flowerpots, and chasing a renegade squirrel that dared to venture too close to the stairs.

Aileen reappeared carrying a tray on which sat two acrylic glasses and a bottle of white wine along with a selection of cheeses and crackers. Two padded chair-cushions were tucked under one arm in a neat balancing act.

"You shouldn't have gone to this trouble." The standard phrase sat dry in my throat.

"No trouble at all. I'm happy to take a bit of a break."

"You're Jimmy's wife?" I said, sounding even to my own ears like the village idiot.

She laughed and poured the wine. "I've heard so much about you. From your mother. The dear woman. She was so proud of you, you know. Talked about you all the time."

"Nice wine," I said. And surprisingly it was.

"I know that Jim was a bit of a wild one in his youth. But I hope I've tamed him a bit. You'll find him changed. At least I hope so." She laughed again and popped a slice of Brie into her generous mouth.

I didn't want to admit that I didn't remember a thing my mother had told me about her, like where she came from and how long she'd been with my brother. Which left precious little for me to say. Fortunately Aileen seemed to be able to fill any uncomfortable silence.

"Thank you for the wine. It was lovely," I said when I could actually get a word in. "But I have to go into town. Dad expects dinner. Are the stores open, do you know?"

"The supermarket in Hope River is open on Sunday afternoons, yes. That's closer than driving to North Ridge. Even this town has finally joined the twentieth century. Just in time for the twenty-first. Can I bring anything tomorrow?"

"No, please don't."

Sampson and I managed to make our escape, backing along the drive with much tooting of the horn and waving. I liked Aileen and looked forward to spending more time with her. Was it possible that she was actually married to my degenerate of a brother?

Chapter 6

The town of Hope River hadn't changed much. The supermarket was bigger and a restaurant stood on the site of the old lumberyard, where my dad had found work, on and off, when he was temporarily off the bottle. There was a tiny antique shop, a gas station and a hamburger stand, a T-shirt emporium, and a craft shop, all of which, except for the gas station, were closed. A sign in the window of the hamburger stand announced that they were closed for the season. A new two-story professional building appeared to house only a real estate office and the government-owned liquor store, which was a great deal larger than it had been in my youth and was much spruced up. Sign of the times, that. The Royal Canadian Legion, of course, looked exactly as I remembered it. As if it had stood there since time immemorial. Which for me, it had.

I parked in front of the professional building and told Sampson to stay. She curled up in the back seat and promptly fell asleep. Neat skill, I've always thought.

I walked up the street, heading out of town, letting the memories wash over me. Past the end of the business district—an extreme exaggeration—a tiny bridge crossed a tiny river. This was the Hope River, a tributary of one of the many larger rivers that criss-cross this area that is almost as much water as land. Hope for whom, I never knew. "Hopeless" we called it when I was a kid, as probably every child who ever grew up here called it. Every one of us certain that we were being terribly witty and original.

Hope River has always been nothing but a working class town in an area without much in the way of work at the best of times. And no work at all in the worst of times. Past the bridge, one street curved along the lazy bend of the river. A handful of Victorian era stone houses with double stories, crisp gingerbread trim, substantial lots, and huge gnarled old trees lined the gentle slopes leading down to the riverbank. It was a nice day. The sun felt warm on my back.

Today, in the early part of the twenty-first century, the town's hopes for economic salvation are pinned on waiting for the urban creep of cottage country. Hoping to be the next Bala or Port Carling. Waiting for big cottages, big wallets stuffed with big bucks to spend. Still waiting.

The trees lining the street were deciduous, bare at this time of year, but showing off their first hint of buds, like proud prospective mothers with barely bulging bellies. In autumn the street would be a glorious display of northern color.

But I didn't intend to be here to see it.

I went to the supermarket.

Today's copy of the *Gazette* was prominently displayed. A different picture of Jennifer. The headline screamed: SEARCH CONTINUES. POLICE: ARREST IMMINENT.

I ignored the paper and went in search of something to cook for dinner. I would pick up something to serve the family tomorrow as well as for Dad and me tonight. You can always fake it with chicken. Dessert would be a bit tricky: you can't disguise packaged desserts as homemade. I settled for an angel food cake wrapped in plastic, strawberries, and whipped cream. Add real whipped cream to anything and people will think you spent all day working on it. Tonight we'd have spaghetti, which was one of the few things my mom taught me to make that I could still remember.

I unloaded my groceries and tossed in a chocolate bar and a copy of the *Globe and Mail,* which calls itself Canada's national newspaper.

"Becky McKenzie." The clerk placed her hands on her ample hips and stared at me. She was considerably overweight, verging on obese but not quite there yet, and hawk-beaked with far too much makeup and a bad perm. One of Shirley's friends?

"Yes. That's me." I forced a smile. "Back home again."

"Don't you remember me? Kim Wright, I was then."

"Oh, my god. Kimmy. Of course I remember you." This was cute little Kimmy? The envy of every girl and the desire of every boy at Wilfred Laurier High? The Kimmy Wright who reduced even my brother to a slobbering fool? How I had wanted to be allowed access to her sacred circle, but I had been rebuffed at every pathetic attempt.

She smiled, showing stained teeth. Several were missing from the back of the bottom row. "Been a long time, Becky."

"It has. But I'm called Rebecca now."

She started checking through the groceries. "Rebecca. I'm sorry about your mom."

"Thank you."

"Heard you live in Vancouver. You're an executive with a bank, your mom said. I've heard it's nice in Vancouver."

"It is. Uh, what are you doing these days?" Stupid question. The pride of W.L. High was checking groceries.

She smiled and told me what I owed. "I have two kids. Samantha and Clint. All grown up now."

"That's nice."

"Are you staying for long? Maybe we could get together one night. Go for a beer or something?"

"I don't think I'll have the time. I'm busy with my family, you know? Lots to do."

"I know. Well, nice seeing you, Becky. You look real nice."

I loaded the bags of groceries in my cart. Kimmy Wright wanted to go out for a beer with me. And I had said no. Hot diggidy dog.

But somehow the moment wasn't quite as satisfying as I would have imagined it back in high school.

Two men had come into the store as I was packing my groceries back into the cart. They checked out the girlie magazines placed discreetly behind high shelves on the top of the rack, but our conversation caught their attention and they moved to stand blocking the end of the checkout aisle.

"Excuse me," I said.

"Becky McKenzie, is it?"

"Rebecca actually, but yes. I don't think I've had the pleasure." The one who spoke was a big man, heavily muscled through the arms and shoulders but flabby around the belly. His worn jeans were slung low beneath his pot and he hadn't bothered to shave in several days. His hair needed a good wash.

"No pleasure of ours."

"Do I know you gentlemen?" Ray always said my lip would get me into trouble one of these days.

"Stop it, Jack," Kimmy said. "Not here."

It was okay to try to intimidate me somewhere else?

"We're wondering what your brother's up to these days."

What a strange comment. "Uh," I said.

"We don't take too well to scum messing with our girls."

"A noble sentiment."

"You tell Jim McKenzie we're watching him. The cops might be afraid to move, but the men of this town aren't."

"And very admirable too, I'm sure."

"Are you taking the piss, lady?" The second man spoke for the first time. He was small and neatly dressed. But his narrow dark eyes chilled me in a way the other man's bulk failed to.

"Who me? Perish the thought."

"You guys," Kimmy hissed, her voice low, meaning business. "You stop this now, or I'll get Nancy out of the back. And she'll call the cops."

"Keep your shirt on, Kimmy. We're leaving." They didn't take their eyes off me. "You tell him. We're watching." The bigger man almost spat, but caught himself in time and they both marched out, tossing their magazines on the counter as they passed. A pair of mammary glands that would do an elephant proud stared up at me.

I exhaled heavily.

"Are you okay?" Kimmy asked. "They shouldn't have involved you, Becky. Not fair."

"Involved me in what? I have absolutely no idea what all that was about."

"People are upset about the disappearance of Jennifer Taylor."

"So. That has exactly nothing to do with me." The men had scared me, badly. But the fear was receding and along with it the smart attitude. All that was left was an icy shiver.

"A lot of folks around here remember that Jimmy spent time in jail. People like Jack think maybe he wasn't in long enough."

"Well you can tell 'folks' that my brother is absolutely not my problem." My heart thumping with memories of fear and newfound rage, I pushed my cart out the door. One wheel locked, forcing me to wrestle it back into line.

Jack and his friend were calmly smoking cigarettes on the sidewalk beside the parking lot.

I sailed past, head held high, my shopping cart leading the way. I hoped they were impressed by the size of my car and of my dog. I've lived in the business world a long time—I can play the pissing game as well as anyone alive.

Hanging out the window, Sampson growled low in her throat as we drove away.

Jack and his friend watched us pass.

⌐⌐⌐

"Nice dinner, dear. Thank you." Dad pushed his chair back and rubbed his stomach happily.

"Glad you liked it. Do you have any plans for tomorrow?"

"Probably go to the Legion. Play a bit of pool."

I started clearing the plates. Sampson eyed the meat sauce remains casually, as if not really paying any attention. I stuck my tongue out at her.

"I brought some reading to catch up on." I stacked the dishes in the dishwasher. "So I'm going to take Sampson for a walk and then go to bed early and get into it."

"Becky?"

"Rebecca."

"Right. Rebecca?"

"Yes." I turned at the question in his voice.

"I was hoping that… while you're here…"

"Yes?"

"You would go through your mother's things."

"Me?"

"Someone should."

"Shirley can do it." I returned to the dishes. There was enough sauce left for one person's lunch tomorrow. I scrounged through the cupboards for a plastic container. Cold leftover spaghetti. The best meal of them all.

"I'd rather you did it… Rebecca."

I snapped the lid shut.

"There's her clothes and her personal things. We could give them to the church. Your mother had some nice things."

Bought at the nearest five and dime.

"But in particular I thought you could go through her papers."

"Papers? What sort of papers would Mom have?"

"Letters from her family in England. Old letters from you and from Jimmy when he was away."

"Actually, I was going to speak to you about Jimmy. I ran into some people in town…"

"Her diary."

"Diary?"

Sampson took advantage of my sudden lack of attention to attack the dishwasher. Her long tongue eagerly scooped the spaghetti and meat sauce remains off the stacked plates. Outside, a truck struggled up the hill to the big house. Jimmy.

"You can do with her diary what you think best. I've never looked at it and I don't want to look at it now."

"Mom kept a diary?"

"Yup. Long as I knew her. Some years she wrote in it most every night."

"And you never read it?"

"Nope. She asked me not to. The night we was married. Said it was her private thoughts. Not for anyone else, even me. So I never did."

I sat down in a sticky vinyl kitchen chair, wringing a dish-cloth through my hands, not knowing whether to believe him or not. To have the person closest to you in the entire world keep a diary for fifty-five and more years and never give in to the temptation to read it?

Impossible.

Impossible for anyone else I knew.

But not for him. A man who had lived his life detached from everything happening around him. His wife, his children, his home: Nothing had ever mattered.

"Do you think I should read it?"

"Up to you." He pushed his chair back and stood. "Going to catch a bit of the game before bed." He shuffled into the living room, looking every single one of his many years. "She kept them all in the cellar. Enjoy your walk."

Chapter 7

The Diary of Janet Green. Saturday, January 22, 1944

Dad and Aunt Betty reacted so badly when Bob and I told them that we want to get married that we've hardly said a word since. It has been quite unpleasant around here, so say the least.

I was making breakfast this morning, a bit of bacon and toast. We've come to the end of the strawberry jam. There are no eggs left. Dad came downstairs right after me. He looked all sad, and sort of sagging around the edges. He ate his bacon and toast without saying a word, and then when he was about to get up from the table, he told me that he doesn't want to lose me, and if I marry Bob and go to Canada then he'll lose me. He said that he couldn't bear it, what with Mum leaving and then what happened to my brother, John. So we both cried and hugged each other. That is the first time I have seen my dad cry. Even when we got word about John being killed, Dad just walked out to the yard, whistled for Bonnie, and they went into the wood.

It's only been two years, but since that day my dad has been getting old before my eyes.

Dad said that he will miss me dreadfully if I go off to Canada, but that if this is what I really want to do then I have his blessing. I kissed him and jumped up and down with the joy of it. Then he told me that he would take Bob out to the pub in town the next time he was off duty, and he would buy a drink for all the lads to celebrate that Bob and I are to be married.

I am so happy!

April 20, 1944

Tomorrow is my wedding day!

    After tea I tried on my dress for the last time before the ceremony. It is so lovely. Dad saved every clothing coupon he could manage; some of my aunts even sent coupons so that we would have enough. That was so very kind of them! Mrs. Beeton has made me the most beautiful dress. It is all white, not long with a flowing train like I have always dreamed of wearing, but falling only to the knee. But I wouldn't have anything longer if a fairy offered it to me tomorrow. I have borrowed the veil and shoes that Jenny's sister gave her to wear to her wedding. Jenny is already expecting a baby, so the borrowed veil must be good luck.

    The cake is sitting in the kitchen. It looks lovely, although a bit small. But it is a real wedding cake, like the ones they had at the family weddings we went to before the war.

    My wedding day! Tomorrow will be the happiest day of my life.

Chapter 8

I took Sampson for a long walk and got back as the game Dad had wanted to watch was ending. He mumbled good night and shuffled off to bed. I turned out the lights, locked up, and made my way to my own bed. The night was pitch dark, the way I like it, but my eyes remained wide open, staring at nothing but blackness. Sampson snuggled against the curve of my body as she had every night since Ray's death, the night she was first allowed up on the bed. My mother's diary was almost certainly nothing more than a litany of schoolgirl dreams followed by a lifetime's worth of long lists of groceries needed and chores to be done. I didn't want to read them. They'd be sad, nothing but sad. Dad had no interest in them, so tomorrow I would find the lot and toss them into the trash.

But something nagged at the back of my mind, an irritating infinitesimal whisper that wouldn't be hushed and sent off to sleep, so in the early hours of the morning I succumbed, crawled out of bed, and crept down the rickety old stairs to the cellar.

The light over the landing did little to penetrate the darkness. In this old house, the basement was not a recreation room, as might be found in a modern suburban home. It was a real cellar, lined with handmade shelves made out of cheap wood groaning under the weight of jars of homemade jam and preserves and bulk purchases bought on sale at the supermarket. A few root vegetables, the remains of a winter's worth of supplies, were stacked in farmers' market bushel baskets in the corner. My mother had been dead only a few days, but already the damp, dark room was assuming a miasma of dust, mold, spiders and abandonment.

Tea chests.

Wooden tea chests were used for packing.

My mother moved into this house in 1946, the day she arrived from England with nothing but a cardboard suitcase, a squalling Shirley, and her dreams. She would have had no further need for packing crates.

Prying the lid off the first one, I peered inside. Too dark to see anything. I ran upstairs for the flashlight Dad kept on top of the fridge.

The light's strong beam revealed a box crammed full of books. Not books from the bookstore or library, but mostly loose-leaf binders, a few spiral-bound notebooks, one or two proper journals.

I leaned up against the freezer and shone the flashlight into Sampson's eyes. She didn't like it and snapped her jaws to scare the light away. "I don't want to do this, dear dog." I told her. The box was nearly full and there were two other tea crates behind this one. That's a lot of writing.

I pulled out the book on the top. It was a good quality journal, and on the cover there was a pretty picture of a young girl with a long summer dress and big sun hat standing in a field of yellow flowers. I opened it to the first page. The *From:* was filled in with a date only a few months ago. The *To:* was blank.

I hoisted myself onto the freezer and lifted my flashlight higher in order to see better. I flipped to the last written page. Sampson sat in a far corner, scratching at I didn't want to know what.

I hadn't been home for thirty years, but in all that time my mother had written to me almost every week and often more. Her handwriting was as familiar to me as my own. More familiar. It's been years since I've written anything more involved than a shopping list or directions to a friend's summer home. Like almost everyone else in my world, I type, and then click "print."

It was dated six weeks ago:

> *Bit of a pain in my head again today. Came on me*
> *sharp as I cleared the front step. But then it passed.*
> *Maude keeps saying that she'll drive me to see Dr.*
> *Richardson in North Ridge, if I only make the appoint-*
> *ment. That's kind of her. She's become a good friend,*
> *Maude. But I don't like to go to Dr. Richardson.*
> *He's pleasant enough but seems much too young to*
> *be a doctor. I do miss old Dr. O'Malley. Winter will*
> *be over soon, thank goodness. After fifty-some years*
> *one would think that I would be accustomed to these*
> *horrid Canadian winters. Letter from Rebecca today.*
> *So nice to hear from her. She doesn't write much any*
> *more. This was the first letter in months.*

Did I really want to read this? But I could no more climb back up those stairs, turn off the light and go to sleep than Sampson could tell me that she would read them and give me a précis.

> *She took Ray's death so hard. I wanted her to come*
> *out here, for a nice long visit. But she won't. Too*
> *proud. It would have been better if she and Ray had*
> *had children, then she would have someone to live for*
> *now that he's gone.*

Enough!

The book slammed shut with sufficient force to distract Sampson from a thorough washing of her private parts. The journal landed with a thud in the open tea chest, and I jumped down off the freezer.

The treads shook with every step as I stomped up the stairs. The light was switched off so fast that Sampson had to make the last bit of her way in the dark.

I found it hard to sleep that night. All the years of my accumulated guilt rose to the surface and I tossed and turned until daybreak.

I was a bad daughter. My mother tried to be a good mother. She was a good mother. I was a bad daughter. I'm a bad person.

So what, I asked myself? This was my life's lesson: no good deed goes unpunished. The good finish last. I'd learned that at the hand of the master: my grandfather.

Monday morning. For most people, a working day. For me, the day of the dreaded family dinner. I stared up at nothing as the sun conducted dust mites in Viennese waltzes across the ceiling. My parents had slept in this bed. Making love. Yuck! Conceiving Jimmy and eight years later, me. Yuck again! Why were there so many years between Jimmy and myself, when Shirley and Jimmy were fairly close? If I read my mother's diary I might know.

I pushed the thought aside. Who wants to know the details of their own conception?

Not me.

Of course, I told myself as I padded to the back door to let Sampson out, being my mother she wouldn't have written such an impolite thing down. Would she?

"Morning, Dad." He came in as I was measuring out the coffee I'd purchased yesterday. "Sleep well?"

"As well as can be expected, Becky. Without your mother beside me. But thank you for asking."

"Rebecca," I said automatically.

"Coffee. How nice." He pulled out the remains of yesterday's newspaper and settled in at the table. No one would see today's papers until someone walked up to the mailbox on the road to get them.

I briefly considered doing just that. And telling my dad that I would be back in a few minutes and I would have my eggs over easy, thank you. And lightly on the toast. I don't like it burned.

Instead I pulled out sausage and eggs and sliced generous pieces off the loaf of twelve-grain bread. "What time's the funeral tomorrow?"

"Two."

"Fried eggs okay?"

"Yup."

"Do you know Jennifer Taylor's family?"

"Who?"

"The girl who's gone missing. The one I read about in the *Gazette*." Reduced-fat granola and non-fat yogurt were laid out on the counter for my own breakfast. The sausages smelled great, all bubbling and hissing away in the frying pan. One or two wouldn't hurt, and when was the last time I had indulged in a fried egg? Before yesterday, that is? I returned the unopened container of yogurt to the fridge and tossed three more sausages onto the pan.

"Her father owns the hardware store. Fawcett's. Old John Fawcett died long ago. His son didn't want the store, sold it to the Taylors. They never changed the name."

"Do you know the girl, Jennifer?"

"Seen her in the store once or twice. Don't go there as much as I used to any more. Just for a light bulb or a bunch of nails now and again. Getting too old to be doing chores around this place. Janet worried that I would fall and break something." He smiled at the memory. "Said she didn't care if I broke my fool neck, 'cepting that then she would have to look after me."

I turned back to the stove and cracked eggs into the hot fat. The smell of sizzling sausages, fresh coffee, and browning bread filled the kitchen.

"But Jimmy knows them well. He gets lots of work over the summers these days, building cottages, fixing up the old houses. More work than he can handle. He hires on the Taylor twins, Jennifer's older brothers, when school's out. Jimmy told me she tags along some times. Said she wants to learn a trade. Funny world this. People woulda laughed themselves silly in my day, girl thinking she could be a builder."

I put the sizzling plates on the table. "She spent a lot of time with Jimmy?"

Dad shrugged and turned his attention to his plate. "Funny bread this. What's these little things?" He poked at the toast with his fork.

"Seeds."

"Seeds. Imagine that. Your mother never served up toast with seeds." He took a cautious nibble. "Good though."

Eventually Dad finished his breakfast and, leaving the dishes to me, walked up the road to get the papers: the local *Gazette* and the *Sun*, a Toronto tabloid. When he got back he tossed them on the counter as I folded the dishtowel over the oven rail to dry. I glanced at the front page of the tabloid.

PARENTS PLEAD FOR JENNIFER'S RETURN. Must be a slow news day in the Big Smoke. A middle-aged couple, faces sagging with a worry verging on despair, filled the front page. A pair of teenage boys flanked them, looking equally grim. Dad had told me they were twins, but otherwise I never would have guessed. The boys were the same height and they had the same narrow eyes. But one was lean and wiry while the other had either never lost his puppy fat or had already grown more. Jimmy's helpers. Two black labs sat at the fat boy's feet. Even the dogs looked lost and confused. The grief-stricken family stared back at me. The man was identified as Dennis Taylor, Jennifer's father. I thought I remembered him from school. And not at all fondly. I folded the paper and placed it on the counter, face down.

I spent the morning tidying the house before indulging in the luxury of making myself a cup of tea. A real cup of tea, leaves steeped in the brown betty and poured through a silver strainer. I drank my tea out on the deck, standing up because the chairs hadn't been put out yet, watching Sampson dash about the lawn and under the trees as she followed one fascinating scent to another. The sun caressed my face with the soft, polite warmth it only shows in spring. Sampson dashed around the side of the house, probably heading for the woods.

Since Ray's death, I had tried to learn to whistle. Two fingers at the edge of my mouth, the way he did when calling the dog home. What came out usually managed to be no better than a feeble squeak, but this time I managed a full blast. I felt rather pleased with myself, particularly when the big dog rounded the house and climbed up the steps to stand at my feet.

"What a good girl." I scratched behind her ears. I had no worries that she would get lost in the woods. She wouldn't go far. We lived in a condo in Vancouver, a high-rise like so many others, in a very good part of town. Most of her days Sampson lived the life of a city dog, kept inside, walked by a professional dog walking service because my working hours were so long. But we—now just me, me and my dog—owned a vacation home near Whistler. To which, when my husband was alive, we had escaped as often as we could.

In summers past Ray golfed, and I sat out on the big wooden deck overlooking the rainforest with either a good book or papers from the office. In the winter we skied. Ray on the slopes of Whistler and Blackcomb, me—too afraid of heights to ride the ski lifts—cross-country, often with Sampson somewhere off to one side following tiny animal tracks and sniffing at patches of yellow snow.

Only once since Ray's death had we driven back into the mountains. It rained constantly and I spent most of the time staring out the big bay window watching the trees drip water. The place went up for sale the day I arrived back in the city.

I looked at Sampson's mud-encrusted feet, legs and belly. At her wagging tail and smiling face. I plucked a dead twig out of her bushy tail. As soon as it reached a reasonable time in Vancouver, I'd call the agent and tell her to take the property off the market. Sampson needed it.

And so, I now realized, did I.

Energized a fraction, I reluctantly entered into the simple, emotional, gut-wrenching, heart-breaking task of sorting through my mother's clothes, as Dad had asked me to do. He'd made the bed, or at least he'd tried. The quilt was so lumpy it obviously had been dragged up over a tumble of sheets. It was a beautiful quilt, lovingly constructed of tiny squares of fabric in myriad shades of blue ranging from almost-white to near-black but blending so slowly from shade to shade that it was almost impossible to determine where one color ended and the next began.

I opened the cupboard and went through the drawers, making three piles. Things too old, too stained, or too horribly out of ,fashion for anyone to want headed for the garbage. Mom had few nice things—a couple of good dresses, a new pair of shoes, two old but serviceable handbags. These would go into a box for the church. And then there were the things to be kept. Of which there was precious little. Shirley might like a few pieces of Mom's jewelry. None of it was good—she never spent money on herself, and Dad never had a nickel to his name. But some of it had sentimental value. It was nice to see that she still used the wooden jewelry box that I bought her for her birthday a long, long time ago. I picked up a brooch. It was large and perfectly ugly, but she liked it. When I was young, she wore it on her best coat, the one that she wore to church every Sunday in winter. It was silver plate pounded into a hollow circle, rimmed with rhinestones and with a rhinestone tail dangling down. The tail had become partially detached and waved from side to side as I shook it.

I remembered sitting in church. On the hard wooden seat, the heat in the building turned up way too high. The minister—I forget his name—droning on and relentlessly on. The poor man had not the slightest inflection or emotion in his voice; he might have been reading the yellow pages for all he seemed to care. I was the youngest in my family, so I was always plunked between Mother and Grandmother. Jimmy and Shirley sat on Grandmother's other side and wriggled as far away as they dared get. On occasion, Shirley tucked a Nancy Drew inside her Bible and read all through the service. I wanted to tell Mom, but the look my sister gave me when she caught me watching was enough to chill my blood. Father and Grandfather didn't normally come with us to church. There were never many men in church, except at Christmas and Easter or something special like the baptisms. And even then nothing approaching the numbers of the women. Usually it was only the oldest of the men, the ones who drooled and fell asleep during the service and woke up shouting "Who? What?" The ones who came in their wheelchairs or walkers, and had to be helped up the ramp and down the aisle by wives as old as they or a succession of daughters or daughters-in-law. About once a month my father would come, leading his family down the aisle, nodding at all the neighbors. But never Grandpa. Church was for children and women. I don't remember the actual occasion when he said that, but the memory of the words is there, spoken in his deep voice, the one that would accept no argument. But he could be quick to quote the Bible, and I assumed that he had also spent his childhood Sundays confined to the stiff wooden pews.

When he turned sixteen, Jimmy simply stopped coming with us. Nothing was said, at least not in my hearing, but I knew that my grandfather had decided that Jimmy was now a "man."

I'd promised myself that I also would escape, one day.

The silver circle lay in my palm, the too-red rhinestones watching me. One finger caressed the floppy tail lightly. I would take this one piece only home with me. It would be enough.

As I worked through a lifetime of belongings, the edges of my mind kept returning to the three tea chests nestled in the cellar, in the same way that a tongue seems instinctively driven to seek and probe a sore tooth or a raw cold sore.

This room, my parents' bedroom, was nice. The cream paint was fresh, the curtains thrown back and the windows wide and full of soft, gentle sunbeams, the blue quilt glowing on the bed. The room had long ago banished the ghost of its childhood resident.

Banished, but not defeated, Jimmy now having ownership of the big house.

The walls were hung with a multitude of photographs of us three children in every stage of our lives. At first I paid them no attention, concentrating on the task at hand, wanting only to get through it. But my self-control had broken and I'd spooked myself by thinking thoughts long forbidden, of that hard church pew and my hated brother and grandfather. And of my father. I hadn't hated *him*, but simply loved with a clear childish emotion that was more often than not met with a wall of indifference and the whiff of alcoholic fumes.

Sampson nudged my thigh as the tears threatened to flow. I gratefully scratched behind her ears, and my eyes wandered down the rows of photographs. My brother, Jimmy, in the uniform of the high school baseball team. Cock-of-the-walk as always. Two of his teammates flanked him, taller and heavier than he, but almost insignificant, props to the main event.

How easy life would be if one could judge a book by its cover, a person by their looks. If, like the angels and devils they had taught us children, good people had pure white wings and flowing golden locks, and bad people hooked noses, long fingernails, and foul breath.

Sampson nudged me once again. I swear she's equipped with a tear-o-meter, ready to jump in and protect me from my own emotions. My husband was—had been—a professor of medieval history, of all obscure topics. But he looked like a prizefighter. Six foot two, a heavily muscled two hundred and twenty pounds that came from a genetic gift, not from any desire on his part to be formidable. His nose had been broken more times than he could remember, the first when as a seven-year-old he fell off his bike, his attention having been distracted by a library sign advertising a reading by a visiting author of whom he was fond. And there he hung, beside my brother Jimmy. Jimmy is eight years older than I am—and eight years was a good many when we were children. But no matter how young I was I had always known why the older girls at school wanted to be friends with me.

Girls would wander by our house and pretend to be lost. *Oh, dear, Mrs. McKenzie. I seem to have taken the wrong road home from school. If I can come in for a moment I'll call my mother to come and fetch me.*

Mom would sigh and stand back to let them in. And the poor girl's eyes would dart around the kitchen seeking some memoir of the object of her desire. And if Jimmy did condescend to appear, he would stroll into the kitchen, help himself to the contents of the fridge, and then walk away munching on a cookie or a piece of fruit cake without giving the poor lost girl a single glance. For Jimmy—Little Jim, as everyone except my mother called him because my grandfather was Big Jim—was even to this day the most handsome man I have ever known. I hadn't seen him for thirty years, and still didn't particularly want to, but the pictures on my parents' bedroom wall told me that he had scarcely changed. Shouldn't one's evil deeds be reflected in the eyes or in the skin?

Well, they aren't.

My brother had the darkest of dark hair, always worn slightly long to show off a mass of tousled curls, eyes so black they offered only hints at the mysteries that lay beneath, a smile around straight white teeth that would charm the angels right out of heaven. Taken one at a time each pristine feature might amount to a face too feminine, but on Jimmy everything coalesced perfectly into a deeply masculine whole.

He was the image of my grandfather. So much so that one might be forgiven for thinking that my great-grandparents had had one of a pair of twins cryogenically frozen to be thawed out years later. As if my grandmother and my mother's contributions had been ignored by the genetic pool.

As a child I thought of Little Jim as an exact replica of Big Jim, although a bit smaller. For, unlike the adoring girls who collected flowers along our driveway in the spring, and in the winter decided that our stretch of the lake was the only one suitable for skating in the entire county, I knew that my brother was just as mean, just as vicious, and just as emotionally dead as his adored grandfather. Today we would call them sociopaths. Back then we stayed out of the way.

If we could.

Is it genetic, did the vicious streak come with the curly hair and the innocent smile? Or did Grandpa's complete adoration of his only grandson fertilize and water a seed that would otherwise have remained dormant?

Chapter 9

The Diary of Mrs. Robert McKenzie. July 8, 1944. Two AM.

It is very late. I have lit a candle to break the darkness. These nights are so terribly dark. The blackout curtains are pulled tight. I peeked out before lighting the candle and couldn't see a thing. There is not a light anywhere. I might be the only person left in the world and I would not know it. I had a dream, a horrid dream. I woke up with my heart pounding. Bob has gone, of course I don't know where. The radio is talking about the invasion of France. I hope he isn't there. Maybe they sent him up to Scotland, for work with the radio or something. He is very talented with electronics, he told me. Too valuable, I am sure, to be sent to the beaches of France.

Before he left, Bob asked me if I wanted to go to Canada. Now that we were married, he said, I could get a ship to Canada, and stay with his family until he got home. It would be safer for me there, he said, in Canada. But how could I? Can I take the chance of his getting leave and coming here to find me gone? Can I leave Dad and Aunt Betty? There is no one else to help in the shop now. All the village girls have gone to war work. And can I abandon the hope that my mother might come looking for me? If she hears that I'm married, she'll want to wish me well.

I am afraid. My monthlies did not come. They are now three weeks overdue. That is not much, but I have always been so regular. The girls at school said that they could be delayed by worry. I do not think that I am ready.

Chapter 10

I pulled my thoughts back to the present: Sampson sniffing at Mom's jewelry box, welcome spring sunlight spreading in through the big, new windows, the sound of a heavily loaded truck bouncing down the country road at the bottom of the hill. Jimmy would be here for dinner in a few short hours. My heart pounded and my palms gathered sweat. I was eight years younger than my brother, but even as a child that hadn't been enough to protect me from his vicious tongue and his sadistic streak.

On this wall of family memories, there was only one picture, an extremely old one, of my paternal grandmother. She looked quite splendid in a fancy hat with a moth-eaten bird perched in one corner that almost, but not quite, disguised the shadow of fear in her tiny dark eyes. There was not one single picture, I was glad to notice, of my father's father.

Too many sad and difficult thoughts; it was time to abandon Mom's possessions. Only by concentrating on the task at hand and ignoring the photos dotting the walls had I managed to accomplish anything at all. But once I stood up to look at them, the memories brought to the surface by that simple collection of family photographs amounted to more than my stomach could handle for one day.

Dad came down the hall as I emerged from the bedroom.

"Everything sorted out?" he asked in his typically detached way.

I wanted to slap him; instead I said, "Not yet. It'll take a couple of days."

"Okay."

"By the way, Dad." I aimed to wound. "I was wondering when Jimmy got out of prison the last time. Can't have been too long ago. I assume he didn't get time off for good behavior." Or maybe he did. Man or woman, it didn't matter. If they had something he wanted, Jimmy could charm their pants off.

"That's over and done with. We don't talk about it any more. It was all a misunderstanding and he and Aileen are very happy together."

"A misunderstanding," I said. "Like all the other bloody misunderstandings?"

My father looked at me. The skin on his face was as thin as Japanese rice paper, the bones so prominent they threatened to burst through any moment. God, he was getting so old. A wave of red shame washed over me like a tsunami. I tried to choke the words back.

Too late.

"That sort of language isn't appropriate, Becky. Your mother wouldn't like it."

I was ten years old once again. The topic avoided, the guilt assigned.

"Sorry, Dad."

"I'll be out in the shed for a bit."

"Do you want lunch?"

"No thanks. I had a sandwich at Tim Horton's. Have to eat something to digest the claptrap that bunch of old buggers keep putting out. Everyone and their dog has an opinion on what has happened to young Jennifer. Norm Berg's granddaughter thinks she's been kidnapped by aliens." He pulled a soft drink bottle from the fridge door and walked out of the kitchen.

When I thought of my childhood I always picture a bottle in my father's hand. And certainly not a bottle of Coke. When I first got here there was only a six pack of beer in the fridge, which was now down to four. I'd searched the kitchen looking for a bottle of vodka or rye. Nothing.

I dialed into the office and printed a position paper off on my portable printer. My eyes remained fixed on the little letters, but my thoughts wandered like fairies caught in an unexpected updraft of summer wind. I found myself constantly glancing at my watch, wondering if it was time yet to start dinner. We would eat incredibly early, by my standards scarcely past lunchtime.

I read about global oil revenues and thought about tea chests in the basement. Judging by the number of notebooks in the one box I'd opened, my mother must have been writing for most of her life.

Was it up to me to consign to the rubbish bin what she had kept for—what, sixty, seventy years? And if not me, then who?

As I sorted through these thoughts and wondered what to do, I finished my tea, disconnected from the Internet, shut down the computer, packed it away, and walked like a zombie to the top of the rickety, dark, dank stairs.

I started at the end of the top-most book, reading once again that she thought I should have borne children. Well, duh. Whose mother doesn't think that? I read about the touches of headache. That wasn't what killed her—she'd had a heart attack while standing outside the supermarket with her bags of groceries waiting for her husband to pick her up because she'd never learned how to drive. But if she had gone to the doctor about the headache, who knows what else might have been found. And if found, perhaps her death could have been prevented.

I flipped to the front of the book.

The entry was from the beginning of the winter before last.

Jim and Aileen came to shovel the driveway and
stayed for supper. I won't let Bob shovel any more.
They say that it's too dangerous for a man of his age.
Of course we could hire one of the boys from town,
but Jim volunteered. So thoughtful of him. I made
ham and scalloped potatoes for supper. That always

was Jim's favorite meal. And I served a peach pie that
I had put up in the summer. The last of the pies for
this year. Aileen brought a squash soup for starters. It
was lovely, very thick and creamy. She's a good cook,
although her meals are sometimes a bit unusual for
Dad and my tastes.

I tossed the book back into its box.

As I suspected.

A litany of recipes.

Time to start a dinner of my own.

Jimmy and Aileen walked the short distance down the hill from
the big house to arrive right on time. Aileen wore a fantastic
dress, reminiscent of the best of the hippie era, swirling in layers
of flowing blue. She had tied her lovely black-and-gray hair into
a wild spray at the back of her head, and a long string of clear
blue beads hung around her thin neck. Rows of silver bangles
running up both arms clanged in greeting as she held out a huge
wooden salad bowl.

"You told me not to bring anything. But I can't resist. And I have
found with this family you really can't have too much food."

I said nothing, simply stared past her, and she mumbled
something about taking the salad into the kitchen.

"You look good, Rebecca. Aileen told me you like to be called
Rebecca now, rather than Becky. It suits you better."

"Jimmy." The word choked in my throat. He was as amazingly good-looking as ever, although he showed every one of his
years. His hair was not quite as long as when we were young,
but it was still long enough that the thick curls danced around
his ears and tickled the back of his neck. By conventional standards he would have been considered too thin and too short,
like his father and grandfather, to be truly attractive. But his
size never seemed to matter, and since I'd seen him last he'd
bulked up considerably. Instead of going to middle-aged fat, as
I had hoped, a line of muscles bulged under the sleeves of his

clean white T-shirt and his stomach was as taut as my mother's washing line. But the years had not all been kind: his hair and moustache were streaked with gray, and some of the intense color had faded from his remarkable eyes. Lines reached out from the corners of his mouth and were carved into the delicate skin around his eyes. His face held none of the anger and arrogance I had been expecting.

Thank God he didn't try to hug me. Instead, he took my hand in his. "It's been a long time."

"Yes." I pulled my hand away.

I've negotiated contracts with billion-dollar companies and stared down men worth almost as much, but under the strength of my brother's blue eyes I looked at my feet.

Chapter 11

The Diary of Mrs. Robert McKenzie. September 1, 1944

I found Aunt Betty working on a lovely piece of yellow wool this morning. I have finished at Barnum and Son and have been helping out at the shop, but today I felt so sick that Dad insisted I go home. Will this horrid nausea ever end? I think not. I believe that I am condemned to throw up everything I eat until the end of time. It is too awful for words. Aunt Betty was embarrassed to see me, and tried to hide the needles and wool. But I saw them, and I also saw her trying to hide a slight smile.

January 19, 1945

Bob is here on leave. It seems so very strange, to have my husband with me. I feel like a real married woman. Somehow Mr. Fitzpatrick heard that my Canadian soldier was coming on leave and he sent his motorcar to take me to the train station to meet him. Can you imagine? Me, riding in a motorcar with the Fitzpatrick driver. Dad came, of course, because he wanted to greet Bob. But also I suspect that he was rather afraid of leaving me to old Bert's driving. Almost all of the young men have left, except for a few like Mrs. Maitland's Hugh with his withered leg and bad eye. Years ago all the women felt so sorry for Mrs. Maitland. All except for Mum, who said that Mrs. Maitland got what she deserved with a freak of a son like Hugh. But now the women seem rather envious of her, although of course they would never say so. She is the only woman in the village to have her son still at home with her. The old men have to take over jobs like driving Mr. Fitzpatrick and Lady Helen into Woking or to the train station. Dad says that Bert can't see much beyond the end of his nose. It is wonderful of Mr. Fitzpatrick to spend precious petrol coupons on me! Dad says that he made a lot of his money in Canada after the Great War and still has a soft spot for the Canadians.

I was so nervous. I haven't seen Bob for months and months. Would he still love me, I wondered. Now that I am all fat and awkward with legs swollen to the size of an elephant's. Aunt Betty has gone up to London to visit Aunt Joan. Joan's feeling poorly, she said. I haven't heard from Mum, but I know that she will come, once she hears the news of my marriage. The post is so terribly bad, since the War started.

Bob was so happy to see us. He grabbed me in his arms and swung me around and around, until I shouted for him to stop. He said that I look wonderful and placed his hand on my stomach so gently. The little devil has been quiet this past week, and he wouldn't move for his daddy. I have decided to name him Arthur, after Dad. I wrote to Bob and asked if he agreed. He said Arthur is a wonderful name. Of course, it might be a girl, and if it is I will call her Shirley. For no reason, just because I like it. But it will be a boy, I am sure. A boy just like his dad.

⌒⌒⌒

He's asleep now and I'm writing this by the light from a bit of candle. The stub is almost burnt down, and I don't have much more time. I don't want to switch on the lamp. It will wake him. He looks so handsome, sound asleep. His right hand is under his cheek and he is curled up like a baby under the old blanket. Dr. Mitchell said that we could still have relations, right up to the last month. I feel so ugly, with my hideously swollen belly and my ankles almost as bad. So I told Bob that the doctor said I mustn't. That is my first lie to my husband. He said it was fine. He understood. But I lied. I will make it up tomorrow. I'll get up early and make a lovely breakfast. Mrs. Beeton gave me a bit of ham. She had a twinkle in her eye and I was so embarrassed. But it was kind of her. Dad went to the pub after dinner. He was all embarrassed too, and I think he wanted to give us some time alone. I love my dad so much, I don't know if I will have the strength to leave him when it comes time for me to go to Canada.

The candle is flickering now. Time to slip back into bed. I will lie next to my husband, with our son wrapped up in my body warm and safe between us.

Chapter 12

The cheerful sounding of horns saved me any further regression into emotional babyhood. A tiny convoy consisting of Shirley and Al's car followed by a late-model van pulled into the driveway.

Sampson ran out to greet the newcomers. Buried under an avalanche of emotion, I forgot she was at my side, and now that my senses were coming back, I cursed her for not sensing danger and sending Jimmy scurrying for cover.

"Oh, wow! What a nice dog." A boy of about ten, all freckles, tousled red hair, and gigantic feet, fell out of the van and grabbed Sampson around the neck before I had time to open my mouth and warn him to approach her gently.

But she didn't disappoint. Dogs always seem to know that they are to treat children differently, and she politely allowed her ruff to be rubbed before she wiggled out of his grasp and stepped away.

"Leave that filthy animal alone," Shirley shouted. "You don't know where he's been."

Which got the evening off to a great start.

"I'm sure its okay, Mom." A young woman jumped down from the passenger seat of the van. "The dog seems perfectly well behaved."

"He's dirty."

"Mud washes off, Mom."

Shirley marched up the steps without another word. She thrust a foil-covered pie plate into my hands and plopped herself down on the couch.

"You would be Rebecca. The baby of the family." The young woman who approved of Sampson—I'd taken an instant liking to her—grinned at me. "I'd give you a hug, but I see you've got your hands full. I'm Jackie, your niece."

"Pleased to meet you, Jackie. At long last."

"And this rascal is Jason." My niece rubbed the head of the ten-year-old as he wiggled past her, in hot pursuit of Sampson, now heading back into the kitchen, knowing that that was where the food was headed.

"Your son," I said, inanely. "My great-nephew. How amazing."

"I see you've met Jackie." Al reached for my hand, apparently not noticing that I still held a pie. Rhubarb by the smell of it, and straight out of the oven. Fruit rich with the flavor of the good earth, pastry redolent of steamy kitchens, wooden rolling pins and clouds of white flour.

My mother had made rhubarb pie every spring.

Al pumped my right hand with enthusiasm as I balanced the pie in the other. He was a nice antidote to my sister's far-from-warm greeting. "And this is Jackie's husband, Dave."

"Dave." I nodded and he forced a smile in return. My niece's husband was fat and bald. He looked to be much, much older than his wife. "Pleased to meet you, Dave," I lied.

"Nice to meet you," he lied in return.

A third car pulled up as we were still standing in the doorway exchanging greetings. My brother took a seat in the living room beside his older sister. Dad, Al, and Dave joined him and they were soon chattering on about the latest hockey game, and who would make it to the finals, but Jimmy watched me, his ocean blue eyes filled with a calm silence. I pretended not to notice.

Two little girls bounded into the room and squealed in delight at the sight of the great dog now returning from the kitchen. These were the great-grand twins my mother had written about so proudly. Jessica and Melissa, as alike—to quote a well-worn but appropriate cliché—as two peas in a pod. They both were dressed in pink denim overalls (since when did denim come in pink?) and white T-shirts. Pink ribbons, chosen to match the overalls, shone in their pale hair. I smiled at the girls, but they scarcely noticed me in their eagerness to greet, in this order, Sampson, Jimmy, and my father.

The twins' mother, presumably my niece Elizabeth, followed them in. She nodded at me, said nothing and plunked her fat body down on the chair nearest the TV.

That left me standing at the open door, all by myself, clutching a warm rhubarb pie. Even my dog deserted me as the twins descended on her and started rubbing every available patch of her great, furry body. The traitor.

The tops of the big trees lining the driveway swayed in the rising wind. They didn't have any leaves this early in the year, so their movements were soft and quiet, like a ghostly orchestra, all tuned up and starting to play but trapped behind the barrier to the outside world, a barrier beyond which sound and life would not pass. The sky stood stark and gray behind the row of moving branches and solid, grounded trunks.

I slammed the door shut with one foot and carried the pie into the kitchen. Dad had switched the TV on and he, Al, and Dave were thoroughly engrossed in some sort of game. The overweight woman on the couch struggled to her feet and followed me into the kitchen. Jimmy watched us go.

"You must be Liz?" I said brightly, holding out my hand, having finally relieved myself of that rhubarb pie. "Shirley's youngest daughter?"

"That I am." Her handshake felt as limp as a fish left in the market at the end of a long, hot day. The family resemblance was there: She was short, with her mother's fine pale hair and contrasting dark eyes. But where Shirley and her eldest daughter, Jackie, were thin to the point of scrawny, Liz was, to put it rudely, a barrel.

Shirley followed Liz into the kitchen and greeted Aileen. I knew that I couldn't really blame my sister for being cold and distant toward me. But it annoyed me, nonetheless.

"Isn't this nice," Aileen bubbled. "All the McKenzie women together at last."

I smiled at her, overwhelmed with gratitude. A hideous platitude but at least the poor woman was struggling to bring us together.

Mostly they ignored me. And I was happy about it. These people saw each other almost every day. Every child was bounced on every knee and the women popped into each other's kitchens with tomatoes straight off the vine and squash picked that morning. The men watched hockey in the winter, baseball in the spring, and football in the fall while the women prepared thick stews, rhubarb pie, and roast turkey brimming with sage and walnut stuffing.

But it was not a world I wanted to be part of, I reminded myself. A world of women in the kitchen, children dancing around their varicose-veined legs. Of men watching the game on TV or on special occasions standing over the barbecue as if they had tracked down the wild animal and then killed it with their bare hands.

I didn't belong here.

Funeral tomorrow, then a day or two to finish sorting out Mom's possessions. Even I couldn't expect Dad to do that.

And Sampson and I would be on our way back to the West Coast.

Aileen reached into her enormous tote and produced a bottle of red wine. A lovely Australian Shiraz. "Care to join me, Rebecca?"

I grinned. "I do believe I will."

"Ladies?"

My female relatives nodded in unison. Jackie pulled glasses out of the cabinet. She knew her way around this kitchen. We consumed the Shiraz quickly and Liz pulled another, cheaper, bottle out of the plastic shopping bags she had brought and refilled our glasses.

I didn't dare ask why Liz's husband hadn't come. She might not even have one, and Mom would not have wanted to mention such a tender detail in her letters.

Aileen pulled cutlery and glassware out of the cupboards and carried them to the dining room. Liz took her glass of wine and waddled back to the TV. Jason flew into the kitchen shouting that they needed more beer in the living room. Jackie joined her nieces in their admiration of Sampson, and Shirley stared out the back window at the gathering storm clouds.

I followed Aileen into the dining room. The table was new since my day, and a good deal larger than the one that had been used mainly as Mom's sewing table. We always went to the big house for Christmas or Thanksgiving and the occasional family birthday. Otherwise, like every other family in the Hope River area, we took our meals at the chipped Formica table in the kitchen. This new table had been carved out of a beautiful dark wood and was surrounded by matching chairs with high backs and deep, colorful cushions. The wood felt as smooth and cool as lake water under my fingers.

"This is a lovely table. Must have cost Mom and Dad a lot."

Aileen laughed her light, tinkling laugh. "Only the price of the wood. Your dad made it."

"Dad?"

"That's right."

"My dad only ever made cheap picnic tables with benches that broke the first year they were used."

She continued placing knives and forks in neat formation, tucking a paper napkin under each fork. "Some things have changed since you lived here, Rebecca."

I shrugged. "I guess. Tell me, is Liz married?"

"Oh yes. But it's no surprise that her hubby hasn't put in an appearance. He doesn't like family things much. He might make it tomorrow, to the church, but if he does that will be a stretch. His name's Ralph."

"How long have you been married to Jimmy?"

"Three years. Don't assume that everything here is the same as the way you left it, Rebecca. It isn't. I haven't known your family for long, only since I married Jim. But I am aware to some degree of what things were like, and, well, things have changed. And people not the least of all."

"Perhaps. This house has changed. Some money has been put into it. But people don't change."

"Some do."

"Not in my experience."

She set the last place and straightened the knife in a proper line. Only then did she lift her head to look at me. Difficult thoughts swirled behind her eyes, and she hovered on the verge of opening her mouth, struggling to find the right words to say.

"When's dinner?" One of the twins bounded in. "Grandpa says if dinner isn't ready soon, can they have a bag of chips?"

"No, they can not. Your grandpa shouldn't be eating chips no matter when dinner is."

"Okay, I'll tell him."

"No, don't." Aileen laughed. "Tell him that dinner is almost ready."

The girl scurried off, intent on her errand, her long pale ponytail bouncing behind in a swirl of pink ribbons.

Jackie stuck her head around the corner. "Something needs attention in the oven, Aunt Rebecca."

I rushed to do my duty. A bit of sauce had bubbled over the edges of the pot and hissed on the oven floor.

Jackie peered over my shoulder. "No damage done. It'll clean up. But maybe you should put a cookie pan on the bottom shelf to catch the drips. If it needs to cook much longer."

I checked the timer on the microwave. "Twenty minutes?"

She pulled a cookie sheet out from under the sink and waved me out of the way.

"Smells good."

༺༒༻

And, to my surprise, it was.

"Can I come visit you in Vancouver, Aunt Rebecca?" one of the twins asked, spearing the last bit of chicken off her plate.

"Of course you can," I said. "If your mother will let you."

"Can I, Mom? Can I?"

"Can we, Mom? Can we?" The second girl added her voice.

"Certainly not." Liz tossed me a malevolent glare. This niece of mine had decided the moment she laid eyes on me, and probably long before that, that she didn't like me. Her loss.

I returned her glare with a bright smile. "When the girls are a bit older, they could fly out by themselves. Children travel unaccompanied all the time. I have a vacation home near Whistler. Do you ski, girls?"

Two pairs of matching brown eyes opened wide. "No."

"No matter," I said. "You can learn." I wasn't trying to be difficult. Simply feeling all caught up in the warmth of family, a hearty dinner, and the soft evening light fading to darkness outside, the expected storm having failed to materialize. At that moment I really did think it would be nice if the twins could visit.

Liz's eyes narrowed to nasty slits. "Don't think I'm going to allow my children to travel the whole way across the country to visit a stranger. We'll hear no more about it."

The girls deflated.

Jason innocently stirred the pot. "I can ski, Aunt Rebecca. My mom and I go skiing all the time. Don't we, Mom?"

Jackie nodded.

"Can I come visit you in Whistler? My friend Rob went to Whistler last winter with his whole family. He said it was the best."

"No point in talking about that now," Al interrupted. "In case you have forgotten, your great-grandma's funeral is tomorrow."

"Sorry, Grandpa." Jason bowed his head. His mother tossed him a sympathetic smile.

"A place in Whistler, eh?" Jimmy said. "You've done all right for yourself, baby sister." I looked for the traces of spite in his expression but couldn't find them. In prison you learn, I would imagine, to hide your thoughts very deep. He'd barely said a word all through the meal. But his blue eyes watched me constantly.

Jackie rose and started collecting the plates. Aileen followed in a graceful, liquid movement that set her bangles clanging.

I assembled the dessert while the two women scraped the few remains into the garbage and stacked the plates in the dishwasher. Jackie dipped her finger into the whipped cream and licked it off with a mischievous smile. "That all looks perfectly lovely. Bit early for strawberries isn't it? They must have cost a pretty penny."

I shrugged. "What's money when it's for your family?"

She laughed heartily. "That's what I say. Unfortunately, Dave doesn't agree. The skinflint."

The dessert turned out to be a beautiful, sculpted arrangement of cake, berries, and cream. Everyone suitably *oohed* and *aahed* as I carried it in.

Jason slipped scraps of cake under the table to an eager Sampson. Even if I hadn't seen the movements of the boy's hand, the thumping of the dog's tail would have been a sure giveaway. I pretended not to notice.

The children were excused to watch TV while the adults settled back into their chairs.

Once again, Jackie and Aileen got to their feet to gather up the dirty plates. "Now you sit and relax, Rebecca," Aileen said, although I had made no move to get up. I did the cooking. Someone else would do the dishes. Doesn't everyone's household work that way?

"Coffee, everyone?" Shirley asked.

They mumbled in agreement.

Dad asked Jimmy how things were going with his work. Jimmy made a non-committal reply. Jason stood behind his great-grandpa and put one arm around the thin, stooped shoulders. Al smiled at his grandson. Generations of McKenzie men. A lump formed in my throat, and for the first time in my life I felt a slight twinge of family sentimentality.

Then I imagined that I could see my grandfather, Big Jim, standing behind the little tableau, an eavesdropping ghost. The burgeoning pang of sentiment disappeared in a flash, replaced by the sour taste of bad memory.

My mother had made something new for Thanksgiving dinner one year. A butternut squash casserole, runny with streaks of melting butter, dark brown sugar not yet fully mixed in, tiny pools of maple sugar forming on the top. I'd watched her make it and was practically drooling at the thought of actually eating it. Imagine—a child looking forward to squash. She had carried it up the road to the big house where Grandma was preparing the traditional turkey dinner.

Even as child, it was perfectly obvious to me that my grandmother didn't enjoy the work. That there was no joy in getting the celebration meal on the table. Years later I would flip through cooking magazines and be shocked to discover that for some women preparing the holiday meal offered a pleasure all in itself. I still only half-believe it.

For some reason my grandfather objected to the squash. Indian food, he called it. Then he picked up my mother's Corningware pot (one of her very few good things), held it high above the table, looked my mother in the eye, and threw it. I can still see the dish shattering in a spray of white porcelain and tiny blue flowers and orange squash dripping down the pattered wallpaper.

Everyone continued eating and my dad downed his beer. I might have seen a single tear form in the corner of my mother's eye. But maybe I didn't. Every bite of that dinner stuck in my throat, not even trying to make the long journey down to my stomach. When we got home, I slipped into the bathroom, stuck my fingers down my throat and brought it all back up.

"Now what are you thinking about there, Rebecca?" Al's cheerful voice dispelled the ghosts of dinners past. "You look all serious like."

I forced a smile. "I'm wondering what I'm missing back at the office."

"I'm quite sure they can get along without you for a day or so," Liz said, placing a perfect sneer around the word *you*.

I smiled at her as I might at a shark or a corporate head-hunter come to plunder my department. "No one is indispensable, for sure. But in my experience, some are more so than others."

She stared at me, a blank expression on her podgy face. I felt a tiny twinge of guilt at striking back at someone so out-matched.

Tough.

Jackie, Dave, and Jason left first, Liz and the twins following on their heels. Tomorrow would be a long day for us all.

My mother's children settled around the kitchen table nursing mugs of coffee, while Dad, Al, and Aileen plopped themselves in front of the TV. Sampson snoozed at my feet.

"Funeral tomorrow," Shirley said. As if we didn't know.

"Hard to believe that we won't see her again." Jimmy sighed and peered into his cup.

"Not to come through that door ever again. With an apron full of tomatoes or peas."

"I'll miss her letters," I said. "I already do. Those letters were so… her. Her personality came out on paper perfectly."

"I tried to talk her into getting a computer," Jimmy said. "Told her that it would be an easier and faster way to write to you. But she wouldn't hear of it."

"Too expensive," Shirley said. She peered into the fridge. "There's a bit of cake left. Anyone?"

We shook our heads, and she cut a slice for herself. "Wouldn't have thought you could cook like that, Becky."

"Well, I can," I snapped. *Fooled her.*

Al poked his head around the door. "Time to be going, Shirl."

My sister gulped down the last forkful of cake and put the plate into the dishwasher.

We all trailed out to the front porch. Dad, Jimmy, Aileen, and I waved goodbye as the lights of the car dipped down the hill. Sampson dashed into the dark woods in hot pursuit of some small, nocturnal animal. I hoped it was small.

As I turned to call after the dog, my peripheral vision caught Jimmy giving his wife a slight nod. Aileen took Dad by the arm and guided him inside. "Have you laid out what you plan to wear tomorrow, Bob? Shall I check it over, make sure everything is as Janet would expect it to be?"

The night muffled his reply.

Jimmy cleared his throat. "I'm glad you're home, Rebecca."

"Where else would I be on the day before my mother's funeral?"

"I only mean that it's been a long time since you've been here."

"Nothing to come for. Mom gave me all the news."

"Look, Becky." He turned abruptly and gripped my upper arms, his handsome face a picture of—what? Could it possibly be pain? His fingers were strong, the muscles of his arms well-exercised and powerful.

I broke out of the grip with an abrupt upward slice of both arms. "Don't you touch me."

"Listen to me."

"No. I don't have to listen to you. Not now. Not ever. I'll sit with you at my mother's funeral, because Dad expects it. But then I never want to see you again."

"Everything okay?" Aileen stood in the doorway. The living room lights shone softly behind her. The fabric of the blue dress swayed in the light wind coming off the lake.

"Fine, dear, fine." Jimmy smiled, his perfect white teeth shining in the moonlight. Growing up in a family without much money, and in a town without much of a dentist, lucky Jimmy always had perfect teeth. I had suffered through years of adult orthodontistry as soon as I scraped together the money to pay for it.

"Good." Aileen took his arm and hugged it to her side. "Nice night. Full of promise for the beauties of summer yet to come, don't you agree, Rebecca."

"Perfectly lovely."

"We'll be on our way," she said. "We'll be here at 1:45 to pick you and Bob up."

Jimmy looked at me.

I looked at Aileen. "We'll be ready."

"Good night then." They walked down the steps, and their silhouettes merged with the scented velvet night.

"I was thinking, Jimmy," I called.

"Yes." His voice sounded particularly deep in the darkness.

"I heard that you know Jennifer Taylor. The girl who disappeared. Terrible, eh? Her family must be so worried. They'll never find her alive. Don't you agree?"

Aileen sucked in her breath. A pebble rolled down the hill, and their footsteps faded away—hers soft and hesitant, his hard and angry.

I didn't feel any better.

Chapter 13

Leaving the last of the cleaning up for the careful attentions of the house fairy, I crawled into bed. Dad watched TV for a long time, and I lay awake listening to the incomprehensible mumble coming from the sports channel. The lacy curtains on my bedroom window were open wide, and outside a full moon shone, round and white. Light flooded in. At last Dad switched the TV off and padded about the house in his going-to-bed routine. Sampson shifted her bulk under the covers, and I actually smiled, thinking of my mother's horror at the sight of a dog allowed up on the bed. In a moment of sheer, unadulterated madness, I'd offered to speak at tomorrow's funeral, and I still had no idea what I was going to say. I'd started to work on a speech on the plane from Vancouver, but it was so full of greeting-card sentiment that I deleted it with disgust as the pilot commanded us to put up the seat trays and straighten our chairs in preparation for landing. A reference to the dog on the bed might be a good opening.

What else could I say about a woman who had struggled to protect me from the vicious savagery of her own family but couldn't protect herself? Who saved every penny she earned so that her youngest daughter could escape? Who buried her head in her chest when her husband buried his head in a bottle? Who taught her children about common decency and good manners while they listened to a rising crescendo of swearing and shouting from the back shed?

What could I possibly say about the mother who encouraged me to apply for every scholarship that came up? Who kept a secret bank account and handed it all over to me when I left town never to return? Yet who had stood by and allowed her oldest daughter to be married off to the town nerd because she was, in my grandfather's sainted view, a disgrace to this family.

I glanced at my bedside clock. Well after midnight. Dad's snores echoed down the hall. Sampson twitched and chased rabbits and cats in her dreams.

I still didn't have a speech.

Suppose I dissolved into tears and had to be helped from the podium? Would anyone mind? Probably not.

My feet felt the cold hardwood floor. Sampson came awake instantly, jumping off the bed to stand beside me.

Once again, we made our way down the dark staircase. I decided to dig back a bit. Into the murky past. I pulled the top off the second crate. The dust rose in a gentle cloud, visible in the strong beam of my flashlight, to dissipate like the flimsy memories it protected.

I started to read.

> *I hate him, I hate him. I hate him so much. Oh,*
> *God, what have I done to deserve this? What have I*
> *done that You would punish me so?*

I slammed the book shut. I was looking for some emotion, to be sure. Some understanding. But this was not meant for me.

But if not me, who? My mother must have known that she would die some day, probably soon. She was seventy-seven years old when her heart gave out. Why then did she leave all these notebooks in these old tea chests? So her children would consign them to the rubbish heap, unread? Or so her youngest daughter would find them. And finding them, read them?

Perhaps even she didn't know.

I pulled out another book. This one was a good quality journal with a picture on the cover of the scrubbed, smiling, mundane faces of the Brady Bunch, dating it nicely.

*The house seems so lonely now that Rebecca is gone.
I miss her more than I thought possible. Bob too,
although he would never say so. Poor Bob, he has
missed so much in life, shut off from all emotion the
way he is.*

*But Rebecca writes all the time, and she seems to be
having such a grand time. I do wish I been given the
chance to go to university. Unthinkable, of course, in
my day, for a girl from a shopkeeper's family. Still, it
would have been nice. I only hope that Rebecca isn't
having such a wonderful time, all the boys she must
be meeting and all the parties she will be going to,
that she neglects her studies.*

I am so proud of her.

"Wow," I spoke aloud. Sampson assumed that I was talking to
her and abandoned her attention to a dishrag that had become
trapped between the freezer and the wall. She cocked her big
head to one side and gave me an inquisitive look. I rubbed her
chin. My mother loved me. And she was proud of me. Wow!
Not that she had much to worry about in the boy and party
department. I had been a frightened, shy, unattractive girl, all
long awkward limbs and bad haircut, from a poor family in one
of the poorest parts of the province. I didn't go to university for
the social life. Just as well, because I didn't have one.

That day's journal entry went on to talk about Liz's success
in earning her baking badge at Brownies.

The best place to start is at the beginning.

I replaced the Brady Bunch journal and pulled the first tea
chest out, the one tucked away at the back. It was covered by a
solid layer of dust. Good thing I don't have allergies.

The books in this chest were older, plainer, packed in reverse
order, the newest at the top. The first journal would therefore be
found at the bottom. A few were moldy, some showing traces of

insects and damp. I dug down, piling the fragile books carefully on top of the other two chests. At last, I reached the bottom-most book. It was plain brown leather, small, about five inches by seven, and surprisingly heavy for its size. Even through the miasma of years, damp, and neglect, my fingers felt the quality of the little book. A quality that didn't appear to be repeated in any of its later fellows.

The spine cracked like a gunshot as I pulled back the cover. I winced and loosened my grip. The ink on the first page had faded to an ugly brown, the color of old dried blood.

The Diary of Miss Janet Green. July 17, 1943

The words were large and bold. The journal was the only place in her world that this girl, daughter of shopkeepers, could be bold. Forthright. Unleashing the universal female desire for self-expression. I imagined a teenage Neanderthal girl crawling away from the family fire to carve her diary on the cave walls.

> *Today, I met HIM. HE is the most wonderful, perfect,*
> *handsomest, smartest man in the entire world. I am*
> *IN LOVE. Is it mere happenstance that only last week*
> *I received this diary from Aunt Joan for my 17th*
> *birthday? It can't be. I am sure that I was meant to*
> *start the rest of my life in the pages of this very book.*

Gee. This was embarrassing. The paragon of virtue no doubt didn't spare a second thought for the tall, gangly, so-young Janet Green. We've all done it. Fallen hard for the biggest jerk in town, school, club, church…whatever. The one who never looked at us again and for whom we ate our tender, innocent hearts out. My mom was seventeen when she started this book. To modern ears she sounded more like a twelve-year-old. But times were different.

I turned the page. It was filled with two words, over and over again. *Bob McKenzie, Bob McKenzie…*

The paragon of manly virtue was my father.

There were no windows in the cellar to mark the passage of time or the rising of the sun. I read on and Sampson chased dishrags and moths until my father's feet tracing the well-worn path to the bathroom sounded overhead. Instead of heading back to the bedroom once the toilet was flushed and the water turned off, his footsteps moved into the kitchen.

Morning.

The morning of my mother's funeral.

I still didn't have a speech. But I had a lot to think about.

The church was full, nearly standing room only. It was a small church, to be sure, for a small community. When Ray's grandmother died at age 102, the huge cathedral was almost deserted and the aging priest's voice echoed around and around in the cavernous chamber. At the time I thought that there is not much in life sadder than the funeral of someone so old that they have outlived all friends and most relations.

My mother's coffin rested at the front of the church, surrounded by stiff, formal bouquets, the wood buffed so highly that one could see one's face in it. If anyone was brave enough to put their face that close.

The minister droned on. I paid no attention, thinking of nothing but Ray's funeral. There *is* something sadder than an empty funeral, and that is the funeral of a man so young that everyone he worked with, the men on his recreational sports teams, his wife's colleagues, even neighbors and old school friends, pack the tiny funeral parlor and spill out into the hallway. Ray had had no religious beliefs, having abandoned the Catholic church long ago. His death had been so sudden, and threw me into such shock, that I exerted no control over anything that happened in the few days after. His sister arranged for her own priest to perform the service, although the man had never met Ray. My husband would have hated every second of his own funeral.

Sharp elbows in the ribs from Dad on one side and Shirley on the other. Time to pull out of remembrances. I was on.

I climbed the two steps to the lectern, cleared my throat, wiped my palms on the skirt of my designer suit, and wrung the white cotton handkerchief I'd found in the back of my mother's dresser drawer between my hands. And spoke my mother's eulogy.

I didn't have any notes, having never managed to prepare a speech. So I spoke from my heart. About the dog on the bed and how angry that would have made her. And about the modest bank account she kept untouched so that all the money would be there for me when I was ready to go to university. How she sat up late helping me fill in forms for the scholarships I needed to supplement the bank account. About her bus trips to Toronto to visit me. And about her joy in seeing the sea again after so many years, the first time she came to visit me in Vancouver.

I returned to my seat in a daze and Dad gripped my hand as I sat down.

At last it was over. The family filed out first, as was the custom, and stood blinking in the soft sunlight falling on the fresh green grass. The carefully tended flowerbeds were bursting to life in carpets of purple and yellow and white crocuses. A handful of adventurous tulips and daffodils struggled to push their fragile, soft moss-green heads above the rich black earth.

New life all around me. Birth of a different sort—plants pushing themselves free of the dark comfort of the nurturing soil and into the wider, welcoming world.

Death is a part of life.

The cotton handkerchief, well worn to begin with, was now in shreds. Full of my own pain, I paid no attention to the river of mourners pouring out of the church. The family, even the great-grandchildren, lined up beside me to shake hands. But I didn't see my brother Jimmy.

Liz's husband, the reclusive Ralph, did put in an appearance. He stood beside me on the lawn, all four hundred some pounds of him. The man was a mountain. A short, fat mountain, constantly wiping rivers of sweat from his forehead. It was a sunny but cool spring day. I didn't want to be around to see Ralph in the heat of summer.

We drove in a dark procession to the graveside. Funerals should always be held in the rain, the colder and heavier the better. But for my mother's interment the sun shone brightly in a cheerful baby-blue sky.

The graveside service was, thank goodness, short. The ritual of the words was comforting, even to someone who has no religion. At the end, Al supported my dad, who was sobbing silently. My dad so rarely showed any emotion that as a child I didn't think he felt any. It had all been beaten out of him. Young.

Service over, I stood by myself, shaking hands, most of which were liver spotted and gnarled, as the crowd broke up and people walked to their cars. Everyone stopped to say a word, every word kind and tinged with sadness, condolences heartfelt. I wondered what people will find to say at my funeral.

Kimmy Wright hugged me closely, like we were best friends or something, before introducing me to her mother. "If there is anything you need…" Kimmy said, the tone and words as ritual as the graveside service.

Actually, Kimmy, I need you to tell me that you were a perfect bitch in high school, and announce to those here assembled that I didn't let John Ferrar stick his tongue down my throat and put his hand up my skirt behind the bleachers. Or anywhere else for that matter.

I smiled and thanked her and her mother, so frail that she looked as if a strong wind would have her flat on her back on the graveyard lawn, for coming.

Chapter 14

The Diary of Mrs. Janet McKenzie. April 2, 1945

Shirley. Her name is Shirley. She has dark eyes and almost no hair. But her nose is exactly like Bob's and her skin is dark, like his. I am sure of it. I am sure I remember right. It has been so long since we were together, that sometimes I have to struggle to picture his face in my mind. It was an easy birth, the sister told me. I certainly didn't think so! But it is over and I am A MOTHER! Imagine that. Me, Janet MCKENZIE, nee Green, is a MOTHER. I only wish that Bob could be here. I have no idea where he is. Oh, I wish that this horrid war would be over. They say it can't go on much longer. They say our soldiers are almost in Germany.

Bob's mum wrote me a lovely letter last month. She welcomed me into their family. Bob told me that he is an only child, and it was really hard on his mum when he joined the army. (He spells it Mom. *I am going to be a Canadian so I will have to learn to call her Mom.) I will write to her tonight. And tell her all about Shirley. A first grandchild! And there will be lots and lots more. I would like six babies. Six Canadian babies, little Misters and Misses McKenzie. All of us on our lovely farm in Canada. I haven't heard from my own mum. I hope she is safe. The bombing has been something fierce in London and now they have these horrid rockets falling all the time. I worry sometimes that she is hurt and calling for me. But they can't find me.*

Dad came to visit earlier. It took all my courage but I asked him if he had word from Mum, if she knew she was a granny. His face just clouded over, like it always does when someone mentions her, and he said no. Aunt Betty came to visit also. She brought a perfectly huge pile of knitting. Tiny, perfect cardigans and booties. She made a great fuss over Shirley, but I know that she is afraid of the day we will leave for Canada.

December 25, 1945

You would think that with the war being over it would be the most wonderful Christmas ever. But it isn't. We didn't have much for Christmas dinner. Dad killed one of the chickens and Aunt Betty made a lovely doll for Shirley but still everyone seems so down. I miss Bob terribly. I thought that when the war ended we would be together, forever. But it has been seven months already. There is no more food in the shops than ever there was. Everything is still rationed. I hate it! I hate it all! Bob has left for Canada. I understand that we can't travel together. But I want to be gone. All this waiting is perfectly awful. I have been getting letters from the Canadian Wives' Club. Other wives and children have left for Canada already. Why not us?

Bob was here for two days only. Two days! Then he was gone again. In all our married life I have had not much more than a few weeks with my husband. I have more acquaintance with the pathetic, crippled Hugh Maitland than with my own husband.

Happily, this time we were able to engage in marital relations. It really is quite wonderful, when you can relax and forget about how ridiculous it all is. Bob was just getting started, so to speak, when Shirley began to cry. It was Aunt Betty's own suggestion, that she care for Shirley for the night and we move the cot into her room. When I heard my baby crying, I wanted to get up to go to her, but Bob told me to let her be. Of course I worried about her the whole time but some part of my mind still liked Bob's attentions. The next night it was much better. Shirley slept the night through. But then he was gone again. At least not to the war this time. Back to Canada. Safe. Waiting for me. And for our daughter.

Chapter 15

The reception was held at Jackie's house near North Ridge. Everyone who had been at the church and then at the graveside, as well as a handful of stragglers, packed into the thoroughly modern house. Totally without character, it would have fit into any suburb of any city in North America. Like all of its fellows, lined cheek-to-jowl down the long straight street on which only the houses were big—the trees were nothing but overgrown twigs. Sad to see such a house and such a street in a town as distinctive as North Ridge. But it was no business of mine how North Ridge handled its growth.

The twins had been assigned the task of making sure their great-granddad was taken care of. They ensured that he was settled comfortably in the settee in front of the cold and empty gas fireplace and, as instructed, scurried off in their matching navy blue dresses to fetch tea and sandwiches. A few women close to his age, unaccompanied by men, settled down near him.

A half-remembered line from *Hamlet* teased the edges of my brain. Something about the funeral baked meats not yet being cold.

Tea was the order of the day. Tea and enough sandwiches, salads, casseroles, cakes, and squares to sink a battleship. But I found Jackie and Liz and a couple of their friends out on the back porch sharing a bottle of red wine. I swallowed my tea in one gulp and held out the rental-supply cup.

"Now you mustn't tell anyone, Aunt Rebecca," Jackie giggled, pouring a generous slug. Liz grunted once, put her glass down on the wooden railing and walked into the house. She forgot to say hello.

"I don't think Liz likes me."

The friends mumbled their condolences and scurried for safety.

"She doesn't not like you," Jackie said, once we were alone. Night was moving in. Soft and gentle like a cloak of the best black velvet. Clouds covered the sky, hiding the moon and stars. Crickets chirped in the distance, a single frog croaked, heralding a chorus. A thick line of fully grown trees bordered the postage stamp slice of backyard. Judging by the development around here, they wouldn't last much longer. And the frogs and crickets would disappear along with them. "My sister doesn't like many people."

I shrugged. Her problem. "Have you seen Jimmy?"

"Why do you ask? I get the feeling you and Uncle Jimmy don't get on too well, either."

"Inquisitive little thing, aren't you? I would say that most of this family doesn't get on with me *too well*. What about you?"

Unasked, she refilled my glass. "I like it here, in North Ridge. I went away for a while. To the big, bad city. To the University of Toronto, on a full scholarship which I was exceedingly lucky to get because my parents couldn't afford it otherwise. I managed to get my degree but didn't like the life much. I missed Hope River. I missed my mom, and my grandma, I even missed my sister. Probably a first in the history of the world."

I smiled.

"So I came back. And I met a nice man here in North Ridge and I married him and we had a nice son and bought this house only a few miles up the road from Hope River, where I grew up. But at least I did have the chance to see something of the bigger world. And although it might not be the place for me, I do envy anyone who can walk boldly into that world and make it work for them."

"Mom, Mom. Can we go and catch frogs? Can we?" Jason danced in the doorway, scarcely able to contain his enthusiasm.

"Who's 'we'?"

"Matthew. Me and Matthew."

"Matthew and I."

The boy scrunched his freckled face in confusion. "I guess you can come, if you want to."

Jackie laughed and reached across me to rub her son's head. Exactly the way I did to Sampson. "You know what I mean. Say hello to your Aunt Rebecca first."

"Hello, Aunt Rebecca."

"You can go with Matthew. But only to the swamp. You hear me? No further."

"Okay." He disappeared in a flash of ill-fitting suit and red curls.

"A nice boy," I said.

"I think so."

"I was asking if you'd seen Jimmy."

"So you were. I took a plate of ham and salads out to him about fifteen minutes ago. He's in the garage. The die-hard smokers have set themselves up out there. Which coincidentally happens to be the location of Dave's beer fridge."

I walked through the house, placing my tea—turned wine— cup on the crowded kitchen counter as I passed.

A thin line of crocuses lined the concrete pathway running along the front of the house to the double driveway and attached garage. The flowers were folded in upon themselves, petals snuggled close together. Night was falling slowly as it does in this part of the world at this time of year, wrapping the gentle hills and calm lakes in a blanket of dim purple light, delicate odors, and muffled sounds. When I lived here as a child I loved the twilight hours the best. I still do, on the rare occasion I have time to enjoy them. Today I didn't.

Jimmy had loosened his tie and undone the top button of his white shirt. The fold lines were so perfect that it was obvious the shirt had only recently been released from its store wrapping.

Dave held his can of beer up to me in a question.

I shook my head.

He finished his beer with a long swallow and crumpled the can in his fist. "Back to work," he said with a huge martyred sigh. "Jackie will be looking for me."

"Nice speech, Becky," Jimmy said. He was drinking from a bottle, not a can, and studying the decoration on the label as if there would be a test later. "You did a good job."

I shrugged.

"I suppose I shoulda done it. Being the only son and all. But I didn't know what I could say."

I snorted. "Were you there? In the church? I didn't see you. Aileen sat up front, beside Jackie. With the family."

"I sat at the back. To be honest, Beck, I was afraid I'd break down and I wanted to get out of there fast, if I had to."

"My name is Rebecca. Not Becky and certainly not Beck. And God forbid any of your macho friends would see you crying at the funeral of your own mother."

"Well pardon me, *Rebecca*. Look, you think I was a real shit to Mom. And I was, a long time ago, God forgive me. But you haven't been home for years, and you don't know what's been happening around here. Things change. People change." The look in his amazing eyes was one that I never thought I'd see. Not defiant, not gloating. Not proud and mocking. Almost as if he was asking for my understanding. Perhaps even my friendship.

And leopards change their spots every day. And pigs fly and snakes shed their skin and never grow any more.

Maybe he took acting lessons in jail. He'd never had the need to act before. His charm was natural and unforced, so powerful that everyone who fell under his spell assumed that they'd misinterpreted the briefly glimpsed streak of cruelty. Until it was too late.

"Stow it, Jimmy. I don't really care."

"Sure you do. Why else did you come back? You didn't have to. You could have sent a big bunch of flowers and a fat check to cover the funeral. That's all anyone expected, you know."

That hit home. My brother always knew where to strike.

"I didn't come out here to fight with you."

"No, you didn't. You came out here with a chip on your shoulder so big it's crushing you. I've told you that things are different now. And Aileen has told you. If you won't listen, then it's your problem."

The beer drinkers had scattered at the first of our angry words. Further down the driveway and out on the road, cars were starting up. The first of the mourners, probably those who had traveled a long way, were leaving.

"I came out here because I'm going home soon and I wanted to ask you what's going to happen to Dad. I'll have this same talk with Shirley."

"You could always take him with you." He tossed his beer bottle into an open trash bin. Missed by a mile and the bottle rattled off into a dark corner of Dave's garage. He jerked the fridge door open and pulled out another. Visible under the starched shirt, the muscles in his back and shoulders were tense with strain.

"Well, I'm hardly going to do that, now am I?" I said, while at the same time begrudgingly admitting to myself that this was a first. The Jimmy I knew disdained to absorb any tension into his own body. Why should he, when he could always lash out at the nearest available target? Which sometimes happened to be my mom.

"Can't afford it? That's too bad, *Becky*. I could always send you a little bit every month. To help out, you know."

"Fuck you, Jimmy." I turned and took the first step back to the comparative safety of Jackie's house.

"Run away, *Becky*. It's what you do best, isn't it?" His voice dropped and took the cruel edge with it. "Christ, this is stupid. We have to talk about Dad; there's no getting around that. Maybe this isn't the best time for it."

"Is there ever a good time?"

Two men detached themselves from the group of smokers gathered by the front door out of earshot of our family squabbles.

They spoke to each other in low voices. They looked familiar. Boys I had gone to school with? All grown up fat and ugly?

Jimmy paid them no attention. "No, there will never be a good time. But for some completely strange and unknown reason I want you to believe that things have changed with me. Mom wrote to you all the time; she visited you a year or so ago. She never complained about me the last few years, did she?"

"Jimmy," I sighed and turned back to face him. "Mom never complained about you. Never. Maybe to her god but not to me. Christ, she never even said a word against Grandpa."

I hate him, I hate him, I hate him. Those bitter, angry words told to the confessional of her diary. Which "him" might she have been thinking about?

Jimmy's eyes darkened with what in anyone else I would have taken for pain. The look passed so quickly it might not have been, and my intuitive wariness returned. He wasn't looking at me. He was looking over my shoulder.

"We've been wanting to talk to you, McKenzie," the larger of the two men said. I recognized his voice. Jack, with his skinny, frightening friend. The men who'd accosted me in the grocery store. Today Jack had dressed in a cheap, badly fitting suit, once-white shirt, and thin black tie and had combed his greasy hair. All in honor of the funeral. How thoughtful of him.

"A lot of people in this town are mighty upset about what's happened to the Taylor girl," Jack's pal said. He was small but his voice was very deep, not quite fitting the scrawny frame. His suit fit him a good deal better than his friend's did.

Jimmy smiled. The way a shark smiles. "I'm upset too. She's a nice girl. But I hear that the police are working full out on it. They've even brought in detectives from Toronto."

"We think that maybe you should be helping the police with that," Jack said. Neither of the men paid me any attention. Probably not a good thing.

"I would if I could." Jimmy spread his arms out in supplication, the beer bottle firmly clenched in one fist. "But I'm sorry to say that I don't know anything about it."

"Some of the men in this town think maybe you know a whole lot about it," said Scrawny. His right hand was pushed firmly into his pants pocket. Clenched. Holding something?

They both stepped forward.

"Do they, now?" Jimmy swung his beer bottle against a wooden shelf that held an array of shiny, pristine, never-used amateur tools. The brown bottle shattered and the body fell away. He balanced the jagged-edged neck comfortably in one hand.

Chapter 16

The Diary of Janet McKenzie. September 12, 1946

At last it is almost our turn. We are now in London, waiting in the hostel until they tell us it is time to get the train. It has been so many years since I was last in London. Not since that Christmas so long ago, when Arthur and Raymond were perfectly bratty and Mum was still with us. We heard all about the bombing of course, and saw the terrible pictures in the magazines and newspapers. And, night after night, we only had to look up to see those German bombers flying over Surrey, toward London and the north, our brave English fighters after them. But nothing quite prepared me for how much devastation there is.

I would love to go out and see the sights. But Shirley is poorly and she fusses all the time, night and day. Teeth, the Red Cross woman told me. But I know it's more than that. She is a sensitive baby, very intelligent. Things were terribly difficult at home these last weeks. Dad was remote, cold almost, like I don't remember him ever being before. Aunt Betty came over all crying and moody, saying that she couldn't bear to part from the baby. Which, of course, had me crying no end and then Shirley all in an uproar. I almost considered not going. Not going to Canada. Not going to Bob. Of writing to him and telling him that I had changed my mind. But then what would become of me? A divorced woman, with a baby, in a little village in the south of England?

But then I got another lovely letter from Mrs. McKenzie (Mom!) and everything seemed fine again. Her letter said that she is getting the spare room ready for the baby and that her friends have given her clothes for a little one, warm sweaters and thick pants and a snowsuit and boots for the winter. (It gets extremely cold in Canada, I have heard.) Of course I don't expect that we will be living with Mr. and Mrs. McKenzie for long. Just until Bob has our own home finished and ready for Shirley and me. And all the babies who will soon follow.

Chapter 17

For the first time, Scrawny looked at me. His eyes were narrowed to nasty slits. "I think you're needed in the kitchen, lady."

"Actually." I found my voice. "No one has ever needed me in any kitchen. So you must be mistaken. Are you two friends of my mother? Thank you for coming to pay your respects."

Jack looked at me, slack-jawed. Clearly he thought me quite ga-ga. Irony and sarcasm were no doubt concepts not to be found in his vocabulary.

I smiled my best business-cocktail-party-reception smile. "Did you have enough to eat? There's plenty more."

"Becky, you're not helping," Jimmy said, his voice low. "Please leave." He balanced the shattered bottle in his right hand.

"One day, lady," Jack said, "someone's gonna put a fist in that big mouth."

"We want to talk to your brother, that's all," said Scrawny, his fingers moving as he caressed whatever he held in his pocket. "You should go back into the house."

"I don't think that's really what you want. To talk, I mean. But no matter. Now, I am particularly famous for my loud piercing voice, as I am sure you noticed. So if you gentlemen don't leave right away I might have to actually start screaming. And that will be embarrassing for us all, won't it?"

"Shut up, you loud-mouthed bitch." Jack's limited patience broke and he took one step toward me. Jimmy gripped the bottleneck tighter and stepped forward, balancing his weight on the balls of his feet. He was half Jack's size. Scrawny looked from each of us to the other; he was losing control, unsure of what to do.

I kept talking. It's what I do best. "I'd rather you didn't call me that, please. After all, we are here to pay our respects to my mother."

"Uncle Jimmy, Uncle Jimmy. Look what we got." Jason and his friend Matthew burst into the garage. Their faces were streaked with dirt, their eyes bright with excitement. Jason's funeral suit was soaked and mud-splattered, and a jagged gash tore the fabric of his left pant leg.

Together the grinning boys held out a jar. A fat frog sat inside, looking none too pleased at being the center of attention. My sympathies were with the frog.

"Get outa here, boys," Jack growled. "We got business here."

The boys looked at him in confusion. The man didn't want to see the big frog?

"Time to be on our way, Jackson," Scrawny said. "Too many women and kids around to allow us men to have a nice polite conversation."

Jack Jackson (could that actually be his name?) growled again but did as instructed. Scrawny pulled his hand out of his pocket and turned to leave.

"You tell the cops where she is, McKenzie," he tossed over his shoulder, as he headed down the driveway. "Or it won't be our fault what happens to you."

He stopped, turned, and looked at me. "And don't you be around, lady."

Jimmy threw the neck of his beer bottle into the garbage with an inaudible sigh and a pronounced relaxing of his shoulders. "That's a really great frog. But it won't live long in that jar. You should take it back to the swamp, where it belongs. It'll be happier living free. Don't you think?"

"I guess," Jason sighed.

"Time for dessert." A smiling Jackie appeared, bearing a silver tray covered with a large assortment of squares, cookies, and slices of cake. "Dave said you two were catching up on old times, so I guessed that you wouldn't come in for something as unimportant as food. Jason Warzak, what have you done to your suit?" She handed me the tray and sighed mightily. "Boys. What's a mother to do?" The twinkle in her eye belittled the seriousness of her words.

"What on earth were those two doing here anyway?" she asked. "Heard about the free food, I suppose."

"You know them?" I asked.

"Sure. Jack Jackson and Pete Hartman. Scum of the earth. Drifted into town years ago when their truck broke down on the highway and they never quite managed to do us all a favor and drift out again."

"Did they know your grandma?"

"It seems sometimes as if Grandma knew everyone in this town."

"Where do they work?"

"Keep out of it, Becky, please. They're none of your business." Jimmy scooped a handful of cookies off the plate. "Time for us to be going. I'll get Aileen and we'll say our good-byes. Thanks for doing all this, Jackie."

We watched him go. I was left holding the dessert tray.

"What's none of your business, Aunt Rebecca?"

I looked at Jackie's thin, serious face and handed back the tray. "Jimmy thinks I insulted the big one, so he's worried about me."

"Well, don't you get on their bad side. Jack's as thick as two short planks, but Pete isn't. Crafty as a fox that one."

"Looks like people are leaving now. You'll have a lot of dishes to do. I'll give you a hand."

We walked silently back to the house. The cloud blanket dispersed as night settled in, but the moon had not yet risen. With no high leafy trees to shade them, the harsh yellow light from the streetlamps shone far too bright, blocking any sight of stars on this clear night. That didn't seem right. This far away from the crowded south, the show of stars should be wonderful. On the summer nights of my childhood we could sometimes even see the Northern Lights in all their haunting, colorful glory.

Cars pulled away from the side of the road, and loud good-byes and final condolences echoed through the dark street.

Old women and a few men filled the living room, gathered around my dad, who remained seated in the best chair, the one close to the unused fireplace. Deep lines were carved through the tough old skin of his face, and his eyes were moist and vacant. He held a delicate china teacup in one shaking hand. Jackie removed it with a silent smile.

In contrast the kitchen was full of chattering, laughing middle-aged women, washing and drying dishes, covering serving platters, rooting through cupboards in search of plastic containers, rinsing out the utility-size coffeepot borrowed from the church. The garbage bag under the sink, overfilled, had toppled over, and Liz bent over a mop to wipe brown mush off the floor.

"You must give me the recipe for that bean dip, Kay," one woman said to another. "It was absolutely wonderful."

"It's so simple, you won't believe it." Kay rhymed off a list of ingredients.

The women watched me out of the corner of their eyes as if I was some strange exotic specimen. Catching sight of me, Kimmy squealed and dragged a heavily made-up woman wearing a short skirt and tight blouse out of the corner where she had been trying to stuff serving platters into a cabinet.

"Becky, you must remember Norma. Norma Fitzgerald what was."

Norma managed to control her own enthusiasm. "Becky McKenzie." She breathed a cloud of booze and cigarette smoke. "After all these years."

It was an effort, but I politely refrained from waving my hand in front of my face. "So nice to see you again, Norma." I was fast becoming a world-class liar. Despite popular misconception, lying is not a requirement in the world of business and corporate relations. But it sure seems to be a necessity when returning to the small town where one grew up. I remembered Norma well enough. One of Kimmy's sycophants, always following the popular girls around with her tongue hanging out, desperate to be considered part of the in crowd. One step above lowly Becky McKenzie, who was totally out, Norma could be, and was, meaner and nastier than any Kimmy. The politics of the lives of teenage girls: a better preparation for the world of business than any MBA program.

"Isn't it nice that Becky's home again, Norma?" Kimmy said.

Norma nodded and forced a smile, but her thickly painted, dark eyes gave another message. One rainy November day I had come across her in the girls' washroom during math class, the period right after lunch, sticking her fingers down her throat, too occupied to notice that the stall door wasn't latched properly. I laughed until tears ran down my cheeks and my sides ached. And then, of course, I proceeded to tell the entire in crowd. Horrified, not at the act, but that she had been caught by nerdy Becky McKenzie, they ignored Norma for weeks. A trace of hostility narrowed her black-rimmed eyes, confirming that Norma remembered the incident as well as I.

Thankful not to have to play at being friends, I turned to Jackie. "You have more than enough help here. It looks like Dad is ready to pack it all in. I should be getting him home."

"I'm sure he's comfortable where he is." Shirley walked in from the deck, her arms laden with glasses, teacups, and plates. "Surrounded by all of his old friends. But if you want to leave…"

"In my opinion, whether you want it or not, I don't think he's comfortable at all. He's just buried his wife of more than fifty years and the poor man is quite worn out."

Shirley placed her load carefully on the countertop, squirted a stream of yellow dishwashing liquid into the sink, and turned the tap sharply to hot. "Well, my *opinion*, having seen the man every day for the last fifty years, is that he is quite happy in his circle of friends and that we should leave him be until they have all left."

"Jesus Shirley, lighten up." Once again the assorted friends scattered, but this time they moved not quite out of range. Kimmy and Norma retreated to the hall but no further, and there they stood, practically horizontal, their heads leaning into the kitchen in order not to miss a single word. "I said he looks tired, that's all. And he does."

"I would appreciate it if you didn't swear every time you open your mouth."

I stood in the center of the ceramic floor, beside the wooden butcher's block, gobsmacked. "My language is hardly the issue here. And this isn't the right time to get into the real issue, whatever you may decide that it is."

"And when would be the right time, Miss High-and-Mighty, Miss Big-City Girl? Sorry, I should have said *Big-City Woman.*" She threw a glass into the sink and turned to face me. Rage mottled her thin face; her eyes had narrowed to hostile slits.

"You come dancing in here after thirty years and everyone is so happy to see you. Good old Rebecca. Isn't she clever, isn't she beautiful? Hope River's success story. Well some of us have stayed here to look after what's important. Our family. How much did that suit cost you anyway? More than my husband makes in a month, I'll bet."

"We don't really want to talk about your husband's salary right now." I tried to make the comment light, friendly. I failed.

"You think you can laugh at Al? Al's a good man. So he's out of work right now, lots of men are. He'll get a job, come tourist season. We had to get married. So what? It's worked out, hasn't it? Better than your marriage did, anyway."

I saw red. I gripped the edge of the butcher's block. It was good wood, the grain straight and smooth beneath my fingers. "My husband is *dead*, you stupid bitch. And don't you dare imply that it was my fault."

"I didn't say anything about fault. I said that because you've made a mess of your life, don't come back here trying to mess up ours."

A cloud of acid rage covered my eyes and filled my heart, and I lashed out. At the edges of perception I could almost hear the silent gasps of our eager audience, feel them stretching forward so as to not miss a single moment. "Like I would even be bothered to interfere in your petty, insignificant life. That would surely—ha! get it?—*surely*, be too stupefyingly boring for words."

"Stop this, right now," Jimmy stepped between us, his eyes dark with anger. "You two are putting on a display for the whole town."

The crowd behind me shuffled and turned to discussing other topics.

"You told me you were leaving," I snapped.

"I wanted to, but Aileen said we should stay and help clean up." He nodded to the dining room door, where his wife stood with a pile of dirty plates and an embarrassed grin.

A high voice snickered. I whirled around. "Don't you people have anywhere to go? Something exciting must be happening in Hope River on a pleasant night like this. Raccoon shooting or raiding the town dump come to mind."

"Aunt Rebecca." A strong, cool hand took my arm. Jackie smiled into my face: She is the only one in my family who even approaches my height. "You're absolutely right. It's time Grandpa went home. Can you help him, please?"

I recognize applied psychology when I see it. And I was glad to see it. "I would be happy to. I wouldn't want to outstay my welcome here. Good night Jimmy, Aileen, *ladies.*" Head held high, I stalked out of the kitchen.

"Mother!" Behind me Jackie hissed at Shirley. "You were so out of line!"

In a re-enactment of the parting of the Red Sea, the crowd of eager onlookers dispersed as I passed into the living room surrounded by a virtual roar of good-byes, coat-gathering, and the sound of the front door slamming.

My father sat amid his circle of old friends, most of them unaware of the drama they'd missed in the kitchen. Conversation and reminisces ebbed and flowed around Dad. He sat by the fireplace, as oblivious to conflict raging around him as if he were the eye of a hurricane or a whirlpool.

"Ready to go home, Dad," I bent over him.

The old ladies rose to their feet in a wave of concern. The old men, fewer in number but no less vocal, waved their hands and snickered at the very idea that Bob might be ready to be taken home and put to bed. Like a puppy, or an overeager child after a birthday party. I held my father's arm as Aileen slipped his coat over his shoulders, and we walked out into the night.

I had parked the SUV on the street, knowing that getting out of the driveway would be a nightmare of organization, finding the keys for this car, locating the owner of that. A cat sat under the nearest streetlight, watching us. This street was trying hard to grow up to be a big-city street, but I could hear the mating cry of the crickets in the long grass behind the houses and the bellow of frogs from the woods beyond.

"A nice party," Dad said as I held the passenger door open for him. He hesitated at the step. The SUV wasn't designed with seniors in mind. I gripped his arm firmly and helped him clamber up. "Your mother would have liked it, Becky."

"Yes, she would."

"Nice of Jackie to invite all of your mother's old friends."

"Yes, it was." I climbed up into my own seat and started the engine. The headlights caught a raccoon crossing the road on the way to Jackie's house in search of party residue. He was huge, fat, and arrogant and barely gave my car a sideways glance or let me think that I was inconveniencing him in the slightest. I watched him waddle into the darkness at the side of the house before pulling away.

"Too bad she missed it." Dad chattered on as I maneuvered the big vehicle out of the narrow streets. "I'll tell her all about it, of course. But I won't make it out to sound quite as nice as it was. So she doesn't get jealous, you understand."

"I understand."

"Not that Janet is ever jealous of anyone's good fortune."

"No."

"I'm gonna suggest that we drive out to Joe Armstrong's place tomorrow. He's been laid up with a broken leg, you know. His wife, Margaret, and Janet were always the best of friends."

I remembered a Joe and Margaret; they'd lived not far from us when I was growing up. The Armstrongs have been dead twenty years or more. Killed in a head-on collision on the way to the hospital to visit their newest grandchild, Mom had written to tell me. I don't know anything about psychology, but at a guess, I'd say that his mind had simply shut off the overflow of emotion caused by Mom's funeral, and the only way he could cope was by unconsciously pretending she was still around.

It was so sad.

Dad talked as I drove, about plans for tomorrow's visit to the Armstrongs, and worries as to if he should buy a piece of property, located I didn't understand where. As we drove up to the house, and I helped him out of the SUV, he talked about Jimmy, wondering if he would be able to find a good job having quit school so young.

Chapter 18

Diary of Janet McKenzie. September 14, 1946

At last I am here. On this huge ship. It is all quite horribly fright-ening but exciting at the same time. Imagine me, on the Queen Mary. *I remember when I was a tiny girl, looking at a magazine with a beautiful picture of the* Queen Mary. *Someone royal was boarding her, but I don't remember who.*

It wasn't like this for her, the Royal, I'm sure. There are so many of us. Women just like me, some with babies, some with older chil-dren, some on their own. Everyone seems quite frightened. Like me. Shirley has a touch of a cold, not much of one, ordinarily not any kind of a worry, but I don't want her crying and acting up on the ship and upsetting the other women.

It came quickly, this order to get ready for the trip to Canada.

I am so frightened—I have forgotten his face. I don't know if I will recognize my own husband.

Mr. Fitzpatrick sent his motorcar again. Not Bert this time, instead Albert Grady drove. Albert, not yet twenty years old, with half his face burnt away. Everyone in town knows that Elizabeth McCallum, who he was engaged to practically since they were in the cradle, took one look at his ravaged face, fainted dead away, and caught the next train to London.

Aunt Betty packed so carefully for us. All my best clothes, and Shirley's tiny things. Dad left us at the station. He said he was too busy in the shop to travel up to London with us. But I don't think that is the true reason. He buried his face in Shirley's soft blanket, and muttered words of love and caring. I have not heard from my mother, and as the train pulled out of the station and my father stood on the platform, his face as ravaged with loss as that of Albert Grady with fire, I cared no longer.

September 16, 1946

I haven't been sick even once. All around me, the other brides are lying in their bunks moaning, unable to eat a thing. But I feel fine. Shirley's cold is finished and she is as bright as a button. Perhaps we were born to enjoy the sea air. Some of the poor mums are suffering dreadfully; they can't even look after their little ones. We all pitch in and try to help and the Red Cross nurses are wonderful. This ship is so lovely. Such luxury: thick rose-colored carpets, beautiful upholstered chairs, white tablecloths in the dining room. I would like chairs like that in my house and crisp white cloths on the big dining room table. Not right away, I understand. Bob doesn't have that much money. But when we are settled and his farm is prospering, I will remember those chairs. And the eight of us (our six children and Bob and I—the McKenzie family!) will be sitting around a huge wooden table with a sharply ironed white cloth and silver polished until you can see your face in it.

As well as all the war brides and their children there are Canadian soldiers on board, heading home. They have their own decks and we brides are absolutely forbidden to fraternize with them.

The food is absolutely wonderful. White bread, as soft and fluffy and as pure as snow. Apples and oranges. As much as anyone can manage to eat. After the first meal the brides were stuffing bread rolls and fruit into their pockets and up their sleeves, afraid that it would all be gone the next day. Too bad for the sick ones who can only groan with envy as we healthy ones recount every mouthful.

September 18, 1946

Sea travel is wonderful. I have promised myself that Bob and I and our family absolutely must travel to England one day. We'll take the children to meet Dad and Aunt Betty. So many of the other war brides are still in bed, simply being sick. I do feel sorry for them. Those of us who are well are doing our best to help with their children. I have taken charge of a dear two-year-old, all tousled blond curls and big smile, whose mother hasn't kept a thing down since we left Southampton. The dear child pretends that she is helping me take care of Shirley.

The Red Cross nurses are perfectly wonderful and have organized feeding the children, preparing bottles for the babies, organizing the nappies and other laundry, and caring for the children whose mothers are sick.

In the evenings they show movies up on the deck. I would love to go, but I don't want to leave Shirley. She is so wide-awake and active during the day that she sleeps all the night through in her hammock over the foot of my bunk. But what if she wakes up and I am not there?

September 23, 1946

Will this trip ever end? Or will I keep on traveling, until I have gone all around the world and am back home in dear old England? To find Dad meeting me at the station with wide-open arms, and Albert Grady standing beside the car.

We arrived in Halifax at long last. Everyone was so happy to be there. A few husbands and new families were at the dock in Halifax to meet the ship, but most of the brides, including me, still have a long train trip ahead of us.

This is all so different than the train from Surrey to London. There we saw neat well-ploughed farmland and towns and small villages and then the outskirts of the great city itself. But here in Canada we can go for hours without passing a single house or a plot of cultivated land. The woods are lovely, starting to turn color with the change of the seasons. But sometimes at night there is not a light to be seen. Not a farmhouse or a village or even a car on the road. Sometimes I think that we are back in England where the war is still on and the blackout is in effect. But then suddenly we come to a station and lights burst all around us. One lonely bride disembarks, a pile of luggage placed at her feet, perhaps clutching her sleepy baby. Fortunately most of the women who have stepped off the train have had someone (sometimes whole towns!) out to meet them with a good deal of laughing and singing and heart-felt cries of welcome. I have seen entire families, mother, father, grandparents, numerous aunts and uncles, break down in tears. But we left one poor soul standing on the platform all by herself. As the train pulled out, the stationmaster switched out all the lights but one, and she was left standing alone in a thin pool of light.

September 24, 1946

Toronto! We are almost there. I am all ready; Shirley is wide-awake, fed, washed, and dressed for the big day. Mrs. Morrison, so much older than the rest of us, heading all the way to Victoria, is playing with her, showing her the countryside as it passes by. I have taken the opportunity to write a few words in my diary. I am so excited I can scarcely hold my pen straight. Those of us who are to get off in Toronto were up before sunrise, washing and doing each other's hair. Putting on a bit of makeup and perfume if we were lucky enough to have some and slipping into our best clothes. Thank goodness I am disembarking in a big city. I'm sure I'll have nightmares for the rest of my life of that poor girl standing on the platform in the middle of Quebec, her small scraps of cheap luggage around her, while the lights in the station go out one by one. Mrs. Beeton sewed up a lovely traveling outfit for me. I thought it was wonderful, when I first saw it. But when I see what the other women have to wear for their husbands I know that my dress is cheap and shabby, and too obviously put together by a village widow. Nothing I can do about it now. The clothes I have worn on the voyage are certainly no better.

Farmers' fields and forests are behind us now; we are passing rows of small factories and neat houses. Toronto. I must stop writing and fetch Shirley and make sure all our possessions are ready.

I am so afraid.

Chapter 19

What bit of sleep I managed to get was rough and disturbed. Sampson, confined to the house the entire day of the funeral, woke me by pushing her cold wet nose into my face and scratching at the sheets before the sun had even crested the horizon.

I made myself a cup of coffee, sipped barely a mouthful, and took Sampson into the woods. It was colder than it had been since my arrival, and dark clouds were gathering low overhead. But the cool air of a fresh spring morning felt perfectly wonderful on my bare face and hands. The woods are beautiful up here in the spring, the forest floor an ocean of delicate white trilliums, the occasional red bloom thrown in to add a splash of color. The deciduous trees were not yet in leaf, but their buds were so ripe that I believed that if I held my breath long enough I would be able to hear them grow. Sampson bounded on ahead, sniffing at every twig and under every tree, yet still managing to cover ten yards for each one of mine. Birds and squirrels watched us from the tops of the tallest trees, and a hawk circled high overhead. These woods aren't part of my family property. All we have is the two houses, their yards and the stretch of road that joins them. This was government land, and it was good that no one had bothered to develop it. Many times in my youth, I'd escaped here, running as if the hounds of hell were after me, to bury my tears in the decaying leaves of the forest floor, seeking comfort and solitude that they did not have to offer.

To my surprise, when Sampson and I got back to the house, Dad was still asleep. He'd never been one to lie in after the sun came up. Yesterday's ordeal must have taken quite a toll on him.

It was close to noon when he stuck his head into the living room, nodded briefly and shuffled down the hall to the bathroom. My Discman was on my head—*Crash* by the Dave Matthews Band playing—my laptop plugged into the phone line as I finished sending a pile of e-mails.

A few minutes later he walked into the room, washed and dressed, his hair neatly combed. "It's late. Long past breakfast."

I pulled off the headset and smiled. "You deserve to sleep in once in a while. This must be the only day in your life you've ever missed breakfast."

"Missed breakfast the day after I married your mom."

"Oh."

"Don't want to sit around here all day. I'm going out to the shed for a while. A bit of work will do me good."

"Do you want something to eat first?"

"Nope. I'll eat in the shed. But not breakfast. Too late for breakfast. I'll have a sandwich."

"I'll bring it out to you, then."

Why was I doing this, I asked myself as I sliced twelve-grain bread and loaded on the cheese and pickle. And a dash of English mustard. Considering that traditional English cooking is so terribly bland, how have they managed to invent the wonder that is English mustard? I made the sandwich with a good dollop of resentment along with the mustard. When Ray had been marking papers or working on the last draft of a book with a deadline looming, I would bring him his meal on a nicely arranged tray. But I expected the same when I had a presentation to give the next day or a board meeting to prepare for. But this was different: Dad had to learn to cope somehow, didn't he?

A glass of milk would go nicely with the sandwich. I rummaged under the sink in search of a tray on which to carry the lunch. I hadn't been out to the back shed yet and had no desire to do so now. It had been such a gloomy place in my childhood. Tiny windows that hadn't felt the caress of a damp rag since McKenzie King was Prime Minister. Nothing but spiders and mice, as well as the occasional rat, scurrying around in the corners.

A neat brick path, twin of the one in front, led the way from the kitchen door and wound its way to the shed, passing through the dug-under vegetable garden waiting for the warmth of the spring sun and the feeling of my mother's sure fingers. The shed was bigger than I remembered, the door nicer, made of good wood finished and varnished. Hands full, I kicked the door with my foot. Dad pulled it open and stood back to allow me entrance.

"Gee, Dad. This is nice. Really nice."

And it was. A clean cement floor, a long neat workbench, rows of tools and wide, new windows admitting the soft spring light.

He was working on a rocking horse, and several others in different stages of completion lined the far wall. They were beautiful: carved out of warm, soft blond wood with curly woolen manes and tails, huge brown painted eyes, and cloth saddles.

"Those are wonderful," I said.

He looked at his hands, embarrassed, and accepted the tray.

The room was neatly divided into two. One half, my father's woodworking shed, then a high divider, and the other half lined with shelves containing piles of cotton fabrics in every color imaginable. A late-model sewing machine sat on a table.

My throat closed.

"A few years ago, we demolished the old shed and put up this larger one and moved your mother's quilting things in here. So we could be together." He coughed and kept his eyes downcast, embarrassed. "Janet had to work hard to keep the sawdust off her cloth, but she said she liked working in here."

"That's a good sewing machine. Much better than the old one she used when I was young."

"Yup."

"I don't see any finished quilts."

"Everything made over the winter went up to the store a month or so ago. Then she wasn't feeling too well and didn't start anything more."

"What store?"

But he wasn't listening to me. "Lonely in here, without her. Sometimes I turn my head to tell her some stupid joke I heard in town, or ask what those twins are up to. And for a moment I almost see her sitting there, her head bent over that sewing machine, concentrating on the feel of the cloth. But she isn't there, is she?"

"No, Dad."

I left him to his cheese and pickle, rocking horse and memories.

Not only the sewing machine, but the sloped drafting table installed so Mom could cut fabric without having to bend over, the woodworking equipment, even the quality of the wood used in the making of the rocking horses, was at odds with my ideas about what sort of materials my parents should be able to afford.

As much as I didn't want to, I had to confront Shirley about what was to become of Dad. Today was Wednesday; my return ticket was for Saturday morning. I would like to get it over with today. But Shirley was at work. I'd go over there after dinner.

To pass the time, I returned to the cellar.

Chapter 20

The Diary of Mrs. Janet McKenzie. September 24, 1946

P.S.

    We are here. And it is as wonderful as I imagined. I simply cannot get to sleep; my heart is still pounding with all the excitement. He was waiting for us at Union Station in Toronto. He looked so strange dressed in a plain brown suit instead of a uniform. But he is as handsome as I remembered. Now that we are together again, I can admit that I was terrified that he would be different than I remembered—less, somehow. As we came off the platform, there were so many people to meet the brides and the soldiers, such a crowd. Shirley cried out in terror and buried her head in my shoulder. I had a wild thought of running back to the train and telling the conductor to take me back to England.

    But then he was there.

    And it was perfectly wonderful.

    He came in a car to collect us. A car as nice as Mr. Fitzpatrick and Lady Helen's. And no need for a driver. Bob drove it himself. I was so proud.

    He told me that it wasn't his car; we were to spend the night at his friend Charlie's family home. Charlie, who walked with us the night Bob asked me to marry him, had been killed in France. He was an only child, and Bob explained to me as we drove north through the neat, tree-lined streets of Toronto, his parents were devastated by his death. They welcomed his best buddy into their home and were waiting eagerly to meet Shirley and me. We would spend the night in Toronto, so I could rest. Then catch a train further north, to Bob's own home.

I have absolutely no recollection of Charlie. I met him once. And that on the wonderful night Bob proposed to me. So Charlie was gone from my consciousness like the trace of a dream. But I pretended to his mother that I remembered him fondly, and she welcomed Shirley and me into her home and her family. Mr. Lombard is a cold, distant man. I didn't even meet him until dinnertime. He stood at the head of the table and carved the roast of beef with a face that might have been made of stone. All the while his wife chattered on about what a lovely baby Charlie had been, and what a perfect scholar and athlete. Shirley was asleep upstairs in a lovely bedroom with delicate rose-patterned wallpaper and a maid assigned to watch over her all the night. I wanted nothing but to be with my husband, and close to our baby. Instead we stared at the cold, empty eyes of Mr. Lombard and listened to Charlie's mother describe his childhood in great detail. It was perfectly horrid.

The dining room was huge; the table would have comfortably fit three times our number. It is only September and still mild, but an enormous fire had been laid in the stone fireplace at the end of the room. A maid, dressed in crisp black and white, slipped silently in and out of the room, changing plates and producing new courses. For dessert she served a pie. I almost groaned in delight at the taste of melting pastry, tart apples and the light touch of cinnamon and nutmeg.

Mrs. Lombard smiled at me. "Apple pie. My Charlie's favorite."

Before the war her words might have caused the delicate pastry to stick in my throat. But now I knew the value of a good meal. I smiled at her and chewed.

The maid kept Shirley all night. Bob and I slept in a bed so big it would have filled Dad's whole bedroom in our house back in Surrey.

This is my diary and I have promised it that I will always be honest, so I will. Bob and I didn't get a good deal of sleep.

I had been so afraid. Afraid he wouldn't want me any longer, afraid that he would find me horribly plain and boring. Afraid I wouldn't belong here in Canada. Afraid that when I saw him I wouldn't love him any more. That I would be embarrassed that he is shorter than I am.

We have been married for a year and a half; we have a child together. Tonight we made love as if nothing had gone before.

I wonder if this will be the pattern of our lives together: Bob asleep in an enormous four-poster bed, snoring lightly, the baby lovingly cared for by the maid; me still up, taking advantage of the quiet to write in my diary.

January 1, 1947

Shirley is asleep at last. She has been crying for days, probably with her teeth, and Mr. McKenzie has been simply horrid about it. You would think that Bob had never been a baby, but was born full-grown and brought home from a pumpkin patch or something.

We have to get out of here. This horrid house is so small. The baby cries and Mr. McKenzie gets angry. Mrs. McKenzie tries frantically to hush her, and her urgency upsets Shirley even more. Then Bob tries to calm Mr. McKenzie. With as much success as his mother has with the baby.

It is the first day of 1947. A new year. I opened my diary this morning wanting to write something to mark the start of this New Year. I couldn't believe that I hadn't written in it since the morning after I arrived in Toronto, before we set out to come here. Was that only a few months ago? More like a lifetime.

This 'farm' is scarcely more than a patch of what in England we would call 'wasteland'. Mrs. McKenzie (who I simply can't call Mom) keeps a few chickens and rabbits and a good-sized vegetable garden of which I caught the briefest glimpse before a foot or more of snow buried it. The house is small, badly heated, and ill furnished. If I weren't so proud, I would write to Dad and ask him to send me Granny's tea trolley. Anything to have a decent piece of furniture.

How happy I was, on that long train trip through the endless Ontario panorama of rocks and trees. So different from the farm-lands and sleepy villages of Surrey, from the bombed-out shell of London and the slums of the Southampton docklands.

Mrs. McKenzie was there to meet us at the station. Bob stepped off the train, cradling a dozing Shirley in his arms, myself standing proudly by his side. His head was high and his eyes bright and he was so happy.

I was so proud.

Then he saw his mother.

His father hadn't come, she said. Too much work. Bob passed me the baby and took his mother's thin shoulders in his hands. Skin in all different shades of yellow and purple colored her face down the left side and the eye was nothing but a slit peering though puffy flesh. She held her right arm awkwardly to one side. She moved as if she wanted to touch the baby, but a spasm of pain passed across her face and the arm fell away.

She looked at her son's feet. "A fall," she said, her voice so soft, I had to strain to hear her, "down the stairs all the way to the cellar. The light was burnt out. Lucky I didn't break my neck, eh?"

"Heavens," I cried. "You could have been killed. I hope you've fixed that light. I'm sure we will be over to visit all the time, and I wouldn't want one of the children getting hurt."

"Not to worry," my new mom said. She braced against the pain and reached out her left hand to stroke Shirley's pink cheek. "I'll make sure she's kept safe."

Shirley shifted on my shoulder and opened her eyes wide. She tossed her grandmother a huge, drooling smile.

It was at least a month or more before I noticed that Bob was not talking about 'our home'. That instead he was full of plans about building an extension onto his parents' house, to make a bit more room.

We are easily five miles or more from the nearest town, called Hope River. And that is not much more than a couple of dark little shops, a decrepit pub, and a white frame church.

Mr. McKenzie seems to spend a good deal of his time chopping wood, when he's around, which fortunately isn't often. I don't see a sign of fields or of crops (although we arrived here in the autumn, I remind myself, constantly). There isn't a barn.

In fact, in this whole area I haven't seen sight nor sound of a prosperous farm. Leaving Toronto, our train passed oceans of beautiful *land: tall barns, stone farmhouses, fat cattle grazing, rich black fields ploughed under for the coming winter. I sighed in contentment. Shirley guzzled at her bottle and Bob smiled at me from beneath his thick eyelashes.*

Then we passed through the town of Barrie and continued on north past some other towns I can't name. And almost before I knew it, we might have entered a different world. The fields ended and the dark woods closed in upon the tracks. The open spaces where livestock grazed were gone. Only hard, bare, naked rock remained. For the rest of the journey I waited for the sky to open once again. But the forest and the rock closed in even more. And the train pulled to a stop in a station that is even smaller than the one in the middle of Quebec where we stranded the war bride. And my husband announced that it was time to get off.

A neighbor brought Mrs. McKenzie to fetch us in his truck. Mrs. McKenzie and I (with Shirley in my arms) struggled to fit in the seat beside him. Good thing she is so thin. Bob had to sit in the open back of the truck with my trunk. The man didn't say a word the whole trip and when we all finally got out, Bob handed him some money.

I honestly thought that he had deposited us in front of the servant's quarters. But no, this falling-down wreck is my new home.

Mrs. McKenzie went to the kitchen immediately to start dinner; Bob took Shirley out of my arms and showed me to our room. I scarcely knew what to say. My bedroom in England was nicer than this. The bed is small, the wallpaper tattered, and a huge water stain makes an ugly blot on the ceiling. At the foot of the bed there is a crib for Shirley. It is the only nice piece of furniture in the whole house, a rich dark wood, carefully sanded and stained. Covered by a beautiful blanket in cheerful yellow and blue. I had selfishly hoped that Shirley would have her own room, like she did at the Lombards'. So Bob and I could have our privacy.

When Bob's father came through the door that first day, Shirley was playing on the floor with a pile of wooden blocks Mrs. McKenzie gave her. He scarcely glanced at her, but he eyed me up and down all right. Like he was trying to memorize every inch of me. Examining me like a prize heifer. That is, if anyone in this barren country knows what a cow is. I flushed to the roots of my hair and held out my hand. He continued to look at me, until I dropped my hand in embarrassment.

"You're a big one," he said at last. I didn't think he had been working any too hard. He scratched his belly. "Still breast-feeding, eh?"

I was mortified. It is simply unheard of for a man to mention such a thing. Of course I wasn't breast-feeding. I had given that up before leaving home. Good thing, too. They didn't like it on the ship and encouraged all the mothers to switch to the bottle.

"Dad." Bob's voice was low and tinged with an anger I hadn't heard before. "This is my wife, Janet. And my daughter, Shirley."

At that my father-in-law stepped toward me and held out his arms. He was welcoming me into the family. He hugged me and pressed his crotch up against my hip. I recoiled in horror, sure I had misunderstood, terrified that I would react badly and embarrass everyone. He only grinned at me and turned to my husband.

"Make sure the next one's a boy, eh."

Chapter 21

I left Sampson behind at the house with Dad. Shirley didn't seem too terribly fond of her, and I expected this visit was going to be difficult enough.

Al opened the door with a beer in hand and a friendly smile of welcome. Shirley didn't bother to move off the couch or to look away from the TV. She grunted a less than enthusiastic welcome. "Beer, Becky?" Al said.

"That would be nice, thanks," I replied, more to accept hospitality than because I wanted one. I sat in a worn old armchair; the springs settled under my weight.

"The service was nice," I said to my sister.

"Yes."

"And Jackie did a great job of the reception."

"Yes."

"She's a lovely woman. You should be very proud of her."

"I am."

Al handed me an icy glass, the deep-colored beer perfectly poured, and grinned widely at the thought of his eldest daughter. "Yup, she's a great girl. She went to university, you know. University of Toronto."

"But then she came home, back to where she belonged." My sister kept her eyes glued to the TV. It was a movie; I recognized the handsome face of Kevin Costner.

"I've come over because I thought that this would be a good time to talk about Dad."

"What about him?"

"What's going to happen to him, now that Mom's gone. I'm going home on Saturday."

There was a long pause. Al went back into the kitchen and returned pulling open an oversize bag of barbecue flavored chips. Shirley watched Kevin Costner.

I'd always fancied Kevin myself, but this wasn't quite the time. "Shirley, do you think you could turn that off so we can talk?"

She looked at me for the first time. Age had carved deep circles under her eyes, and she looked nothing but tired. "I want to see the end."

"Please, Shirley. I know how busy you are with your family and your job, so I assumed that this would be a good time to drop over. The movie will be on again. It's not very good anyway. It was a huge flop at the box office."

"Oh, pardon me. I should have realized that you would know all about what's worth watching and what's not. But I like it."

I put my beer glass onto the coffee table and struggled out of the sagging chair. "Suit yourself. I'll be here until Saturday morning. If you find the time, come on over for a visit and we can talk about our father's future."

The lovely Kevin was silenced in mid-speech. Shirley glared at Al as he twisted the remote control in his callused hands. "We've seen it before. It is awful, but we like the water scenes. Shirl's always wanted to go to Hawaii, but we could never quite manage it. You two should talk. I'll be in the kitchen."

"He's a nice man," I said once Al left. And I meant it.

"Oh, yeah. Like you've ever thought Al Smithers was worth dirt."

"I didn't say he's the man for me. But he's still nice." I sat back down.

She leaned across me to pick up the remote. The neck of her dressing gown flapped open and offered an unwelcome glimpse of her limp, sagging breasts. She fingered the device but didn't turn the TV back on. "So, talk."

"Do you think Dad can live on his own in that house? He doesn't cook, probably has no idea of how to operate the washing machine. He left a pot of water on the stove the other day until it boiled dry. I've been thinking that maybe we could get him a housekeeper, someone to fix his breakfast and clean up and keep an eye on the place."

"Well, I'm not doing it."

"I didn't say you should. I meant we could hire someone."

"And who's going to pay for it?"

"We can work something out. I'll help if Dad can't afford it himself."

"I'm sure you will."

"Do you have any better ideas?"

"You could take him to Vancouver. He can live with you there."

"That's ridiculous and you know it. He doesn't know anyone in Vancouver. He would never want to leave his friends, his home, his routine. He's lived in this area his whole life."

"Then you can move back here and take care of him yourself."

I debated grabbing the remote out of her hand and turning the TV back on. Even that horrible movie made better sense than this conversation.

"That isn't going to happen, and you know that too. Why are you being so difficult? Why won't you talk about this with me?"

"Because you left us before. You owe me. It's your turn to do something for this family. I've done enough." She was yelling now, and Al popped his head through the kitchen door, a question on his lips. Wisely he thought better of it and remained silent.

"You went off to the big city and the good life and left me to rot here in this horrid town."

"Christ, it's hardly my fault if you messed up your life."

"You think you can come in here after all these years and sneer at my husband…"

"You used the word 'rot,' not me. And I didn't sneer at anyone. I said Al was a nice guy." I looked at him, standing in the kitchen doorway, a bottle of beer in one hand, a handful of chips in the other, and a shocked expression on his face. "I did, really. That's what I said."

"She was so proud of you." Shirley's thin, lined face was turning an unattractive shade of splotchy red, and spittle gathered at the corners of her mouth. I rose to my feet again and took a few steps toward the door. She stood up as well. "Nothing but 'Rebecca this' and 'Rebecca that.' Year after goddamned year."

Al found his voice. "Stop this, Shirley. That's ancient history."

"I looked after the old man, did you know that, did you? After Grandma died Mom wouldn't go near him. She hated him. Did you know that? She absolutely hated him. So who else was there to look after the old goat? Good old Shirley, that's who. Jimmy was living in the big house again, but you couldn't ask Jimmy to wash the sheets or clean up the mess, now could you?

"He was a pig. He felt me up one day when he was collapsed sick in his bed. Apparently he wasn't as sick as he appeared."

That did shock me. As much as my brother mocked and ridiculed me, he'd never laid a hand on me. "Jimmy abused you?"

"Are you a total fool? Of course not. The old man did. It was disgusting. Disgusting." She burst into tears.

Al reached for her, but she swatted him out of the way. "No one from around here would look after him, for love or money. Dad would come in sometimes and try to clean up a bit. But he was working long hours, and not around much. So it was up to Shirl, good old Shirl, to clean the house and listen to Grandpa complain about what a bad job I did, to step in his vomit in the morning when I came in to fix his breakfast, and to feel his filthy old hands on me when he pretended to be too sick to get out of bed to reach the toilet.

"It was the happiest day of my life, the day he died."

"For God's sake, why did you never say anything?" Al's words were a cry of anguish. He dropped his chips onto the floor and they crunched under his feet as he reached for his wife.

"You don't talk about your family to outsiders. Never. No matter what. Isn't that the way we were raised, Becky?"

"I'm your husband. I'm not an outsider. I remember that year, when you were looking after your grandfather. You went over there every day, you never complained."

She glared at him in contempt and swatted his hands away.

"Why did you think I never let the girls come with me? They were old enough to help. I didn't want them anywhere near the old bugger."

"Dad's not Grandpa, Shirley," I said. "You know that. And he's not going to turn into Grandpa all of a sudden, just because he's old."

"That's right," Al said. "Becky's right. Bob's a good man."

Her legs gave out under her and she collapsed into the couch, tears running down her face, sobbing in great gulps. "And where were you all that year, Miss High-and-Mighty, Miss B.A., Miss M.B.A.? You would have known that Grandpa couldn't look after himself."

"No one told me. Mom never told me. I guess I assumed he was okay after Grandma died, or that Mom would take care of it. Mom told me that Jimmy went to live there after he left Margie."

"After Margie kicked him out, more like. But never mind that, whatever you thought, you thought wrong." She blew her nose on a paper napkin. "And now you can get out of my house."

Al sat beside her on the couch, and finally she allowed him to wrap his arms around her thin shoulders. She buried her head into his chest and wept.

I left.

～～～

I went back to the house long enough to collect Sampson, grunt a greeting at Dad, and hit the road. I wasn't leaving, not yet. I hadn't picked up any of my things, only my dog, my companion, but I needed to think, and the dark country roads seemed a good place to do it.

I would have to call the airline and move my departure back another week. They wouldn't be too pleased at work; I had some important meetings scheduled for the following week, and a major project waiting for the go-ahead based on the results of those meetings, but I couldn't leave Hope River now.

I had felt like a piece of dirt standing in Shirley's living room as she lashed out at me with thirty years of bottled-up anguish. But as the night woods rolled past my windows and I felt the hot wind of Sampson's breath on my neck as she leaned over my shoulder, sniffing at heaven knows what, I scrubbed most of the dirt away.

Shirley had been an adult when Grandpa died in 1982. More than an adult—a married woman with grown children. She could have refused. She could have told Mom and Dad and Jimmy that she wouldn't do it. Don't make me feel guilty for not helping out. If they'd asked me, I would have told them to let the old bastard rot in his own filth.

But Shirley knew him better than me. Grandma and Grandpa lived in the little house with them throughout most of her child-hood, only moving to the big house when I was young. I have almost no memory of my grandmother, never anything more substantial than a shadow. But after all these years, I still hated my grandfather. What memories of him did my much older sister have that I (thankfully) had been spared?

I was surprised to hear that Mother had let Shirley bear that burden alone. She'd done so much to protect me from him, why did she let Shirley face the beast on her own?

Regardless of what had happened in the past, I decided, turning the car back toward home, it was now up to me to make arrangements for my father.

Chapter 22

I dreamed last night about Charlie Lombard. A man I met once only and don't even remember. I dreamt that I had married him, not Bob. And that Charlie hadn't died in Normandy but instead brought me to live in a beautiful house. A home with fine furnishings and lovely paintings on the walls. A home with big rooms and warm fireplaces. With a nanny for Shirley and a maid for me. A home like his parents have.

I woke up feeling overwhelmed with despair and longing. Because the dream forced me to understand that that it was in the Lombard home that I spent the last happy day of my life.

Yesterday I told Bob that we have to move. I can't live with his parents any longer. His father insults me constantly (I'm too tall, my accent is funny, my cooking is horrible) and he watches me with a look I don't like, one that reminds me of the time Jenny and I walked home alone after a dance and those two soldiers (Englishmen, I am ashamed to say!) stepped in front of us and said they would give us cigarettes if we would do horrid things with them.

Mrs. McKenzie tries to be kind but she is such an insipid, insignificant thing. She loves Shirley, which is about the only good thing I can say about this place or my new family. She plays with Shirley for hours on end, and Shirley loves her in return.

I told Bob that we have to move. And he said that he doesn't have enough money saved up yet. I said I didn't believe him, and we had the most dreadful row. It was the first fight we have had. I said that if he couldn't find a home of our own for his family, then I would get a job and help out. Of course, he said that no wife of his would work and I said that if he was so proud why were we still living with his parents? That set him straight, sure enough. But I wasn't proud of it. I had hurt him. Badly. A man needs to be the head of his household. But how can Bob? When we're living here? We hardly even have marital relations any more. I just can't. Not with Shirley in her crib at the end of our bed, and his parents the other side of a thin wall. I can hear his father snoring all the night long.

And now Bob is drinking more than I would like. He stays out late some times, more and more all the time, and he comes home hardly able to stand up straight. It's my fault, because I won't let him touch me. But I can't. I just can't.

April 3, 1947

Shirley was two years old yesterday. We had a little party for her. Mrs. McKenzie made a lovely cake, and decorated it so nicely, with pink icing and lovely red roses and two candles. Bob gave me a bit of money and drove me into North Ridge so that I could buy a present. I got her a dress, so pretty, all frills and ribbons. Like the dresses on the girls before the war. I bought her some books as well. She is so terribly smart. I love reading to her.

And I bought a new journal for me! This one only has a few pages remaining. I considered stopping my diary. Burning everything that I have written. But I couldn't do it, and then I understood that I need it now more than ever. This book is my friend, my companion. I have need of a friend. I haven't really made the acquaintance of any of the women around here. They live so far away, too far to walk for a visit. I miss the village so much. It seemed horrid and provincial when I lived there, but now I wish, more than anything, that I was living once again on a neat lane with houses and cottages close by, a pub at one end of the street, my father's shop at the other. And the ancient stone church only steps beyond that.

Perhaps in the summer, when the snow is gone, Shirley and I can get out more. Bob and Mr. McKenzie never come to church.

On Christmas Eve Bob put on his suit, the first time I've seen him wear it since the day he met my train at Union Station in Toronto. I almost wept, to see that he could be handsome, still. He'd had a few drinks in the afternoon but at least he came with us to the service. But not Mr. McKenzie. He was at a bar somewhere, no doubt drinking heartily to the birth of our Savior, and he came home after midnight roaring for Mrs. M. to get out of bed and fix him something to eat, before he fixed her good and proper. Bob got up to calm him down and soon she was banging pots around in the kitchen. Bang them over his head, would be a good deal more to my liking.

There's a loose floorboard under the dresser in our bedroom. I found it when I reached for a ball Shirley dropped. It makes a nice hidey-hole for my diary. Never before have I felt the need to hide my diary. No decent person would ever dream of reading a woman's private diary. But HE is no decent person and I don't trust him.

I saw a robin this morning. It gave me some hope. Everything will be better, as soon as it is spring. Bob has been saving as much as he can of the money he is making at the plant. He doesn't talk about it, but I'm sure he is putting it aside for a home of our own.

Of course, with Shirley being two it made me realize that she should have a brother or sister soon. But Mrs. McKenzie is NEVER out of the house! I do mean NEVER! Oh, she goes shopping on Saturday morning and to church on Sunday but I am expected to go with her and Bob has to drive us. Sometimes on the weekends when he is home and his mother is working in the kitchen or sewing in her bedroom, and Shirley is having a nap, Bob will give me a look and nod toward the bedroom, but I would simply DIE before I would take my husband and sneak off to our bedroom in the middle of the day. With his MOTHER in the house.

It has been a long time since Bob has given me that nod.

She doesn't seem to have any friends, except for the women she talks to after church. And she never goes out. Of course HE is out more than he is in. And we're all the better for it. He's rude and rough. He pays no attention to his granddaughter; a few times I have been almost afraid that he was going to strike her. But instead he says something mean and walks away. He mocks his son and I don't know why Bob puts up with it. He pretends that he hasn't heard and pours himself another drink.

But my husband loves his mother. I have heard that that is a good sign: A boy who loves his mother will make a good husband. They were wrong. About that as about so many things.

If only I had a friend. Someone to talk to. I have received a few nice letters from the brides I met on the ship. Their letters are full of exciting news about a home overlooking the ocean in Vancouver, a husband going to university in Montreal to study for a lawyer, a baby on the way, large and welcoming new families.

I don't write back any more. What can I say?

Chapter 23

Immediately after breakfast the next morning, Sampson and I set off up the hill to the big house. I didn't know what sort of hours Jimmy kept, but I hadn't heard his truck pulling away yet. If they weren't in, I would leave a note asking him or Aileen to call me.

My brother and his wife were sitting on the front porch finishing breakfast. It was sunny, but the air still held the sharp bite of early spring, and they were dressed in thick, colorful, hand-knitted sweaters. Aileen greeted me as if I were truly welcome. Nice of her after my considerable rudeness, which had served to mark the end of the funeral reception.

"Coffee, Rebecca?" She held up the carafe. "You'll need something to keep your hands warm."

"Thank you."

"You sit right here and I'll get another cup. Have you eaten? I'd be happy to bring out more."

"I'm fine, thanks."

She patted Sampson's huge head with much enthusiasm and went into the house to get the cup. Unasked, the big dog followed, tail wagging. She was never one to turn down an offer of breakfast.

This deck gave them a spectacular view of the lake and the hills beyond. The house sat just short of the crest of the hill. The road running in front of the house ended at the driveway, as there was nothing beyond but bush and swamp. A natural garden of trees, brush, and stone ran downhill to the rocks lining the shore of the lake. Closer to the house a scattering of flower beds, lined with neatly placed red bricks, had recently been turned over, made ready for the planting of colorful annuals.

"Morning, Jimmy."

"Morning." He picked up his newspaper.

"Any more news about Jennifer Taylor?"

"No."

How long did it take Aileen to get one coffee cup?

"Look, Jimmy. I'm sorry about what I said the other night. It was uncalled for, and I'm truly sorry."

"That's okay."

"It's not okay, not really. But I am sorry."

"Forget it." He looked up from his paper. "I was a jerk when I was younger. Actually I was pretty much of a jerk when I was older, too. I don't blame you for not liking me."

"Maybe we can start over." I myself didn't wholly believe what I was saying. After all these years the pain that this man caused still had the power to cut me like a knife. But I needed an ally in my search for arrangements for Dad, and I would be gone in a few days. I could fake forgiveness.

The edges of his eyes crinkled in a tiny smile. "I'm willing."

Aileen slipped back into her chair. "I brought some leftover toast for Sampson. Do you mind?"

"Don't mind at all."

"So, what brings you two out this lovely morning?" Aileen poured the coffee. "Going for a walk?"

"No. I came with a purpose. We need to talk about Dad. About what he's going to do now that Mom isn't around."

"Good," Aileen said, rolling up the sleeves of her sweater. It was a beauty in good wool all the shades of an autumn forest—rust, yellow, and brown—with long, wide sleeves and a rolled neck. "Jim and I want to talk to you as well."

I let out a laugh of relief. "That's a better reception than I got yesterday from Shirley. She doesn't want to think about it at all."

"Shirley's an angry woman," Aileen said thoughtfully. "I feel sorry for her. She's had a hard life."

"No harder than a lot of people," Jimmy said.

"Oh, pooh." Aileen laughed, light-hearted and full of warmth. "Like you're so hard done by. Sitting out on this beautiful deck on this perfect morning while your dutiful wife caters to your every whim."

He flashed her a grin of such unadulterated adoration it was almost embarrassing to witness.

Sampson snapped in canine irritation and we laughed. Aileen had forgotten to offer the leftover toast.

"I'm worried," I said, "about Dad living on his own."

"We are as well," Aileen said. "We asked him to move up here, into the big house with us, but he refused."

"Point blank," Jimmy said. "He told us that he has lived in that house his entire life and doesn't see any reason to move now. He doesn't want to be, in his words, 'beholden to anyone.'"

"Old men," I sighed. "He was happy to be beholden to Mom all these years, but that probably doesn't count."

Aileen grinned and reached across the table for Jimmy's hand.

He lifted her hand, touched it to his lips, and checked the watch on his other arm. "We need to talk about this, for sure, but I've gotta be on the road before much longer. A load of lumber's being delivered to the site at nine and I have to be there to sign for it."

"Site?" I asked.

"A cottage I'm working on, going up on Lake Ramsey."

"It's a massive place," Aileen said. "What they're calling a vacation home now because it's too big to be called a cottage. Jimmy's doing the carpentry. Built-in kitchen cabinets, shelving in the library—can you imagine a cottage having a library?—hardwood floors, a deck. Woodwork in the guest rooms over the boathouse.

They even want hand-crafted Muskoka and lounge chairs. The works." She smiled at her husband, pride shining in her eyes.

"And they want to start using the main building this summer. So I've got my work cut out for me. But Dad…"

"Would he accept a housekeeper, do you think?" I asked. "Not a live in, but someone to come over every day and clean up and fix his meals?"

"I think he'd agree to that." Aileen glanced at Jimmy and he nodded.

"That's going to cost a lot," I said.

"Dad never talks about money, you know that," Jimmy said.

"Well this time he's going to have to," Aileen said. "He can afford it. He and Janet never spent a penny they didn't have to, and the business has been doing extremely well the last few years."

"And you know, if anyone does," Jimmy replied.

"Back up a minute, here." I was getting confused. "What business are you talking about? I can see that there's been money spent on the house. I assumed that they were getting some help from old-age security."

Jimmy finished his coffee in a gulp and pushed his chair away from the table. "I'll leave Aileen to fill you in on all that. Time for me to be on my way. Someone has to bring home the bacon."

Sampson barked her agreement. Aileen rubbed the dog's head.

"This business of theirs? Is that what Dad meant by a store? He said that Mom's quilts had all gone to the store. I assumed he meant the church bazaar."

Aileen smiled. "Your parents have done very well for them-selves over the last few years."

Jimmy bent over and kissed the top of Aileen's head. "Thanks to my dear wife," he told me. "She's a marvel, this one." Then he went into the house in search of the keys to his truck.

I looked at her, full of questions.

"Perhaps later I can show you what we've done," she said. "But I also have to be off to work soon. I'll get a piece of paper and we can start jotting down some ideas for Bob's housekeeper. There are lots of elderly widows in this area who would be more than happy to take care of your father. But I fear that as soon as they find out that marriage and taking possession of the house are not part of the deal they won't prove too reliable."

"That might be the best option of all."

"But not something we can count on."

Jimmy emerged from the house waving his keys and kissed his wife once more before bounding off the deck and rounding the path to the garage at the back of the house. Sampson trotted off at his heels, hoping for a car ride. I called her back.

A huge flock of Canada geese flew low overheard, heading for open water, their loud honks full of delight at the return of spring. The battered old pickup he used for his business roared to life and tires crunched on gravel. Jimmy reached the road as another car climbed the hill. It was a white sedan with the colors and emblem of the Ontario Provincial Police. The police car flicked its lights and gave one blast of the siren at the sight of Jimmy about to pull away.

"Oh, for heaven's sake! Not now." Aileen dashed down the steps and ran across the lawn. Her feet were bare and her colorful skirt flowed in a soft river around her ankles. Sampson, always happy for a good romp, took off after her. I yelled, but she paid no attention.

The police and my brother. Some things never do change. But if they were headed for a confrontation, I didn't want my dog in the middle of it.

Chapter 24

The Diary of Janet McKenzie, who wishes she was still Janet Green. April 14, 1947

I won't be posting my letter to Dad and Aunt Betty. I have it all written. Days of thought and effort. I decided to tell them straight that my marriage isn't working. That Bob seems to care only for his mother, a bottle of beer, Shirley. In that order. That his father is a lout and I haven't seen another woman to speak to for months. And if we move into our own home in the next year, I'll eat my hat.

Thank God I haven't posted the letter yet. Because I got one from them first. Dad is getting married! I can't believe it. Mum hasn't been heard of in more than seven years, so Dad has taken steps to declare her dead. And he is marrying an aunt of Albert Grady. Maureen is her name. She is a widow, of course. Lost her husband during the blitz. She came to Woking to visit Albert and his mother, met Dad and they fell madly in love (he didn't say that, but I read between the lines), and are about to get married. And to top it all, Aunt Betty (no longer needed and probably not wanted) and Aunt Joan are pooling their substantial savings and purchasing holiday accommodations in Brighton where they plan to cater to war-and-rationing-weary families seeking, in Aunt Betty's words, 'peaceful respite by the sea'.

Dad writes that he is broken-hearted that I won't be at his wedding and won't get the chance to meet Maureen. He knows that we would get on famously, he says. Aunt Betty enclosed a letter of her own, saying that perhaps one day Bob and I and our family will be able to take a holiday in Brighton. She also mentioned, in a roundabout way, that she is perfectly happy to be free from the duty of caring for my father and willingly hands that task on to someone else.

I am happy for them both. But it would seem that there is now no place for me.

April 17, 1947

Bob has lost his job. And I have lost all hope. The plant closed, all of a sudden, and all the men were let go. He came home in the middle of the day, looking all downcast. His mother wept and carried on as if he had died. Fortunately it is a bit milder today and most of the snow is gone, so I scooped the baby up, put on her coat and took her out for a walk. We couldn't go far, because of all the mud. But I had to get out of there. There aren't many jobs around here. Most of the young men go to North Bay or Toronto to get work. That's an idea! Maybe things will work out for the better—at last Bob will realize that we can't stay here. He might have to go to the city to get a job. Wouldn't that be a wonder!

Of course Mr. McKenzie didn't help matters any when he came home. I don't even know what he does all day. I suppose he has a job. He goes out every morning, and comes home for supper sometimes, but some days he doesn't come home until after we have all gone to bed and I hear him slamming doors and then Mrs. M. tiptoes down the hall to make his dinner. You would think that he would be kind to his son who has lost his job. But not him. He said mean things to Bob. So mean that I left the room without even finishing my dinner. But Bob just sat there eating his beef stew and potatoes. And his mother got up and poured him another beer.

Chapter 25

Jimmy climbed out of the truck, and two police officers got out of their car. One was in uniform, and one in plainclothes but still managing to look every inch a cop. Jimmy waited by his truck as they walked toward him. Aileen flew up, apparently heedless of the gravel of the road under her bare feet.

"This is completely out of line, Sergeant." Aileen spoke as I arrived, silently gesturing for Sampson to come away. The dog ignored me. The long hairs on the ridge of her back stood at attention and her tail flicked slowly back and forth, full of warning. Something unpleasant was happening and she stood at the ready.

The plainclothes officer looked at her. "Please control that dog, Ms. O'Connor. We don't want any unpleasantness, now do we?"

"Not at all," I said as I grabbed Sampson's collar.

His stare shifted to me. "Heard you were back in town, Becky. Nice to see you."

I had no absolutely idea who he might be. "Nice to, uh, see you too."

The uniformed officer was young and handsome, tall and well built, looking quite splendid in his crisp black uniform and wide-brimmed hat, his hand casually resting on the gun at his side. He glanced at Sampson out of the corner of his eye. "Why don't you put that dog in the house, Miss? We need to talk to Mr. McKenzie."

"Never mind the dog," Aileen snapped. "She's harmless. We have nothing more to say to you. We told you everything we know the last time you were here. Which is precisely nothing."

"It's okay, Aileen." Jimmy placed one hand lightly on his wife's arm. "We all want Jennifer to be found. Sergeant Reynolds is only doing his job."

Reynolds. Now I placed him. Bob Reynolds. His sister, Ruth, same age as me, had been one of the in crowd in school. But he was much, much older than we were. He'd gone away to Police College when we were still in junior high. Ruth had scarcely been able to bear the shame.

"Well, he's done quite enough of his job on our property. I'm sure there are clues to be found elsewhere, if he would only take the time to look."

"You're not helping, Ms. O'Connor. Becky, perhaps you could take your sister-in-law and that dog up to the house."

"My name's Rebecca, Bob. And Aileen doesn't need me to take her anywhere." I neglected to mention Sampson, brimming with hostility, convinced that her new friend was under some sort of threat.

"Please, Aileen," Jimmy said, his eyes on his wife's face. "Go with Rebecca up to the house. You haven't finished discussing Dad."

I expected Aileen to stand her ground, but instead she sighed. "If you insist. But much more of this, *Sergeant* Reynolds, and you'll be looking at a harassment suit."

She stomped off toward the house, as furiously as one can stomp in bare feet on spring grass. I followed her, and Sampson followed me. Aileen plunked down on the chair Jimmy had recently vacated, the one facing the road. The look on her face would freeze water.

"Are you okay?" Stupid question. I sat down as well.

"They won't leave him alone. They keep coming around asking us the same questions. I do have a mind to call a lawyer, get some advice."

I looked toward the road. The men were still talking. Jimmy's hands were clenched but hanging loose at his sides. They were too far away for us to hear what was being said. The lake shone behind them, dazzling in the sunlight. Small clusters of white clouds gathered together on the horizon, like old friends meeting for a tea party around a table draped in an antique cloth of heavenly blue.

The tableau broke up without warning. The police climbed back into their car and disappeared down the hill. Jimmy didn't stand watching them leave; he turned to us with a wave and a smile and climbed into his truck. The wheels kicked up a cloud of dust on the dry roadbed and he was gone, following in the dust the police had stirred up.

"I'll be on my way if you have to get to work." I got to my feet. "I'm glad we had this talk. Call me when you have some time and we can decide on our plan of action. About the housekeeper, I mean."

"They think he's responsible for Jennifer Taylor's disappearance." Aileen's voice broke. "Half the people in town are ready to convict Jim, and Bob Reynolds is happy to go along with them. Saves any actual thinking on his part."

I sat down again. Sampson spied a squirrel crossing the lawn and set off in hot pursuit. She didn't even come close, and the black squirrel sat at the top of a juvenile pine tree, laughing. "Small town people have long memories," I said.

She looked at me sharply. "Memories of what!" she snapped. "Jim wasn't a saint."

To put it mildly.

She read my mind. "I know he caused a lot of trouble. I know he spent some time in jail. I met him in prison. Did you know that? He has no secrets from me. But you tell me, did he ever have any trouble—legal trouble—with girls? Did he, ever?"

"No."

"Right. So he spent time in jail for what, drunk driving and assaulting the arresting officer? I know that. Robbery? I know that, too. But some of the narrow-minded people in this town,

Staff Sergeant Reynolds foremost amongst them, won't forget for a second. As if a conviction for a fucked-up robbery attempt automatically makes a man a child-rapist and murderer. This is the very reason why a lot of men can't go straight once they get out of prison, did you know that? The so-called law-abiding, tough-on-crime, hang-em-high crowd simply won't let them." She brought her hand down on the table with enough force to bounce the crockery and distract Sampson from the treed squirrel. She trotted back to sit under the table.

"You said some pretty mean things yourself the other night, Rebecca. Can't you believe that Jim has changed?"

"I'm prepared to let go of the past. I told him so, while you were in the kitchen."

"I guess that's all we can ask." Her shoulders sank, and she rested one elbow on the table, closed her eyes, and rubbed at her forehead. Thick strands of black and gray hair escaped from the bun to fall in loose curls around her hand.

"Look, I have to get to work. Why don't you drop by again later, after dinner, and we can draw up a list of places to advertise and women who might be looking for that sort of work. And don't worry about the money. Bob can afford to crack open that wallet of his. She tried to smile. "I'll bet moths will fly out when he does. It's not as if he needs to save any longer for his old age." The smile faded, and her eyes welled up and threatened to overflow.

She seemed like... she was... a nice woman. But she was Jimmy's wife. I had always thought that tears went with the job description. There was little or no comfort I could offer her. I excused myself and called for Sampson, who had disappeared once again.

We left Aileen gathering up the remains of breakfast with one hand, while trying to wipe away the tears with the other.

Instead of taking the straight way back and walking down the dirt road, we cut through the woods. Aileen's words echoed through my head and I paid scant attention to the trilliums, the new grass underfoot, or the budding leaves on the old trees.

You tell me, did he ever have any trouble—legal trouble—with girls? Did he, ever?

Legal trouble, no. Jimmy had never needed to force any girl, and he had a sufficient sense of self-preservation to stay away from the too-young ones. But trouble. Yes, there was always lots of trouble.

~~~

I was seventeen years old in 1972, when Jimmy came back to Hope River. I don't remember if it had been when his first marriage broke up, or the time he lost his job in North Bay for punching his supervisor, or if he was just out of jail. He was 25 and my mom had been pleased, although she tried to hide it, that he hadn't wanted to move back into our house. Instead, like a rat returning to the nest, he settled in with Grandpa and Grandma. By this time my mother hardly ever walked up the dirt road to the big house. Thanksgiving and Christmas Day she would make the effort, but that was about all. She cooked sometimes, when Grandma felt under the weather, but Shirley, now married with two children, or I was called upon to carry the heavy dishes up the hill. We were always told to return immediately, not to dawdle. Like we would want to. And Dad had fallen so far into the bottle that he was just about useless.

My best friend had been a girl named Linda Richards. I didn't have many friends; I guess Linda was my only friend. She and her family had arrived in Hope River less than a year before, straight from England. My mother absolutely adored her. Linda's father was a doctor, and she was a real beauty with masses of red hair and the most amazing green eyes. Like the very fields and hedgerows of Surrey, my mother exclaimed in one of her rare flights of imagination. I was surprised that our friendship lasted more than a few weeks. With a doctor for a father, an exotic accent, and being a beauty, the in crowd tried to swallow Linda up. But she liked me, and I liked her: She was a genuinely wonderful person.

The day after Jimmy moved into the big house, Linda and I were in the kitchen eating thin sandwiches and cookies—*biscuits* as Linda and Mom corrected me, collapsing together into giggles—and drinking tea out of the best china cups.

Jimmy walked into the kitchen as if he'd never been away, pecked Mom on the cheek, patted me on the head as he would the family dog, and turned the force of his full-watt smile onto Linda.

Walking through the spring forest these many years later, I wondered if I had imagined it. Did she really fall head over heels at that instant? Did I actually feel my world grind to a halt beneath me? Or do I remember it that way only in retrospect, when we see everything so much more clearly?

Regardless, nothing would ever be the same again. Linda still came over, but her green eyes darted around the house like a bee in search of pollen, across the yard, up the dirt road to the big house. She had no further interest in breathless discussions about the boys at school, or about whether we still liked John Lennon, or in exchanging the latest thrilling gossip about girls from town. For a while, Jimmy would be at our house when I got home from school, and Linda walked with me every day. But I knew it wasn't because she wanted my friendship. Mom, who never appeared to have had any illusions about her son, seemed to have gone blind and happily set a place for him at tea.

Of course, Linda was seventeen years old, and as unable to keep a secret about herself as to stop dreaming of romance. One day after lunch when we were in the girls' washroom she confessed to me breathlessly that she was "madly in love" with Jimmy. News flash! Like it wasn't written all over her lovely, open face.

I told her all about him, in the utilitarian girls' bathroom, at the district high school. The white tiles on the walls had been scrubbed until they gleamed, and the smell of disinfectant hung heavy in the air. I watched her reflection in the large mirrors, all red hair and innocent green eyes. And I told her about the other girls. About the phone calls that disturbed our house until my dad shouted at the poor girl on the other end, about the irate fathers banging at our door. I told her about the failed marriage and the stint in jail resulting from a bust-up in a bar that put the bouncer in the hospital.

She brushed her red hair until it shone, called me a fat, jealous bitch, and walked out the door.

Three months passed before she next came to my house. It was late at night and her frantic pounding at the kitchen door dragged us all out of bed. That time she wasn't so pretty. Her eyes were as red as her hair and snot flowed freely from her swollen nose. She begged my mom to tell her where Jimmy had gone. As if Mom would have the slightest idea. Mom gathered Linda into the kitchen and made tea—the solution to every crisis—but they didn't laugh over the cookies. I stood in the shadows and watched.

She had been to the big house, she told us, trying to find Jimmy. She hadn't seen him for almost a month. He'd said he'd call, but he hadn't. Grandpa laughed at her and told her to stop bothering them and shut the door in her face. Grandma crept out the back door and stopped her in the road. She told Linda that Jimmy left for Toronto, where a friend had found him a job. Grandma told her to forget Jimmy. But Linda swore at the old woman and called her a liar and ran down the dirt road to our house. To Jimmy's mother.

Mom and Dad insisted that they didn't have an address for Jimmy, that they didn't know where he'd gone, but if they heard from him they would let him know that Linda was looking for him.

She screamed at them. As in a fairytale, but not the part she had dreamed of living, Linda truly turned ugly before my eyes. Understandably she thought they were lying to her: A family in which parents didn't know where their son lived was well outside the experience of her tidy world. But they were telling the truth. Even before he turned sixteen, Jimmy would disappear for months at a time and then walk through the door one day expecting that a place would be set for him at supper.

Dad offered to drive her home, but she shoved him aside and bolted into the night.

"Oh, dear," my mother said.

Linda hung around school for another couple of months, her previously shiny hair, the envy of us all, hanging lank about her shoulders, her eyes heavy and swollen with tears. And that wasn't all that was swollen. The girls began nudging each other and giggling when she passed, wrapped in a heavy sweater although it was warm for May that year.

At least once a week, usually more, she would stop me in the hall and ask if I'd heard from Jimmy. My own pain at her quick abandonment of our friendship was as sharp as that of any woman rejected by her lover. The last time she asked, I laughed in her face and aimed to wound. "Like he would ever call me. He didn't even tell my parents when he got married. I'm sure he's found a new girlfriend by now and they are very happy together." It gave me a perfectly wonderful glow of well-deserved revenge to say the words, and I laughed at the look on her face, but the laughter died soon enough, leaving nothing but an empty hole in my belly as I watched Linda flee down the hall, drowning in her own sobs as everyone stood aside to watch her go.

She stopped coming to school and missed the last few weeks before the end of the year. The girls whispered behind their hands and nodded to each other in wide-eyed satisfaction.

On the last day of school, a day that should have been full of the promise of long, hot, free summer days to come, we heard that she was dead.

Sampson ran up to show me a branch she found. She dropped it at my feet and danced in excitement, every muscle in her big body trembling with anticipation as she waited for me to pick it up and throw it.

I stopped walking.

Nothing official was ever said, of course. But one of the girls in my class, whose sister was a friend of Linda's sister, made sure that the news that Linda had killed herself got around. She had swallowed a bottle of her mother's sleeping pills and a good portion of her father's liquor cabinet before going for a midnight swim in the lake.

Mom and I went to the funeral. It was a huge affair; most of the town attended, the deeply grieving as well as the mildly curious. Dr. and Mrs. Richards were pale and shocked. But not too shocked to cut us dead as we approached them after the service, Mom's hand held out to offer her condolences. Mom retreated, the weight of her shame dragging her head low. A few of her friends from the quilting society gathered closely around her as if she needed as much support as the grieving parents.

As perhaps she did.

The Richards family moved back to England before the summer ended.

The image of Linda's wild auburn hair, red eyes, dripping nose, and swollen belly as she sped down the crowded school hallway, trying to escape from the echo of my taunting laughter, still haunts me in that out-of-consciousness space that lies between wakefulness and dreams.

The path we were taking ran jaggedly from the back of the big house east through the woods and abandoned farmland to turn south again and run parallel to the main road, part of a patch of land owned by the government. Speculation was ripe that the government-owned property—a good deal of it lake front, with a gentle west-facing slope, close to road and power lines—would be soon be divided into lots and put up for sale. The boon to this area would be enormous. But it would open up the land north of the big house, and Jimmy and Aileen wouldn't be too happy about that.

The demand for cottages, anything on water and the more open the lake the better, to the north of Toronto was spreading like a modern version of the black plague. Anything reasonably close to the city had long ago been priced well out of the range of the middle class; some undeveloped properties on the more desirable areas went for a million dollars or more. And so it spread out, further and further from the populated centers, the endless search for a perfect bit of woodland paradise.

Reaching a fork in the path, Sampson and I turned south, to where there was nothing at all desirable about the land. No one would be so desperate as to develop anything between my family property and the highway. The ground here lay low and flat and was thoroughly saturated with spring rains and the remains of snowmelt. To the west of me, toward my parents' house, it became a near-swamp. Unpleasant for people, perhaps, but greatly beloved of dogs. Better not to think of the grooming job awaiting me when I got Sampson home.

These woods were pleasant, waking up to the warmth of spring after a long, severe winter. Handfuls of dirty, wet snow still hid in the bottoms of the darker crevices of the wood and in the shadows of the larger trees, trying to escape the warming reach of the sun for as long as possible. The forest floor was coming to life with bright green shoots and wildflowers popping up out of the thick mud. Most of these plants were grasping at the only bit of sun they would get all year; the forest canopy would soon grow thick and dense. The woods were lovely, quiet, peaceful, but in some indefinable way too civilized. Nothing like the thick, overgrown, ropy forests of B.C., where the trees grow so tall you can't see the top, even with your head thrown right back and your mouth hanging open. Where moss and vines fill every space with every imaginable shade of green. The rain forest: I hate rain, but I love the rain forest.

I couldn't hear Sampson breaking small branches and crushing the decaying piles of leaves underfoot. "Sampson, come here. Come here! There's a good dog," I called and called, my voice rising with every plea. I stepped off the higher ground and my running shoes sank into the mud.

Her whine came from my left, low and serious. "I'm coming," I cried, wading deeper into the muck.

She burst from the swamp with a flurry of stinking water and even stinkier mud.

"Oh, for heavens' sake," I shrieked. "You're a bad dog as well as a completely disgusting mess of one!"

Not chastised in the least, she merely shook herself off, sending a good deal of swamp water flying in all directions, before proudly dropping her discovery. A scarf, long and thick, good wool by the look of it, thoroughly soaked in mud and swamp water, despite which the cheerful colors of blue and gold managed to shine through.

"Ugh. I suppose you think this is a lovely present for me." She wagged her heavy tail in agreement. "Fool dog." I pushed the dripping mess with my foot. "Nice scarf. Someone will be missing it. But I don't need a scarf and I don't want to carry this wet horror all the way home. Thanks anyway, girl." No need to worry about Sampson's feelings being hurt at the rejection of her gift. I hadn't finished talking before she bounded off in search of fresh adventures.

I left the scarf where it lay and walked on. A chipmunk broke cover and dashed across the path. Something unpleasant scratched at the back of my mind. The newspaper article discussing the disappearance of young Jennifer Taylor had described the clothes she was wearing when last seen walking away from her friend's house. A blue wool coat with matching cap and scarf.

Chapter 26

The Diary of Janet McKenzie. July 12, 1947

I have the house to myself. And the quiet is wonderful. Bob has taken his mother and Shirley to the potluck supper at the church. I complained all day of a headache in order to get out of it. Bob was quite concerned; before they left he made sure that I was comfortably settled in front of the wireless, wrapped in a blanket, with a cup of tea at hand. Once they had gone, I threw off the suffocating covering and headed straight for the bedroom and my beloved diary.

I have a plan. I will give my father one year to settle into his new marriage, Aunt Betty one year to set up her holiday home. And my husband one year to find us a new house. Or in July of 1948, Shirley and I will be on a ship back to England.

Oh, no! A car is pulling up outside. It's Mr. McKenzie, home early. To ruin my lovely peaceful evening alone.

July 13, 1947

I pulled out this book from its hiding place and held it in my hands. There is a small pile of books under the floorboard. I can see the journal that Aunt Joan gave me for my seventeenth birthday, so full of my hopes and dreams. Was I ever that young? That innocent?

I carried this book over to the stove. It is hot today, very hot. Much hotter than it ever got in England. But I was going to start a fire in the wood stove. A fire to burn hotter and hotter. A fire hot enough to consume my dreams.

But I couldn't do it. Instead I turned away from the stove and took up my pen and opened my book. I will write it all down, like I promised myself so many years ago.

Bob has taken his mother and Shirley to church. After ensuring that I was perfectly comfortable and had everything that I might need until their return. His father hasn't been home all night, but that is of no concern to my husband and his mother. And less to me.

I gather that last night's potluck was a huge success. Mrs. McKenzie proudly carried home an empty pot.

When they got home, Bob took one look at me, cowering in bed, the blankets up to my chin despite the heat of the July evening, and did everything he could to make me comfortable. He put Shirley to bed, after his mother gave her a bath and put her into her pajamas, and brought me tea and some biscuits. He sat beside me and rubbed my back through my thick flannel nightgown and whispered soft words into my ear.

Do I still love him? I think perhaps I do. Sometimes I catch a glimpse of the man I know him to be and the love of him catches in my throat. He is a kind man, a good son to his mother. But he is not a good husband. In the balance of things, what weighs more? I do not know. I considered telling him what happened last night while he and Mrs. M. were at the potluck. And perhaps I would have. If he hadn't been so kind, so concerned. If he hadn't been a caring man. I pulled myself deeper into the blankets and drank the overly sweet tea. Bob laid his hand on my forehead and said that I had a fever. He didn't want to disturb me. He would sleep in the living room, on the couch. He would listen for Shirley, and fetch her if she awoke.

I do have a fever.

But it is not a fever of the body.

It is of the soul.

And it will burn inside me for the rest of my life.

July 20, 1947

Once again, I am sitting up writing in this journal while my family sleeps. Nothing is as I imagined it would be, when Shirley and I first stepped off the ship in Halifax, so full of hope and dreams. How ironic that all my hope died once we arrived here in Hope River. What an inappropriate name. My family is asleep. All of them: my precious daughter, my husband whom I still love, God help me, my mother-in-law, as mindlessly vacant as a sheep wandering the fields, my father-in-law. For whom my hatred has no words.

To my everlasting shame, I lured my husband to the marital bed tonight. Fortunately for some reason he hadn't had anything to drink. I can still see the stupid smile on his face once he realized what I was suggesting.

God help me.

My body still aches, my wounds are raw. Internal, hidden, known only to me. But if, God help me, I have conceived—and at this time of the month, such is possible—it must be disguised.

He can never know.

April 5, 1948

Of course I can't ask Bob to climb under the dresser and pull up the loose floorboard to fetch my diary. So this bit of paper the nurse brought will have to do. I haven't written in my diary for many months. But in here the days lie heavy on me. They bring me the baby every few hours. I hold him to the breast and they take him away again. Until the next feeding. I feel like a milk machine.

The other mothers in my ward seem perfectly happy with this arrangement. They are content to send their babies away, so they can fix their hair and makeup and ensure they look nice when their husbands come to visit.

I would rather visit with my son.

The nurse has been around. Bearing samples of formula, telling us all about the benefits of bottle-feeding. I have decided to breast-feed this time. The nurse is quite scandalized. Unsanitary, she told me.

I am the only mother in this ward who wants to continue breast-feeding. They think it is my strange English ways.

Let them think so.

Bob was in earlier. Looking quite like the cat who swallowed the cream. His mother is minding Shirley, he said. That, at least, I know I can trust.

I want to name him after my father, I said.

Arthur.

He agreed. Arthur McKenzie.

A good name.

Chapter 27

I stopped walking. Sampson trotted back down the trail wondering what was keeping me. That might be the very scarf. Evidence. Should I pick it up and take it home, or call the police and bring them here? They would want to see the site, wouldn't they? But would I be able to find the place later? Granted this wasn't the spot where the scarf had been found, that was somewhere back in the swamp where only dogs, adventurous children, and fools would ever go. And murderers.

I retraced my path, all the while imagining the polite scorn if I called the police about finding a clue and then managed to lose it. I decided that I had to hold onto the evidence. This path wasn't heavily traveled, but it was a path, meaning that people walk on it. Anyone could pick up the scarf; I might not be able to find this spot again. Best to take the scarf with me and leave something to mark the place where Sampson emerged from the swamp.

What to leave as a marker? I didn't have a bag with me, nor a scarf, hat, or mittens. I didn't even have Sampson's bright blue leash; it hung on the coat hook by the kitchen door. I struggled out of my coat, a lovely chocolate brown shearling with cuffs and collar of contrasting beige fur, and hung it on a tree branch. Ray's present to me the Christmas before last—our final holiday together. I had nothing else to leave behind.

I sprinted down the overgrown trail, Sampson bounding ahead, thrilled at the exercise. The ground felt solid and familiar underneath my running shoes. The path divided again, going east to join up to the highway, where it crossed over and moved erratically on toward town, but heading west it was a short distance to the road that led toward the lake and our house.

Dad wasn't home, for which I was extremely thankful. No need to explain why I was so out of breath and why I was calling the police.

The number of the OPP detachment was posted beside the telephone in my mother's neat handwriting. "Staff Sergeant Reynolds, please." I said the only name I knew, gave my own name, and held on, listening to empty air while Sampson swallowed the contents of her water dish.

"Reynolds here."

"Rebecca McKenzie. We talked earlier today?"

"I remember. What can I do for you Ms. McKenzie?"

"Are you the officer in charge of the Jennifer Taylor disappearance?"

"For now."

"In that case, I've found something that might interest you. I'm at my father's home."

"Is this to do with your brother, Ms. McKenzie?"

"Absolutely not. Are you interested or aren't you?"

"I'll be there shortly. Don't leave until I get there."

"I called you, remember? I'll wait." Jerk. I hung up the phone without bothering to say goodbye.

They made good time. I'd scarcely rubbed some of the mud off of Sampson and put the kettle on before I heard the high-pitched scream of the siren coming down the road and pulling into the driveway.

I unplugged the kettle and walked out to the front porch in time to open the door to Bob Reynolds and his handsome sidekick. "Tell the whole neighborhood you're coming, why don't you?" I said.

"You have something to show us, Ms. McKenzie?"

"It's in here. My dog found it." Said dog didn't appear to have forgotten her earlier confrontation with these men. She guarded the kitchen door with her teeth bared and hair on end, her voice low in her throat. I stifled a smile of pride as the constable edged gingerly around her. Good dog.

The scarf sat in the middle of the kitchen table, soaking into a bed of hastily gathered newspaper. We all looked at it.

"I found this while out walking. It might be nothing, of course. But the paper says that Jennifer wore a blue scarf when she went missing. So I called you." I held my breath, willing them to laugh at my female hysteria and tell me that this was a bit of discarded rubbish and had nothing at all to do with the disappearance of any teenage girl.

"Can you show us where you found it?"

"I think so."

We trudged back through the silent woods. The earlier sunshine had gone, and thick clouds gathered in the west. The chill enveloped me. I missed my coat. I hadn't bothered to pick up another. Reynolds demanded that Sampson stay behind, and I'd reluctantly left her in the house, scratching at the wooden kitchen door and whining with enough force to shake the house down if the scratching didn't work.

We said not a word as we tramped through the silent woods. Reynolds walked beside me and the constable, finally introduced as LeBlanc, followed like a lumbering ghost.

The walk back took longer than I expected, and I worried that I wouldn't be able to find the spot, and they would arrest me for wasting police time, or some such nonsense. But at last we rounded a corner and there it was, my beautiful coat, hanging from the naked branch of a dying jack pine.

"I left my coat as a marker. Sampson, my dog, brought the scarf to me. She dropped it right there, under the tree. I don't know where she picked it up."

The constable reached for his radio and Bob Reynolds did a 360-degree scan of the area. "Where did the dog come from," he asked, "with the scarf?"

I pointed into the growth of trees, most of them dead or dying, the swamp beyond. He swore and then turned back to me.

"Thank you for your help, Ms. McKenzie. Can you see your way home? We'll wait here."

"I'd like to stay."

"That wouldn't be advisable. This is a matter for the police."

Well, la-di-da. Like I thought it was a matter for the Women's Christian Temperance Union.

Sitting sullenly in the house, nursing a cup of overly sweet tea, I could hear the sounds of considerable activity on the road. Cars arrived, doors slammed, men talked in loud voices. Curiosity got the better of me and I crept out the door and back down the narrow path.

A row of police cars lined the road, red lights flashing in the deepening afternoon gloom. Shapes of people moving through the trees and dancing flashlights broke the dreariness. I wasn't the only onlooker, by far. Locals with nothing better to do were attracted to the potential crime scene like moths to the proverbial flame. My interest, of course, was completely different. I, after all, was the finder of the clue.

A fact that had no effect whatsoever on the shiny-faced, pony-tailed, uniformed constable guarding the path. "No one is allowed down here, Miss," were her only words.

Dad arrived home, almost breathless with excitement as he relayed news of what was happening up on the road. My euphoria at finding the "clue" and the excitement at being involved in the police investigation had died long ago, leaving me nothing but bad tempered and irritable.

I waved him off with an angry gesture. I was on the phone with my secretary, trying to get enough work done to salvage some credibility from the cancellation of next week's crucial meeting. Dad crept into the kitchen, downcast.

The next interruption was the arrival of Bob Reynolds and the handsome Constable LeBlanc.

"I have to go, Jenny," I sighed into the phone. "One crisis after another here. Christ, it's more peaceful at work."

"Is your father all right?" She was a great secretary, Jenny. Young and exceedingly pretty in a flirty vacant-eyed way that discouraged a lot of people from taking her seriously. Their mistake. To my great good fortune she had been assigned to me as a temporary replacement when Norah, who had been my secretary since my promotion to V.P., quit the day after her husband won five million dollars in a lottery. I was happy for Norah, but sorry for myself. She'd been with the company practically forever and I was a newcomer to the rarefied air of the executive floor. But Jenny proved to be a dream of an assistant once I no longer needed anyone to guide me through the intricacies of being a vice-president.

"He's fine," I said. "But there is so much other stuff going on around here, you wouldn't believe it." I held up one finger to Reynolds, fidgeting from one leg to another at the front door. "I'll tell you all about it when I get back. Call me after you've spoken to Ling."

"Will do."

"Ciao."

"Ciao, Rebecca. And don't worry. We can manage here without you for a while."

"That's what I'm afraid of." I was only half-joking. I hung up and opened the door to the police.

"I don't appreciate being left standing on the front stoop while you gossip on the phone, Ms. McKenzie."

"That *gossip*, Sergeant Reynolds, could buy and sell this entire town. With yourself and your friend here thrown in as chump change."

The constable grinned, the first expression I'd seen cross his striking face. His teeth were small and badly stained, the smile thin-lipped. What a disappointment.

Dad wandered out of the kitchen carrying a can of pop. "Bob. What brings you here? Did you find that girl? What's with all the police cars up on the road? Folk said you're searching the swamp."

"We were. Your daughter found a scarf up there earlier today."

Dad looked at me in amazement. I shrugged.

"Can I offer you and your friend a beer, Bob?"

"No. Thank you, Mr. McKenzie. We still have work to do. Sorry about your wife."

"Thank you."

I got off the phone for this? "Do you have something to tell me, Sergeant?"

He turned his attention in my direction. "Mrs. Taylor has positively identified the scarf as belonging to Jennifer. Apparently Mrs. Taylor's mother knitted it herself, last Christmas, so it's an original."

"Oh."

"Wanted to let you know that we've finished, for now. We didn't find anything else significant in the area, but we'll be back tomorrow at first light. We appreciate your help in this matter."

"My pleasure."

"I have to ask you to stay out of that area until we've finished. But otherwise, when you're out walking your dog, keep your eyes open for anything out of the ordinary. That goes for you too, Bob."

Dad nodded enthusiastically.

"That scarf could have come from anywhere, couldn't it? I mean Sampson brought it to me; another animal could have deposited it in the swamp."

"We're aware of that."

"Good."

I closed the door behind them and rested my back against it.

"That's real exciting, Becky," Dad said. He sat in his favorite La-Z-Boy and picked up the remote. "I wish I'd been here to see this scarf." He pushed a button and the sound of an overloud commercial filled the room. "What's for dinner?"

"Actually, Dad, it might be more excitement than we want. The cops are already nosing around here a bit too much. It's not good that something has concentrated their attention even closer."

"What do you mean, nosing around? It's what they're sup-posed to do. It's their job, investigating. That girl lived not far from here, and her family store is down the road a bit. The police will be looking everywhere." His eyes drifted back to the TV, where a car chase of some sort was going on. Much squealing of tires, crunching of metal, and shooting of guns.

"Dad. They're talking to Jimmy. That's not good. Aileen's pretty upset about it."

"Jimmy didn't have anything to do with this. The police will find that out soon enough and then leave him alone."

Not for the first time, I wondered in what dream world my father lived.

And was there any room in there for me?

"Now, what's for dinner? I'm hungry. Didn't get any lunch."

I took the empty can out of his hand. "Let's go out for dinner, okay? I don't feel much like cooking."

Eating out turned out to be a bad idea. There is only one res-taurant in Hope River. It sits on the main street across from the grocery store and is a run-down old place with cracked plastic on the chairs, an ancient linoleum floor, stuffing popping out of the booth seats, ceiling tiles stained with damp, poor ventila-tion, and the heavy smell of frying food. A souvenir clock from Sudbury and a calendar from the Jones Brothers' Auto Body Shop were the only wall decorations.

Every face in the room turned to watch us walk in. Dad smiled and greeted most of the customers by name as we made our way to a vacant booth. They nodded in return, but there was no small-town friendliness filling the grease-tinged air. No concern for the recent widower's welfare. The faces were closed, cold, verging on unfriendly. For a few moments I struggled to understand what was going on. Many of these people had been at my mother's funeral—was it only two days ago?—commis-erating with Dad on his loss and drinking their fill of Jackie's tea and Dave's beer.

But soon enough I got the picture: News of the police search of the swamp near our property must have spread through town, greatly enhanced, no doubt, as it passed from mouth to mouth. And if the police were suspicious of Jimmy for no other reason than his past, what might the town be thinking?

The waitress slapped two menus down on the table. "Evening, Bob," she said. "Sorry about your loss."

"Thank you, Maggie." Dad buried his head in the menu. I don't know why—it had scarcely changed in all the time I'd been away.

She tapped her pencil against a grease-spotted note pad, waiting for us to make up our minds. "Meatloaf's the special tonight. Comes with mashed potatoes and peas."

"A hamburger, please," I said. "And can I have a salad instead of the fries?"

She shrugged and wrote something down.

"The meatloaf is always great here. I'll have that. Thank you." Dad smiled and handed her his menu.

She smiled back and patted her over-colored, permed, and sprayed hair. She wasn't wearing a wedding ring. "Back in a jiff."

We looked at the paper place mats and twiddled with our cutlery. My dad and I have never had much to say to each other.

Maggie brought glasses of ice water. Faint remains of a smudge of red lipstick marked the rim of mine. I pushed it to one side. At least my knife and fork were sparkling clean.

I cleared my throat. "We were thinking, Dad, that it would be a good idea to get a housekeeper for you. Someone to look after the house, get your breakfast, that sort of thing. What do you think of that?"

"Who's 'we'?"

"Jimmy, Aileen, and I."

"Can't you do it?"

"I won't be staying much longer. Another week and I have to go back to Vancouver."

He looked genuinely surprised. Had he actually thought that I'd come home for good?

"Here we are." Maggie carefully placed two brimming plates in front of us. Mine didn't have the requested salad, just a limp slice of half-green tomato nestled beside an enormous pile of fries. The potatoes were thick and brown, singed until crispy around the edges. In any restaurant in Vancouver I would have protested, vigorously. Here, I sighed and picked up my fork. Dad's meatloaf was bathed in rich brown gravy, and his potatoes were fluffy and running yellow with melting butter. Maggie carried a squeeze bottle of ketchup under her arm, and when her hands were free she plopped it in front of me.

"Now what's this housekeeper you folks talking about?" Divested of her burden she placed her hands on her ample apron-wrapped hips, settling in for a chat. "You looking for a housekeeper, Bob?"

"No," Dad grunted.

"Yes," I said. "Do you know someone who might be interested?"

"Depends on the hours. And the money. But I've been thinking about getting out of this place. I been here too long. You know how it is, honey? Gets to the point where you don't even know why you stay on, you just do."

A shout from the counter interrupted her. "Maggie, more coffee."

"Hold your horses. I'll be there." She scribbled on her pad, ripped off a sheet of paper and held it out to me. "That's my number. Call me. I'll be happy to talk to you."

I took it. "We'll talk."

She scurried away to get the coffee.

"She seems nice."

Dad snorted and dug into his meatloaf.

I drenched the fries in ketchup, picked up my hamburger, laden with pickles, tomato, thick red onions, and lettuce, and looked around before biting down. Most of the patrons had gone back to their own meals, and their own business. But a few were watching us. I stared at one old bag until she had the grace to flush and look away.

We finished our meal in silence.

I pulled out my wallet and was checking the bill when a middle-aged couple stopped by our table. I'd seen them at the church and later at Jackie's house. "I hear the cops found something mighty interesting up around your place earlier, Bob," the man said.

Dad continued pouring cream into his coffee. "Norm. Audrey. That's what they say."

"Some folks in town are wondering if that son of yours has anything to do with it."

"No," said Dad. "It was my daughter, Rebecca here, who found it and called the police." I looked at him in surprise. No one could possibly have misunderstood what these people were implying. Could they?

The couple looked at each other and walked away without another a word.

Dad put down his cup with a world-weary sigh. "Time to go home, Becky."

I tossed a few notes on the table rather than taking the trouble to scrutinize the check and calculate the gratuity.

All conversation stopped as we walked through the restaurant, heading toward the door. Maggie waved cheerfully and one old man said, "See you around, Bob." Everyone else simply watched us go. I'd bet good money the place hadn't been so quiet since the day it served its first slice of meatloaf.

We stepped out onto the cracked and broken sidewalk and the chill night air. The street was deserted, not so much as a piece of garbage moved in the wind. Dad wrapped his scarf around his neck. Sorrow lined his old face, his cheeks were sunken, his eyes small and dark, full of pain.

I took his arm. "It'll be okay, Dad. I'll make sure it is."

He patted my hand. "I know you will, Janet. You always do. What would I do without you?"

Chapter 28

"Sorry, Aileen. I am absolutely all in. All I want to do tonight is crawl into bed with a good book and a warm dog. Do you forgive me?"

She giggled. "Of course I do. Absolutely. I often feel like that myself. But at least I have a fiery man rather than a warm dog."

Her tone was so friendly that I laughed. A week ago I would have taken that comment as an insult.

"Do you know anything about what was going on down there today?" Aileen asked. "I stopped at the grocery store on the way home and the clerk said something about the police finding something to do with Jennifer."

"They found her scarf, that's all. I'll tell you about it tomorrow. By the way, I have a lead on a housekeeper."

"You work fast, Ms. McKenzie."

"That's what my husband tells me." The laughter died in my throat as I realized what I'd said.

"Why don't you come to work with me tomorrow?" Aileen said, her voice quick and high-pitched, trying to cover up the silence that fell between us like one of Sampson's particularly smelly indiscretions. "We can make plans about this housekeeper, you can tell me all the police gossip, and I can show you the shop."

"I'd like that."

I was down by the lake with Sampson when Aileen drove up in her little car. She tooted the horn and started when I tapped the window from the passenger side.

"Come and join us, if you have a minute."

The thin, tender skin at the edges of her eyes crinkled as she smiled at the invitation, making me wonder how old she was. Jimmy was well over fifty, and I had assumed Aileen to be much younger. But the light of the harsh morning sun danced off the hair on her head, revealing more gray than black, and cast deep shadows around the lines drawn under her eyes and in the corners of her mouth.

"What a lovely morning," she said. "The weather channel says storms will be moving in this afternoon."

"I've found that it never pays to listen to the weather reports. They're wrong as often as they're right."

"So true." She wore a different sweater today, one perfectly suited to this fresh spring morning in shades of yellow and green with a dash of cobalt blue. As before, long silver and glass earrings framed her face, and a colorful skirt flowed around slim ankles. Her sandals were thick and practical.

We stood in silence, watching Sampson chase the tiny lapping waves. A large black bird flew overhead carrying a length of straw in its beak. A cardinal called from the branches of the maple at the front of the house.

"This is quite the mystery trip." Sampson had been stowed in the house with Dad, and Aileen's foreign compact had pulled onto the highway, heading south. "No one has told me a thing about this store of yours. I don't even know where it is."

Aileen laughed. She rolled down her window and loose tendrils of long hair fluttered in the breeze. "Huntsville," she said. "It's quite a drive, but there's a market there for the sort of things we sell, something that there isn't much of here. Yet. We have a shop in Port Carling also, but it's closed for the winter. I'll be opening it up May long weekend."

"Who's 'we'? Do you have a partner?"

"It's a family thing. Your family, Rebecca. Jim and I own the stores, but Janet and Bob contribute a good portion of our stock." She glanced at me out of the corner of her eye. "You look surprised."

"I am rather."

"You'll see when we get there. I'm hoping to be able to open a store in Hope River one day. If the cottages keep moving north the way they are, we'll be right in the middle of cottage country before too much longer."

"Is that a good thing?"

"For Jim and my finances, great! For the dying town of Hope River, wonderful! For the enjoyment of our home, and the peace we get sitting out on our deck or working in our garden, I'm not so sure."

All around us the woods were starting to shrug off their winter garb of stark tree limbs and dry, brown undergrowth. The beginnings of new life blanketed the forest floor, soft and clean. I shuddered at the memory of blackflies, the scourge of the North. I hoped to be long gone from Hope River before they made their voracious, but fortunately short-lived, appearance.

"I was sorry to hear about your husband, about Ray," Aileen said, in her typically blunt way. "When was it, about a year ago that he died?"

"After the New Year before last."

"How did it happen? Do you mind my asking?"

"No, I don't mind. A car accident. A stupid car accident. Late night, heavy rain, the road slippery with wet leaves, a car skidding out of control on the steep hillside, straight into Ray."

"How awful for you."

"How awful for Ray." I wiped at my eyes. "He was a truly good man. In a world of not-very-nice people, Ray was a genuinely good man. He hung on for three days." Days full of over-brewed coffee, gnawed and ripped Styrofoam cups, snatches of tormented sleep, ancient magazines, too-bright lights, the patient hum of machinery, and whispered conversations. A broken body in a room of coldly efficient equipment. Outside the ICU, a waiting room full of fresh-faced students, good friends, faculty, family, all whispering their prayers, offering their hopes and crying their fears. Ray's mother, so tiny and frail you wouldn't think anything else could diminish her. But those three days did.

"The doctors fought so hard to save him. As if they knew his was a life worth saving. But there was no hope." No hope. I sobbed and turned my face to the window.

We drove in silence for a long time. The clouds moved closer.

"How did you meet my brother?" I asked when at last I thought that I could speak without my voice breaking.

"In prison."

"Uh, right."

"I don't tell most people that, believe me. I know perfectly well how it sounds. But it's not quite that bad."

"You don't have to explain."

"I'm a psychologist. My area of specialty is, was, anger management. I worked in the prison system for over twenty years. Let me tell you, I've met some men and a few women that I would be more than happy to condemn straight to hell if I believed in such a place."

"Why'd you give it up?" Time to change the subject. I didn't want to hear about her infatuation with the handsome, charming, "misunderstood" inmate.

"A long story, as most stories worth telling are. But I didn't fall in love with Jimmy when he was my client, if that's what you're thinking." Aileen looked straight ahead, watching the road. A bug hit the windshield and splattered its guts across the glass. She kept her voice under control, strong and steady, but her hands, resting on the steering wheel in the proper ten-and-two position, were clenched, the knuckles white.

"When then?"

"As I said, it's a long story. I quit the prison service. Burnt out doesn't begin to describe it. The job destroyed my first marriage. And eventually it came close to destroying me. I received a small inheritance from a childless aunt, so I decided to take some time off, try to find my way through the rest of my life."

"And…"

"And I ran into Jim, quite by accident, in Huntsville one fine day in the height of summer, years after we'd first met. He'd been out of jail for some time, had gone back to live in Hope River, and started up his own carpentry business. He came into town for some shopping and was standing on the bridge watching the river and a family of ducks swimming below. I jumped out of the path of a kid on a bicycle and bumped right into Jim. We recognized each other, talked and went to lunch. And here I am today."

"Happy?" I asked.

"Completely."

The green highway sign announced our turnoff, and Aileen concentrated on crossing into the right lane.

In early May the town of Huntsville is small-town quiet. But that's the lull before the storm. The rush comes over the long weekend at the end of the month, when people arrive to open up their cottages. But even on this day there were plenty of enterprising people around, getting in supplies, searching for hardware, electrical, and plumbing equipment, getting a start on the season. It gave the town a nice, bustling mid-week air.

Aileen pulled into an alley to park behind a row of stores. Then we headed down the main street to Cottage Art and Design. The front door was propped open and a young woman stood guard over the counter. She tossed a huge smile of welcome for Aileen and, incidentally, me.

"My sister-in-law, Rebecca," Aileen introduced us. "My dream of an assistant, the best in the whole-wide-world, Chrissie."

Chrissie beamed at me and shook my hand with much enthusiasm. Taken piece-by-piece her face would be considered plain—heavy features, nose and lips overly prominent, thick eyebrows, chin too chiseled for a woman. But all together it coalesced into a stunning whole, accented by a river of lush chestnut hair falling past her shoulders. Close to six feet tall, maybe more, she dwarfed not only my tiny sister-in-law but also me, something I am not used to in a woman. Her style of dress was similar to Aileen's: hand-knitted sweater, long skirt, exquisite jewelry.

"I thought Rebecca'd like to have a look at some of her mother's work," Aileen said.

Chrissie took both of my hands in hers. I almost jerked them back, but conscious of the offence that would give, I stoically endured her touch. She smelled of fresh laundry, herbal shampoo and (before lunch?) pot. "Janet was a true artist," she breathed. "That rarest of all people. A true artist. I am so sorry to have missed her funeral. But it fell on one of my days to work at the coffee shop, my other job, and they wouldn't give me the time off. Uncultured swine."

"There isn't enough business in the off season to keep Chrissie on full time," Aileen explained. "As much as I would like to. She opens up for me and looks after the store when I'm on shopping trips as well as on Saturdays, but that's about it until summer."

Chrissie pressed my hands together once more and then released them. I tried not to wipe them on the seat of my jeans. "Such is the fortune of commerce," she whispered. "But please, Rebecca. You're here to look around." She waved one hand expansively, swept her long skirt aside, and returned to the stack of papers she had been examining behind the counter.

Aileen grinned at me, her eyes sparking like a mischievous elf. "A great saleswoman," she whispered. "The summer people absolutely adore her."

The bell over the door tinkled and a woman entered the store. Aileen fixed her smile in place and moved to greet the potential customer.

The store was small, but filled to bursting with goods for sale. Handcrafted items, most of them, everything perfectly suited for lodges, holiday cabins, cottages, and vacation homes. I spotted a rocking horse, a twin to those currently residing in my father's workshop, and nicely arranged groups of plain wooden benches and tables, which on a first glance might appear to be plain but were made out of the finest wood, carved as delicately as if composed out of clouds of lumber. There was a collection of wide-limbed Muskoka chairs, ubiquitous in this part of the country, but these were special, perfect, the wood glowing with light from within. I ran my fingers lightly across the arm of a chair as soft and smooth as good leather. I flicked a price tag: priced to match their quality.

Wooden shelves piled high with quilts lined the back of the shop. Bed-sized quilts and artistic wall hangings draped the walls in waterfalls of vibrant color. More quilts accented the wooden chairs and tables, the fabric warm against the grain of good wood. Leaning close, I checked out another price tag. And almost choked. But it was a beautiful piece—a king-sized quilt in almost every shade of blue imaginable, each hue fading gently into the next. It was the twin of the one on my parents' bed.

"Lovely, isn't it? That's one of Janet's."

"It's amazing. Stunning. I had no idea she was doing this sort of work. She quilted when I lived at home, and she occasionally mentioned it in her letters. But they were things for the annual church Christmas craft sale, presents for friends, for our beds."

"I miss her dreadfully, I do," Aileen said. "But the business-woman in me is simply frantic wondering where I will ever find another artist. Your mother did most of the fabric art here.

"Janet sewed all her dreams into scraps of fabric. See that one there, the tiny one? It might be you, when you were little. Or some other girl from her past. What do you see in it?"

"A girl. Afraid of the touch of cold water."

"Afraid. Yes. But she will touch it, won't she? Don't you see it? She's frozen in time, but when she's released, when time gives way, as it must, the girl will put one toe in, only one big toe, and that only for a second. But the sensation of cold water on that one toe will liberate her to explore the world."

"You see more than I do."

"Perhaps."

"That rocking horse over there looks the same as the ones in Dad's workshop," I said. "Did he make it?"

"He certainly did. We had quite a rush on them before Christmas. Sold every single one. The people who come up here for the holidays love to have locally crafted items for their children and grandchildren. And bless them, so they should. Most of the woodwork here is your father's."

"Is everything in this lovely store made by someone in my family?"

"No, although it would be wonderful if it were. The wood carvings and the bowls? A Muskoka man makes those. Bob does wonderful work with larger pieces but he has no eye, or patience, for details. The pottery is from an assortment of potters near and far. Some of the jewelry is mine." She waved her long-fingered hand toward the display cases. Chrissie waved back at us.

"You made those lovely things?"

"By no means all. But some of them."

"You are a wonder, Aileen," I said, and I meant it. Businesswoman, artist, former psychologist, tamer of the untameable Jimmy McKenzie. All I ever made was money, which for most of my life was the only thing that mattered. Now it looked pale in comparison.

"Not a wonder, not I," she laughed. "When I was a practicing psychologist, a large part of my approach involved working with my clients using the therapy of art and crafts. Working out anger, encountering your feelings by toiling with your hands, creating something out of rage and hate. I totally believe in that. I've seen it work, time after time. I've seen the worst criminals break down at the sight of a lump of clay they molded into what they see as an image of their late mother, even though to everyone else it still looks like a lump of clay.

"And like all of us, I have my own demons. Working with glass and metal tames them. I started making jewelry seriously when my first marriage broke up. It helped me through a hard time. Your niece Jackie is experimenting in stained glass. She made this." Aileen opened a display case and picked up a pair of earrings. Tiny, beautiful pieces of glass, glowing with perfectly clear green light as if they had been plucked directly from a medieval church window.

"Stunning."

"These pieces are beautiful," Aileen said. "And I'm proud to put them up for sale. But Jackie has a long way to go yet. She has perfected one style and tries desperately to stick to it. She is afraid of trying something new."

"I'm off, Aileen." Chrissie waved from the front door. She'd put on a coat, too heavy for this weather, mittens, and scarf, and had pulled a woolen hat tightly down over her ears and forehead. "Nice to meet you, Rebecca. Ask Aileen to bring you over to the café for lunch. Perfectly hideous food and horrible psychic energy, but a nice view." She disappeared with a wave and cheerful tinkle of the doorbell.

I laughed, "That's certainly a ringing endorsement."

"That's Chrissie. Never stops hinting that she would like more hours in the store. But what can I do? This is a seasonal business. Nine months of the year it's all I can do to keep the wolf from the door.

"But lunch is still a good idea. I have a lot of paperwork to do. You're welcome to stay here, or take a stroll through town, not that that's likely to prove dreadfully exciting. Take the car if you want to go somewhere further. Then we can catch up over a late lunch."

"Can I help at all?"

"No. It's paperwork mostly. The odd customer might drift in. But there are unlikely to be many serious buyers, it being a Friday in early May."

"Fortunately I never go unprepared. I have a paperback in my bag. I'll take a walk and perhaps find a coffee shop somewhere. Is there one?"

Aileen laughed. "All the modern amenities."

"I'm sure I'll amuse myself. It's been a long, long time since my last appearance in this town."

Like the forest that surrounded it, Huntsville struggled to wake up after a long winter. The sidewalks were thick with mud and dust, not yet washed away after being left behind by the melting snow. I walked slowly through the light foot traffic, stopping now and again to peer into the shop windows. Several were closed, either for the season or permanently, signs still in place but with windows covered by newspaper or cardboard. Algonquin Park outfitting stores were doing a light but steady business. A pretty ice cream store, perfect in the traditional pink and white, beckoned. But storm clouds were gathering, the wind was rising, and the air hung heavy with moisture. It didn't seem like an ice cream sort of day.

I stopped in the middle of the bridge that crossed the river running through the center of town. The water level was low: A bicycle and several hubcaps littered the shallow water at the edges of the river. The middle of the channel was green and impenetrable.

Presumably this bridge marked the spot where Jimmy and Aileen had met after his release from prison. The bridge that started their romance. A romance that, wonder of wonders, appeared to have lasted longer than the first bedding.

I spent a pleasant, relaxing afternoon exploring the town, watching the traffic pass by, and reading my book over a frothy cappuccino. For the first time in a long time, I had no particular place to go and nothing in particular to accomplish. It felt nice.

I held the door for a customer as she bustled out, clutching a shopping bag and quite obviously thrilled with her purchase.

"A sale. Congratulations," I said to Aileen once I was inside the shop.

"One of Janet's. Part of the last batch I got from her." She pulled two paper bags out from under the counter. "I called Chrissie and asked her to bring some sandwiches and soup up from the café. We've had more customers today than I expected, and we can eat here while I keep an eye on the store. Is that okay?"

"Great. Whatever's in that bag smells wonderful."

Aileen handed me my lunch and peered into her own bag.

I pulled out a sandwich, a container of soup, a bottle of juice, and a pile of napkins. We ate standing up, leaning on the counter.

"I love your store, Aileen." I bit into the thick, juicy turkey, tomato, and sprout sandwich. "Wow, this is good." I peered between the layers. "This dressing is wonderful. I'll admit that I was rather worried about what I'd get. Chrissie sort of implied that the café food is dreadful."

"She didn't imply, she came right out and said it." Aileen spoke around a mouthful of her own generous sandwich. "The food there is great. It's a hugely popular place with the locals as well as tourists. She doesn't like working there, and makes sure everyone knows it."

"Why do they keep her on then? Nothing worse for business than a disgruntled employee."

"The owners are her parents."

I burst out laughing and took a sip of my soup—lentil, thick and hearty. "I appreciate you bringing me out here, to see the store and all. I had no idea my parents were doing this sort of thing."

"You knew it all along, Rebecca. Your mother always quilted for the church ladies' bazaar, and your dad has been carving in his workshop for years. But as long as they only made things for charity bazaars or for use by the family no one thought their things were of any value." She held up one soupspoon-clutching hand. "Hear me out. I don't mean 'you' as in 'you, Rebecca.' I mean you, everyone. When I first met them, Bob was selling his furniture for a fraction of the price he could get in Toronto considering the quality of the work. But it brought in a bit of extra income and he was very proud of that.

"Your mother's work, of course, didn't earn her anything. She made it for all for charity or family. No one considered it to be art. It was something that women make, therefore not real art. It was crafts."

I made a ball of my empty sandwich wrapper and stuffed it back into the paper bag. "Was the store your idea?"

She laughed. "Forgive me if I get on my high horse sometimes. It makes me so mad, the way that our world devalues women's traditional art. But to answer your question, yes. I've always wanted to own a craft shop. I love to make jewelry, but I work very, very slowly. There is simply no way I could ever produce enough to make a living out of it. When Jim and I married I still had a bit of my aunt's money left, and the idea was growing in the back of my mind that I should open a shop. The first time I saw what your mom and dad had sitting out in that shed I almost died. Janet didn't like the idea of putting her work up for sale. She was afraid she'd be embarrassed, that no one would buy it if they didn't think they were being altruistic and making a donation to the church at the same time.

"But Jim and I persevered." She lifted her arms and held out her hands. "And here we are."

I was literally speechless. In my real life, I'm a vice-president with an investment bank. The people who work for me lend hundreds of thousands, millions, of dollars every day of the year, and all of it moves under my supervision. My people have a good reputation, a great reputation, of being solid, reliable, honest, and their reputation extends through them to me and through us to the bank. Most of our deals are good—only a few turn belly up, and it isn't often, if ever, because of something we missed or didn't follow up on. I wasn't kidding when I told Bob Reynolds I could buy and sell Hope River and every business in it with a phone call.

Yet all the while my family had been struggling to put together this business. This lovely shop that gave my parents pride in their old age along with much-needed income, which put the sparkle into Aileen's eyes, and some purpose into Jimmy's life.

"We've talked all day about this shop and how Jim and I met, but I still don't know much about you, Rebecca. And me, the psychologist! What sort of work do you do? Jim told me you're with a bank."

"Yup. Bank of Western Canada. Small business loans, mortgages. Boring stuff, but it makes the world go round." Aileen must have been good at her previous profession, she actually looked interested.

"Tell me, Aileen." I studied my hands. "Does Jimmy ever talk about our grandfather? Big Jim we called him, when I was a child. And my brother was always called Little Jim? To everyone except my mother, and me. She forbade me to ever say Little Jim."

The bell over the door tinkled. I was standing with my back to the door and paid it no attention, willing the customer to leave, concentrating on getting an answer to my question. Until I saw Aileen's eyes open wide and all the color drain out of her face. I whirled around.

"Afternoon, ladies."

The very last people you would expect to find in a store with a name like Cottage Art and Design.

Jack Jackson and his skinny friend.

Chapter 29

The Diary of Janet McKenzie. April 12, 1948

James. They called him James.

I don't think that I can bear it.

I took ill while still in the hospital. Pneumonia, I was sick for days. They took the baby and held him to the bottle. Of course he likes it—it is so much easier for him. Now he refuses my breast and my milk has dried up. So I have to give him the bottle. The nurses and the other mothers smirk.

While I lay ill, Bob and his father went to the courthouse and registered the birth. James Arthur McKenzie, they wrote.

I will choke every time I say that name.

April 15, 1948

Home at last. That was a joke. The hospital was better than this. Mrs. McKenzie, of course, dotes on the baby. Little Jim, she calls him. I tried to tell them that his name is Arthur, but none of them will listen to me. Little Jim, my father-in-law said, all the while eyeing me as if I were a prize sow at the autumn fair. Little Jim, he said looking me straight in the eye. And to my everlasting shame, I flushed and looked away.

Once the baby is old enough to travel we will leave. I will take Shirley and Arthur back to England. My father and his wife will be happy to take us in. I know they will.

June 1, 1948

Dead.

> *Dead.*
> *Dad*
> *is*
> *dead.*

A letter this morning from his wife. Her words so drenched in sorrow that I'm sorry that I've never met her. An accident, a stupid, stupid accident. He was walking down the road from our house, taking Bonnie for her morning walk. Bonnie, so old now that she couldn't get out of the way of a speeding motorcar. My father, Arthur, ran into the roadway to save her.

And there they both died.

I have not seen my father for several years, but he is still a presence in my life. His letters have reminded me that I am loved in the world. I have always known that I have someplace else to go.

Now he is gone. And I am alone.

No, I must not think that. I have Baby Arthur and Shirley. And I believe that Bob loves me still.

In his own way.

Chapter 30

Aileen moved around the counter in one liquid movement, all long earrings and flowing skirt. "May I help you? Gentlemen." The last word was an afterthought, bitter on her tongue.

"Nice place you got here." Jack casually flipped over the oval sign that hung over the door. It was hand-painted with two scenes of the same lake. One side showed the lake at midnight, the moonlight sharp on the still water; the other, a view in the daylight, children splashing in the sun-sprinkled water. One side said *Closed*, the other *Open*.

"Are you looking for a gift?" Aileen asked. She held onto the countertop as intensely as she earlier had gripped the steering wheel of her car when she feared that I would criticize her for her relationship with Jimmy.

I looked at my watch. "Will you look at the time? Almost closing time, already. Clay will be by in a few minutes to pick us up."

Jack and Pete ignored me and walked into the store. Never before had I really appreciated the phrase "bull in a china shop." Here we had one bull and one nervous piglet. Jack touched the edges of one of my mother's bed-sized quilts hanging on the wall. It was made of intersecting circles in shades of orange and brown I don't find attractive.

"Pretty blanket," Jack said. I felt the need to pull it down from the wall and wash it.

"What do you want, Pete?" Aileen said.

"Nice store you got here," the scrawny one said.

"Thank you. If you're interested in buying a gift for your mother I'm happy to help, but otherwise, I would like you to leave. Please."

Mistake that. Never say please. A polite word. A woman's word, therefore a sign of weakness. Always a mistake.

Jack abandoned my mother's quilt and picked up a glass carving of a duck. It showed nothing but the bird's rear end in the classic feeding position: tail up, head buried underwater. He tossed it from one huge paw to the other, his ugly face twisted in confusion over what the carving was supposed to represent.

"No need to be rude, Mrs. McKenzie," Pete said. He wasn't distracted by the wealth of trinkets; his eyes were only for Aileen, with a peripheral glance for me.

"Well," I said, "time for me to be on my way. I told them at the police station that I would be back soon to make a report on the theft."

Pete stood in my way. He was smaller than I, shorter and lighter. But I have never been in a fight in my entire life. And we both knew it. For a wild, insane moment I considered asking him if he wanted to bargain for the rights to the funding deal for a computer company so red-hot the business press were calling it the Canadian Microsoft. Everyone on the West Coast wanted a piece of the action but my top lender, Ling Wong, was on the verge of closing the deal.

Pete sneered at me. Better not to mention the loan. "You got a big mouth on you, lady."

"You've said that before. And I'm tired of hearing it. Tell us what you want and get the fuck out of here."

"Rebecca, please, let me handle this." Aileen's voice sounded small and thin.

Jack tossed the glass duck, caught it. Tossed it and caught it again.

"Me and Jack want to let you know, Mrs. McKenzie," Pete drawled, "real friendly like, that folks in Hope River are getting tired of that husband of yours fooling around with the girls."

"My husband isn't fooling around with anyone."

"Shut up, bitch!" Pete yelled. His thin face turned red in an instant. The small, dark eyes grew narrow and hostile; the veins on his neck bulged with tension.

"Leave us alone, you jackass." I made a dash for the phone, prominently displayed behind the front counter. Jack dropped the duck and grabbed me as I passed. The delicate glass carving hit the floor with a crash and shattered into a thousand bits. I stared at it: this duck would surface no more. Jack's strong fingers dug into my arm. "Going somewhere, lady?" He leered into my face. Beer fumes washed over me.

He held my arm while Pete wandered around the store, picking up a few items and placing them back again, neatly, exactly where they belonged. Aileen watched him, her face so white I thought she might faint.

"If you want something from us, tell us what it is and then get the hell out of here," I shouted. Jack raised his right hand, the one he wasn't using to hold me, and struck me hard across the face. I would have fallen if he hadn't been holding me up. The pain spread though my body, but as bad as it was, the humiliation was worse. Far worse than the pain. No one had ever hit me before. Words were the weapons of my childhood. Hands and fists, never. At least not directed against me.

Aileen gasped and the last of the color drained from her face.

"Me and Jack," Pete said, "thought that it might help Jimmy-boy recover a bit of his memory, if we paid you a visit. Didn't know loudmouth over there would be here. But that's just a bonus, eh? Two of us. Two of you. We can have a nice party, and you can tell Jimmy-boy all about it, later. How's that sound?"

The bell over the door tinkled once again.

"I see your sign, Aileen, please don't be mad at me, but the door is unlocked, so I knew that it would be all right to pop in for a quick moment." A woman filled the doorway, large and round, her face shining with the exertion of walking down the street, her mop of thin gray hair almost standing on end from the force of the wind. Behind her stood a younger woman, a teenager, probably her daughter judging by the similarity of their features. The girl was tall and lanky, with long fingers and a bird-like neck, her chin and forehead dotted with acne, and her mouth stretched in a grin of embarrassment. She, if not her mother, recognized the scene in front of her, not for what it was, but certainly as something private.

"Come in. Come in," Aileen stepped forward. "Pearl, you are always welcome. This must be your daughter? So pleased to meet you. Your mother talks about you all the time. Here to collect our contribution for the Police Retirement Fund are you? And how is your dear husband, the M.P. for this district?"

Pearl looked at Aileen as if she had grown another head. Her daughter grinned. "Daddy is perfectly fine, thanks for asking. He's busy down in Ottawa, and we miss him. But the work of the government never ends, don't you agree?" she asked Pete, straight to his face.

Without a word he pushed past the women and headed out the door. Jack dropped my arm and followed.

I leaned against the counter and sighed with relief.

"I'm sorry, Aileen," Pearl said, "but we aren't here for the police fund. Are they soliciting? I hadn't heard. I was rather hoping that you might have something to contribute to the auction we're holding in June for the women's shelter. It's a wonderful cause, you know. The poor women are..."

"I think we've come at rather a bad time, Mother," the girl said. "Ms. O'Connor doesn't look at all well. Do you need some help here, Ms. O'Connor?"

Aileen reached the front counter and me. She hugged me tightly and I hugged her back. Her thin frame quivered beneath my arms.

"No. Thank you. We'll be perfectly fine. My friend had a bit of a fainting spell, which gave me quite a shock." She smiled up at me. If you could call it a smile. "But she seems perfectly all right now."

"Oh dear," Pearl quivered in sympathy. "Pardon us for interrupting. So very sorry. But as long as I'm here… Can I count you in for a contribution?"

"Not now, Mom. Let's go. I'll come back later."

Pearl withdrew reluctantly. The bell tinkled behind her. The girl looked at Aileen. "Would you like me to call someone, Ms. O'Connor? The Police Retirement Fund, perhaps?"

"Thank you, sweetie," Aileen said, "but no. Please don't."

The girl left.

My legs gave way and with my back against the counter, I slithered to the floor like a vertical crab. My face throbbed like a punk-rock drummer on acid. Aileen scurried to the door. With a loud snap the lock fell into place before she collapsed beside me.

"Who were those women?"

"The dumbest woman in the district and her daughter, the smartest girl. Everyone says that she has the inside track to a full scholarship at Queen's next year."

"I trust they don't collect for the Police Retirement Fund?"

"Don't even know if there is such a thing."

My mind wandered and observed us from above. We were babbling about inconsequentials, thus not having to face the facts. "The mention of the M.P. was a touch of brilliance."

"Believe it or not, I didn't make that up. Pearl is indeed the wife of the esteemed Member of Parliament for Huntsville-Bracebridge. Dammed if I can remember his name."

We burst into gales of laughter. Which stopped all too soon. I rubbed my face—the throbbing wasn't going down—and struggled to my feet. "There's a police station only a few blocks from here." Aileen crawled over to the shattered remains of the glass duck. "Don't touch anything. I'll go and get them," I said.

"No."

"Eh?"

"Don't go to the police. I need to clean up." She picked up a shard of glass, one of the duck's lovely tail feathers. Aileen's beautiful skirt formed a soft puddle on the floor around her.

"Of course I'm going to get the police. That jerk attacked me. Shit, it hurts like hell. They threatened you and your property. God knows what else they would have done if Mrs. M.P. and her clever daughter hadn't arrived."

"I don't want to talk to the police."

"Aileen, listen to me. We were saved by the bell, quite literally. They might try it again."

"I don't want Jim to know."

"What?"

She gathered the pieces of glass up into one hand, and felt all over the floor with the other, searching for invisible shards. She cried, silently, the sobs shaking her shoulders.

I turned my back to give her the privacy she seemed to need and fingered the sign on the door. *Closed.* Let it stay that way.

"I don't want the police involved in this. We have enough attention directed our way these days. We don't need any more. And I don't want Jim to know. He'll go after them, Jack and Pete. He's not a young man anymore. Jim forgets that sometimes." She took a deep breath, straight from the diaphragm, pulling air into her back and shoulders. "I don't want him to get hurt."

"I might not be here next time, Aileen, not that I amounted to any help at all. But the Huntsville version of Superwoman might not be here either. And then what?"

"There won't be a next time." She looked up at me, crouched on the floor, her full skirt all around her, and held out her hands. Shards of glass sparkled on her palms. Only the tip of the duck's tail was recognizable. "They'll get the person who took Jennifer and then those two will leave us alone."

The argument died on my lips. There was nothing I or anyone else could say to Aileen. "If you're sure that's what you want, I won't say a word to Jimmy, or anyone else. But you're wrong. Let me lay a complaint with the police against Jack. I won't even mention Pete. That'll leave you out of it. If the cops are onto it, Jimmy won't dare go after Jack and Pete."

"He will. He will. And the police won't stop at a charge against Jack. They'll want the whole story. And they'll wonder what Pete knows about Jim." She struggled to her feet and dropped the pieces of glass into a dustbin. The tip of her index finger dripped blood. She sucked at it without thought.

"Was that duck worth much?"

"No. It's worth nothing."

Aileen locked up the shop and we drove back to Hope River in silence. I gazed out of the window and watched the dark forest slide past my window. I had no doubt that if we told Jimmy about what transpired at the store this afternoon he would be after Jack and Pete before we even finished speaking. And that would probably end up putting him in jail, the severity of his stay depending on the injuries inflicted. That was the Jimmy I knew. Quick with his fists. Fight now, think later. Manly honor above all. It made me sick. Aileen and I would go on living with the facts of the assault and the threats, but we couldn't do anything about it because Jimmy couldn't deal with the idea. A lot of men would approve of any action he took. But not the law. So Aileen was right to be afraid.

My mind drifted. The forest rolled by. A deer watched us pass. I scarcely noticed her.

Jimmy. My brother Jimmy. Did he have anything to do with Jennifer Taylor? Aileen didn't want to draw police attention toward her husband. Did she have reason to be afraid? In my mind's eye, my brother smiled at me over his breakfast table. Handsome as ever, the crooked smile, the eyes as blue and as deep as the lake sparkling over his shoulder, hard muscles bulging under his hand-knitted sweater. But wrinkles were crinkling the edges of his eyes and pulling the skin down around his mouth. His hair was streaked with gray. He grunted softly as he got up out of a chair.

Jennifer Taylor. She was what? Seventeen years old? Young. Innocent. She knew Jimmy; she wanted to be a carpenter, just like he was. Some might think that a strange choice for a girl who might rather be expected to dream of being a movie star, or a pop singer. A doctor or a lawyer. Perhaps a firefighter or a cop. Maybe even an investment banker. But not a carpenter in a two-bit Ontario town. A town so insignificant that it wasn't even marked on some maps.

Jimmy had never had to force a woman in his life. What with his charm and his looks, he needed nothing else.

That was the man I remembered. But how long ago was that? He was now over fifty. To me he is still heart-stoppingly handsome, but in a few short years I'll be facing the dreaded big 5-0 myself.

What might Jimmy look like to a seventeen-year-old girl?

Like a joke?

Like an old man who couldn't keep his pants zipped up?

Did she laugh?

I peeked out of the corner of my eye at Aileen. She was concentrating on the road as dark rain lashed at the windscreen. Did she know anything? Or did she simply fear everything?

⌒⌒⌒

"Home. We're here." Aileen shook my shoulder and I struggled out of sleep. The rain fell with its full strength, and the wind bent the trees until they moaned, begging for relief. The lake tossed gray and white waves, angry and restless. With nowhere else to go they headed for the shore.

Dad opened the front door to greet us and Sampson shot out, tail wagging, beautiful face open wide in greeting. I hurried to get out of the car, shaking sleep from my groggy head, fumbling with the seat belt release, tripping over the door frame, afraid that my dog would scratch the car's paint in her eagerness to get to me and that Aileen would be mad at her. At me.

"Have a nice day?" Dad called from the doorway, all smiles and baggy pants.

"Wonderful. Except for this horrid rain." Aileen waved cheerfully. "How was your day, Bob?"

"Fine, thank you, dear."

"Have to run. Thanks for coming with me, Rebecca. It was lots of fun. See you tomorrow."

It wasn't a standard-shift car, but Aileen still managed to clash the gears as she pulled away. Cold rain dripped down my neck, and Sampson muddied my coat as I watched Aileen's car pull onto the dirt road and disappear up the hill.

———

Saturday morning, I eyed myself in the mirror over the dresser in my room. Lovely shades of purple and green decorated one side of my face.

I hadn't brought any makeup with me from Vancouver. Makeup, like high heels, power suits, and leather briefcases, was for business meetings. I'd have to drive into town as soon as the stores opened and get something to cover the bruise. Too bad I couldn't walk around all day with a paper bag over my head. But even Dad would notice that. I struggled to think up a good excuse for my appearance. Walked into a door, tripped over the dog? A frustrating exercise. Why do women feel that they have to make themselves look like idiots in order to hide the evidence of men's brutality?

Sampson whimpered, her nose held to the crack under the bedroom door. I crouched down and gave her a big hug. "You love me no matter what I look like, don't you, dog? You don't even notice. Could have used you yesterday. I won't leave you behind again." She squirmed out of the embrace. Dad was up. Kitchen cupboards were opening and closing. Sampson had more important things on her mind.

Ling and her husband had had dinner with the prospective clients last night. I told Jenny to give Ling the number here and have her call me first thing to let me know how it went. It was now 8:00 a.m.; the stores opened at 9 o'clock or maybe 9:30. If I went into Hope River I might not be back until ten. Which was seven Vancouver time. Ling has small children. She would be up early, even on a Saturday. I wanted to be here for her call, but decided to chance the shopping expedition. Even Ling would surely have breakfast with her family before calling me.

Sampson continued to whimper and was getting louder at it. The moment I opened the door she dashed out. Dad was making noises in the kitchen; he would let her out.

I picked two of my mother's diaries off the floor and stacked them neatly on the night table. I'd fallen asleep reading through the selection that I'd carried up from the basement. They made for pretty tough reading, some of them, but now I was hooked.

I'd let Dad get the breakfast, wouldn't that be a treat? I sat on the edge of the bed and returned to the page I'd been reading last.

When I looked up again it was almost 8:30. Time for a coffee and to head into town to be there when the drug store opened. The house was quiet; I assumed that Dad had taken Sampson out. Perhaps I should get him a dog. A big friendly mutt, a stray from the pound, a companion, something to keep him from feeling too lonely. He and my mother had been married for almost sixty years. Once I'd gone back to Vancouver and Dad's life had settled into some sort of routine surely his loneliness would be unbearable at times.

I sighed. My nose twitched as it sensed something foreign in the air. Something wrong.

Smoke?

Smoke.

I threw aside the journal and ran.

Chapter 31

Waves of thick, gray smoke rolled out of the kitchen and down the hall. I burst into the kitchen, my eyes watering, my lungs already gasping for air. The smoke was coming from the stove. There was a frying pan on it and the element underneath shone with a fierce red light. Something black and unrecognizable popped and sizzled in the pan. A dishrag, placed on the counter with its tip resting on the edge of the stove, ignited with a whoosh as I stood stupidly in the middle of the kitchen, looking for something to use to pull the pan off the heat. I leapt back in shock.

Outside, Sampson barked. They were returning from their walk.

I arched my arm around the spitting grease in the pan and the fire-hot element, reaching for the knob. A few spots of hot fat splattered on my bare skin, but I managed to switch the element off before running to the sink. A drinking glass sat on the draining board. I filled it with water and threw the contents onto the dishcloth, now crinkling around the edges and releasing cheerful red sparks into the thick air. Not enough. The dishcloth continued to smolder, and another piece burst into flame. More water. The second glass did the job. I grabbed a drying-up towel from the rack and used it to cover my hand while I pulled the frying pan off the element, which was gradually fading from enraged red to dull, safe black. I turned the burnt scraps with a fork. Bacon. These were the charred remains of rashers of bacon.

"In you go, girl." My father held the door open to allow a sodden Sampson entry. The dog's thick coat bore testimony to the fact that it had rained all through the night. She tracked a trail of muddy paw prints across the kitchen floor as she made her way to her water dish.

"Morning, Becky. Sleep well?" Dad pulled off his raincoat and hung it on the hook beside the door. Only then did he sniff the air. "Smells like smoke in here."

"Dad, what were you thinking?"

"About what?"

"About breakfast. Remember breakfast? Bacon cooking on the stove?"

"Bacon would be nice, thank you, dear." He used his right hand to wave smoke away from his face, pulled up a seat, sat to the kitchen table, and unfolded the newspaper.

I propped open the back door with a chair, stopped to take a coughing fit, and then opened all the windows.

Sampson sneezed.

"Dad!" I cried, once I had regained control of my breathing. "Did you want to burn the house down?"

"What are you talking about, girl?"

"You left the bacon cooking, Dad. And a dishcloth beside the stove to top things off. If I hadn't been here, the whole house would be in flames by now."

He looked up from the paper and glanced around the kitchen. "No harm done. Have you seen the sports section? It's not here."

It was an effort, but I managed to control my rage. "I'm going into town to do some shopping. You can clean the dog while I'm gone, she's covered in mud."

He looked at Sampson. "So she is. Stores aren't open yet. You have time to make us breakfast. Eggs would be nice. And there's some bacon in the fridge. Leastways there was the end of a packet yesterday."

"Dad. There is no bacon left. You started cooking it before you went out with the dog. Don't you remember?"

"Sausages'll have to do. Get some bacon when you're in town, will you. There's a good girl."

I know when I'm beaten. On the bright side, I didn't have to lie about the condition of my face. Dad hadn't even noticed. With a good deal of ill grace I rubbed Sampson down with a towel and threw sausages into a fresh pan. The burnt one I'd stuffed into the garbage can, the handle sticking out, pointing back at me like an accusing finger. It could accuse all it wanted: I wasn't going to make the attempt to salvage it.

I plopped the sausages onto a plate with two undercooked fried eggs. My father smiled at me. A genuine smile, full of appreciation for the food and love for me. I collapsed into the other chair. It was now well after nine.

"Someone from my office might call while I'm out," I said. "Can you take a message? It's important. I need to know where I can reach her."

"Isn't it a Saturday? Why would your work be calling you on a Saturday?"

"What on earth does that matter? Can you take a message or not, for heaven's sake? It's important."

"Don't shout, Becky. Not in the house. Your mother never would abide shouting in the house. Of course I can take a message. I'm not completely an old fool, although everyone around here seems to think I am. I can be trusted to take a phone message."

"Sorry, Dad."

"Off you go now. Take as long as you like, dear."

I checked that I'd remembered to switch the stove off. It was cold and nothing rested nearby that shouldn't be there. Dad sipped his coffee and read the paper. I kissed the top of his head and he smiled up at me.

Sampson and I dashed through the rain to the SUV. At least I dashed. The dog took her time to chase a squirrel up a tree and sniff at a patch of grass. She was once again a sodden blob of good humor by the time she leapt into the car.

I made it into town before the store clerks did, and sat in the car cooling my heels for a good half hour before the lights of the tiny drug store came on and shapes began to move around inside.

Pulling my coat over my head I made a dash through the rain and tried the door. Locked. The clerk looked up at the sound of someone pounding for admittance. She scowled fiercely and tapped her watch. I pounded some more. To little effect. My own watch said 10:02. A small river ran down the sidewalk, soaking into my running shoes.

Realizing that any more attempts to gain entry would only get the clerk's back up and then I might never be allowed in, I tried to find a bit of shelter from the driving rain in the lee of the building.

The woman drew her eyebrows together in the manner of a particularly ferocious grade school teacher as she pulled back the latch on the door. She looked me up and down, clearly unimpressed, and walked away without a word.

As quickly as possible, I tossed cheap makeup into a shopping basket. Get the job done and get out of there. Foundation, face powder, blush (too pink? too bad!) and brush. As an afterthought a chocolate bar for Dad joined the contents of the shopping basket. He always had a weak spot for chocolate. And what the hell! One for myself.

The sullen clerk was ringing up my purchases when, of all the people I didn't want to meet, in walked Kimmy Wright, shaking her umbrella to dislodge the raindrops.

"Becky. How nice to see you. Isn't it a perfectly dreadful day?" She folded the umbrella up neatly and tucked it into her tote.

"Absolutely."

"How are you and your family managing? My mother wanted to drop by with a casserole the day after the funeral, but I suggested that she wait until you've left. Your dad'll need it more then. Do you agree?"

"Yes. Very thoughtful of you." I pulled money out of my wallet and slapped it down.

"Don't you have anything smaller?" the clerk said.

"Eh?" A pink fifty-dollar bill lay on the counter. "Oh, right." I dug through my wallet and shoved a green twenty into her outstretched hand. She had a bad case of eczema, red and scabby, on the pad of her thumb. She handed me my change and slipped the receipt, makeup, and chocolate bars into a plastic bag.

"Lovely to see you, Kimmy. Do keep in touch. Have a nice day." I snatched the bag and bolted for the door.

"Excuse me, Miss," the clerk called. "But don't you want this back?" She waved the pink bill at me.

With a forced grin that must have looked as bad as it felt, I sheepishly returned, accepted the money, and stuffed it into my pocket.

Kimmy followed me out the door. "That's a terrible bruise on your face, Becky."

"It's nothing, really. I tripped over my dog and fell into the edge of an open door."

"If you say so. But if you want to talk… I volunteer sometimes at the women's shelter in…"

"Thank you. That's kind of you. But I fell into a door. And speaking of the dog, she's waiting in the car right now. I have to get back, my dad's also waiting for me."

Kimmy watched me from behind the big glass windows of the drug store as I drove out of town pretending not to notice her.

"Aren't you the complete and utter jerk," I spoke to my reflection in the rear view mirror, once we were back on the highway. The bruise was developing very nicely, thank you. I juggled the thought around in my head for a while. A jerk, an idiot, a fool. It was a foreign feeling. I like to be in control, in my work, my home life. And until Ray's death, I always was.

And now Kimmy Wright believes that someone in my family is hitting me. Suspicion will almost certainly not fall on my gentle, soft-moving father. The most likely suspect is the former bad-boy, the quick-with-his-fists renegade Jimmy. The news would be all over town by lunchtime.

But perhaps not. If Kimmy really did volunteer at a shelter then she would well know the importance of privacy. Did I care what Kimmy Wright and the citizens of Hope River thought of my family and me? To my considerable surprise I found that I did.

The situation was so absurd I actually laughed out loud. Sampson stuck her cold wet nose between the front seats in an attempt to join in the joke. I rubbed her chin. Before leaving Ontario, I would make sure that Kimmy heard the real story. If only because Jimmy appeared to be having a tough enough time going straight.

I pondered the direction of my own thoughts as I simultaneously drove and scratched an appreciative dog. Did I really think that Jimmy was going straight? Perhaps. He seemed sincere, and Aileen was no bubble-headed bimbo. I decided right there, as I slowed down to allow a tiny brown rabbit with a cotton-ball tail time to scurry safely across the road and disappear into the dense brush, that I would give my brother the benefit of the doubt.

The decision made, I felt a good deal better, and I finished the journey with a touch of a smile on my face.

An old compact, almost as much brown rust as blue paint, sat in the driveway. Shirley's car.

They were sitting in the kitchen with Mom's favorite everyday brown teapot and an empty packet of cookies in the center of the table.

Responding to an impulse, doubtless on account of the previous promise to make the most of things with my brother, I planted a kiss on the top of my sister's head and smiled at my dad.

"Shouldn't you wash that dog off before she tracks mud all over the house?" was Shirley's response.

"Tea's still hot," Dad said, returning the smile. "Pour yourself a cup why don't you."

"In a minute. Did anyone call for me?"

"Yes. I took a message. It's right here." He peered through the bottom half of his glasses and read slowly, concentrating. "Some woman named Lynne? *Great night. It's in the bag. Guaranteed.*"

"Ling," I corrected him. That sounded like Ling all right. Everything was always "guaranteed" in her optimistic world. And she was so good at her job that it usually was.

"Mean anything to you?"

"It does, Dad, and it's good news. Thanks."

"What's the matter with your face?" Shirley said.

Amid the turmoil of my thoughts on the drive home and then the pleasure at receiving Ling's message, I'd completely forgotten the bag of makeup clutched in my right hand, and the bruise it had been purchased to conceal.

Involuntarily my hand rose to touch my cheek. "Nothing. I tripped over Sampson and fell into an open door."

She snorted, her thin face pinched with righteous justification. "Don't know why you put up with that dog. It's nothing but a slobbering mess. You look like you've been in a fight or something. Suppose someone sees you. What ever will people think?"

"She's my late husband's dog," I replied, struggling to keep my voice level. "She loved him very much, and now she loves me."

Shirley had the grace to flush an unbecoming pink and look away. She ran her finger through the crumbs at the bottom of the cookie box.

"It will look worse tomorrow, dear, believe me," Dad said. "I remember when I was in the army. In a bar in London, it was, not long before I met your mother. A fight broke out. Some fellow had been paying too much attention to someone else's girl. It had nothing to do with me, I never was one for throwing a punch, but in trying to get out the door I found myself in the way of a wild swing and took a fist straight to the eye. The next day I was fine, although a bit sore with the start of a bruise. But the day after that I was a real fright, got quite the teasing from the other lads." He chuckled at the memory. My memories aren't quite so amusing. They are of my father's black eyes and bruised cheekbones and limping walk in the days that followed one of my grandfather's temper tantrums.

When I was a child I sometimes wished that my dad would turn into "one for throwing a punch." Do something to protect himself. But as far as I knew he never so much as raised his voice to his father. And so the abuse went on.

Would striking back have stopped it? Or would my grand-father, bully to the core of his black heart, have turned his fists on someone else? Someone who couldn't throw a punch if they tried? Like my grandmother.

No wonder my dad had been a drunk.

I escaped to my bedroom to apply a bit of the newly pur-chased makeup. I looked in the mirror, checking my face from all angles. The makeup did seem to make a bit of a difference. It smoothed the tone out and de-emphasized some of the darker color, if nothing more. Remembering Dad's wartime story, I shuddered to contemplate what I might look like tomorrow.

"I was in town earlier and I heard that Maggie Kzenic is coming to work for Dad," Shirley said as I was settling down at the kitchen table with an empty cup for the tea.

"That's not decided yet. She's jumping the gun a bit."

"Work for me?" Dad said. "Doing what? I've got no work to offer anybody."

"You may not think it's decided, but Maggie told her euchre club, and from there it got all over town, that she's going to be Dad's housekeeper. I think you should put her straight, Rebecca."

"If she wants the job, great." I poured myself some tea.

"Don't need a housekeeper," Dad said. "Any cake left, Becky? Cookies seem to be gone."

I pulled out a tin that I had discovered earlier. It was a fruit-cake, and it looked moist, rich, and delicious. I took down side plates and forks and a cake knife and placed the whole lot on the table.

"If Dad needs a housekeeper," Shirley said, "then I'll find him one."

I spluttered in indignation. Did I not try to talk about this with my sister? Was I not very politely shown the door? "We can talk about it," I said, as I passed Dad a serving of the cake. It was very dark and rich with fruit. I could smell the brandy it had been soaked in. Sampson thumped her tail.

"Nothing to talk about. I'll handle it."

"Jimmy and Aileen and I…"

"Jimmy," Shirley snorted. "I wouldn't ask Jimmy to find a kennel for that wretched dog." She tossed her head at Sampson, who was still waiting for cake crumbs to fall. "Never mind someone to come into my father's house every day. And as for you, Miss Vice President…"

"Is that what all this is about, Shirley?" I asked. "Not about Dad and what's best for him, but about not wanting me to be in charge? Well let me tell you, I don't want to be in charge of anything, thank you very much."

"I'm going to take the dog out for a bit of a walk," Dad said. "The rain seems to have let up for now, so this would be a good time."

The emotions raging through the house fascinated Sampson so much that she ignored the beloved word "walk."

"Come on, there's a good girl." Dad took his raincoat down from the hook by the door, and man and dog trudged out into the muddy yard. But first Dad carefully shut the door, not making a sound.

My sister and I faced each other, across the narrow room and the chasm of years. Ten years apart in age, we'd never been playmates. Scarcely even sisters in the sense of girls sharing clothes and toys and dreams. I hadn't thought of her more than five times in the thirty years since I left. I had escaped, made a good life—a great life—for myself, left it all behind without a backward glance. I wondered what I'd left behind for her.

"Shirley," I said.

She scraped her chair across the kitchen floor and stood up, her thin chest heaving. "Why don't you just leave, *Becky?* You're not needed, or wanted, here."

Unlike our father, she slammed the door on her way out.

~~~

The rain started up again in the night, accompanied by a full orchestra of rolling thunder and a spectacular display of jazzy bolts of lighting that filled my bedroom with light and sound.

Sampson hates a thunderstorm; it turns her into a quivering mass of furry jelly. Long before the first blast of thunder shook the house, she had crawled under my bed. And there she remained, all through the night.

The next morning the ferocity of the storm had abated, but the rain continued to fall, a steady, quiet torrent.

True to form, Dad had said not a word about the scene in the kitchen when he and the dog returned from their walk. He brought Sampson in, dried her legs and belly off, and announced that he was off to the Legion. I didn't see him again until suppertime. I spent the remainder of the dismal day down in the basement, lost in the distant echoes of my mother's thoughts. Spiders were moving in already, spinning their delicate webs in the dark corners of the cellar, no longer kept at bay by Mom's fiercely wielded straw broom.

I was in a dreadful quandary about what to do with the diaries. Was it right for a daughter to know so much about her mother? To peer into her secret dreams, her hopes, her fears? Mom had been old when she died: not dreadfully old, not incapacitated by old age, but old enough to be aware that she didn't have a whole lot of years left to her. She must have known that someone would read the diaries if she left them behind. Did she think it would be me? Or was it more likely that she assumed Shirley would be the one to go through her things? Perhaps it was her way of apologizing to her oldest daughter. Apologizing for taking her away from a warm, adoring family and a comfortable middle-class home in a pleasant English village only to replace it with a hardscrabble life of poverty, strife, and abuse.

Perhaps my imagination was getting the better of me and I was reading too much into it. Maybe Mom didn't even think about the future. She got pleasure, enormous pleasure as well as strength—it was obvious to me that the diaries kept her going when nothing else could—from keeping a record of her days. So she kept on writing with never a thought of someone finding them after she'd gone.

And what should I do with them, once I finished reading and took Sampson and myself back to the West Coast? If I decided to keep them, would I ship them to Vancouver, all three tea chests full? Eventually all would come to a dead end. There would be no one to cherish them once I was gone.

A sobering thought.

⌒⌒⌒

The weekend passed in a peaceful blur of leaden skies and liquid air. Aileen and Jimmy came for lunch on Sunday, which appeared to be a bit of a family ritual. Fortunately Dad remembered to tell me in time.

While in the cellar with the diaries, I'd also discovered a treasure trove of frozen food in the freezer. All of it homemade, either wrapped in aluminum foil or freezer bags or packed into sturdy plastic containers. A few of the packages were marked in my mother's neat handwriting, but the rest were in all sorts of different wrappings and markings. Some were unlabeled. People must have been arriving the entire day after Mom's death bearing casseroles. And Dad put them carefully away in the freezer and forgot about them.

I dashed downstairs to pull out a large package marked *chicken pie*. Even I could manage to do mashed potatoes, and there were still plenty of vegetables to throw together to make a good salad. At the last minute I called to invite Jackie and her family. Jason was in a hockey game and his dad was driving, but my niece sounded delighted at the invitation. I might be fighting with her mother, but I liked Jackie a great deal.

Before the guests arrived, I patted makeup onto my face, which was now reaching its full colorful glory, sort of like the woods in autumn. Jimmy noticed; the question darkened his eyes but he said nothing. Hopefully he would blame the dog and a sharp door. Aileen tossed me a thankful smile, and Jackie fussed over her grandfather.

Conversation over the dinner table was mostly about the store. Aileen had enough of Mom's quilts to see her into the summer, but she needed to find a new supplier. I was not part of the conversation, so it seemed odd to me that they could talk about Mom's work with so little emotion.

But then my own business life is as far from my emotions as it can get and still occupy the same body.

Jackie sheepishly confessed that she only had two pieces of jewelry ready to offer for sale. Aileen was disappointed, but she hid it behind a bright, encouraging smile. They decided that Jimmy would bring the truck around after lunch and they would load up Dad's winter collection of rocking horses to take to the shop in the morning.

I cleared the dishes and brought out dessert. Apple pie, another bereavement offering found in the freezer. I served the pie with huge scoops of vanilla ice cream on the side. It didn't seem proper to serve pastry for the main course and also for dessert, but the alternative was my cooking. No contest.

It was a lovely lunch. After coffee Aileen, Jackie, and I did up the dishes while Dad and Jimmy switched on the TV to see what sports might be on. Wrapped in the warm companionship of the women of my family, the chore didn't even seem like work.

Aileen excused herself to go to the bathroom. I handed Jackie, in charge of the washing, a burnt pastry-encrusted cookie tray. I'd managed to cook the chicken pie a bit too long. She coughed lightly and scrubbed vigorously at the baked-in crust. Then she dropped her voice. "They're saying some nasty things about Uncle Jim. In town. I heard it this morning. I forgot to get bread for Dave and Jason's sandwiches so had to make a quick trip to the grocery store."

"What sort of things?"

"I was standing beside the bread, debating between the whole wheat at full price or the white on sale. And on the other side of the shelf two women were gossiping. I couldn't see them, I could only hear what they were saying." Her eyes darted about, wary of Aileen's return. "One of them said that Uncle Jim molested Liz's daughter Melissa. But that the police wouldn't prosecute because he paid them off."

"Do you wonder that I hate this damn town?" I slammed my fist into the countertop, imagining that it was someone's face.

"I snatched the first loaf of bread that came to hand, and hurried around to the other aisle. They stopped chattering mighty fast, you can imagine, once they saw me. I didn't know what to do then, Aunt Rebecca. I glared at them and they hurried away. Should I have said something?"

"Probably best not to. Anything you say will only encourage gossip."

On her way through the living room Aileen asked Dad if he wanted more coffee, and Jackie and I changed the subject. But the quick conversation left me worried. This wasn't a good time for fabricated rumors to be circulating about Jimmy. Even the gossip in this town was stupid. As if the police weren't waiting to jump on Jimmy McKenzie if he so much as crossed the street against the light, never mind him paying anyone off to cover up child abuse.

I enjoyed the family Sunday lunch very much, but I spent the rest of the afternoon with a knot in my stomach as if I'd eaten that whole apple pie.

Monday morning the cats and dogs continued to fall, but despite the rain my own restless dog needed a walk. I made breakfast for my father and decided to brave the elements early in order to be at my computer by the start of business, Vancouver time.

The police had spent a good part of their weekend poking through the woods behind barriers of yellow tape. But Sunday afternoon the tape came down, and the patrol cars drove away.

We set off through the woods toward the swamp. I soon realized what a huge mistake that was. Sampson was covered, from her belly down, in mud and indeterminate guck.

The spring rains had raised the level of the bog very high indeed. Paths that I'd walked down days ago were now virtually under water. I scooted around widening puddles in search of higher ground. Of which I could find precious little.

Sampson burst out of the bush, lifted a dripping muzzle to me and grinned from ear to ear before dashing back into the quagmire. *A bath for you, my girl, when we get out of this.* I smiled at the memory of the voice in my head. She hates the water, but up at our chalet, after a romp in the rain forest, Ray would throw her in the shower and clamber right in with her. Afterward, the bathroom would look like a tornado had swept through.

Getting into the tub with her was one thing I wouldn't do for the silly dog. She would hate me for it, but I would make her stand under the shower all by herself, until she was once again shiny and reasonably pristine.

She disappeared into the swamp, and I kept walking, seeking some sort of path. No point in turning back now. She couldn't get much muddier and neither could my boots. She would find me, soon enough. But instead of bursting out of the under-growth in hot pursuit as soon as I faded from sight, the dog started barking.

Cornered a ferocious squirrel, I assumed and whistled for her to join me. Not that I can whistle, but I sort of push air through my lips and hum at the same time, and Sampson seems to understand.

But this time she didn't respond. I called and whistled and called some more. And she alternately whined and barked but didn't appear. With a curse I stepped off the high ground; my boots sunk immediately into the muck. I ploughed through, cursing every step of the way, the mud dragging down my steps like an affectionate bog-creature asking me to stay and play. For me, all this rain might be a curse, but for the forest it was the source of life. Spring flowers and grasses grew with wild abandon in the rich, muddy soil. A bullfrog croaked a throaty greeting (or was it a warning?) as I stepped over a rotting log covered with soft green moss.

"Sampson," I bellowed. "Come here."

She barked some more.

My anger faded to be replaced with a growing sense of worry. She didn't sound in any sort of pain, thank goodness. But she might be stuck, and she is pretty darned heavy. Particularly when soaking wet and coated in mud.

I passed through the last line of trees clinging to solid ground. The swamp stretched out before me, stunted trees, thick mud, slimy water, long grasses. Thoroughly inhospitable. By this time next month it would be far worse—a paradise for breeding insects.

Sampson stood on a patch of slightly higher ground, surrounded by swamp. She saw me and barked once. She stood over a log, half of it submerged in the water, half resting on land.

I waded into the muddy water, hoping that Sampson had found nothing more than a struggling puppy, caught in the rising waters. I imagined myself drying it off in front of a roaring fire, pouring a small helping of dog food into a saucer and fresh water into a bowl, all the time receiving excited licks of gratitude from a soft, wet tongue. But the back of my mind warned me that this expedition wasn't fated to have a happy ending.

I got closer and form took shape. A mud-encrusted foot stuck out from under the side of the log nearest to me. A pair of legs rested on the high ground, partially hidden by the log. One foot still wore its boot; the other was bare of boot and sock. The naked toes stuck up out of the mud at the round bottom of the rotten log, like little oyster mushrooms. The head and torso stretched down the slope and disappeared in the thick water, an arrangement for which I was profoundly grateful.

Sampson rubbed her big head against my hip. I sunk to my knees and hugged her tightly.

Chapter 32

The Diary of Janet McKenzie. December 14, 1953

My son dropped a glass of milk onto the bedroom floor today. It was a full glass, too full, and it rained glass and milk all over the floor, the liquid dripping under the big old dresser. I pulled the dresser away from the wall to get at the drops of milk and found the loose floorboard. I had actually forgotten about it. Too many bad memories, no doubt. I waited until the children and Mrs. M. were asleep, and Bob was in the front room listening to the news on the wireless, and then I pulled out my diary. I haven't written in it for more than five years. It's been a long five years. Aunt Betty is dead as well as Dad. So I really am alone in the world. I have thought a lot over the past years of what might have been. If Mum had stayed with us, if my brother John had lived. If Mary Jones hadn't taken sick, so that I went to the dance with Jenny. If I hadn't met Bob.

But what's done is done. And no use crying over spilt milk as Aunt Betty always said.

It's time to start writing in the diary again. I did like keeping it. But I'll never show it to my daughter now, as had been my intention, so long ago.

As bad as things are, I do have my children. And if things had been different, then I wouldn't have them. So maybe it is all worthwhile after all. Shirley is so smart, like I knew she was when she was a baby. She does so well in school. Jim is a little terror, but Mrs. M. says that all boys are like that, so I'm glad. That he's normal, I mean. I learned early that there was no point in calling him Arthur. Can't have the poor boy growing up confused about his name, Mrs. M. said one day. The only bit of sense I have ever heard come out of her mouth.

Sometimes they call him Little Jim and then they call Mr. M. Big Jim. That I'll never say.

Bob built a bit of an addition onto the house. So we could finally move Shirley and her brother into their own room. Not that there is likely to be anything going on in our bedroom that the children shouldn't overhear, let me tell you! That part of our marriage is long over. Bob reached for me one night a few weeks after the baby was born, and I actually jumped out of bed and ran to the bathroom to be sick. I won't allow him to touch me in that way again.

So he continues to drink.

A second room went onto the main house as well. "Shirley will want a room of her own once the next baby arrives." Mrs. M. smiled at me. Stupid woman. But it's hard to hate her. She's like a particularly innocent child herself, so timid and frightened, scurrying about, trying to guess what her husband wants before he bellows for it.

Him, of course, it isn't hard to hate at all. At least he pretty well stays out of my way. Since the time Bob took his mother shopping and the children were napping and he caught me in the kitchen. I pulled a knife out of the drawer and told him I'd use it if I had to. I would have too, and he believed me. I wish sometimes he hadn't. Then I could have used it. I don't think I'd even mind going to prison, if it meant that my children would be free of him. He has no more time for Shirley than he ever did, thank God. But it worries me sometimes, the time he spends with Jim. Trying already to 'make a man out of the boy'.

There will be no 'next baby', so I turned the new room into a sewing room. No one ever goes in there. I will move my diaries and bury them in a drawer under a pile of fabric.

After Jim's birth and then the news about Dad, I thought I might die of sorrow and loneliness. But shortly after that a new minister arrived in town and his wife turned out to be nothing at all like the old one. She is terribly nice, not at all like the stuck up old prune face who would scarcely give Mrs. M. and me the time of day. As if it was our fault that we live in a shack with a bastard of an old man and his son who drinks himself into oblivion. But the new minister's wife, she is nice. She invited me to the quilting circle she started at the church. I didn't really want to go. Sit around in that freezing old church basement with that herd of stuck-up cows sewing a bunch of rags? No thanks. But Mrs. Burwell talked me into it (she doesn't take no for an answer, that woman). There is no one left now in the quilting circle but Mrs. Burwell and I. And the quilts she taught me to make are certainly not bunches of rags.

So now I have a lovely sewing room of my own. I don't get much in the way of housekeeping money but I've managed to save a bit of what Bob gives me for the children's and my clothes by making them myself. I am making a quilt for Shirley's bed. In my own sewing room.

Chapter 33

Not until long after, when the shock started to fade and it was me, not a rescued puppy, sitting in the warm kitchen, wrapped in a blanket, food and drink pressed upon me, did it occur to me that perhaps I should have checked the body for signs of life. I have never seen a dead body before, not counting those dressed in their best, neatly made up and laid in a casket, but I found that a person knows. This one was well and truly dead.

I'd grabbed Sampson's collar, keeping my eyes averted from the half-submerged object. The dog followed me, reluctantly, and we waded back through the swamp to the path. Once again, I stripped off my coat and hung it on a branch before sprinting through the woods for home, Sampson loping ahead of me. She didn't even pause to chase a squirrel that crossed her path.

We stumbled through the back door, a stream of mud marking our progress. I grabbed the phone and dialed 911. My father sat at the kitchen table, a cup of coffee frozen on the way to his mouth, the Saturday newspaper spread out before him. Upside down, I recognized the face of the Prime Minister, who was shaking hands with some foreign dignitary.

The conversation was brief. I declined to stay on the line and, after offing the pertinent info, hung up before collapsing into a hard kitchen chair. Sampson gulped back stomachfuls of water. My father looked at me, open-mouthed, his eyes reflecting the confusion and despair in my own. Without a word he pushed his chair back and left the room, to return moments later with two thick, fluffy towels. He pressed one into my shaking hands and lowered himself on arthritic knees to kneel on the floor beside my dog. He murmured softly to her, all the while rubbing her coat vigorously with the towel. I followed suit, rubbing at my own face and hair. Sampson attended to, Dad poured the remnants of the morning's pot of coffee into a chipped mug, took the towel out of my hands, and replaced it with the mug.

It was awful, the dregs of the pot, and lukewarm to boot. I drank deeply, wanting only to soak up the warmth. Then Dad knelt again, his face wincing with the pain in his knees, and loosened the laces of my shoes. I held my feet out, one after the other, and allowed him to peel off the dripping socks and rub my feet with the towel. I closed my eyes and luxuriated in the feeling of being truly cared for: the one thing that money can't buy. You can purchase a day at the spa or hire a masseuse, but when your time is up or your money runs out, you're shown the door, ready or not.

Sound of a car on our road, tires crunching the gravel driveway. Doors opening and slamming shut.

Too soon.

Groaning, Dad pulled himself to his feet and went to open the door, Sampson following at his heels. I shook my head and tried to pull myself back to reality.

Two OPP officers marched into the kitchen, holding their wide-brimmed hats in their hands. One female, one male. I didn't recognize either of them. He was young, fresh faced but prematurely balding; she had long black hair gathered back into a perfect French braid. In my younger, much younger days, when I had long hair, I tried so hard to do it like that. Weeks of trying and buckets of tears of frustration passed before I gave up.

"I was expecting Bob Reynolds. He came the last time I called. You've heard about the scarf I found?"

"Sergeant Reynolds is in court in North Bay today, ma'am," the female officer said in a voice as high-pitched as a child. Internally I cringed. That voice will kill her professional future in what is still a man's world as surely as a round of tears at a crime scene.

"If there is anything to report, we'll let him know," the young man offered.

"Well let me assure you, you'll have more than enough to report. It's out that way." I waved my arm in the vague direction of the woods behind our property and through them to the swamp. "I left my coat as a marker. Can you bring it back please? It's rather a good one."

"If you could show us what you saw, ma'am? That would be more convenient." They looked at me.

"One minute," Dad waved his hands in the air and hustled out of the kitchen. He returned with a handcrafted cable-knit sweater, two pairs of thick woolen socks and high rubber boots.

"Thanks, Dad." He was smaller than I, but his feet were bigger. With both pairs of socks my feet fitted into the ugly boots, although leaving a bit too much wiggle room for the toes. They would do.

Sampson made no effort to follow us. I almost wished she would: this was starting to become a habit. I led the police through the woods and into the swamp. There hung my lovely shearling coat, hanging on the branch of a naked tree.

Past the coat and down the incline to the moving boundary of the rising swamp, I stopped at the water's edge and pointed.

"There, there it is. That log. Do you see it?"

"I see lots of logs," the male officer said, taking a few tentative steps into the water. The squelch of mud as he pulled his boot free with each step was clearly audible.

On the patch of high ground there was a flash of movement at the sound of our voices as something, some animal, scurried away from no-need-to-contemplate-what.

His partner followed, the edges of her mouth turning down and her nose crinkling in disgust, as she put one foot into the water. "We see it, Ms. McKenzie. You don't have to come any further. If you could stay at your home for a while? Someone will be around to take your statement." She looked over her shoulder at me. The other officer waded through the muck. Frogs and birds and early insect life set up a cacophony of protest at the human invasion of their muddy paradise. Part of the evidence was visible from where I stood, particularly that one foot held down by the log. But regardless of my revulsion, I felt a twinge of regret for the creatures that called this swamp home. The invasion had only just begun.

"I'm not going anywhere." I stumbled back through the woods, cursing the police for leaving me to find this… thing… after they'd supposedly spent the weekend scouring the swamp, and trying to keep from throwing up until I was out of sight of the two officers, although I had no reason to care about their opinion of me. My heaving stomach held out until I reached the tree holding my coat, and there I vomited into the soft mud around the roots. A lifetime passed, but my stomach did eventually settle, and my panicked breathing returned to a semblance of normal. With one hand holding the small of my back I straightened up.

I kicked mud over the puddle of vomit until it was completely covered. A nice meal for the insects burrowing around the tree roots. The thought brought on moments of dry heaving. But nothing remained in my stomach to come back up.

I gathered my coat and stumbled up the path to my family home.

I never again wore the lovely chocolate shearling coat with the beige cuffs.

—◦—◦—

Naps make me bad tempered and grumpy. Give me six to nine hours in the dead of night, and I'm a happy woman.

But on this day, I walked through the house in my father's mud-encrusted boots without saying a word. His worried eyes followed me. I slammed the bedroom door in my dog's face and collapsed fully dressed onto the bed, remembering only to pull off the boots before I hit the sheets.

I slept badly, disturbed by the sounds of the house. Dad turning on the TV. Sampson scratching at the door. Her toenails clicking dejectedly down the hall. The phone ringing. A heavy knock at the back door. Dad grunting as he pulled himself out of his best chair. Murmured voices. The sound of a car engine starting up and the crunch of gravel as it pulled away. Then gentle tapping at the bedroom door and my father's soft voice.

Thinking about it made me realize that his voice is soft. Soft and gentle like the man himself. "Girly man" my grandfather called him once, in my own hearing. My father had flushed and looked at me, embarrassed. Not at the insult but at his daughter overhearing it. Of course I didn't know what a "girly man" might possibly be. A man who liked to play with girls, perhaps? Nothing wrong with that. Men were fun to play with—not Grandpa of course, never Grandpa—they would swing me around and around by the arms until I screamed with delight. Or push me on the swing that my brother Jimmy, in a rare moment of kindness, had made and hung under the biggest tree that could be found for miles around. Push me so high I both feared and hoped that the swing would break and I would fly over the lake and into the setting sun. Men played in a way that women never did.

The door squeaked open on a hinge in need of oil and Dad smiled in. "Time to wake up, sweetheart. I've brought you a bit of toast and some tea."

I struggled to consciousness and tried to sit up. "Come in, Dad. What time is it?" Sampson landed on the bed with enough force to knock the breath out of me. I scratched behind her ears.

"The police wanted to talk to you earlier, but I sent them away. They said they'd be back at five and it's almost that now. Some tea and toast will help you get yourself up."

I settled a mound of pillows behind my head, and Dad put the tray onto my lap. The toast had burnt and he'd tried to scrape most of the black bits away. An open jar of cheap, mass-produced marmalade sat to one side, the knife stabbed into the sticky, aromatic depths. A tea bag floated in the cup. If Mom could have seen it she would have passed out. My throat closed.

Girly man.

It should have been offered as a compliment.

Praise of the highest order.

"Thanks, Dad."

He grinned shyly and his cheeks burned. "Better hurry up and eat that, my girl. The police said five o'clock and you can be sure they'll be here right on the dot."

I nibbled at my toast. "Anything happening at the swamp?"

"Too much. Too much. Cars coming and going; people and dogs tromping through the woods. Everyone and their dog phoning me to ask what's going on. I wish your mother was here, Becky. She'd know what to do."

I doubted it. My mother could handle almost anything, but a dead body would be out of even her league. I smiled anyway. "That she would, Dad. That she would."

We stopped talking to listen as a car drove down our road and pulled into the driveway. Sampson lifted her head and pricked her ears up.

"Guess they're back." Dad sighed. "You finish your tea there. They're early. They can wait a while. Oh, by the way, your office called. Girl named Jenny, sounded real nice."

"She is."

"I told her you couldn't be disturbed."

I pushed aside the tea tray and swung my legs over the edge of the bed. Dad left the room in a rush, no doubt to avoid seeing me in my dishabille. I was in no mood to dress for company. The cops would have to interview me in the clothes I'd slept in. They were professionals: They should be able to stand the shock.

They were waiting for me in the living room. Sergeant Reynolds and the female constable with the enviable hair and cringe-inducing voice.

Cups of tea sat on the coffee table in front of them, accompanied by generous slices of the wonderful fruitcake laid out on a plate. Despite the seriousness of the situation, and my thick head, I smiled to myself. My dad might make it on his own after all.

"Thank you for meeting with us, Ms. McKenzie," Reynolds said, licking the last of the cake crumbs from his fingers. The constable pulled out a notebook.

Nice of him to make it sound like I had a choice. I went straight to the point. "Do you know who it is?"

"What time did you discover the body?" Reynolds also could come straight to the point.

"I'm not exactly sure. We, my dog and I, left the house around nine this morning. Found the… it… on our way out. I ran straight home and called 911. So it was probably about ten minutes before the 911 call, I'd say."

"Did you touch anything?"

I shivered at the thought. "Are you kidding? I took one look and ran for home."

"Did your dog touch it?" the constable asked. Her high voice made it sound like a question asked during story time at nursery school.

"She might have. She got there several minutes before I arrived. I went to see what was going on because she was barking and wouldn't come when I called. But I didn't see anything in her mouth."

"Did you pick anything up at the scene? Leave anything behind? Drop anything?"

"No. Only my coat as a place marker, but your constables saw that."

"Did you walk up to the body, look around a bit?"

My laughed came out broken and strained. "Dad, do you think I could have another cup of tea, please?" He rose from his chair reluctantly. He'd been hanging on to every word. "Certainly not. I didn't even get to the high ground. Soon as I could make out what Sampson found, I ran. Like any person with half a brain."

The constable wrote furiously. "You'd be surprised," she mumbled under her breath, probably not intending to be overheard.

Dad brought more tea and cake, and the police asked a few more questions. Basic stuff: Did I see anyone in the woods today, did Dad or I hear anything unusual in the last few days?

Finally Reynolds got to his feet and thanked us for our time. The constable put away her notebook.

"I have a question, if I may?" I asked.

He eyed me suspiciously. "Yes?"

"Have you identified the body? Is it Jennifer Taylor?"

"We can't say at this time."

"Can't or won't? Come on, Sergeant. The news will be all over town by breakfast time tomorrow, you know that better than I do."

"Unfortunately, yes. It is Jennifer."

I would have been surprised if it wasn't. "Thank you for telling me. If—when—the news does get around, it won't be from me."

They paused at the door to struggle into their coats.

"One more thing."

"Only one, Ms. McKenzie?"

"Why didn't you find her before now? Your people have been all over the swamp the past few days. How did they manage to miss such a tiny detail as the dead body they were actually out searching for? You even had dogs. We heard them. Drove Sampson here nuts."

"At first glance, it would appear that the body was held down by that log you saw. What with all the rain we've had lately and the last of the snowmelt running off into that swamp, the log rose to the surface. And what was under it, rose with it."

"It seems to me that my dog is doing a good deal of your work for you, Sergeant. Perhaps I should start billing you for her time."

The constable grinned. Reynolds didn't.

"A homicide inspector will be in town tomorrow, Ms. McKenzie. You can be sure that he will want to speak with you. Please don't leave without informing us first."

"Wouldn't dream of it."

"I have a question for you, Ms. McKenzie," the constable said. "How did you get that nasty bruise on your face?"

Instinctively my hand reached up and touched my cheek. "Tripped over the dog and fell into the edge of a door."

"Is that right?" she said.

"Yes."

"If you ever want to talk about it…"

"About tripping over my dog, I don't think so. Goodbye."

I stood at the window watching them go, the would-be police dog by my side.

For dinner I heated a can of soup and threw together cheese sandwiches. Neither of us ate much. From the kitchen window we caught the occasional glimpse of dark shapes moving through the woods. The rain started up again. The police were in for a miserable evening.

After we finished eating, Dad collapsed into his chair and switched on the TV to a black-and-white movie. I have no interest in old movies, but to keep him company I curled up on the couch with the intention of reading the last of the business press newspaper clippings that Jenny had thrown together for me. But the clippings were boring, and the movie soon caught my attention. It was *Casablanca*, which I had certainly caught bits and pieces of but had never seen in its entirety. Dad fell asleep about half way through, but I watched to the end, loving it.

When I get home, I might look up some more old movies. People in those days really could act.

"Wake up, Dad." I shook my father's shoulder. "Time to go to bed."

He stumbled down the hall mumbling goodnights, and I returned to my papers.

Sampson, like Dad, was on the verge of collapse due to the excitement of the day. But that wretched nap had ruined my sleep pattern. I went into the kitchen to make more tea and peered out the back window. It was dark now, the activity in the woods had ceased, but the police would be back tomorrow. I gave a thought to poor Jennifer Taylor and particularly to her parents. I hadn't known her, but I had seen her dead body, wet and muddy and so vulnerable. Those five little white toes. I shook my head in an effort to dispel the image.

I wondered if her father was the Dennis Taylor who had been in my class at school. Nasty boy, tiny eyes, too long limbs, greasy hair, acne-spotted face. I'd dated him a couple of times—yes, I was that desperate. One night when he had been walking me home from a dance at the school, he'd suddenly pulled me into the bushes at the side of the road and knocked me down. He fastened his greasy lips onto my mouth and stuck his tongue down my throat. Then he stuffed his hand up my skirt and sort of moved his fingers around over my panties. It was disgusting. I wanted to pee. Instead I yelled and gave a good solid push to get him off of me. I was no shrinking violet even then: I'd grown up fighting with a much older brother. Dennis rolled to one side and just sat there watching me scramble through the woods back to the road. He tried telling everyone that I had put out on the first date and been really hot for it. Fortunately for me, no one had believed him. He'd tried that story too many times before.

But regardless of how nasty a teenage boy he had been, Dennis Taylor didn't deserve to live to see his daughter murdered.

As I returned to the living room with my tea, a set of head-lights drove by, heading up the hill to Aileen and Jimmy's house. They passed and all was calm and dark once again. For once my work held no interest for me. I hadn't checked my e-mail all day, nor returned Jenny's call. They could do without me for one day. I flicked through the TV magazine. I hadn't watched TV in so long that none of the programs listed meant anything to me. And the paperback that I bought at the Vancouver airport was boring when I was high in the air and fresh for the journey. It would be excruciating with my mind as restless as it was. My thoughts full of dead bodies and feeding insects, I wasn't in the mood to venture back into the cellar to get more of the diaries. I'd made sure to slip the volumes I'd brought upstairs back down as soon as I finished them, worried that Dad or someone else might find them.

The ringing phone pulled me out of my self-pitying funk.

"Rebecca? You have to come. Now. Please."

"Aileen, what's the matter? Are you okay?" A stupid question. The woman was obviously not okay.

"Please." Her voice broke on the word, and she swallowed a sob. "They've taken Jim."

The lights on the road. Jack and Pete. Aileen had a right to be terrified. "I'll be there as fast as I can. I'll bring Sampson. Have you called the police? They won't get far."

"The police took him, Rebecca. They've arrested him for killing Jennifer Taylor."

Chapter 34

The Diary of Janet McKenzie. September 20, 1954

Today I did the most incredible thing. I actually yelled at Mr. M. Even as I was saying the words, and looking right into his hateful old face, I knew that I would run into the sewing room as soon as I could safely get away, and pull out my diary.

He arrived home late from work for some unknown reason. (I am being sarcastic here—he smelt like a brewery.) The dinner stew was painfully thin tonight. Nothing like we had in the war, of course. How Aunt Betty could make an egg stretch! I never thought I would need to know all her tricks once I came to Canada! Bob is out of work again and meat is so expensive. I added lots of potatoes and vegetables but it was hardly enough. The children, particularly Jim, wanted more. So I gave them more. He wasn't here to eat his share. Let the children have it. They need it.

Finally he came stumbling in and shouted for his dinner. Mrs. M. pulled the remains of the stew out of the oven—mostly gravy and potatoes and carrots and turnips—and put plenty of bread on the plate, but he started yelling to beat the band. "A man needs his meat," he shouted at her. And he actually threw the plate full of food onto the floor. Bob and I were just getting into bed, but we could hear the crash from our room. Bob ran into the kitchen and for some crazy reason I followed. Well, there she was, down on her arthritic old knees, cleaning up the mess and him looming over her all red in the face and still yelling curse words and insults. Bob spoke all soft and comforting (like he always does) and offered to make some bacon and eggs for his dad.

After all these years, I finally had enough. I pushed (pushed!) Bob out of the way, and pulled Mrs. M. to her feet.

"Enough food has been wasted in this house tonight," I said. I looked down at Mr. M. "Why don't you just go to bed and sleep it off? You can have eggs for breakfast."

He turned even redder, if that were possible. Then he slapped me across the face. It was a shock that. The pain seemed to radiate right down to my toes. Mrs. M., of course, started to cry and ran out of the room, a tea towel held to her face.

His face twisted with an expression I still can't describe. Angry, yes. But something deeper. Even more frightening than his anger. I stepped back and felt behind me for the cutlery drawer.

Bob stepped forward and touched his father's shoulder. "Time for bed, eh, Dad?" he said. "Little Jimmy's asleep. Don't want to wake him up."

I pulled open the drawer and touched a knife. But, to my surprise, Mr. M. deflated right before my eyes. Instead of slapping his son's hand from his shoulder and slurring something insulting, he simply walked away.

It's late now. Mrs. M. crept out of her room to clean up the kitchen, but Bob and I had already done it. We looked at each other over the broken dish. I swear that my heart leapt and I had a flash of a vision of Bob at that dance so long ago, stepping forward ever so hesitantly, wanting to ask me for a dance, but afraid I would turn my nose up at a man shorter than me. Better I had, I reminded myself, as I scooped up a lone piece of potato and smiled back at my husband.

June 2, 1955

I will call her Rebecca. I loved the book Rebecca. *I read it long into the night in my father's house. I don't remember if it was before the war, or during it. The book itself captivated me so, I was scarcely aware of what was happening in the world around, war or no war. Rebecca, of course, wasn't a very nice person, not someone you would choose to name your child after. But I loved the name, if not the woman. Therefore I will name my daughter Rebecca. Mrs. M. doesn't like it (so… Jewish, she says in her thin voice). Mr. M. doesn't care. It isn't a boy. And Bob wouldn't voice an opinion to save his life.*

So Rebecca it is. She is beautiful. Beyond beautiful. She will be tall, like me. The nurses measured her and weighed her and said that she was 'long'. Tall, like me. But she will be strong, where I am not.

If I were strong I would be long gone from this place. Off to the city to make my fortune. But that's a dream and nothing more. For what could I accomplish in any city with three children in tow? I dream sometimes that it is suddenly discovered that I am a great actress, or an opera singer of incredible power, and my children and I are whisked away to a life of luxury and favor.

But then Rebecca dirties her diaper, or Jim rips the head off Shirley's best doll and I am brought back down to this dismal, hopeless earth.

May 8, 1956

A letter arrived this morning. From Anne Johannsen. A name I scarcely remember. It will be ten years in September since we all came across on the Queen Mary. Anne has this idea of everyone writing down everything that has happened to us since we parted and she will put together a collection to send to us all.

After I read the letter, I left the children with Mrs. M. and went for a long walk. To my surprise, I find that I have quite fallen in love with these woods. There is usually no one about and I can walk and think in peace. It is spring now, so around me everything is growing. The tiniest of buds are spreading on the waking trees; grass and the first few trilliums are poking their heads up from the forest floor. I can hear birds again, and it is wonderful. I hate this horrid place and long constantly for the tidy green fields of Surrey. But when I am in the woods, alone, I know that I am longing for my father's home, and my Aunt Betty's cooking, and the warmth of their fireplace, and their love. All that is gone now. And miles and miles of neat hedgerows, perfectly cultivated fields, and contented cows can't bring it all back.

I imagined, as I walked, what I might say for the Queen Mary War Brides letter. "Things are better here since I held a kitchen knife to my father-in-law's throat and told him to stay away from me. My husband has a job now; fortunately whenever he loses one job he finds another quickly, but he doesn't make much money. I suspect that what little there is goes to help his mother with the housekeeping. He can be sober for weeks at a time, but then he falls off the wagon, and when he's on the bottle he scarcely glances at our children. We still live with his parents, my husband and I and our three children. He has no ambition to leave this dead end of a town and better himself. But he doesn't beat me, and I suppose that's a blessing."

I was composing the never-to-be-written letter in my head when a deer, a beautiful doe, stepped out of the woods directly into my path. She looked at me for a long time, studying me with her wonderful, expressive brown eyes. I looked back, struggling to communicate. But then we heard a truck, grinding its gears as it drove up the hill. She flicked her tiny white tail and with a flash of dotted rump disappeared.

I hate this place with all my might. But I love these woods. Is that possible?

Chapter 35

I flew into my bedroom for my car keys. Sampson yawned and lifted her head off the pillow, jumped off the bed, and stumbled after me.

I scribbled a note for Dad, in case he woke up, and put it on the kitchen table under the pepper shaker, half of a set of particularly unattractive ceramic pigs. They were so out of synch with my mother's taste that they could only have been a gift from a friend, probably made by said friend.

"You stay and look after Dad," I told Sampson. She yawned and didn't look particularly disappointed at the command.

This wasn't the first time the police had come in the night for my brother.

I ran out the door.

Aileen had left the house and walked down the road to meet me. She opened the door and clambered in before the SUV came to a full stop. She still wore her pajamas, cheerful, cuddly polar bear cubs skating and tobogganing and skiing across the white flannel. A colorful shawl had been tossed over her shoulders, and her long hair tumbled wildly around her head, half in and half out of its bun. Her eyes looked like those of a horse I'd seen once—rearing back in terror as a car rounded a corner in front of it. The driver saw the horse in time and pulled out of the way. I wasn't so sure that disaster could be avoided this time.

I made a three-point turn and headed back down the road.

"Did they actually arrest him? Formally, I mean, with a legal warning and such?"

"No. They said they wanted him to come in and answer some questions. They've talked to him before, but this is the first time they've taken him to the station. That's not good."

I agreed. But what the heck did I know? My sole experience with criminal law could be found between the pages of a Peter Robinson mystery.

The sun had long ago taken its nightly bath in the smooth orange waters of the lake, and the stars hung like the most precious of diamonds over the black water. There was no moon.

There was also no traffic on the highway, and I pushed the car as fast as it could go. Dark, foreboding pine trees lined the roadway in a solemn, macabre honor guard.

"Thank you for coming, Rebecca," Aileen said, the words muffled, her face turned to her window, to the forest lying beyond the reach of our lights. "Jim told me not to drive because I'm too upset. He told me to call you, said you'd help. He said I could count on it."

"He did?" Imagine that.

"Your brother loves you very much indeed. I don't know exactly what happened between you when you were kids, but I have a pretty good idea. He wants to make amends, if you'll let him."

"Let's leave the past for another time."

"You're right, there are far more immediate matters to worry about. But you and he have to deal with your history someday."

It seems to me that I have been dealing with my past with perfect success all these years—mainly by ignoring it. "Tell me what they have on him. Why did the cops take him in? They questioned me in my living room. It was all terribly civilized. Over tea and fruitcake, of all things. Perfectly Agatha Christie."

A flash of light as we drove through Hope River, marking a tiny outpost of human habitation in the vastness of the wild. A Monday night in May, not much happening in town. Lights and canned music spilled from the bar, but there were only a handful of cars parked outside. We drove past the restaurant.

Maggie Kzenic stood on the steps putting on her hat and mittens as inside someone extinguished the last light. She looked up, without much interest, to watch us go by.

"They said they found Jennifer's body in the swamp."

"Unfortunately I found her. Or rather Sampson."

"You found her?"

"Yes. Buried in the muck."

"How awful for you. Are you all right?"

"Thanks for asking, but we aren't here to worry about me, are we?"

"No. That was the psychologist in me, always struggling to rise to the surface. The police found something on her. A necklace. Like one Jim has."

"Is there something special about this necklace, Aileen?"

"Yes." She choked on the word. We had passed Hope River; the OPP detachment wasn't in town, but a good bit further north, the other side of North Ridge. There were no other cars on the road. My headlights carved a path out of the darkness, illuminating the thin white line leading to the vast, empty North. Beyond the confines of this rented monstrosity of a vehicle lay nothing but the gloom of the primitive forest. By the lakes there would be a few summer cottages, owned by people who didn't mind the distance from Toronto, and some homes like ours, built in the days when lakefront property didn't cost too much more than anything else. But inland there wasn't much at all: a scattering of farmhouses on the rare bits of land suitable for agriculture, the homes of people who liked their privacy.

"What's special about it?"

"It's one of a kind. I can testify to that. Because I made it myself, in honor of our first anniversary. Two broken hearts linked by a thin chain. At the time I thought I was being so clever."

"Can't you tell them it isn't Jimmy's?"

"The cops came directly out and asked him if he had one like it. They described it, all the details perfectly. Obviously they knew it was his, lots of people have seen him wearing it. So, yes, he said he owned a necklace like that, no point in denying it.

And when they asked him to show it to them, he had to confess that it had been lost."

"Did you know he'd lost it?"

She hesitated before answering. "No."

"Did they tell you where they found this necklace?"

"No, but we were certainly given to understand that it had something to do with the finding of Jennifer's body."

A flash of light shattered the black night as we rounded a corner. The OPP station. Aileen was out of the car and running for the door the moment the car edged into the driveway, before I had even started to look for a parking spot.

By the time I parked and made it into the building, she was standing in front of the desk, tapping her toes, bare and wrapped in open sandals.

"He said I have to wait here."

"Did you talk to someone already?"

"They were waiting for me. He told me to wait."

"So we'll wait." I took her arm and guided her to a row of institutional chairs lining one wall.

And there we waited, as instructed.

Aileen pulled at the loose threads on her shawl as if she could unravel it all and knit herself a perfect world in which murder never reared its ugly head and love lasted forever and the police sat around all day playing cards and eating doughnuts because they had nothing else to do.

I touched the back of her constantly moving hand, and she gripped me with a ferocity of which I wouldn't have believed her capable.

"Let's go, babe."

We looked up and Aileen released my hand. She rose to her feet in her characteristic gentle, flowing movement and studied her husband's face. "Are you okay?"

"Perfectly. Let's go home."

I'd fallen asleep in the rock-hard chair, clutching my sister-in-law's hand in mine. For the second time that day my head felt as thick as the mud in the swamp. Thicker.

Sergeant Reynolds stood in the background watching the touching little family tableau. No emotion cracked the lines on his face. "The inspector will be here tomorrow. He'll want a few words with you, McKenzie."

"I heard you the first time."

"Consider it a friendly reminder. Don't leave town."

"I have no reason to." Jim shifted his grip to his wife's waist. She melted into his arms and he half carried her out the door.

"Ta ta for now, Sergeant Reynolds," I said in a failed attempt at frivolity.

"Always a pleasure, Ms. McKenzie, always a pleasure." He sounded as sincere as I did.

We drove home in silence. Jimmy and Aileen sat close together in the back, not saying a word. We passed through Hope River, the town dark and silent except for the bright lights spilling from the bar. There were a handful more trucks and cars in the parking lot than when we had last passed. Even on a Monday night in May in northern Ontario, there are bound to be some people out in search of a good time.

We were minutes the other side of town when a deer leapt across the road in front of the car. A gleam of immense brown eyes reflecting the harsh light of headlight beams, a clean movement as liquid as a fish floating under the surface of a lake tinged red by a new dawn, a flash of brown and white rump, and she was gone.

"Come in, please, Rebecca," Jimmy said as I pulled up to their house. "We won't be going to sleep anytime soon."

He led the way through to the living room and immediately set about preparing a fire in the enormous stone fireplace. I hadn't been in this room since my childhood, and if I'd stopped to think about it I probably would have refused to step foot over the threshold. And that would have been a mistake. Even before the fire flared to life, the room was seductive and inviting. Tapestries and woolen wall hangings in autumn shades of rust, gold, and all the colors of green imaginable warmed what once had been cold, beige walls. The old shag carpet was gone, replaced by good hardwood flooring and a scattering of colorful area rugs.

Aileen moved around the room, lighting candles in wall sconces and on the mantle, which was of stone so carefully laid that it might have risen directly from the solid rocks of the Canadian Shield lying beneath the foundations of the house. She selected a CD from a full rack and popped it into the player. Muddy Waters. I love the blues.

I sank into a leather chair the color of caramel and the consistency of butter; Aileen took a wooden rocking chair opposite. Once the fire was blazing, Jimmy slipped out of the room and returned with a bottle of excellent brandy and three crystal balloon glasses. He poured with a generous hand and handed the drinks around before collapsing on the floor to sit at Aileen's feet. She stroked his hair.

"This is wonderful. All of it. What you've done with this room. I remember it as being the most perfectly awful place. And it was always so cold. The grandparents never wasted any money on heat."

"See that piece over there?" Jimmy pointed to a small china figurine of a shepherdess guarding one sheep. The top of her staff had broken off, and a poorly glued crack ran up the other arm. "Recognize it?"

"No."

"One of Grandma's pieces. Most of it was hideous stuff, but we saved a few things to remember her by. I think of her as that shepherdess. Trying to do some good for her sheep, but her crook is broken and her spirit as badly patched together as that statue."

I swallowed my brandy.

"I think of her a lot these days," he said. "She was a good woman, Grandma. She wanted to do good, but she was, sadly, simply too timid."

I studied the frail shepherdess with the concentration I normally give to a company prospectus or my own investment portfolio. That was a startling statement, coming from Jimmy.

To me, Grandma had been just plain weak. As weak as a single drop of water taken from the lake outside. Nothing else. A woman I'd wanted to get as far away from as I could. I hadn't even cared enough to come home for her funeral.

Jimmy smiled at his wife over the rim of his brandy glass. The smile was strained. He tried hard to make the effort: to smooth over her worries. She rubbed one finger across his hand, lightly. Aileen asked him if he was warm enough, or if she could bring him a sweater. He replied that he was fine.

Of all the people who made up my family, I was the last living soul who knew the story of Jimmy's parentage. Not for the first time, I wondered if I should tell him what I had discovered in the diaries. My answer always came back the same: Leave well enough alone. But if I was comfortable with the answer, why did I keep asking the question? Should I burn the diaries before I left? Take my mother's secret to my own grave? The ultimate question again: Why had she left them to be found?

"Rebecca?"

I looked up.

"How's the brandy?"

"Wonderful, thank you. Sorry, I was thinking about what a wonderful job you've done with this room. You've managed to chase all my ghosts away."

Aileen smiled at me, a tiny smile, just the edges of her mouth curling up. Her face was brittle with fear, but she enjoyed the compliment.

I sipped again. "This is good stuff."

"Aileen has taught me to appreciate some of the finer things in life," Jimmy said.

She burst into tears like a dam breaking open under an earthquake. "Please, please," she sobbed, "we have to talk about it."

Jimmy looked stricken. He lifted himself to his knees and gathered his sobbing wife into his arms. "I'm so sorry, dear heart. That's the McKenzie way of dealing with a problem."

"Ignore it and it'll go away," I said.

"But not this time, unfortunately. You both deserve to know what happened tonight." He released Aileen and resumed his place at her feet. He looked deep into his brandy glass and swirled the golden liquid around and around. "They found Jennifer Taylor's body in the swamp behind Dad's place earlier today. That bit of news is no surprise to you, Rebecca. I guessed that it was your dog that came across her. When they inventoried the items on the body they found a necklace, identified instantly by Constable Rosemary Rigoloni as similar to one owned by me."

Aileen sobbed, quietly but steadily. Jimmy patted her knee. "Rosemary is a friend of Aileen's," he explained. "She's been here several times as part of Aileen's book club. I wear the necklace my dearest wife gave me every day, proudly. In the summer it's more visible under T-shirts. If not Rosemary, anyone else in town could have told them that it belonged to me."

"The curse of a small town. No wonder I hate this place."

Jimmy grinned, his familiar disarming grin. "Today I agree with you, little sister. But if it wasn't for this town, I sometimes wonder if I would be doing real hard time."

Aileen sobbed again. Jimmy slipped out of the room and returned with a box of tissues.

I indicated that perhaps it was time for me to go. He signaled to me to stay. "Aileen has to hear this, Rebecca. And I'd like you to hear it as well. More cognac?"

I held out my glass. In the fireplace a log broke in half and collapsed in a shower of yellow sparks.

"Do you know how Jennifer came to be in possession of this necklace?" I asked.

"Yes, I do. Jennifer was a great girl. And I mean that. She wanted to be a carpenter, she loved to work with wood, really loved it. Her hands were born to it. Her brothers help me out for the money, but they have no heart for the work. Jennifer does… did. Her father was staunchly against it. I can't stand the man, a supercilious asshole of the first degree. You didn't know I can say words like supercilious, did you, Becky?"

"I've never underestimated you, Jimmy."

"Perhaps you should have. Anyway, Mr. Taylor didn't approve of her working for me, but he permitted it as long as there was money to be made. There aren't a lot of jobs for a school kid around here that last any longer than July and August. But he wouldn't hear of her taking up carpentry as a career. Jennifer told me many times that he thinks it not a suitable occupation for a woman. Fellow is living in the nineteenth century."

"Sounds like the Dennis Taylor I went to school with, all right."

"Anyway she was a great assistant. Far better than those lazy brothers of hers. I would have sacked the both of them in a flash, if anyone any better came to hand. She showed up on time, early more often than not, and worked like her heart and soul were in it. Course she is… was… still going to school, so she only helped out on holidays and on the weekends when I was busy." His voice changed, and he turned his head to stare into the fire. "Dead. Do you know, I haven't really even thought of her that way. I knew she hadn't run away. As tough as her old man is on her, she isn't the type to up and run. When Reynolds told me they'd found the body, it didn't come as much of a surprise. But dead. She was so young, she had real promise." He got up to toss more pieces of kindling onto the fire. The flames reared up hungrily. We all watched the wood be consumed. Muddy Waters sang about love.

"But…"

"No flies on you, are there baby sister? But she was interested in more than just the carpentry. Christ. Only because I'm probably the only man she'd ever met who told her to follow her heart and her talent. She and her brothers worked for me last summer. Remember, babe, we had that big job on that place with the gazebo and the guest house?"

Aileen nodded.

"We were finishing it up, putting the last touches on the gazebo. You should see it; it's absolutely fantastic. The lady of the house saw one in a garden in England and had to have one just like it. One day, the last week of work, Ryan is off sick and

Kyle has a dentist appointment. Me and Jennifer are having a perfectly great day. It was real hot, sweltering, so when we took our lunch break I stripped off my shirt and dove into the lake. And Jennifer did the same. I tried not to notice, really I did, babe. But she swam up to me and started rubbing herself against me and saying things I didn't want to hear."

Aileen blew her nose.

"I told her that lunch was over and it was time to get dressed and back to work. She was embarrassed, but she put her shirt and bra back on, and we finished the gazebo. Her brothers were back the next day; we moved on to the guest house and I thought it all ended then."

"But it didn't?"

"I got a few odd jobs in the fall, and the twins and Jennifer helped out on weekends. She didn't say anything about what happened and everything between us settled back to normal. Over the winter I do work indoors, making furniture and the like. No need for help, so I hardly saw the kids. Last month I started back to work up at Lake Ramsey, and I called them. Their dad had been sick over the winter, so Ryan was working at Fawcett's Hardware. But Kyle and Jennifer were available."

He stopped talking and poured out another round of drinks. Good thing I only had a few hundred yards to drive home. The brandy was excellent. Ray loved good brandy and he taught me to appreciate it as well. It was one of his few extravagances. Would my husband and my brother have gotten along? Would they have found something in common?

"First day of work, Kyle hit his thumb with a hammer. I don't like the kid, take your eye off him for a second and he's slacking off, but I had to admit that his thumb was a real mess. His mom came to collect him. They were scarcely out of sight before Jennifer turned it all on. Told me that she missed me all winter and she was so glad to be working close to me again. I told her that I'm a married man and I don't believe in fooling around on the job. If she wanted to learn to be a carpenter she would have to act a pro and not mess up the best chance she was going to get. She said she understood."

"But she didn't?" Aileen croaked. She had shrunk so far into herself that she was in danger of disappearing altogether if something didn't pull her out of it. I didn't know what could.

"I wear that necklace every day. I want to be buried in it, you know that Aileen. Don't you?"

She didn't respond.

"But I have to take it off at a work site. No jewelry on the job. That's asking for trouble. So every day, soon as we arrive, I put my wedding ring and the necklace into my lunch box. That day Jennifer's mom came for her early. They didn't approve of their precious daughter alone with the likes of me all day. Christ if only they knew."

"Parents worry," said I who had no experience whatsoever. My mother worried. But never of anything that lay outside of our own family.

"Yeah. With cause, eh? I don't like them, the Taylors, they're both a piece of work. They both remind me of Grandpa. All piss and wind and not an ounce of human kindness in their shriveled up bodies."

I swallowed and focused on the flames dancing in the grate. "I always thought you got on great with Grandpa."

He looked at me with those lovely eyes the color of the lake on a summer's morning. At the present storm clouds were moving in. "I never believed in Santa Claus or the Easter Bunny, you know. Grandpa told me straight out that stuff was for girls and babies. And he told me that I wasn't a baby and I was certainly not a girl. But I was a kid, little sister. I needed to believe in something."

"I don't give a goddamn right now about Santa Claus," Aileen whispered, her voice struggling to regain its normal pitch. "Tell us what happened. Please."

"The necklace was gone from my lunch box when I finished up for the day and got ready to go home. My ring was there, in the pouch where I always left it. But the necklace was gone.

"I didn't ask her the next day, I didn't know what to say. I couldn't accuse her of being a thief. Particularly as Kyle was back. I didn't want to say anything in front of her brother. I should have said something, Aileen, I should have told you I'd lost it. But I suppose I hoped that she would have a change of heart and give it back to me and we would laugh about it. Because I still like her. She is…" His voice broke on a choked sob. "…was a nice girl, and she would have made a great carpenter."

Aileen reached down from her rocking chair and held him close.

I looked at my empty glass, the firelight shining through it, catching the few remaining drops of brandy in a shimmer of spun gold.

"You need a lawyer, Jimmy. Do you have one?"

"There's Kowalski, who I've used before. Don't know if he's still in North Bay, though. Last I heard he was up on some charges. Might even be disbarred."

Lovely. "My company has a whole stable of lawyers in Toronto. First thing tomorrow morning, I'll call someone."

"I can't afford…"

"It's on me. Let's say it's thirty years of Christmas and birthday presents all rolled into one."

A touch of color crept back into Aileen's face. "That's not fair. Then we'll owe you thirty years' worth."

"A tapestry similar to that one." I pointed to a huge delight, a northern forest scene, each stitch picked out in shades of gold and crimson with a touch of icy blue. "It would look wonderful in my cottage in B.C. And a promise that you'll both deliver it, of course. I can't be bothered to wrap it up myself."

"Done," Jimmy said.

"Agreed," Aileen said.

I wouldn't know a criminal lawyer if one leapt out of the woodwork and waved his checkbook at me. But my company keeps plenty of corporate lawyers on hand. They would be in contact with colleagues who did criminal work. Wouldn't they?

"They've taken the truck," Jimmy said. "I gave them the keys so they could check it out."

"Check it out?" Aileen said. "What for?"

"Just routine," my brother said. "I told them that Jennifer's been in the truck plenty of times; a few days before she disappeared she used it to pick up a load of lumber. They'll return it in a couple of days. And as this is now officially a murder investigation, a homicide inspector will be arriving from the big city tomorrow. I'm sure I'll be hearing from him."

"Let him know that you won't speak to him without your lawyer present," I said. "Tell them he has to travel up from Toronto, so it may be a while."

Jimmy and Aileen nodded. From different sides of the fence, they both had plenty of experience with the criminal justice system.

I drained my glass, resisted the urge to throw it into the fireplace, and staggered out to my car. The night air had a definite chill. A full moon hung low over the lake, a perfect white ball against the black sky. It shone so brightly that only the brightest stars could be seen.

Aileen hugged me closely, her fragile bones quivering under her shawl. Jimmy slipped his arm around her waist, and they waved in unison as I pulled away.

I stood at the back door waiting for Sampson to sniff out the residue of every creature that had ventured onto our property in the hours since she'd last made her rounds. Finally satisfied, she settled down to do her business.

No point in trying to phone anyone at this time of night. I set the alarm to wake me at first light, so I could get on to the business of finding a lawyer.

Chapter 36

The Diary of Janet McKenzie. March 2, 1958

Of all the things. The Reverend and Mrs. Burwell drove over today and she got out of the car grinning from ear to ear and acting like she had some great secret. And then Mr. Burwell pulled her sewing machine out of the boot and she said it was for me.

I could have fainted dead away. I insisted that I couldn't accept it. And they insisted that I must. So eventually I relented and Mr. Burwell carried it through to my sewing room—which is unfortunately now the kitchen table, since Rebecca grew out of her cot and moved into the children's room and Jim needed to have a room of his own. But someday I'll have a real sewing room again.

The men were at work. Mrs. M. was napping; Shirley and Jim were at school, and Rebecca (for once) was playing quietly with her doll. Mr. Burwell admired the almost finished quilt spread out on the table and then they both stood there, looking at me. I offered tea, and they accepted. I cleared the sewing, brought out the best pot and cups (meaning the ones not chipped) and some biscuits I baked the day before. Mr. Burwell asked me if I was managing. I told him that we are doing fine, thank you. What else could I say? Could I tell him that my father-in-law is a monster and that I fear that he's trying to turn my ten-year-old son into the image of him? That my husband goes on drinking binges and at the best of times is as weak as water and lets his father yell profanities and insults at his wife and grandchildren and daughter-in-law all the day long, and that he sometimes even takes blows from that father? That I fear that, stuck in this town, in this family, my thirteen-year-old daughter (already failing school) will decide there is nothing more to life than making me a grandmother before she finishes high school?

I said we're fine, thank you very much. Now that Bob has that job at the new butcher in North Ridge.

He said, "Good, good" and concentrated on selecting another biscuit. She was about to say something. I could see it in her face. But right then Rebecca pulled out the kitchen drawer and all the knives and forks clattered to the cracked old linoleum floor.

Chapter 37

I dug through the company directory on my computer, searching for a lawyer with whom I'd done business recently. Found him! I dialed the Toronto number. A flat, emotionless voice asked me to leave a message and I did so: my name, my position, my reason for calling, the number of my cell phone as well as the house.

I then went in search of breakfast. Once again, yogurt and granola didn't quite seem to be up to the task. A package of fat sausages smiled up at me seductively. Giving in without any trace of a fight, I pulled out the frying pan and threw them in. Eggs soon followed.

I carried my plate into the living room and hooked up my computer to read the morning papers, although my mind was hardly on it. Government budget crisis, war in some dry forgotten country, bombings in the Middle East. It never changes. Murder in small-town Ontario. Jennifer made the Toronto papers. It will be a sad day when murder is so commonplace in this part of the world as not to be reported. I soaked up the last of runny egg yolk with a slice of sausage and held it up to my mouth. If Ray could see me eating like this, he would have a fit. Probably snatch the plate right out of my hand. God, I miss him. Even in this situation, Ray would know exactly what to do. He would have Jimmy's name cleared, his necklace returned, and the murderer behind bars before dinnertime. I tossed the egg-coated sausage to the dog and buried my head in my hands. Sampson nuzzled me lovingly, after scarfing down the treat.

Then her attention shifted and she barked once and ran to the door. A car pulled up outside.

Perfect. Visitors.

Shirley and Jackie, both of them dressed for work. My sister marched through the door without a word. Jackie mumbled "Hello" with an embarrassed grin.

"I'm not even out of bed before the phone is ringing off the hook. It seems that the police arrested our dear brother last night for killing Jennifer Taylor. When were you planning on informing me, and where is Dad?"

Another reminder, not that I needed one, of why I hated this town. "I wasn't planning on informing you at all, Shirley, considering that Jimmy wasn't arrested for anything and certainly not for murder. And I suppose that Dad is still sleeping, unless you've woken him up, which is entirely possible."

"I'm awake, girls." Dad walked into the living room, still in his pajamas. They were old and worn to tatters, exactly like him. His steps were slow and heavy. "Is someone going to tell me what's going on here?"

"Mom phoned me all in an uproar," Jackie explained. "So I decided that she shouldn't be driving. Dave hadn't left for work yet, so I left him to take Jason to school and went over."

"Why don't I put on a fresh pot of coffee?" I offered, as if I were accustomed to entertaining visitors at this time of the morning.

"That would be lovely," Jackie said, brimming with false enthusiasm.

"Who's been arrested?" Dad asked.

"Your son," Shirley said.

"No one," I said.

"Little Jim?" Dad's face collapsed and for a moment I thought his body might follow, but Jackie took his arm and steered him to the kitchen. "Coffee first," she said.

"Jimmy was not arrested," I repeated, following them. "The police asked him some questions yesterday. That's not so unusual.

She worked for him; they came into contact regularly, so the cops had some questions. That's all."

"Well, I hear that they found evidence, real evidence, that he killed her, right on her body."

"Please, Mom," Jackie hissed, settling her grandfather into a kitchen chair.

"You hear rumor and innuendo, Shirley," I said. "Don't blow it all out of proportion, please."

"I wouldn't be surprised, not at all surprised."

"Mom!" Jackie gasped in horror. Fortunately Dad didn't appear to hear. I put the coffee on, for something to do, not because I wanted to encourage our visitors to stay.

"What happened, Aunt Rebecca?" Jackie asked. "They're saying that you found the body?"

"That, at least, is true. Or rather Sampson found it." In the living room my cell phone shrilled. I dove for it.

"Ms. McKenzie, this is Brian Blanchard. Your message said that you're looking for a criminal lawyer?"

"Thank you for returning my call, Mr. Blanchard." I took the phone into my bedroom and firmly shut the door. "I know you specialize in corporate law, but I'm hoping you could recommend a good criminal lawyer for a friend of mine. It's a murder case. No charges have been laid as of yet, but we're expecting that they may be."

"Good idea to be ready. My wife has been friends since law school with Laura Rabinovich. Laura came over for dinner a while ago. She's top in the field these days. Here's the number. Mention my wife's name, it's Darlene Smith."

We chatted for a few minutes about mutual acquaintances and work he did for my company, while I chafed at the bit to get the conversation over and done with.

"Thanks for the name, Brian. I owe you one. Next time I'm in the Big Smoke I'll take you out for lunch."

"Something to look forward to," he said. "Good luck with your friend."

I broke the connection and dialed Laura Rabinovich's office. Her secretary told me that she was scheduled to be in court all morning. Once again, I left my numbers and my reason for calling. As well as Brian and Darlene's names. I tucked the phone into the pocket of my sweat pants and reluctantly dragged myself back to the kitchen and our cozy family gathering.

"Well," Shirley said, "I hope that was an important call. We're only discussing your brother's life here."

I picked up the conversation as if there had been no interruption. "Shirley, you're spreading idle gossip and speculation like manure."

"Now, girls," Dad said. "Don't argue." Like we were kids again and Shirley was mad at me because I used her makeup to get my dolls ready for a big party they were having. (I'd thought that the dolls looked better in Shirley's makeup than she did.)

Jackie stood at the stove, frying sausages and eggs for Dad's breakfast.

I sat down. "The police took Jimmy in to ask him some questions last night. He worked with her a lot, some of their stuff got mixed up, and they wanted to sort it all out. That's it."

"Are you sure?" Shirley asked, her voice actually sounding a touch hopeful.

"I went to the police station with Aileen. I'm sure."

"Aileen," Jackie said. "Poor Aileen, she must be so upset. Do you think I should go and see how she's doing, Aunt Rebecca?"

"I'll come with you," Shirley said.

That idea needed to be nipped in the bud. "They had a late night, she's probably still in bed. Shouldn't you be at work?"

Shirley looked at her watch. "Family emergency, they'll understand." But she drained her cup and stood up. "Jackie?"

"Ready, Mom. Are you okay, grandpa?"

Dad smiled at her. "Of course I am. You run along now and get your mother to work. Your grandma will finish cooking the breakfast. She's probably down at the road fetching the newspaper. She'll be back in a minute."

My sister and I looked at each other, all animosity forgotten.

"I'll look after the breakfast," I said.

"If you need me to stay…" Shirley said.

Dad waved his hand. "Get yourself off to work, girl. They won't pay you for being late. Now where is that paper? Didn't Janet bring it up?"

"Let's go, Mom. I'm late for work, too." Jackie shooed her mother out of the kitchen. I followed.

"That's only the second time he's said that Mom is around. The rest of the time he seems to know she's gone."

"It's to be expected, I suppose," Shirley said. "For fifty years every time he turned around she was standing right behind him. Hard to get used to the fact that she's not there, I suppose."

"And never will be again," Jackie said.

Shirley and I looked at each other. She held out her arms stiffly as if they weren't quite a part of her body. I stepped forward to return the embrace. Deep in my pants' pocket my cell phone rang. I grabbed for it.

Shirley sniffed. "Time to go, Jackie."

The phone caught in the baggy fabric of my pants. I disentangled it, fumbled for the right button, shouted "Hello" into the phone and looked up to catch Shirley's eye. Too late. She was marching down the path, her shoulders set, her gait stiff with offended pride.

"Ms. McKenzie? Are you there?" The phone shouted, distant and tinny.

"Sorry. I'm here."

"This is Laura Rabinovich returning your call."

"Sorry, Ms. Rabinovich. I dropped the phone."

The voice was deep and authoritative. It chuckled. "Occupational hazard, I've found. But no danger, unless you drop the dratted thing onto your foot. I'm back from court early. I understand you have a potential murder case on your hands?"

"That's right. I'm in Hope River, that's near North Ridge, and I'm worried that a friend of mine is about to be charged, and he needs a good lawyer. Is that you?"

"I'm afraid not, Ms. McKenzie. My calendar is booked solid."

"Oh." I sighed my disappointment into the receiver.

"But I do have a contact for you. Man by the name of Alex Singh. He was a top-flight criminal lawyer in Toronto until about two years ago, when he decided to move to North Bay. Supposedly for the fishing, can you imagine?"

The phone vibrated with the shudder of well-draped shoulders considering the very idea.

"Don't get me wrong, Alex is still practicing. He merely relocated. You might want someone closer anyway. Let me give you the number."

More thanks, sincerely felt, and another offer of a future lunch.

Dad stood in the kitchen door, watching me, his forehead furrowed in an attempt to follow the drift of the conversation. I excused myself and went to my room.

Alex Singh was actually in when I called, and his secretary put me through. An expensive leather chair squeaked as he listened to the details. Singh didn't have many questions, but he promised to contact Jimmy straight away.

"It is my understanding that if I take the case, you will be settling the account, Ms. McKenzie. Is that correct?"

"Yes."

"Your brother will be my client. You understand that my responsibility is therefore to him rather than to yourself?"

"Perfectly. I plan to be going home to Vancouver on Saturday. Send me the bills."

Lawyer found, my job done, I resisted the temptation to hustle up the hill to hear Jimmy's end of the conversation.

"Any plans for today, Dad?" I asked, returning to the kitchen.

"Thought I'd spend some time in the shed." He glanced outside. The landscape was gray, nothing but gray. Land, forest, and sky, all as gray as a battleship on the North Atlantic in midwinter. "Get caught up on a bit of work. Some rocking horses to finish. Kids love those rocking horses."

"Good idea."

"Not a day to go into town. Too wet."

"Right."

"The boys at the Legion will be full of gossip today. Worse than a pack of old women at a church picnic, that lot are."

"Right."

The kitchen phone rang. A double ring, thank goodness, meaning long distance. No one local had called us yet, bursting to catch up on the news of yesterday's events. That was a good sign. Some people still had some respect for my father's dignity. I imagined the phone lines of Hope River and environs bursting into flames through overuse.

"Rebecca, is that you? At last. I have been calling and calling and you don't call back. Is everything all right over there?"

Jenny. How wonderful. A link to my real world.

"I'm sorry for not calling back. My dad did give me your messages. I'm fine, but things aren't good with my family right now, so I'm a bit distracted."

"Oh," she cooed, "your poor father. When my grandpa died, my grandma wanted to die right along with him. But next month she took a cruise around the Caribbean and do you know, she met a man. And they were married a month after that."

I laughed. "I'll suggest that to my dad. What have you got for me, Jenny?"

Dad poured the last of the coffee into a thermos and set off out the back door, heading for his shed. Sampson went with him.

Jenny talked and I made notes. Nothing momentous, nothing requiring my immediate attention. She was merely keeping me up to date.

"Andrew wants a meeting when he gets back on Friday," she said. "Can he conference-call you?"

I asked the time and marked it onto my computer's calendar. "I'll get that on my cell phone. My family is in and out of the house all day; you never know when someone is on the phone. I'll have it on all the time, and if by chance the battery's run out you can call the house next.

"I'll be back on Monday, Jen. Hold the fort until then, can you?"

"It'll be hard, but I'll try."

"Thanks."

I attached the computer to the phone line one more time.

An old pickup truck drove up the laneway, moving much too fast, tossing mud from beneath its well-traveled wheels. It could only be heading for Jimmy and Aileen's place and, now that the Hope River grapevine was in control of the story, it was unlikely anyone was making a social call.

I ran out the door, not even bothering to disconnect the computer. Rain continued to fall, leaving the morning air fresh and clean, the moisture as light on my face as any expensive moisturizer. There was no need for a coat, but as I ran, I realized that I should have stopped long enough to put boots on in place of my slippers.

When I saw the small group gathered on Jimmy's deck, I realized that I also should have brought Sampson. It was Dennis Taylor, Jennifer's dad. His twin sons stood on either side of him. They all bristled with hostility—fists clenched, feet apart, chests thrust forward.

Jimmy stood in the front door, waving his hands and talking. Aileen's face peered over his shoulder, white and pinched tight with fear.

Jimmy continued to talk as I ran up. His pose was relaxed, comfortable, but he balanced on the balls of his feet, ready for anything. "I can assure you, Mr. Taylor, Ryan, Kyle, I had nothing to do with Jennifer's murder. I am as upset as anyone in this town about what happened to her, she was a wonderful girl."

"You liar, the cops know it's you what did it, why else would they have arrested you?"

"That's right," the larger of the twins said, taking a half step forward. He was taller than Jimmy, heavier and much, much younger. His hands were balled into fists and his shoulders stiff with tension. He carried far too much weight around his middle and under his chin for a boy his age. "You can't get away with this, you bastard, the cops might be afraid of you, but we aren't."

Aileen plucked at Jimmy's sleeve. "Come inside, hon. Please. There's no talking to them." She raised her voice. "I'm sorry for your loss, Mr. Taylor, but it has nothing to do with my husband. Please go home. Your poor wife must need you there."

"Don't you mention my sainted wife, you filthy cunt."

Aileen gasped and Jimmy stepped forward, his calm demeanor gone in a flash. "If you want to make something out of this, Taylor, it's between you and me. Leave the women and children out of it."

I walked up the steps. "Now what seems to be the problem here?" I stepped around the smaller boy and reached for his father's hand. "Dennis, so nice to see you after all this time. Please accept my condolences on your loss. And extend my best wishes to your wife."

"Who the fuck are you?" As an adult Dennis Taylor was no more attractive than he had been as a boy. He was a small man, thin and wiry with a few greasy hairs plastered across his bowling ball of a head. He peered at the world through Coke-bottle-bottom glasses, which magnified eyes so bloodshot they looked as if a demented child had gone wild with a red marker. Not even noon and the man's breath reeked of beer.

"This has gone far enough, Dennis. If the police have reason to charge my brother with the death of your daughter, they will do so. Please, go home now and comfort your wife."

"That you, Becky?" He looked me up and down. "You look real good."

"She's right, Dad." The smaller twin took his father's arm. The larger boy, Kyle, was already going to seed, the result of too much fast food and beer, but the younger was trim and fit. Strange to see such different expressions on two otherwise indistinguishable faces. The fat boy was angry, hostile, looking for a fight, his prey in his sights. The lean twin tried to calm his father down, to defuse the situation. Neither of the boys appeared to have been drinking. That was a bonus.

"Fuck off, Ryan," the fat twin said. "Me and Dad have things to settle here."

I looked at Kyle. "You and your father have been asked to leave."

"Come on, Dad." Ryan tugged at his father's sleeve.

The man struggled with his emotions for a moment, he opened his mouth to say something to me, but Ryan pulled at his arm once more. Dennis Taylor deflated and took a step backward.

"Don't think you can get away with this, McKenzie," Kyle said. "If the cops don't do nothing, my family will."

Aileen sobbed with relief.

"Come on Kyle, we're leaving," Ryan said.

Kyle spat at Jimmy's feet but followed his family. Jimmy didn't flinch.

They were halfway down the steps when a rusty old hulk of a pickup truck roared up the hill and pulled to a stop.

Jack Jackson and Pete Hartman climbed out. Two other men leapt out of the back. Jack carried a baseball bat.

The Taylors turned back to face us.

Chapter 38

"Get in the house, Rebecca," Jimmy said, his voice sounding as calm as if we were making arrangements for a stroll in the woods after supper. "Take Aileen with you, lock the door, and call the police."

"Like hell. You two get into the house; I'm going for my car. Be waiting for me at the back door."

"No, Becky. They won't let you get away."

"I can outrun that rabble of walking beer barrels." Of that, I had no doubt. Except for Pete—lean and angry, he could give me trouble—this attempt at a mob didn't look as if they had traveled on foot for any distance further than from a bar stool to the men's room in more than a few years.

The Taylors' departure had ceased abruptly although Ryan, the thin one, continued, with no success, to try to drag his father and brother away. They stood on the bottom step, watching the men approach, walking slowly. Jack swung his bat.

"This isn't a good idea, Dad," Ryan said.

"Go in the house and call 911, Aileen."

"Jim, please."

"Now, Aileen." My brother's eyes were sharp and focused, his body taut, ready for whatever was about to happen. That, more than anything, was what terrified me. Jimmy knew these men weren't here for polite conversation. He was wearing a thick down vest and casually slipped his hand inside. Aileen went into the house.

"Come on Jimmy, don't be a fool," I said. "There's too many of them."

"Go with Aileen, Becky."

"I'll go inside if you do, Jimmy." And then I could head out the back door, through the woods to my father's house and the SUV.

We all heard them long before we saw them, police cruisers, sirens blaring, coming down our road—the proverbial cavalry.

The men walking toward us looked at Pete, doubt and confusion running across their dull faces. Pete raised his hand in the universal stop gesture. Jack tossed his bat under a sleeping rose bush. Jimmy's hand came out of his vest, empty

There were two cars. Two officers stepped out of each, leaving the red lights on the top of the patrol cars swirling round and round in demonic circles. Puddles of muddy water dotted the road and the driveway; they reflected the red light so that Jimmy and Aileen's front yard looked like the entrance to the first ring of hell. As perhaps it very nearly was.

"Trouble here?" said Constable LeBlanc, looking exactly like a knight in shining armor with his crisp black uniform and handsome face partially obscured by the official OPP "Smokey the Bear" hat. Rosemary Rigoloni stood behind him, her hand resting on her nightstick. The other two officers were unfamiliar, but exceedingly welcome nonetheless.

"Just a social call, Officer," Pete said.

"Everything okay here, Mr. McKenzie?"

"Fine, thank you."

"No," I began.

Jimmy drowned me out. "These gentlemen were just leaving."

Pete and his friends headed back toward their truck.

"You dropped something, Mr. Jackson," Rigoloni said, pointing to the baseball bat scarcely concealed by the rose bush. "I'll look after it for you, shall I?"

Jack looked nothing but confused. Pete pushed him toward the truck. "Thank you, Officer, my friend is always careless about handling his things."

They piled into the old pickup, and were gone.

Two of the officers returned to their car and followed the truck. Rigoloni and LeBlanc walked up to the house.

"Mr. Taylor. I'm sorry to hear about your daughter. Is there anything we can do for you?"

Taylor had been emboldened by the arrival of reinforcements, never mind that they'd left so abruptly. "You can arrest this man here." He climbed back up the steps and pointed at Jimmy, spittle forming in the edges of his mouth. The words were slurred. "For the murder of my daughter."

"The matter is under investigation, sir. We're doing everything possible to apprehend the person or persons responsible."

"Yeah, right," Kyle said. "And pigs can fly. Right up your ass, lady."

"If there is nothing further we can do for you, Mr. Taylor?" Rigoloni said. She stepped to one side and gestured down the path to the truck.

Ryan took his father's arm and led him away. Kyle glared at Jimmy one more time and followed.

Jimmy raised his voice. "Oh, Constable LeBlanc, how is the processing of my application for another firearm going? I'd like to be able to pick it up as soon as possible."

LeBlanc looked confused. It was Rigoloni who answered, her tiny voice loud enough to carry through air so charged it might sprout bolts of electricity at any moment. "We can't comment on that, Mr. McKenzie. Firearm permits are out of our control."

The Taylors reached their truck. Kyle helped his father climb in and then took the driver's seat. Ryan leaned out the passenger window and flipped us the bird.

"Do you wish to register a complaint, Mr. McKenzie?"

"No."

"Well, I do," I said. The words came out more as a croak. Now that it was all over, my body was starting to register the shock, my heart beating so fast I might as well have finished a marathon, my throat as dry as ancient parchment. I wiped my hands on the butt of my jeans.

"Please, Rebecca." Jimmy looked at me, his eyes wide and clear. "Let me handle this."

I relented. "Oh, all right."

"We'll request a patrol car to be stationed at the bottom of your road," Rigoloni said. "Until this is settled."

"One way or another." LeBlanc looked at Jimmy with eyes as cold as marble chips. "You'd better watch your back, McKenzie. We won't always be so close at hand, you know."

"Is that a threat?" Aileen stepped out of the house and pulled herself up to her full height. She clutched the cordless phone with white fingers, and the whole of her fragile, tiny-boned body shook.

"Of course not, Aileen," Rigoloni said, giving her a warm smile.

"Take it however you want," LeBlanc said. "Are you in possession of a firearm, McKenzie?"

"Why do you ask?" Jimmy gathered his wife in his arms and held her quivering body tight.

"You have a criminal record, don't you? Yet you referred moments ago to applying for another weapon?"

Jimmy shrugged. "Look it up, Officer. It's a matter of public record. But let me assure you that I am not in possession of an unregistered firearm or of a firearm that is not registered to me. Or to my wife. Satisfied?"

LeBlanc looked anything but.

"Please call us if there is any more trouble," Rigoloni said. "It might be a while before that patrol car gets into position."

"Thank you, Rosemary," Aileen whispered.

"Just doing my job. Let's go, Dave. Dave, I said, let's go."

And they left, walking through the light rain and heavy mud to their car. Rigoloni lifted her hand once, but LeBlanc staunchly ignored us. I had no doubt on which side of that potentially ugly skirmish LeBlanc wanted to be.

But who cares what he thinks as long as he does his job? Thank God we still live under the rule of law.

Jimmy practically carried Aileen back into the house and settled her into the soft leather chair. The fireplace was cold and dark, the candles melted stubs. The unwashed brandy glasses were still on the table, their insides coated with remnants of the heavenly, golden liquid.

"What on earth is going on here?" Dad appeared at the door, his face lined with worry and confusion, rainwater dripping from his cloth cap, Sampson at his heels. I knelt down and gave her a huge hug, ignoring the wet and mud, letting all my fear and tension pour into the dog's big furry body. She licked my face and I burst into tears.

"Becky?" Dad said. "What were all those people doing here? And the police? Why are you crying?"

I scrambled through my pockets and came up with a scrap of previously used tissue. "Nothing, Dad. Nothing."

"You might see a police car on our road a bit more than usual, Dad," Jimmy said. "But don't pay them any mind. They're trying to keep rubberneckers and ghouls away from the area, that's all."

"People these days have nothing better to do," Dad sighed. "In my day we kept out of the way and let the police do their work. I remember when they arrested Corporal Seagal for beating up a whore near the base. '43 it was, or maybe '44. Yeah, '44, just before the Invasion. The English didn't know she was a whore, and they were all in a fine fit, shouting for a charge to be laid."

To forget the horrors of the last half-hour, more than true righteous indignation, I stepped in. "It made a difference, that the woman was a prostitute?"

Aileen laughed. But it was not a good laugh, not a genuine laugh, one full of amusement or mirth; rather a laugh tinged with hysteria. She rubbed her eyes and tucked a stray hair back into its clip, whereupon it immediately escaped. "You McKenzies. I should write you up someday, I could do a wonderful thesis on the fine art of ignoring reality."

Jimmy looked at me, his eyes speaking his concern. "I'll put the coffeepot back on. Dad, care for coffee?"

"No thanks, son. Popped up to see what all the commotion was. I've a mind to get at least one horse finished today. Best get back to it."

"Leave Sampson here, Dad. Please," I asked.

I followed Jimmy into the kitchen. He took off his vest and slipped a knife out of the breast pocket, a big one with a long shiny blade. A Henckels carving knife. Top quality. Razor-sharp. He slipped it back into its place in the wooden stand that sat on the butcher's block in the center of the room.

My brother looked at me. "You learn a few tricks in prison."

I swallowed.

"I won't let anyone touch Aileen. No matter what I have to do." He pulled a packet of coffee beans out of the freezer and poured a handful into the grinder. "I'd like to get her out of here for a while." He spoke over the roar of the machine.

"Where?"

"Her sister lives in Oakville. That's near Toronto."

"I've been there." I searched in the cupboards for mugs.

"They get on well. She'd be happy to have Aileen stay for a bit."

"Think Aileen will go?"

"Not the chance of a bat in hell."

"She can stay with Dad and me."

"I can't see her agreeing to even that."

"What about going to Oakville with her? Seems to me that you're the one who needs to get away."

"I've been advised not to leave the area. You know anyone in this town, other than my family, who'd take me in? Didn't think so. And if they come after me, they won't let anyone I'm staying with stand in the way. And that includes you, Rebecca. Don't be so sure of yourself. No doubt you're a big shot in your business world, but how many fights have you ever been in? Real fights, I mean. Fists, knives?"

"You know the answer to that. Zip, nada, none."

"So please, next time, if there is a next time, don't be so sure of yourself. Do what I tell you."

A tiny glass ball hung on a string in the window. It threw a rainbow of red, blue, and green light to dance across the far cupboards. The sun had come out and chased away the rain clouds. For now.

"Well, Ray always said that my mouth would get me into trouble one day. But so far it has been more likely to keep me out of it."

Jimmy smiled. "I'm sorry I didn't get to meet him. I would have liked him."

"He would have liked you, too." And he would have. The two men would have gotten on great. Yet for all these years I had kept a continent between my husband and my family. Not wanting him to meet them. Ashamed of them. And now it was too late to bring them together.

"I like you too, Jimmy," I mumbled. His back was turned, tending to the coffee and he didn't hear me. I cleared my throat. "Did you get a call from Alex Singh?"

"Yeah. He's going to drive down from North Bay this afternoon. He told me not to speak to the police until he gets here. We have an interview with Inspector so-and-so at four. Thanks for finding him, Rebecca. I mean it, thanks a lot." The coffeemaker stopped dripping and Jimmy poured three mugs full. He reached into the cupboard and pulled out a bottle of brandy and poured a generous slug into each portion. "And thanks for standing by me today. But please. Don't do it again. I can fight my own battles."

"I'm sure you can. But the odds seemed a mite out of kilter to me. You aren't Aragorn facing down a horde of dimwitted orcs, you know."

"Dimwitted they may be. But you're right. Let's get this coffee to Aileen. She'll be thinking we've run away or something."

"One more thing. Do you have a gun?"

"No. I have a prison record and I'm now straight. I don't have a gun."

I stayed long enough to drink my brandy-laced coffee. Aileen lay in the caramel-colored chair, looking as tiny and fragile as an antique rag doll. Her eyes were wide in her pale face, and there were lines carved through the tender skin that hadn't been there when first we met.

"Time for me to be going," I said, standing up. Sampson was ahead of me; she rushed to the door, eager to be heading back outside. "Perhaps I'll take a stroll up to the top of the road, see if our boys and girls in blue have taken up their positions yet. They said it would be a while. Call me if you need anything. I'll send Sampson over."

Jimmy walked me to the porch. "You might want to get Aileen to a doctor," I said as the door closed gently behind us. "She doesn't look well at all."

"When she was nine years old Aileen's father was murdered in front of her."

I sucked in air.

"A robbery gone wrong. Aileen and her dad arrived home early, dance practice cancelled because the teacher was sick, to find a bunch of teenagers tossing their place."

"How awful for her."

"It was. One of the kids panicked, picked up an Inuit stone carving and threw it. A wild shot, unlucky for everyone. It got her dad right in the head and brought him down. Dead on the spot."

"Poor Aileen."

"She has a good therapist, but she's been well enough the last few years to pretty well stop seeing her. This business is sure to be upsetting, to say the least. I might give the therapist a call, make an appointment for Aileen."

"If she needs a drive or anything…"

"Thanks. You'll send Sampson, right?"

"Let me know how it goes with Singh, eh?"

"He told me the bill's taken care of?"

"Yeah, I found the cheapest lawyer in the North. It wasn't easy."

"I'm sure it wasn't. But I'll pay you back."

I shrugged. "As I said: thirty years' worth. Talk to you later."

The promise of a sunny afternoon offered by the sun catcher in the kitchen window had been fulfilled. The lake sparkled blue and gold, smooth and clear and so attractive and seductively inviting that I thought about going for a swim. But, regardless of how it looked, the water would not be warm enough for swimming for another six weeks at the earliest.

A chevron of returning Canada geese passed high overhead, honking their delight at being home again. The dull roar of a motorboat sounded in the distance. Humans also happy to see signs of summer soon to come. Sampson trotted ahead, criss-crossing the path, sniffing out everything that had walked this way since she last passed, separating the safe and the belonging from the hostile and foreign. Would that we could do so as easily.

I no longer had any doubts that my brother had anything to do with Jennifer Taylor's death. Perhaps I'm naïve, but I'd looked into his face as he thought about the girl he admired, and as he talked about the wife he loved so much, I saw how vulnerable he had allowed himself to become.

Yes, I believed him.

Sampson lifted her head, froze for a moment, and then dashed down the road, the hill echoing with the sound of her barking. I trotted after her. Ghoulish tourists or protective police, they were all the same to her. Interlopers to be driven away.

The first time they met, Sampson had accepted Jimmy without question. Time for me to forget the past and do so as well.

I walked up the lawn to my parents' house, my home. The house to which I had been proudly carried on the day my new-born self left the hospital. Where my grandfather ruled the roost with an iron fist and a heart to match. Where his first-born son fell face first into the bottle to avoid becoming him. What sort of man had my father been before he met my mother? I had caught brief glimpses of his younger self in the words of her diary. If he'd married a lesser woman than Janet Green, would he have succumbed to self-preservation and abandoned his mother? It was obvious to me, although Mom didn't come right out and say it in the diary, that my grandfather had beaten my grandmother, badly, the day Dad was in Toronto meeting Mom and Shirley off the train. Probably as a warning to his son of what would happen if he tried to make a life of his own. Was it good that Dad had stayed in Hope River, living in his father's house? If not for the rest of us, at least for Dad's sense of self?

What would we have been, Jimmy and Shirley and I, had we not been raised in that atmosphere of fear and constant anxiety, mixed with the tender love of our mother? Shirley might be less bitter. Jimmy, of course, would not have been at all. And what a gap that would have left in dear Aileen's life.

Thoughts on the scale of "the meaning of life." Far too complicated for a sunny spring day tinged with the miasma of murder and vengeance.

In the middle of the yard, a handful of crocuses, purple and yellow, smiled into the sun from beneath a big old white pine. The flowers had been planted by my mother. Mother loved her garden. Although when I had been a child, she devoted a good deal more time and attention to the vegetable patch out back than to frivolous flowers. But she always managed to put some bulbs in the ground every fall, so she could delight in the most visible sign of spring. At Laura Secord's historic house in Queenstown, Ontario, rose bushes still grow that graced the lawns when she lived there close to two hundred years ago. Perhaps Janet Green McKenzie's crocuses would live as long. It was a nice thought.

Chapter 39

The diary of Janet McKenzie. Sunday, May 8, 1960. Mother's Day

What a perfectly lovely day it has been. Bob and Rebecca brought me breakfast in bed. The food was perfectly dreadful, the eggs the consistency and taste of rubber, burnt around the edges, the yolks hard and dry. Toast so underdone it hadn't even started to color and tea the shade of weak milk. But they picked a red tulip from the garden and put it into a water glass on the tray, and Rebecca simply burst with pride and that made it all taste like a meal prepared in heaven.

At lunch time, Bob shooed me out of the kitchen, saying that Rebecca and he had everything in hand. Much laughing and giggling as they worked. They packed the lunch into a laundry basket, covered it with a blanket and carried it down to the rocks by the lake for a picnic. Shirley made the effort to crawl out of her room and join us. She even waded into the lake with Rebecca for a short while, forgetting that she is too grown up and sophisticated to play with her baby sister. Shirley is only 15 and is devoting far too much attention to her clothes and the bit of makeup she can buy with her allowance. And too much, much too much, time with that Smithers boy. Horrid creature. She has given up any pretence of doing her schoolwork. But I hope that she will get over it in time and return to being the good student that she once was. I would love to see her attend business school. With a qualification like that she could find herself a good secretarial job and get out of Hope River.

But I refuse to let such miserable thoughts interfere with my enjoyment of this lovely day. Jim walked up to the big house to escort Mrs. M. down to the picnic, which was so nice of him. Mr. M. is in jail for breaking some man's arm in a bar fight. Bob said we are lucky that he only got thirty days. Lucky! Better they had thrown away the key! With him not around, Mrs. M. actually manages a smile now and again and my son, Jim, forgets that he is supposed to be hard and mean and sullen. He even joined the girls to play in the water.

It's too cold for swimming yet, but the children waded across the rocks and splashed at each other. Jim chased Shirley, pretending he had a water snake that he was going to put down her back. We could hear him laughing and Shirley squealing as she fled for the safety of the house. They came back and found Rebecca searching through the rocks looking for a snake of her own. Jim told her that he was only pretending, and she looked so disappointed that he promised to teach her to fish this summer. He then tried to talk his grandmother into joining them. She refused, of course, but she was tickled pink to have been asked.

He's a good boy, my son Jim, underneath. I see him every day struggling under the crushing weight of his unknown legacy. I can only hope that he's strong enough to bear it.

Chapter 40

Without warning my legs protested that they simply didn't have the strength to make it up the steps to the deck and carry me into the house. I collapsed on the bottom step and looked out over the yard. My mother's crocuses swayed in the light wind. Beyond the road the blue lake sparkled in the sunshine. We should move that road, I thought, it's an eyesore. It joins nothing but the little house and the big house to the county sideroad. Moving it shouldn't cause any trouble. Then we'd have a perfect stretch of land, the wide yard running straight down to the rocks and the water.

A chipmunk crept out from under the big white pine, looked at me with huge brown eyes and a twitch of its whiskers, clearly wondering if I was in possession of something worth eating. But at a bark from Sampson, it turned and ran up the tree, the chopped-off tail quivering.

I burst into tears. Sampson crept over as if she'd done something wrong, whined, and licked my face to make everything right again. I hugged her close and cried into her fur. Her ruff and belly were thick with dried mud and shedding hair. My fingers plucked at the knots, and I cried some more.

Nothing could make it right.

Ever again.

I cried for the man I loved, the man who loved me with a passion I had never expected and that I believed I could never earn. One of the best men who ever graced this miserable planet.

Ray, why did you have to leave me so alone?

⌒⌒⌒

"Becky, you okay?"

My sister, Shirley, stood in front of me. She scratched through her purse and pulled out a tissue. I took it from her and tried to stand up, so disoriented that for a moment I wondered why my legs wouldn't respond. Sampson lay across my lap.

"Are you okay?" Shirley asked again. She eased herself gently down to the step and sat beside me. Her knees cracked. She tried to keep a bit of distance, but slipped one arm around my shoulders awkwardly. "Are you hurt? Want me to get Dad? Should I call someone?"

"No. I'm not hurt." I crumpled the sodden tissue into a tight ball and twisted it in my hands. She shifted toward me, ever so slightly. I collapsed against her shoulder and broke into a fresh round of sobs.

She was silent for a long time, letting me cry, patting my back, and trying one-handed to open her purse for a fresh tissue. Sampson didn't budge.

It felt nice. The substantial weight of the heavy dog across my lap, a motherly arm around my shoulder. I cried some more.

"Do you want to talk about it?" Shirley said when the sobs died down.

"I loved him. I loved my husband very much."

"I'm sure you did."

"I loved my mother, too."

"Yup."

"They're both gone, and it's too late to tell them how much I loved them."

"It usually is too late, Becky," Shirley said. "And when people have enough time, that's a tragedy all its own. Al's mom died of cancer. It took her months, almost a year, to die. Bit by tiny bit. We had all the time in the world to say good-bye. Too much time."

"You're saying that there is no such thing as a good death?"

"For the person most involved, there can be. If they go at peace with themselves and with how they've lived their life. For those left behind, the survivors, no, I don't think that there is ever a good death."

"How did you get to be so wise?" I smiled up at her. My big sister. Too big, too much older, to ever be a real sister.

"Not wise," she said, her voice distant, her eyes focused far away. "Just a girl from Hope River. But I'm my mother's daughter. She was a good woman."

"That she was."

"And she never knew it."

"Never knew what?"

"That she was a good person. It took a lot of strength for her to stay here, in this horrible town. She must've wanted to run back to England the moment she stepped foot here. Mom never told me any stories about coming to Hope River and starting a new life. All her stories were about England. The village she was raised in, where I was born, the house they lived in. Her father, Arthur Green, our grandfather, owned a shop. Her mother died when she was very young, did you know that? She was raised by her Aunt Betty. Mom told me about the war, the blackouts and the rationing, the German planes flying overhead. But she didn't talk much about meeting Dad and nothing at all about coming to Canada. As a child I certainly wouldn't have been interested in hearing about Hope River anyway, so boring, but I loved stories about the war and how they watched the German bombers on the way to London and the brave RAF fighters chasing after them."

"You don't think she was happy?"

"She hated it here, Becky." Crisis over, Sampson leapt off my lap and bounded across the grass. "Is there any point in going over this? It all happened so long ago."

"It may have happened long ago," I said, "but the repercussions continue to this day. In our lives." The past is always with us, going around and around in ever decreasing circles until it fades into itself like a bit of soap scum finally disappearing down the drain.

I hugged Shirley, perhaps for the first time in our lives with feelings genuinely felt. Her body was so scrawny it might as well have been a museum skeleton, covered in a thin sheet of parchment paper. She hugged me back, awkward, unsure. Her heart was beating hard, very hard. Then, as if she suddenly realized that she was being affectionate toward me, she took back her arm and edged a bit further away.

"Grandpa?" I said. It was time, after all these years, to talk about the shadow that lay over all our lives.

"She never said anything against him, never needed to. He and Grandma lived in the same house as us. You can't begin to understand how awful it was. Even as a child I knew that things weren't quite right. They bought the big house when I was about eleven or twelve years old, not long after you were born, and the grandparents moved in there. It was like someone threw open the shutters and let some light come into our lives. That sounds so stupid."

"No. No it doesn't. It's not stupid at all. I'm trying to understand and you're helping me to do so."

"Mom was happier, lighter, freer. Dad seemed to grow, as if having fought in a world war, reached thirty-some years of age, father of three, he finally was allowed to grow up. But they were still too close." She was staring into space, lost in the memories. "I wished that Grandpa was dead, and then I would lie in bed at night afraid that God would strike me down for being such a hateful girl."

"Oh, Shirley."

Far out on the lake, a boat passed, moving quickly, crossing between one island and another. The roar of the motor was harsh, unwelcome in the soft peace of the afternoon.

"Spring," Shirley said, trying, and failing miserably to sound more cheerful. "I can't wait. You and Jimmy were always great ones for the winter. Do you still love the snow?"

"We… I have a holiday home near Whistler."

"I could have predicted that years ago. I'm more like Mom in that way. Winter is something to be endured, to be suffered through in order to earn the warmth of spring. Mom never even complained about the weather. But occasionally I'd hear her muttering under her breath on a particularly cold night when she couldn't get the house warm, or when the snow prevented her from going to do her shopping, or us getting to school. The crocuses are doing wonderfully. She put a lot of new ones in last year." Her voice fell. "So sad. She'll never see them. I don't imagine Dad'll plant anything this fall."

I twisted to look directly at my sister. "You need to talk more than I do, Shirl. God knows I've always felt so hard done by, growing up in this family. Poor little me. I never spared a thought for how much harder it must have been for you."

She avoided my eyes. "I'm perfectly fine. I've coped with it all and come out fine."

"Have you? Look, Shirley, there is something you should know. Mom kept…"

She jumped to her feet. For a moment, I thought it was fear of what I was about to say. But no. Aileen's car was turning into the driveway. Jimmy was at the wheel. Sampson ran over to offer the visitors a slobbery hello.

When I looked back at Shirley, all traces of empathy, compassion, and trust were gone, as if I'd only imagined them in some fading dream of reconciliation and understanding.

She began to stand up. I reached out one hand and gripped her arm. "I understand only a bit of what you went through, but I lived there as well."

Jimmy climbed out of the car and gave Sampson an enthusiastic greeting, mostly behind the ears. He walked up to the house, watching me, the dog, the house, the yard, everything but his older sister.

"Have you ever thought about him, our brother?" I said. "He's the one Grandpa tried to mold into his own image. Although twist is probably a better word. What hope did a boy have against that?"

She shook my hand off, got to her feet, pushed the door open, and disappeared into the house.

"What're you two doing sitting out on the stoop?" Jimmy asked. "Everything okay?"

"Fine."

"You look like hell, if I may say so."

"You may not."

"I won't, then. Did you have an argument with Shir?"

"No. Shirley's fine. We're cool."

He looked doubtful. "Good."

"Where are you going?"

He laughed, his deep, intense laugh that always had the girls grinning and acting like perfect fools. Despite myself, I actually cracked a smile in return. "I'm not escaping for parts unknown," he said. "I'm off to the store for a few things Aileen has decided that we need. Brie, paté, smoked salmon, champagne. Life's essentials. You think I'm exaggerating, but I'm not. Aileen doesn't handle stress too well." He was no longer laughing.

"Want a bodyguard?"

"Thanks, but no thanks. It's broad daylight and I'm not going to be venturing down any dark alleys. Our friends in blue are parked at the bottom of the road. I'll tell them where I'm headed; they'll keep an eye on the houses. I'll be home in time to meet with Singh before our interview with Inspector Gadget. Shirley okay?"

"I don't know, Jimmy. Is she ever?"

"Probably not. Better she'd done like you and left this damned family long ago."

"Don't say that."

"Say what? Damned? You offended?"

"Of course I'm not offended. But we're not damned. Or cursed or struck by misfortune or any such superstitious nonsense. Don't say that."

He smiled again and bent to kiss me on the cheek. "Right as always. I'll let you know what happens later. If you have a hankering for champagne and paté and French cheese, you know where to find it. Say hi to Shirley."

Shirley was in the shed, silently watching Dad work, her thin face strained and troubled, the dark circles under her eyes pronounced. Dad bent over the lathe, guiding the wood with strong, steady hands. His pleasure in the wood and the work made him look as if he'd discarded thirty weary years.

When I walked in, he straightened his back, turned off the machine, and tossed us a huge smile, full of false teeth. "Both my girls here at the same time. Isn't that nice? Is lunch ready?"

"I can't stay, Dad," Shirley said. "Have to get back to work. I popped in for a couple of minutes to check that you're okay." She headed for the door of the shed. The stiffness was back in her shoulders, the disapproving scowl clamped onto her face, the eyes cold and brittle once again.

"I'll make you a sandwich, Dad," I said. "Come inside in about five minutes."

The lathe roared back to life.

My sister and I walked through the house and out to her car in silence. "It was nice talking to you," I said.

She didn't reply, merely opened the car door and plunked heavily into her seat. The door slammed in my face. I knocked lightly on the window, and she grudgingly rolled it halfway down, turning the key in the ignition at the same time.

"Yes?"

"Why don't I drop by your house after dinner? We can finish talking about Mom."

"We're going out."

"Oh, all right. Have it your way. But we have to talk sometime. With everything else that has been going on, I haven't called Maggie about the housekeeper position. And Aileen has way too much on her mind."

"So?"

"So, if we haven't found someone once I'm gone, it'll be up to you, Shirley."

"Isn't it always?"

This was one for the people at the *Guinness Book of Records*. Caring sister to big-time martyr in five minutes.

"Have it your way," I sighed, stepping away from the open window. "But think a bit about what I said about Jimmy, eh? Think about what a number Grandpa did on him."

She rolled the window up with more enthusiasm than the occasion required and pulled away without so much as a wave.

I had been all set to tell Shirley about the diaries. Now I wasn't so sure. Mom didn't present her only son in a flattering light. Jimmy was struggling to get over his history, with Aileen's help. Would Shirley ever be able to pierce though the miasma of past anger to see what was happening today? She'd be a good deal happier if she could.

Not my problem, I reminded myself. I'd be back in Vancouver by this time next week.

Chicken noodle soup out of a can accompanied by tuna sandwiches served as our lunch. Dad ate without talking and quickly returned to the workshop, eager to get back to work. Reminding Shirley about the great housekeeper hunt had served to remind me as well. Perhaps I should forget the whole thing. Shirley wore her family duties like a weighty cloak of atonement. She wouldn't let Dad suffer.

If we hadn't been through that all-too-brief moment of intimacy sitting curled up together on the steps of the front porch, overlooking the waters of the blue lake, out to the islands and the green and brown woods beyond, I might well have left the job to her. But I'd seen the hurt in her eyes, heard how she still suffered for the past, and felt her thin bones trying to be strong beneath my embrace. I poured the majority of my chicken noodle soup down the sink, tossed the remainders of my sandwich to Sampson, and went in search of my keys.

A single police car sat on the shoulder of the main road, facing the branch that cut off to the McKenzie houses. I tossed what I hoped was a cheerful wave. Two blank young faces watched me.

The restaurant was almost full, but the end of the lunch hour was approaching. Most of the tables were occupied by dirty plates and remnants of meals waiting to be cleared or patrons hurriedly finishing their coffee and pie before heading back to work. Maggie bustled about, collecting empty plates, carrying bills, and scooping up money. I perched on a stool at the counter and pretended to read the plastic menu.

"The soup today is split pea and the sandwich is roast beef on a bun with fries and gravy," the waitress, not Maggie, told me with a disinterested sigh. She was short, with thin, greasy hair allowed to grow too long and bad skin covered with too much cheap makeup. And far too young to be carrying such a bulging stomach out in front of her. She reminded me of the trees in the woods behind our house, proud in the display of their new buds. The girl caught me looking at her belly and lifted her left hand so I could see the plain, cheap wedding band she wore. As if, at her age, pregnant and working in this dump, it would make much of a difference that she was married.

"Coffee please, just coffee." She started to walk away. "And a piece of apple pie with ice cream. Please."

The coffee arrived almost immediately, fresh and delicious. The diner was emptying out. I could smell the pie before it arrived: warm with vanilla ice cream melting around the edges. At the first bite I was swimming in a heavenly bath of cinnamon, warm apples, cool vanilla, and flaky pastry.

I ate my pie with enthusiasm, but sipped the coffee, trying to stretch out my visit. Maggie collected money, wiped down tables, and laid them once again. Finally she had to pass my stool, where I lay in wait, a determined hunter in a duck blind.

"Hi, Maggie," I said cheerfully. "Remember me, Rebecca McKenzie? I came in the other day with my dad?"

She stopped, too polite to shove her way past. Thank heaven for good manners. I have found that you can always take advantage of people by preying on their sense of propriety.

"I remember. How's Bob doing?"

"Not too good," I sighed mightily. "It's hard for him, trying to manage all on his own. Actually I'm glad I ran into you. When we talked earlier you indicated that you might be interested in the housekeeper job we're offering. It's still open."

She looked around, nervous, twitching. "I have a job, Miss McKenzie."

"Oh, right." I lowered my voice, fellow conspirators we. "If you're still interested, that would be great. Why don't you come up to the house when you get off work and we can talk about it?"

"I don't know… Folks are saying…"

"Saying what?"

"There's talk. About your brother."

"So? I'm not asking you to work for my brother. You know my dad, right?"

She nodded.

"You know he's a good man, right?"

"Yes."

"My brother's a good man, too. But that doesn't matter. If you think you would like to work for my dad, that's great. No one's asking you to work for Jimmy."

"Maggie. Tables need setting." A man came out of the kitchen, a stained white apron stretched across his ample stomach.

I raised my voice. "I'll have another piece of that apple pie. With ice cream."

Maggie went to get the dessert, and the bossy fellow returned to his kitchen. The pregnant girl shuffled about the room, pouring coffee for a single man at the other end of the counter and taking the order of a couple newly arrived.

Maggie returned with my pie.

"Actually, Maggie," I said, cutting the pastry with my fork. "To be fair, I should tell you that I stopped by because someone else is interested in taking the job. I wanted to make sure that you weren't still thinking about it before I offer it to her." The oldest, dumbest, cheapest trick in the book.

I should have been ashamed of myself.

But I wasn't. Not in the slightest. It's been known to work on corporate investors.

"Lunch shift is almost over," Maggie said. "I have a couple hours off before dinner starts."

"Good. It's a warm day. Why don't we sit down by the river and have a nice talk? You know the park on Riverside Street?"

"Yes."

"What time do you get off?"

Maggie glanced at the clock commemorating someone's visit to Sudbury. "Soon's tables are clean. Ten minutes? Fifteen?"

"See you then." She returned to her chores and I leisurely finished my pie, rather pleased with myself. Hiring a housekeeper or floating a ten-million-dollar loan. The principle's the same.

I offered Maggie Kzenic the job on the spot. There weren't a whole lot of eligible candidates eagerly lining up to take the position. She explained that she would have to talk to Peter, the owner of the restaurant. She was sort of hoping, she told me, that she would be able to stay on to work the dinner shift. She was finding the morning-to-night workday too hard, problems with aging knees made long hours on her feet a misery, and she had told Peter that she wanted to cut her hours down, but she couldn't really afford to do so. The job with my dad would be perfect for her. We arranged that she would come in four days a week: Monday, Tuesday, Thursday, and Friday. She would get Dad a late breakfast/lunch, do a bit of light housework, have his dinner ready, put it into the oven to keep warm, and be off to her next job by 4:30. I told her that judging by the amount of local home cooking stored in the big chest freezer in the cellar, it would be a long time before she would have to cook. On Fridays she would leave the fridge with enough supplies for the weekend and make up sandwiches and salads or casseroles to be heated in the microwave for his meals.

It occurred to me that after the incident with the bacon in the frying pan the other day, I might ask Jimmy if it was possible for Maggie to disable the stove somehow before she finished for the day.

"I'm going back to Vancouver on Saturday. I'll tell Aileen what we've discussed, and from then on you can deal with her."

She shifted on the uncomfortable picnic bench.

"Is that okay?"

Maggie looked out across the park. Two Canada geese were poking in the brown grass. Not much nourishment, this time of year. In my childhood they all flew south for the winter, great black V formations passing across the clear, blue sky, splitting the rapidly cooling autumn air with their honking chorus, encouraging their friends to keep up. These days, many didn't get any further than Toronto, and there they stayed all through the winter, fed by enthusiastic children with paper bags stuffed full of stale white bread.

"Miss McKenzie?"

"Rebecca, please."

"I'd prefer to deal with your sister, Shirley Smithers."

"Oh."

"Not that I have anything against Aileen, you understand. She's a nice lady, Aileen is. But with all that's going on…" Her voice trailed off.

"Aileen's closer. But if that's what you want, I'll mention it to Shirley. My brother didn't do it. He didn't kill Jennifer Taylor."

"Well, to tell you honest, I don't know. But folks are saying…"

"Lots of people around here don't seem to have anything better to do than gossip. And others don't have the intellect to realize vicious garbage when they hear it."

I didn't have to look at her face to know that I'd made a mistake. I do have a big mouth. One thing I learned early in the business world: It's not a bright idea to insult someone you're trying to get to do something for you. My words stumbled all over themselves in an attempt to make repairs.

"It's been hard the last few days. Hearing what people are saying about my brother. Most people don't have all the facts. They're judging him on his past behavior and that's not fair, is it?"

"I remember Jim when he was a young one," Maggie said. "In all this town there wasn't one person talked about more than Little Jim McKenzie. He was a great one for the girls, your brother."

"That's an understatement."

"There's somethin' you should probably know. Gossip, scuttlebutt moves fast in this town. And most of it's worth nothin' more than the air it's breathed into."

"But?"

"But, some folk are saying that the cops won't do nothin' to charge Jim McKenzie. So they'll have to do for themselves what the cops won't."

"You heard this?"

"Last night, before closin'."

"There was trouble at Jimmy's place this morning. Fortunately it came to nothing. The police are watching the house now. Will you tell me if you hear any more? Please?"

"My brother's in the OPP, stationed over in Thunder Bay. He's a good cop, real proud of what he does." Maggie picked at a bit of dried food clinging to the front of her dress. "He wouldn't take a bribe, look away from a child's killing. No way. The police here wouldn't either.

"Men get to talking when they're enjoying their food. I'll keep my ears open. Let you know if I hear anything worth hearin'."

"Thanks, Maggie."

We parted with a smile. She had to go home and take a nap before the next shift. How perfectly awful must that be? I work hard, but that's different, very different. I'm not on my feet all day. I sit in a nice office, in an expensive chair, and often stop simply to think and look out over the multi-million-dollar view. I love every minute of my job, but even so, I wouldn't want to head back to it a few hours after finishing. Not day after day.

For Maggie the idea of putting in a day helping my father at his house and then going in for a shift at the restaurant seemed like an improvement.

The things Maggie told me, about what she overheard in the restaurant, disturbed me. I walked to my car with a lot to think about. Who did Maggie overhear talking about taking matters into their own hands? The Taylors? It was highly unlikely that the family would be having dinner at a restaurant the day after their daughter's body had been pulled out of the swamp. Jack and Pete? If they had planned trouble last night, they would have consumed more than a few drinks to work up the courage and shown up at Jimmy's after closing time. Not like them to go home and sleep on it.

Suppose the townspeople made a concentrated effort to go after Jimmy? Most of the men in this town were reasonably law-abiding, but the Taylors were a respected family, long-time residents, owners of Fawcett's Hardware Store. Might people follow them? Possible. Particularly on a Saturday night after the bars closed. And my good friends Jack and Pete didn't appear to need any backup in order to make mischief. The idea of the single patrol car sitting at the side of the road seemed rather pathetic. As the saying goes: just because you're paranoid, doesn't mean they aren't out to get you.

In Ontario the bars close at two a.m. Sampson and I would be sitting up late these next few nights.

And after I left?

By then everything would be resolved.

I have always been an incorrigible optimist.

Chapter 41

The Diary of Janet McKenzie. October 3, 1961

Of all the unimaginable things. Shirley today announced that she and Al Smithers want to get married. I can't bear that boy. He is so supercilious and smug. I told her and told her that he was no good and I forbade her to date him. But would she listen to me? Of course not. The fool girl is all of sixteen years old. Younger even than I was when I met her father. And look at what a mistake that turned out to be.

She hasn't said anything, not yet. But I've known for several weeks that she is in the family way. What mother wouldn't know? I am going to be a grandmother. A thought too horrible to contemplate.

It will not happen to my Rebecca. It will not. If I have to move heaven and earth, I will make sure that Rebecca has a chance in this world.

November 24, 1963

In court today. Again. I am about ready to consider myself obliged to invite the judge over for dinner, I know him so well. They caught Jim drinking this time. And him only fifteen. You would think that his family would be ashamed. To have a son in and out of court like he was the revolving door I saw in Toronto back in '46. But Mr. M. just laughs and slaps the boy on the back and says, "A chip off the old block." Poor Mrs. M. knows so little of what is happening these days; she just smiles and packs the boy a lunch of dry bread and a slice of moldy cheese to take with him.

Bob is concerned enough to tell me that he would go to court if he could get the time off work. Of course he can't.

A small fine, and my boy is out the court house door. All of fifteen years old and walking down the main street like the cock-of-the-walk. He is a good-looking boy, and I say that not as his mother, because I think life would go better for him if he had a bit of humility. He is short, like his... father... and ashamed of it, so he works hard to build up his body and strut as if he doesn't care. He is still a good bit shorter than I. Boys his age have a few more growing years yet, but I have seen him eyeing me and then the men in his family and I know that he is worried. Oh, that we lived in a perfect world. Where such things don't matter. And no one will judge my son by the length of his body. But we don't live there, and I can still hear the mocking voice of my husband's own father laughing at him for marrying a woman taller than he. My mother-in-law doesn't even touch five feet. All the better to allow her five-foot-four husband to grind her into the ground.

To top it all off, we had barely arrived home from the courthouse when Shirley announced that she and Al are expecting another baby.

I wanted to cry, although I'd suspected as much. They are still living with Mr. and Mrs. Smithers and Al is spinning big tales of moving to Toronto and getting a good job and moving into one of the new houses that are springing up around the city, acres and acres of them. Bob looked stunned—at least he was surprised. Mr. and Mrs. M. were over at our house, (when is one of them not?). He smirked, of course, and slapped Al on the back as if it were something he'd managed all by himself, and invited Al into the kitchen, and we could all hear the fridge door opening. I don't think Mrs. M. quite understood.

I am going to be a grandmother for the second time. And here I am scarcely thirty-seven.

How did I get to be so old?

Chapter 42

Shortly after dinner I made my excuses and, to my dad's amusement, headed for bed. I set the alarm for two o'clock, but I needn't have bothered—I hardly shut my eyes. When I slapped the buzzing alarm off, everything was quiet. I left Sampson in the house (stealth isn't her strong suit), but closed the door without locking it in case she was needed in a hurry. Creeping down the road to check out the police car, I managed to startle the constable on duty as much as he scared me. My head popped up from behind a rock the very moment he lowered his zipper to take a pee in the bushes.

"Couldn't sleep. Out for a walk. Sorry." My cheeks burned with embarrassment. It must be a great deal easier to be on surveillance in the countryside than in the city. How do female officers manage in the city anyway? I wondered, scurrying backward through the brush.

It was thoroughly dark. Thick clouds obscured any trace of moon or stars. And quiet. Only the distant swamp was awake with the nighttime chorus of deep-throated frogs and high-pitched bugs. I carried a flashlight but kept it switched off. No need to attract any notice. If anyone should be out here to notice me.

I crept up the dark, peaceful road to check on the big house. Every outdoor bulb had been left on so that the yard was as ablaze with light as an Olympic stadium during the running of the 200 meters. But all was quiet. Returning to my father's house, I got my dog and my car (into which I had earlier stowed a blanket, a thermos of coffee, tuna sandwiches wrapped in wax paper, a handful of dog biscuits, a bottle of water, a book, and the tiny reading light I use when traveling) and drove up the road without headlights. I pulled over at the side of the road, switched the engine off, and there we sat.

Not even a deer or a raccoon broke the silence of the night. The frogs had all gone to bed. As we settled into our watch, the clouds abruptly scattered, leaving the sky clear. A full moon washed the big house in white light. It probably washed my car as well, but that didn't matter. The best I could do would be to scare troublemakers away if they came up through the woods, avoiding the police on the road. If they thought I was another cop car, that would be all for the good.

Four o'clock. I started up the engine and drove back to the little house. I certainly wouldn't have deterred any professionals from doing what they came to do, but if a gang of drunks from the bar had been hiding in the woods waiting for me to leave, they would have given up after ten minutes and staggered off home.

The next morning I was sound asleep when Dad knocked on my door and told me that Jimmy wanted to see me. I staggered into the kitchen still in my pajamas to find my brother making coffee and toast. He turned his full-wattage smile on me.

"Good morning, Rebecca. Up late last night?"

"Not her," Dad said. "Hardly finished dinner before she was off. Had to let the dog out myself."

"Hard day," I said.

"Well then, you sit right there and I'll get breakfast." Jimmy pulled margarine and jam out of the fridge. Dad smiled at us both. He loved to have his children around. A touch of guilt shuddered through me at the thought of my thirty-year absence, but I pushed it to the back of my mind and took a seat. My father could have come to visit me in Vancouver anytime. And when we were children he didn't seem to much care whether we were around or not. As I remember, he usually nodded goodnight to me from behind the bottom of a beer bottle.

"What's it like outside?"

"Raining. Looks like an all-day drizzle." Jimmy poured coffee. "Funny noises in the night. Did you hear anything, Dad?"

"Nope. Slept like a log."

"I thought that a car was watching the house, but I might have been mistaken."

"Didn't see nothing like that."

"I must have dreamt it. There was a woman, a really great-looking woman, with a dog in this big car. Drinking coffee and reading. The woman, that is, not the dog. And even before the car arrived someone or something was creeping around in the bushes. Not a dog though."

"A deer?" Dad suggested. "They'll sometimes come pretty close to the house this time of year. Hungry, been a long winter." Jimmy had brought the newspaper up with him. Dad flipped it open to the sports section.

"You're probably right." Jimmy smiled at me. "Toast, Rebecca?"

"I'm only trying to help. Someone needs to be on watch."

"Someone was," Jimmy said.

"Oh."

He poured the coffee. He'd brought his own beans, previously ground.

"However, even the omnipotent someone has to go to work. Fortunately my big job right now is for out-of-towners. They haven't heard the latest news, so haven't called to let me know my services won't be wanted for the foreseeable future."

"Leafs lost again," Dad mumbled from behind his newspaper, while reaching for a slice of toast and jam. "Can't they ever do anything right?"

"Aileen's determined to go to Huntsville. A new line of jewelry arrived at the store yesterday, and she insists that only she can unpack it and arrange the pieces on the shelves. And I would rather she didn't go alone. In case unexpected customers drop into the store, you understand."

"Nice coffee," I said.

"Good idea," Dad said. "All this rain, the roads are gonna be bad."

"Rebecca?"

"I'd be happy to go with Aileen. Her shop is a wonder, and I've been intending to buy some gifts to take home."

"A full day of shopping and girl talk and you might even sleep the whole night through."

That comment deserved only a growl in response. "You okay to look after Sampson for the day, Dad?"

"Course I am. She's a nice dog. We get on real well. Don't we, Sampson?" He tossed her a piece of toast and scratched behind her ears. She threw back the toast and thumped her tail in agreement.

⌇⌇⌇

Jimmy was managing the stress of recent events with an almost unnatural calm. Aileen, on the other hand, was as jumpy as Sampson at a porcupine convention. I offered to drive.

Aileen didn't talk a great deal on the road down to Huntsville, merely twisted her hands together and stared out the window at the passing rocks and trees and lakes. Which were followed by even more rocks and trees and lakes.

Aileen grunted without much interest when I told her that the arrangements were settled with Maggie for the housekeeping job. I said that Maggie would use Shirley as her contact, because they were old friends. (I lied.) I would send Shirley money to cover Maggie's wages. Did she think Shirley would be offended? Aileen grunted again.

The rest of the trip passed in silence. When I turned off Highway 11 to Huntsville, I mentioned that I was thinking about getting some gifts. Something nice for Ray's mother, something fun for Jenny. A token for the neighbor who was bringing in the mail and watering my plants.

She twisted in her seat and turned slightly to face me, for the first time in the long, boring trip. Her hands stopped moving. They were shockingly red, angry, the skin raw, tortured with worry. Her fears come out on her body.

"The heartache that flesh is heir to." *Hamlet*. One summer, so very long ago, before we were married, Ray dragged me to Bard on the Beach, an annual summertime outdoor production of Shakespeare. Nice, but I hadn't given the play another thought. Until now.

"What sort of thing does your mother-in-law like?" Aileen asked, a small, very small, spark of interest flickering across her brown eyes.

"Glass. Stained glass, sculptures of glass, light-catchers. She loves glass." That might have been a mistake: Jack had destroyed the glass duck. But Aileen appeared not to make the connection.

"We have some things like that."

"Good."

The silence hung between us until we pulled up into the alley behind Cottage Art and Design.

Like an ice sculpture sitting out in the sun on a too-warm day, Aileen began to thaw the moment she set foot into her perfect shop. A handful of customers were scattered about, but Chrissie greeted us with much enthusiasm. Her thick hair had been swept off her face and held back in a loose ponytail.

She held up her right hand and made a signal, a code of some sort, something about the customers. Whatever it was, it had Aileen actually cracking a grin.

"I'll leave you to it," she said. "Is the shipment in the back?"

"Yup."

"Rebecca, I've some work to do. You're welcome to browse through the shop for your gifts, or if you'd rather you can look around town. I'll be at least an hour, probably longer."

One of the shoppers, a tall, thin woman, exquisitely dressed in a tan raincoat hanging open over a crisp navy pantsuit, coifed in soft, perfect waves of blond hair, exclaimed over a quilted wall hanging. It was one of my mother's. The forest in winter.

"You do what you have to do, Aileen. I can manage by myself."

She disappeared into the back, and I slid closer to the woman with the perfect hair as she called her companion over to have a look. They *oohed* and *aaahed* in unison. If the shop weren't so small that they likely saw me enter with Aileen and exchange greetings with Chrissie, I would have rushed forward to try (unsuccessfully) to snatch it out of their hands.

I wandered through town, in and out of a few shops. There were some that matched the quality of Aileen's. But nothing to better it. A newspaper rack standing at the entrance of a convenience store held the latest copy of the *Huntsville Forester*. A picture of Jennifer Taylor figured prominently, beside a smaller photo of the swamp, taken from some distance. HOPE RIVER MURDER, the headline proclaimed. I didn't bother to read the copy.

I let an hour and a half pass before returning to Cottage Art and Design. Aileen was in the front, carefully arranging her new purchases. The jewelry might be described as "creative" and "edgy." Much too heavy for my taste. Other than Aileen and Chrissie, the shop was empty. My mother's wall hanging was gone.

"I'll be about another half-hour, Rebecca," Aileen said in greeting. She held up a necklace in front of her face, turning it around and around, examining every angle. It was pewter, sort of representative of a wolf head thrown back against a vague forest background, howling at what was probably supposed to be the full moon. Perfectly hideous.

"No problem. Take all the time you need."

Ray's mother would have adored the duck's bottom, carved so delicately in glass and destroyed so senselessly by Jack Jackson. I avoided anything even remotely like it and selected a sun-catcher, one to join the profusion hanging over her kitchen window. No matter how many she owned, there would always be a place for one more. For the neighbor watering my plants and bringing in the mail I settled on a tiny painting, an original, in watercolor. A boathouse, gray with white trim, an antique wooden boat pulling in at sunset. For Jenny I selected a T-shirt with a picture of a giant mosquito, primed and ready for battle, above the slogan *Huntsville Fighter Squadron*. I pulled the wolf-howling necklace off the display rack. "This would be perfect for someone I know."

Aileen beamed at me. "I wasn't too sure about this artist. Her work is somewhat heavy, too arty, for most of the people who come in here. But if you like it, I'm sure the line will be a run-away success."

"It's different." No point in telling her I hated the stupid thing and was buying it for an incredibly efficient woman whose taste I wouldn't trust to judge tinned soup.

Chrissie wrapped my purchases in tissue paper and rang up the bill. Gifts for only three people. And one of them someone who worked for me. Ray had friends, Ray and I had friends, but once Ray's funeral was over and the suitable period of com-miseration came to an end, I had been left with no one.

Sampson and I had spent the last year in isolation. I went to work; we walked the beach or drove to Pacific Rim Park for long walks in the rainforest. She ate out of a can and I ate out of a microwaved cardboard box. We watched TV together or she snoozed while I worked on papers brought home from the office. Not much of a life. For neither dog nor woman. But then I wasn't looking to have a good time.

Chrissie handed me my packages with a warm smile. "Your friends will love these, I'm sure," she said. Without warning a tear slid down my cheek. "Are you all right? Can I do something? Shall I call Aileen?"

I shook my head. Her concern made it worse, and before I could stop it the tears were out of control. "I'll wait outside till Aileen's finished."

Of course she told Aileen. Jimmy's wife met me on the side-walk in front of the shop. "I'm finished here," she said. "Would you like to get a cup of tea, some pastries maybe? A much-deserved indulgence after a difficult few days?"

"No. Thank you. If you don't mind." I kept my head turned away from her. The tears were finished, and I furiously rubbed their traces off my face. But my nose still ran and my breathing was deep and uncontrolled.

"I don't mind. Thank you for buying your gifts in my store. That was kind of you."

"Not kind," I said, honestly. "You had the best selection."

"Time we're heading home, then. Shall I drive?"

"No. I'm fine. Besides, it's a rental car and the insurance is only good for me. But thank you anyway."

She slipped her arm through mine. "Thank you, Rebecca."

Chrissie stepped out onto the sidewalk to say goodbye. "See you on Friday, Aileen."

"Friday it is. I'll have lunch ready."

"If I don't see you again, Rebecca, have a safe trip home."

"Thank you."

A woman stopped to peer into the window. Frail, elderly, well dressed, every strand of silver hair sprayed into place. Liking what she saw, she came into the store. Chrissie grinned goodbye and followed the customer.

We reversed our mental positions on the way back to Hope River. Aileen put up a pretence of chattering happily while I huddled behind the steering wheel wallowing in my misery. I told her how lonely I'd been since Ray's death, and she muttered words of understanding. I popped *Bruce Springsteen's Greatest Hits* into the CD player, and before too much longer we were both swaying to "Dancing in the Dark." How can you not sway (and sing and tap feet and all that fun stuff) to "Dancing in the Dark"?

I dropped her off in front of the big house. "I'll wait here for a few minutes," I said, "to make sure everything is okay."

"But who will care for you, if everything is not okay with you?"

"I will," I said. "Check the house out and wave with your left hand if it's okay."

"Left hand?"

"Yeah. In case someone is holding you hostage and forcing you to wave. Then you can use your right arm and I'll know someone is there."

"You have seen way too many spy movies, Rebecca McKenzie. No one's hiding in the house. I'm well aware that no one's after me." She sighed. "I almost wish they were, then I could strike back. But I'll wave with my left hand if it will make you happy."

"It will."

She disappeared for several minutes, enough time to do more than a superficial inspection of the house. She wasn't as confident as she tried to make out. But soon, there she was at the door, waving enthusiastically with her left hand and smiling brightly.

Regardless of Jimmy's scorn, I resumed my post the next morning. Two a.m. on the dot. This time I was so tired the alarm had to really struggle to drag me out of bed. I considered throwing the clock across the room and rolling over, snuggling up against Sampson's warm furry body. But the thought of the overwhelming guilt if something bad actually did happen propelled me out of bed. Coffee was in the thermos, cheese sandwiches made and wrapped, and dog biscuits packed.

Except that I didn't stumble across an embarrassed officer taking a leak in the bushes, this night was a replay of the one before.

It was only 3:50 when, thermos empty and bladder full, I started up the engine of the SUV and coasted back to Dad's house. The lights of the big house might have winked off and on for a moment, but if they did it scarcely registered in my weary brain.

Thursday and Friday were to be my last full days in Hope River, so Thursday morning I forced myself out of bed at the crack of dawn. Sampson tossed me the evil eye at the early hour.

Dad seemed to be particularly cheerful that morning. I threw bacon into the frying pan, bread into the toaster, and eggs into a bowl for scrambling.

"Starting Monday morning, Maggie Kzenic will come in around nine. Fix yourself some cereal when you get up, and then Maggie will get you a nice hot breakfast when she arrives. That sound good to you?"

"Waste of money. Any fool can cook up a bit of bacon and eggs."

"Humor me, Dad. I'll feel better knowing that you're looked after."

"For you, then."

I kissed the top of his head. His hair was still thick, the envy of men a third his age, but slick with oil; loose flakes of white skin blended into the gray strands. "Thank you. Any plans for today?"

"Thought I'd get some work done out in the shed till lunch, then go on up to the Legion. You're still leaving on Saturday?"

"Yes. I have to get back to work."

"Then we should have a family dinner on Friday night. Shirley and Al, Liz and Jackie and the kids. Jim and Aileen."

"That's a good idea. I'll call them all this morning."

Dad finished his breakfast and tottered out to the shed. He was so old.

After doing up the dishes I made the duty phone calls. Al answered the phone instead of Shirley, who, he said, had already left for work, sparing me from having to deal with my prickly sister. He accepted the invitation, with pleasure. I mentioned that Maggie had been hired as housekeeper, and asked him to tell Shirley that we could talk about the details tomorrow. No one was home at Liz's house, so I left a message. Jackie responded with enthusiasm. "That'll be great, Aunt Rebecca. I was going to phone you later anyway. Tomorrow's a day off school for Jason. I've taken the time off work to be at home with him, and made myself an appointment at the dentist in North Ridge as well. Now Jason's sulking about having to hang around at the dentist's office, so I was going to ask Grandpa if Jason could come over for a few hours. He likes helping out with the woodworking, and Grandpa loves teaching him. Will you ask him for me?"

"Sure. But if it isn't fine with Dad, I'll be happy to look after Jason."

"I'll bring him by around noon, okay?"

"We'll be here."

Another family dinner to prepare. My minuscule repertoire was exhausted. Imagine the reaction if I phoned Hope River's only restaurant and asked them to deliver dinner for thirteen tomorrow night. Thirteen! I wasn't worried about the traditionally unlucky number, merely the frightening quantity of people to feed.

I needed to make another trip into town. I popped out to the woodshed to tell Dad that I was going out.

He was sitting in a chair beside Mom's sewing table, twisting a scrap of blue fabric in his hand. His eyes were dark and sad.

I knelt beside him and touched the cloth: a pale cobalt background with a pattern of cheerful yellow flowers. "That's pretty. Mom did good work."

"She was a good woman, your mother. She deserved more than I could give her, Becky."

He released the fabric and I ran it through my fingers. Tiny magenta butterflies fluttered above the flowers.

"The day she and your sister got off the train from Toronto was the happiest day of my entire life. Even better than our wedding and honeymoon. We spent the night in Toronto at the house of an army buddy of mine. His family was well off and they were real kind to us. They had a woman come in specially to look after the baby, so Janet and I could have some time alone. Wasn't that nice?"

"It was."

"I was so happy, and so proud. My wife and my daughter were with me at last, at the start of our life together."

"It must have been wonderful."

"The next morning we took the train north. I was bringing my family home. I loved Janet so much, and I was so proud."

I wanted to excuse myself and escape back to the kitchen. And then drive as far as the rented SUV could go. I knew how the story ended, but of course it was impossible to say so.

"The feeling lasted most of the way. The baby was excited, looking out the window, watching the world go by. But then we got close to Hope River and this terrible feeling of dread came over me, like a fist clutching my heart. Worse than anything I'd felt before, even when we were under fire in France. Because I saw Hope River through Janet's eyes. And I was afraid. She'd loved the big house in Toronto, with a fancy car out front and a nanny for the baby. For the first time, I realized that she was expecting me to give her all of that. Instead I brought her here. And I simply couldn't bear the thought of the disappointment I'd become to her. She should have stayed in England."

"Don't, Dad. Don't torment yourself." Of course she hated it. She would have run back to England if not for her pride and the fact that there was no one to run back to. "Every war bride probably thought she was marrying a rich Canadian with an enormous cattle ranch. Like people today think they're going to win the lottery. But when they don't, they get on with it. And Mom did too. Besides, it couldn't have been so bad." I touched his cheek, the scrap of fabric still in my hand. The contrast between his aged, bleached, agonized face and the brilliant flowers and butterflies was heartbreaking. "She stayed."

"Yes, that's true." He clasped my hand in his own. The skin was rough from a lifetime of hard work followed by a retirement spent woodworking.

"Jackie wants to drop Jason over tomorrow afternoon. She said he likes helping you in the workshop."

Dad hadn't cried, but his eyes were moist. They brightened at the thought of his great-grandson and their shared interest in bringing life and movement out of wood.

"I'm teaching him to work in the shed. Toys and small things first. When he's older and more experienced, I'll start him on furniture."

I stood up. "I'm going into town to get things for dinner tomorrow. Everyone's coming. Do you want anything special?"

"A roast would be nice. Janet always did a great roast."

That was an idea. How hard could a roast be?

Dad happy again, I called Sampson and headed into town. One thing I now knew for certain: There was no way I could ever let Dad read the diaries.

Entering the store, I glanced over the racks of newspapers Nothing about Jennifer Taylor today.

Following Dad's suggestion, I bought a roast of beef, some lovely new red potatoes and two bunches of asparagus. I'd pull something out of Mom's freezer for dessert. I remembered a nice appetizer Ray made for friends once: avocado filled with shrimp. That would be easy to make. The asparagus and the avocado cost approximately as much as if they were stuffed with gold, and not knowing anything about cuts of meat, I decided that the most expensive was probably the best. An image of the shock on my mother's face at the expense had me grinning all the way up the aisle.

Kimmy Wright stood behind the checkout. "I'm so glad you've come in, Becky. I was thinking about you last night and wondering when you're going back to Vancouver."

"Saturday."

"So soon." She looked disappointed. "We've hardly had any time to visit. Are you free tomorrow night, maybe we could do something fun? A girls' night out?"

"My family are all coming for dinner. Sorry."

"Oh." Her podgy face collapsed into lines of disappointment. Her foundation had been applied badly, so that it pooled in the wrinkles on her skin and the crevices around her prominent nose. About an inch of black and gray roots showed at her scalp. My conscience pricked.

"How about lunch tomorrow then? At my place? I'll be busy getting ready for my company, but I can stop to make us lunch."

Her smile took twenty years off her face. "That would be great. I usually only get half an hour for lunch, but I'm sure I could get an hour off, seeing as it's such a special occasion. I take lunch at one."

"See you tomorrow then." On the way back to the car, I gave my feelings a thorough analysis. To my surprise, I wasn't all too annoyed at the idea of having Kimmy Wright to lunch. Maybe it would be fun to talk about the old days.

Dad left for the Legion after lunch, and I settled in to spend the afternoon on the computer, either dialed into work or searching for instructions on how to prepare roast beef and vegetables.

Dad's car pulled up as night began to wind itself through the woods. I stretched and got up to switch on the outdoor lights. My brother-in-law, Al, climbed out of the driver's seat and went around to the passenger door. With great care, he helped Dad out.

I opened the door, not yet alarmed, assuming that he had had too much to drink on a pleasant afternoon and evening with the "boys."

Then I saw my father's face.

Chapter 43

The Diary of Janet McKenzie. August 5, 1973

The most wonderful thing has happened. Well not wonderful, I mustn't be TOO happy. But my Aunt Joan, Dad and Aunt Betty's sister, has died. And left a rather substantial amount to me that the letter from her lawyer says was Aunt Betty's originally, what she put into their holiday home and left to Aunt Joan when she died. Good thing that Mrs. M.'s hip is bothering her this morning so she wasn't down at the letterbox the minute the mailman arrived, as she usually is. Instead I went down and there it was. A lovely official-looking envelope all the way from England. As soon as I read it I opened my mouth to tell Mrs. M. But I shut it again, pretty quick. What business is it of theirs that I have come into a bit of money? None at all.

August 6, 1973

I lay awake practically the whole night. While Bob snored on in the bed beside mine. Wondering what to do with my money. Oh, that it were twenty years ago, and I could go back to England in style. Leave this horrid place forever. But then I wouldn't have my pride and joy, my Rebecca.

Regardless, it is not 1953. And there is nothing in England for me. Not even Aunt Joan. So after a long and restless night I have decided to be practical and careful and spend the money wisely. But first, I will take a tiny bit of it for myself. It would be nice to have a real sewing room again, like I had before Rebecca was born and

Jim needed his own room. I can buy some new equipment and the best of fabrics. My quilts don't make any money, I sell them for nothing more than the cost of the material; it's the making of them that gives me such pleasure. If Bob and his father ask me how I can afford such things (like they would denigrate themselves to notice a woman's sewing) I can tell them that I have made a bit of money from the quilts.

But most of it I will put away for Rebecca's education. She is doing so well at school. The teachers tell me that she should go on to university. Until yesterday I worried that we could not afford it. But now we—I—can.

Chapter 44

"Al, what's happened? Is he okay?"

Al half-carried Dad into the house and over to the couch.

"What's happened? Is it his heart? Should I call a doctor?"

Dad's mouth twisted in pain and he was actually crying. Silent tears ran unchecked through the hills and valleys of his wrinkled face, as rumpled as an unmade bed.

"Do you want Becky to call the doctor, Bob?" Al asked. No response. He repeated the question, louder.

"Of course I'm calling the doctor, Al. I'll call an ambulance. He needs to get to the hospital."

"No," Dad whispered. "I'll be okay."

"I hardly think so," I said, moving to the phone.

Al grabbed my arm. "It's not his heart, Becky. Something happened."

"What? Tell me for heaven's sake."

Al still held my arm. "Let's make Bob some tea. We'll be right back, Bob. You wait there." He pulled me into the kitchen.

I wrenched my arm free and whirled around to face him. "What on earth is going on here?"

"He was," Al stumbled for the word, "accosted. In town."

"What! You mean he was mugged? Call the police then."

"Listen to me, Rebecca, please. He wasn't mugged. Some men in the bar started saying things about Jim. About him killing that Taylor girl."

"Oh, no." I sunk into a chair. "What was he doing in that bar anyway? He told me he was going to the Legion."

Al filled the kettle. "Apparently one of the old guys from the Legion suggested they all move on to the bar. They had a few drinks and some men came in, recognized Bob as Jim's father and started tearing into him. I wasn't there, Becky. I don't really know how it all happened. Fortunately a friend of mine, Lance DeLong, was behind the bar. He called me and said I'd better come over. Fast. So I did."

"Poor Dad."

"A couple of Bob's old buddies tried to throw a few punches."

"Good God."

"Gutsy old men. All set to fight for their friend against guys fifty years younger and a whole lot meaner than them."

The kettle whistled. Al poured sugar straight from the dispenser into a mug. No counting out teaspoons.

"Where's the tea?"

I pointed to the appropriate canister. "Did Lance say who these troublemakers were?"

"Yeah. I know them. Everyone knows them."

"Jack Jackson and his pal Pete, I assume."

"No. Not this time. We'd better not leave Bob alone any longer. I'll take the tea out. Can you find a blanket or something?"

"What's the matter with him? Did he get hit?"

"No, Becky. He's in shock. The old guys told me some of what was said before Lance stopped it. Mean stuff."

"What sort of stuff?"

"That Jim's a child killer. Rapist. What the men of this town plan to do if they get their hands on him. We can talk more later. Get the blanket, eh?"

We returned to the living room. Dad huddled on the couch, scratching Sampson's head. Al handed him the mug of tea.

He looked up and smiled weakly. The agony was gone from his face. "Any more of that cake, Janet?"

"No. It's finished," I said.

"It was good. Like your mother used to make back in England, I'll bet."

"Yes." I looked at Al. His face was almost as pained as Dad's had been moments earlier.

"When Little Jim comes in we need to have a talk with him." Dad sipped his tea. "That McCarran fellow came around today, yelling at me to keep Jim away from his Judy. Girl's no better than she should be, anyone can tell that just by looking at her. But there's no need for Jim to get mixed up with trash like that, is there?"

"No."

"Would you like to go for a lie down, Bob?" Al asked.

Dad frowned, his eyes flashed with anger, extinguished so fast I might have imagined it. "I'll fix it when I have the time. I said I would. I've had a hard day at work. I'll do it on Saturday." He looked at Al very strangely, and tried to hunch his shoulders around himself. He rubbed his hands together.

"Oh, God," I said. "He thinks you're his father."

"Time for bed, Bob." Al took the mug from Dad's hand and helped him to his feet.

"But we haven't had dinner yet. Janet? Is dinner ready?"

"Nap first." My stomach churned like a washing machine set to agitate. I swallowed and thought about not throwing up.

Al looked at me, his eyes pleading. I took my father's arm and led him down the hall to his bedroom. Sampson wanted to follow, but I pushed her back with my foot. Dad sat on the edge of the bed and allowed me to pull off his shoes and socks. His toenails were cracked, yellow and badly overgrown, curling around the front edge of the toes. Without prompting he lay flat on the bed, and I pulled the blanket up from where it lay crumpled on the floor and tucked it around him.

"Comfy?"

"I don't feel too well, Janet. I'd like a nap before dinner."

"You do that."

"If Dad asks again, tell him I'll fix the fence on Saturday."

"I'll tell him."

"You have to have a talk with that boy of yours. He can't keep making trouble. People are starting to talk."

I switched off the light and left the door open a crack. Only then did I register what he'd said. *That boy of yours.* Did that mean anything? Or was it merely something to say, the way parents joke that it's "your child" when the little one acts up?

Al was in the kitchen, tossing back a beer.

"Thanks, Al."

"No thanks necessary. What sort of loudmouthed jerks go after an old man and his war buddies?"

"It's good you were there."

"Think I should tell Shirley?"

"Probably not. Nothing she can do, except get upset."

"You're right. And it wouldn't be a great idea to say anything to Jim. He'd be out looking for those guys before I turned around."

I got myself a beer. I rarely drink beer, but right now I needed something stronger than tea. "I'm supposed to go home on Saturday. I've already stayed longer than I planned. But I don't know how I can."

"You can't stay here forever. Who knows how long this thing will go on. Maybe they'll never catch the bastard who killed Jennifer, and Jim'll have to live the rest of his life under suspicion." He finished his beer in one quick swallow. "We're going to Lizzie's for supper and Shirley will be wondering what's going on if I'm late."

I walked him to the door. "You're still coming for dinner tomorrow?"

"Sure. Look, don't worry too much about your dad. It won't happen again. I'm guessing those guys got a real surprise when Bob's friends stood up to them and then Lance sent them packing. Bullies need to think they're impressing people. Now they'll know folks won't put up with it."

I smiled, not believing a word. The next time, they would make sure that no one else was around, that's all. "You're right. Good night, Al."

"Night, Becky. See you tomorrow."

Dad slept the night through, not waking for dinner. I abandoned my two a.m. surveillance, worried that Dad would wake up, confused and disoriented. I couldn't be everywhere, watching everyone. And by the day after tomorrow I would be watching no one.

I simply didn't know what to do. My job was not in peril if I stayed on a bit longer. I worked for a good company, with progressive ideas about family responsibility. But there was a limit; not even my bank would keep me on the payroll forever. And Al was right—it might well be forever before this mess was resolved.

I let Sampson out the back and stood in the doorway listening to her crashing about in the undergrowth.

～～～

Dad got up early Friday morning. The banging of cupboard drawers and slamming of the fridge woke me. Sampson bounded out to greet him, and I stumbled after, having done nothing more to get ready for the day than drag a comb through my hair and pull on a tracksuit. Out the kitchen window, facing east, the horizon was beginning to lighten in vicious streaks of pink and purple. *Red skies in morning, sailors take warning.* Does pink count as red?

Dad looked perfectly normal as he set about filling the coffee pot and pouring cereal. He'd washed, dressed, and shaved. Yesterday's trauma forgotten.

"You're up early, Dad."

"Lots to do. My great-grandson's coming this afternoon. My whole family coming for dinner. Your last day. An exciting day."

I got myself a bowl. Neither of us realized how prophetic his comment would prove to be.

Chapter 45

Sampson needed a walk; I needed to get some work done in preparation for the meetings that Jenny had scheduled for me all day Monday.

We walked up the road to the big house. Last night I counted glassware, dishes, and cutlery, enough for thirteen. It wouldn't matter that they were all wildly mismatched. But I needed to ask Aileen to bring some serving dishes. We took our time. Sampson sniffed under every log and peed on every bush. The sun had risen, a faint yellow blob against a blaze of pink and purple. But in the west the sky over the lake was heavily overcast. High overhead, angry, menacing clouds were moving fast.

Sampson's entire body shivered as she caught sight of a black squirrel, nosing about in winter debris piled under a crooked, half-dead red pine. She crouched low to the ground, ears pointing straight up, haunches twitching. Too spoiled to have the patience required by the hunt, she broke into a run accompanied by full-throated barking when still a full twenty yards from the tree. The squirrel disappeared into the spindly foliage. The canopy of the branches shook as the bushy-tailed animal leapt from one tree to the next.

"It's long gone, you stilly lug," I said. "Good thing your dinner comes out of a can, eh? You wouldn't last long out here."

Sampson's response was cut off by an abrupt shift of her attention. A car was coming up the drive. A police car. Two police cars.

My heart lightened and I set off at a trot, whistling for the dog to follow. Ever the optimist, I believed that this could only be good news. They'd come to tell Jimmy and Aileen that the murderer had been captured and that the watch on their house would come to an end. Life would get back to normal, and I could go home, my mind at rest. Great.

Jimmy and Aileen stood on the porch watching as the officers got out of their cars. Two uniformed men, a man in plainclothes, and a woman dressed in a severe brown business suit mounted the steps. Bob Reynolds, two of his lackeys, and a woman I hadn't seen before.

Aileen's face told the story. This was no goodwill visit. The woman in the brown suit was talking, her voice deep and low. She was exceptionally tall, not much short of six feet, and slightly built. I climbed the steps. Sampson sniffed at Constable LeBlanc's leg. She recognized him; he'd been welcomed into our house. He was, therefore, a friend.

The woman turned to face me. She was over forty, the delicate skin at the corner of her eyes was deeply wrinkled, but her heavy hair, tucked back into a businesslike bun, looked to be a natural ash blond only lightly dusted with gray. She wore an expensive, but most unattractive brown wool pantsuit matched with a plain white blouse, practical earth-colored shoes, and tiny gold earrings.

"I'm sorry, ma'am," she said, her icy blue eyes looking directly into mine. "But this is police business. If you could please excuse us?"

"This is my sister, Rebecca McKenzie," Jimmy said. "I'd like her to stay."

"Very well. But control your dog, please."

Said dog was encouraging Dave LeBlanc to play with her. A touch of color rose up his neck and into his cheeks as he tried to ignore all the unwelcome canine attention.

The woman returned to the subject at hand. She looked at my brother. "If you will come with us please, sir."

"No," Aileen yelled. "You've made a mistake. You can't be serious. I won't let you."

"Please, Aileen," Reynolds said, "you're not helping matters."

"I'm not trying to help," she screeched, her eyes wild, primitive with fear. "I want you to stop this."

"Aileen." Jimmy voice was strong, hard. "Stop it."

She quieted.

"Go inside and call Mr. Singh. Or give the number to Rebecca and let her make the call. Tell him what's happened and ask him to meet me at the police station. Do you understand?"

She said nothing. The officers shifted.

"Do you understand, Aileen?"

"Yes."

"I'll help."

Jimmy sighed heavily. "Thanks, Becky."

I took Aileen by the arm and led her toward the house. She stumbled after me, her legs hardly moving, without conscious thought, simply following my lead. Behind us, handcuffs snapped on my brother's wrists. Fortunately the sound didn't appear to register in Aileen's fuddled brain. It was all so terribly civilized and peaceful that Sampson detected nothing amiss. She wagged her tail good-bye to the visitors and happily followed us into the house.

Aileen collapsed onto the couch, and I found the brandy bottle.

"Where's the lawyer's number?"

She accepted the glass I offered her. "In the kitchen, on the board by the phone."

"You sit there. I'll be right back."

They'd maintained the character of the old kitchen, but accented it with modern cabinetry, solid granite countertops, and ceramic floor tiles. The fireplace in the corner had been used recently—the ash was fluffy, the scent of wood smoke still lingered in the air. An eclectic mixture of fashion and political magazines covered the scarred wooden table. It was a room that I'd be happy to settle into any time, but not today. The scrap of paper with Alex Singh's phone number scrawled in my handwriting was pinned to a corkboard covered with phone messages, postcards, photographs, and reminders.

Fortunately Alex was in and his secretary put me straight through. In a few short words I told him that Jimmy'd been arrested and taken away a few minutes ago.

"Do you know who the officers were who arrested him?"

"Bob Reynolds, from North Ridge. But the woman with them seemed to be the one in charge. Middle aged, very tall, thin, blond hair, hideous suit."

"The formidable Inspector Eriksson. She's tough, but fair. I'll head down there right now. But before I go, can you tell me what grounds Eriksson gave for the arrest?"

"Didn't hear a word of it. I only got here as they were taking him away. But his wife is here, she was with him when they arrived."

He asked me to find out from Aileen what I could and gave me his cell phone number before hanging up.

Aileen was curled up on the couch with her legs tucked under her bottom like a six-year-old girl straight out of the bath, watching TV before bed. Sampson had climbed up beside her and Aileen absent-mindedly scratched the dog's head. She looked quite guilty, caught on forbidden furniture, and moved to jump off. I pressed her rump back down. She was needed right where she was.

"Aileen, did the police tell Jimmy why they were arresting him?"

She looked at me. "For murdering Jennifer Taylor. But he didn't do it."

"I know that, dear. But why did they come for him now? Why not the other night when he was at the station?"

She peered deeply into her glass for a few moments, looking to find secrets buried within the golden brandy. She discovered nothing and with an enormous sigh touched her lips to the rim.

"Mr. Singh is on his way to the police station. He would like to know what they said to Jimmy. So he can think about it on the way."

"They found hair in his truck."

"Hair? Are you sure?"

She shrugged. Her eyes drooped. She was shutting down. only her fingers moved in the dog's long fur.

"Are you sure that's what they said, Aileen?"

She nodded. "Jennifer's hair, in the truck."

"So, Jimmy told us himself that she's been in the truck plenty of times, which is completely natural as she worked with him. There'd be nothing unusual about finding some of her hair. Would there?"

"A clump of hair, they said, with blood on it."

"Blood. The paper said that she was strangled, so there wouldn't be any blood. Would there?"

"She'd been beaten up, they said, her lip split open and one tooth knocked out and clumps of hair pulled right out of the scalp."

"Oh God." These were things I didn't want to know. I struggled to push the image out of my mind. That pretty girl, the perfect teeth knocked loose, the lovely long hair pulled out by its roots. Beaten and strangled and dumped in the swamp.

"Jim cleaned the truck the other night. After she disappeared. But they said that he missed some, 'cause they found the hair under the seat, pushed under the mat."

A cold hand clutched my heart. "Aileen, what are you saying? Do you know why he cleaned the truck?"

"No."

"Well, then, he didn't 'miss' anything. He cleaned his truck. People do it all the time. I've even been known to clean my own car once a year or so. Somehow that hair got into the truck after Jimmy cleaned it."

She put her glass down on the table.

"I have to get back to Singh. Do you want anything?"

"I'd like to have a little lie down, if you don't mind?"

"Of course I don't mind. You go and have a nap; I'll call Singh and then make some tea and bring it in to you. Why don't you take Sampson with you?"

"That would be nice," she said, her voice dull, flat. As drained of emotion as her eyes.

"Can I call your doctor?"

"I'm not sick."

Taking a gentle hold of her elbow, I guided Aileen to her feet and down the hall, gesturing to Sampson to follow.

Aileen settled into the king-sized bed under an exquisite blue and green handmade quilt. Sampson curled around her hip.

After calling Alex Singh and telling him what I had learned, I dug through the contents of the phone table looking for an address book. I found one, chock-a-block with names, addresses, phone numbers, and e-mail addresses. I leafed through every page, reading every line, but nothing jumped out as offering information on the therapist that Jimmy told me Aileen saw occasionally. There was no entry for *Dr. Smith—Aileen's Psychiatrist*. Presumably the shrink was listed by name only. Even if I did manage to locate the number, I wondered if it might be unethical for me to call without Aileen's approval? Not that I much cared if it was. She could be as angry with me as she wanted, but first she needed help.

But that was a moot point considering that I couldn't find the number.

I'd told Singh to contact me as soon as he had any news and made sure that he knew I was good for the bail money. He reminded me, gently, that there wouldn't be any bail on a murder charge.

Tea made, I carried it through to the bedroom. Aileen was sound asleep, snoring lightly, her arm wrapped around Sampson's comforting bulk. Seeing me, the dog eased out from under the woman almost as if she knew not to wake her.

We tiptoed away.

Nothing would do but that I had to stay at least until Aileen woke up. I called the little house to tell Dad that I'd been invited to breakfast, then I searched through the cupboards for cereal, toast, and jam and put the coffee pot on.

I sat at the cozy breakfast nook by the cold fireplace and flipped idly through the magazines. My fingers turned the stiff pages and my eyes noticed the delectable food and gorgeous gardens and a beach party that in my normal life I'd kill to attend. But my mind was traveling the road with Alex Singh and sitting in jail beside my only brother. *Please, Aileen don't fall apart now. Jimmy needs you.* The magazine sailed across the room propelled by the blaze of my anger. Jimmy had worked hard, so hard, to crawl out from under the all-encompassing shadow of his bullying, misogynist, fascist grandfather. He'd thrown off his past to a degree that many people, me most of all, wouldn't have believed possible.

And now this? Wherever he was, the hateful old man would surely be laughing. *You're in more trouble now, boy, tied to your woman's apron strings, than ever you were listening to your old man.*

But Jimmy had a great lawyer; the best that money could buy (up here in the back-of-beyond at any rate). And that great lawyer was on his way right now, a knight in shining BMW. I was confident of my brother's innocence and confident of Singh's abilities. But the names Morin, Marshall, Millgard tiptoed around and around the outskirts of my brain. Innocent Canadian men, all of them, convicted of murders they were later proved not to have committed. In David Millgard's case, after he spent more than twenty years in prison.

And how on earth would I ever tell Dad? This would kill him.

True to the promise of the morning skies, a full-blown storm hit the house, the perfect accompaniment to my gloomy thoughts. Rain lashed against the windows and wind shook the trees outside. The old house moaned and quivered but stood fast on its foundations as it had for so many years and through storms much worse than this one.

⸻

"Rebecca?" Aileen stood in the doorway, her face puffy with sleep, her long hair tumbling around her head like a living thing possessed of a mind all its own. But intelligence and unwilling awareness were back in her dark eyes. Where they belonged for better or for worse. "If you're here then it wasn't all a bad dream."

The coffee was finished, the toast long gone cold, most of the magazines glanced at, if not actually read. "Afraid not. Come sit down. I'll put on another pot of coffee. Would you like some toast? This jam is amazing. Did you make it?"

She shook her head and tried to tuck a strand of hair behind her ear. With as much success as if she were pushing a wave back out to the lake. "No. I get it from a woman who lives in South River and sell it in the shop. It is wonderful, isn't it?"

I took that as acceptance of my offer and started another pot of coffee before popping rye bread into the toaster and laying a second place at the table.

"Did you call that lawyer?"

"Yes. Fortunately he was in the office and he headed to the police station right away."

"Have you heard anything?"

"No."

"When do you think he'll call?"

"No idea. You look better than you did earlier. Are you going to be okay?"

She smiled, not much of a smile, but a smile nonetheless. "Am I going to have a breakdown, you mean? Not yet. I'll wait until Jim is released, then I'll have a proper collapse. Thank you for staying, Rebecca, but I'll be all right now. You'd better get back to Bob's house. He'll be wondering where his lunch is."

I glanced at the clock hanging beside the phone; a bare clock-face mounted on a white wooden panel with black numbers tumbling down the wall. Clever, but hard to read. It was approaching half-past noon.

"I'll pop down to the house, get Dad fed. You can have dinner with us and spend the night at Dad's. I'll make up some story for him."

She shook her head and spread strawberry jam generously over her toast. "No. I have to stay here in case the phone rings."

"I gave Singh my cell number. He'll call me if there's no answer here."

"I'd rather be in my home, Rebecca. They'll release him as soon as they understand what a terrible mistake they've made and he might come straight home without calling."

If Jimmy arrived home and Aileen wasn't here, he would simply turn back down the hill and go to the little house. But he wouldn't be coming home any time soon. The OPP don't make an arrest in a celebrated murder case on a whim. Aileen probably knew that as well as anyone. But if she wouldn't think it, I wouldn't say it.

"If you want. But I'll be up after dinner to check on you whether you want me or not."

Her smile held and even touched her eyes. "Thank you."

I hesitated. "You might want to be careful about answering the phone. News spreads fast, and some people might, well, they might not be calling with words of sympathy."

"Understood."

"Call me if you need me. I put my cell number up there on the board. Do you want Sampson to stay? She's good company."

"That would be wonderful. If you're sure you don't mind?"

"Not at all. But don't forget to let her out occasionally. And if it keeps raining, you'd better have a good towel at hand when she comes in or your floors will be a mess. I'll bring some dog food when I come back."

Aileen saw me to the door. I told Sampson to stay and walked down the hill with a heavy heart.

A whirlwind greeted me when I opened the front door. "Hi, Aunt Rebecca. Where's Sampson?"

Jason. I'd forgotten all about Jason coming to spend the afternoon with Dad. And now that I was reminded of that, I also remembered that in a few hours my whole family would be arriving for dinner. Won't that be a pleasant little gathering?

"She's up at your Aunt Aileen's place. They were getting on so well, I told her she could stay."

"Can we go get her?"

"Maybe after lunch. Where's Great-Granddad?"

"In the shed. I came in to use the bathroom. We're making rocking horses. Granddad lets me cut the wood on the big saw."

"Are you careful?"

He looked terribly serious at the question, his brow furrowed, his eyes intense. "First thing Grandpa taught me was all the safety rules. Besides, he always stands right there watching me."

"That's good then. Go tell him I'm back and we'll have lunch soon."

Jason disappeared in a burst of tousled curls, mud-encrusted jeans, and giant running shoes. He really was a dear. I'd missed out on a lot when I turned my back on this family.

I checked that my cell phone was turned on and fully charged and that the house phone had a dial tone. All of which reminded me of when I was a teenager and would wait anxiously by the phone for some boy to call. (Whomever I might have been thinking of, he never did.)

The last thing in the world I felt like doing was making lunch. And I didn't know what I could possibly say to Dad. I'd have to say something. He'd hear the news sooner or later. Obviously it would be better coming from me than a phone call from one of his Legion buddies. Or someone less inclined to be friendly.

I heated a can of chicken noodle soup and slapped cheese between slices of white bread for grilling.

Dad and Jason stumbled through the back door, laughing at some private joke. Dad rubbed his great-grandson's head. "Come out and see what good work the boy's done, Becky. A chip off the old block this one."

I smiled; my dry lips cracked with the effort. "Dad. I have to tell you something."

"Grilled cheese, my favorite." Jason slid into a seat at the kitchen table.

I chickened out. "I'll see it after lunch."

"Then can we go up and get Sampson?"

"I'll have to think about that. Your aunt Aileen isn't feeling too well and she might be having a nap."

"Then Sampson will be bored and happy to see us," Jason said, making perfectly good sense.

"Lunch first." I flipped the hot, gooey sandwiches out of the pan and onto plates.

"Car coming," Dad said. "You expecting someone, Becky?"

"No." I tripped over my own feet in a rush to get to the front door, prepared to repel invaders. I was surprised that no one had shown up before this, that the phone hadn't rung while I prepared lunch. The Hope River grapevine must be down for annual maintenance.

It was an old car, small and liberally caked with the mud of the back roads. Kimmy Wright climbed out. I'd completely forgotten that I'd invited her for lunch.

She dashed to the steps, holding her raincoat up over her head to give her some shelter against the driving rain.

Kimmy smiled brightly when I opened the door. Raindrops splashed around her feet as she shook the moisture off her coat. "Gosh, what a miserable day. Everyone's so glum in the store, it's a treat to get away for a nice lunch."

Not knowing how to get rid of her, I stepped back and let her in.

Jason wandered out of the kitchen, half a toasted sandwich in his hand. "Hi, Mrs. Michaels. How ya doing?"

"Fine thank you, young Jason. You visiting your grandpa?"

"Yup."

While they were talking, Kimmy pulled off her shoes and walked into the living room. It was past the time I could politely suggest that she leave.

She marched into the kitchen with that small town air of breezy familiarity in any friend's home. My mother's friends always headed straight for the kitchen, and if she was busy they would put the kettle on, set out teacups, and rummage through the fridge for milk without a second thought. Kimmy greeted Dad with a warm smile and pulled up a chair.

"I do apologize, Kimmy," I said. "But I was up at my brother's house all morning, and lunch isn't ready." I looked at her face, searching for a smirk, a sign that she knew why I'd been at Jimmy's.

Instead, she smiled and said, "Don't worry yourself. Jason seems to like that soup. That'll be perfectly fine for me too."

Another can came out of the cupboard.

"Time to get back to work, young man." Dad tossed back the last of his sandwich and stood up. "Nice seeing you, Kimberly."

"I'm sorry for your loss, Mr. McKenzie. Mrs. McKenzie was a nice woman."

"Thank you. Come on, Jason. Wood's calling."

I busied my hands collecting sandwich ingredients. "Any gossip in town today?"

"Nothing out of the ordinary. Linda Jones is expecting her fourth. You won't know the Jones family though. They aren't from around here."

"Do you have any children, Kimmy?"

"Two. Clint and Samantha. Samantha moved to Toronto soon as she finished school, but Clint's still around."

"That's nice."

She dug through her purse and pulled out a pair of photos. An acne-scarred boy with long, shapeless, greasy hair, and a sullen expression, and a girl as beautiful as the Kimmy I remembered.

"Your daughter's lovely."

"Thank you."

"What does she do, in Toronto?"

"She wants to be a model, but it's tough, you know? Right now she's waitressing, waiting for that big break."

"I hope she finds it."

"Thanks." After a fond glance, she tucked the pictures back into her purse, and I served up chicken noodle soup and grilled cheese sandwiches.

Kimmy chatted happily through the meal, commiserating with the Taylor family, then offering news about people we had gone to high school with that I hadn't spared a thought for in thirty years. I waited for my cell phone to ring. Why hadn't Singh called me by now? How was Aileen doing? Should I go home tomorrow or not?

The rain beat steadily against the kitchen windows. Out in the woods, a tree groaned under the force of the wind.

"April showers bring May flowers," Kimmy recited, putting on a childish singsong voice.

The back door flew open on a gust of wind and blew Jason in like flotsam in the storm. "Gotta go to the bathroom."

"I'd better be getting back," Kimmy said with a world-weary sigh. "It was fun talking to you. Can't sit here all day, much as I'd like to."

"I'm afraid that I wasn't terribly good company, Kimmy. I am sorry, but I have things on my mind." I walked her to the door.

"Don't you worry." She bent over to tie her shoes and groaned with the effort. "I understand. I'll be absolutely devastated when it comes time to bury my mom. When Frank died, I woulda died right after him, if it hadn't been for Mom reminding me that I had Clint and Samantha to worry about."

"Frank?" I said weakly. God, how shallow can I get? I hadn't even thought to ask about her children's father.

"My husband, Frank? You remember Frank Michaels from school? He was ice fishing with some of the guys, round about this time of year it was, far too late for them to be out on the ice, but it was a late spring and they'd had too much to drink. They fell in. Frank drowned. Him and Kevin Schneider. Alain Deon lost three fingers to frostbite."

"Gosh, I'm sorry, Kimmy."

"It was a long time ago. The kids were babies. I'm only telling you 'cause if it weren't for my mom, I wouldn't have survived."

I opened the front door, Jason returned from the bathroom asking if he could have a cookie, and Sampson ran down the hill. Jason gave a cry of glee and ran out to greet the dog, heedless of the rain. She was filthy, the long hairs under her belly coated in mud, her feet soaking wet. She barked as she ran, her voice tinged with a panic I'd never heard from her before.

"Jason. Stop," I yelled at the boy.

He skidded to a halt on the steps of the porch and looked from Sampson to me, confusion written all over his freckled face. "Is she okay?"

"No."

Sampson turned and ran a few steps back in the direction from which she'd come. Back toward the big house. She looked over her shoulder to see if I was following. I wasn't. She barked and ran another few yards.

"Something's wrong with Aileen." I flew down the steps. Now that I was coming, Sampson took off, heading back up the hill at full speed.

I splashed through newly formed puddles and over lichen-covered ancient rocks, scarcely noticing that my feet were wearing only socks. Kimmy and Jason followed behind me, and I didn't have the presence of mind to turn and tell them to go back.

That was an oversight I would regret bitterly in the hours to come.

The door was locked and the curtains on the windows were drawn. I knocked lightly on the door and whispered, "Aileen, it's Rebecca. Let me in."

The house was quiet; the only sounds rain pounding on the roof, wind crawling underneath the wide front porch, waves lapping at the rocks lining the shore of the lake, and Sampson scratching at the door with a nervous high-pitched whine.

I knocked again. Louder this time.

No answer.

Something was wrong. I had no idea what, but I wasn't about to walk away just because she didn't open the door.

"I'm coming in, Aileen," I yelled. "Hold on, I'll be right there. Stand back from the window." I picked up a small side-table, left outside with the promise of spring's arrival, and prepared to heave it through the living room window. But that wasn't necessary. The door creaked open and Aileen stood there. Her face so pale she might well have risen from the dead in order to prevent me from breaking her big bay window.

"I'm perfectly fine, Rebecca. Please stop interfering and go away." She didn't open the door more than a few inches but rather she crouched half behind it. Her voice was as flat and lifeless as if she really had recently stepped out of her grave.

My heart fell into my stomach. "Oh, no. What's happened to Jimmy? Please, what's happened to Jimmy?"

Not as well brought up as I, Sampson simply threw her substantial weight against the door and knocked Aileen out of the way. The steps creaked as Kimmy and Jason arrived, the overweight Kimmy panting as if she'd run the four-minute mile.

Aileen fell backward as if she'd been jerked off her feet. I heard an explosion followed by a scream of pain, and smelled a sharp, pungent burning.

Chapter 46

The Diary of Janet McKenzie. September 1, 1974

She is gone. And taken my heart with her. My Rebecca, the child of my dreams, left on the morning bus for Toronto. She has a place at the University and a room in residence. I can scarcely imagine how wonderful it will be for her. I was barely her age when I was Wife to Bob McKenzie and Mother to Shirley. How exciting it all seemed then, and how limiting it really was.

She was so frightened, getting onto the bus. And trying to look so brave. My heart almost broke right there. Bob drove us, and his old mother came. She's scarcely able to get around now but she wanted to come. I'm glad she did.

Mr. M., of course, has done nothing but rant for months about the waste of education on girls, and the better use he could put my money to.

The only thing spoiling the day was Jim's absence. But he will be out of jail in a few months. Shirley would have come, but Elizabeth is down with a bad cold and Shirl couldn't leave her. She's a good mother, my Shirley, I'll grant her that. But she has barely spoken to Rebecca these past months. They are years apart, of course, sisters in nothing but blood. Jealousy is eating Shirley alive. But what can I do for her? The scholarship takes care of Rebecca's tuition, and I pay for her room and living expenses. Even after three years of that there'll be money left over from Aunt Joan's inheritance. But how

*can I give a married woman like Shirley money? That would be to
imply that her husband can't keep his own family.*

*Mrs. M. is poorly and has been so for quite some time, so she has
been spending more and more time here with us in the little house.
She needs care. Mr. M. can't understand why she isn't leaping out
of her chair to attend to his every whim. And so he stomps down the
hill all mad, looking for someone to fix him a sandwich or make a
cup of coffee. I ignore him but Bob, of course, jumps to attention.*

*There is something demeaning about a man in his fifties fetching
his father a beer or making him tea and toast because he's afraid of
the belt if he doesn't.*

October 29, 1974

*I miss Rebecca dreadfully. This house is so dark and tiny and cramped
without her. But I'm glad she is far away from here. She escaped—her
grandfather tried to crush her in every way he could, but she was
strong. Very strong. Since she began to blossom into womanhood
I've watched her with every breath I could spare. Not that I was
afraid of the boys from town or school. She had too much sense to
throw her life away on them. But I caught her grandfather eyeing
her once, and once was too much for me. And my own son Jim is
far, far too much like the old man for me to trust him an inch with
my daughter; although I will admit that he has never shown her
any more attention than if she were the family cat.*

*I hate so much to say it (when I started this diary didn't I prom-
ise to tell it everything?) but I'm glad my son stays away from here
as much as he does. In jail or drinking his way from one town to
another, it doesn't matter to me. To tell the truth, I delight in the
look on the old man's face when he realizes that his precious 'Little
Jim' is so much like him that the boy thinks of nothing but himself
from one minute to the next.*

Chapter 47

The door opened fully and Kyle Taylor stood there, an ugly black gun held in his meaty right hand. Sampson lay in the doorway, red blood spilling from her side in a rapidly spreading pool. Jason ran toward her, but Kimmy's hand reached out to pull him back. "Stay still," she whispered.

"What the hell are you doing here?" Kyle screamed. The gun swayed back and forth between us. "Get the fuck in here."

"Okay, okay," I said. "But let me look at my dog, please."

"Leave the goddamned dog alone," he screamed. "Get the fuck in here."

Sampson whimpered and looked up at me with one large brown eye.

"Can't leave the dog lying here in the doorway." Despite breathing heavily from the unaccustomed exercise, Kimmy was the voice of calm reason. "Anyone passing will see her right away."

Kyle looked at me, then at Kimmy. The gun shook in his hand and finally pointed at Sampson. "Bring it in." He backed up into the house, his beady, dark eyes and big gun watching us. "Kid, you come here."

My nephew slipped past Sampson, his eyes not leaving her. "Please don't hurt the dog, mister. She's a good dog."

"Shut up."

I lifted Sampson's head while Kimmy shoved the hefty hindquarters. The dog's eyes rolled in her head, and she whimpered in pain as she was half-dragged, half-pushed across the floor. But we got her into the house.

"Shut the fuckin' door."

Kimmy kicked the door closed behind her.

"You go and sit over there."

Kimmy did as she was told but I stood my ground. "You've shot my dog. It looks bad. Let the boy run for the vet. We'll wait right here."

"No one's going anywhere. The kid stays here." Kyle's round face was flushed an unhealthy red, and he was breathing almost as heavily as Kimmy. Sweat poured off his greasy hair and ran down his forehead and cheeks. He lifted one hand—not the gun hand—to wipe away a stream of sweat before it reached his eyes. His pupils looked normal—wide and frightened, reflecting thoughts out of control, but as far as I could tell with my limited knowledge of what a spaced-out druggie looked like, normal. He gave off a rancid odor, like he'd slept in a horse stall for a week. Or perhaps out in the swamp. He twitched with tension and nerves, and he burped, straight into my face. He might not be on drugs, but he was well soaked in beer.

Kimmy whispered to Jason to come and sit with her. The couch squeaked as he climbed up onto her ample lap. Aileen whimpered in fear, and Sampson moaned in pain.

"Okay, whatever you say," I said. "But that dog needs attention. I'll get some bandages and towels."

Kyle raised the gun with great deliberation and pointed it directly at my head. "You don't sit down, lady, you'll be the one needing bandages."

"Rebecca, please. Do as he says," Aileen said, her voice breaking.

Kyle wiped another stream of sweat out of his eyes. The room was cool; he wasn't overheating because of the temperature. The hand holding the gun shook so much it was a good thing that it wasn't motion-activated.

Strange how your mind works sometimes. Rather than worrying about my predicament, I considered that I'd never seen an actual handgun before. Like everyone else in the western world, I'd seen many guns, all shapes and colors and sizes, in the movies or on TV. But up close and in real life, from this angle Kyle's gun looked very different from what I would have expected. Cold and impersonal. Unfeeling and angry at the same time.

"Can I sit with the dog?" I asked.

"No, you can't sit with the dog. What's the matter with you, you stupid bitch? I told you to sit over there. Do it!"

"Please, Aunt Rebecca."

I sat on the couch between Aileen and Kimmy. Jason's head was buried deep in Kimmy's wide bosom. There really wasn't enough room on the couch for four, but none of us minded.

Kyle walked backward to a dining room chair and straddled it, sitting down heavily. He faced us, the gun hand still shaking.

"What seems to be going on here?" I asked, attempting to sound perfectly pleasant and full of common sense. "Are you looking for something, Kyle? It's Kyle, isn't it?"

"Yeah, I'm Kyle."

"He's looking for Jim," Aileen said. "But I told him that he isn't here."

"That's right. Jim isn't here. Why don't you go home and we'll have him call you when he gets back."

"Do you think I'm stupid, lady?"

Yes.

"He could be away for a few days," I said. "We can't sit here all day. Mrs. Michaels here is due back at work. They'll be looking for her, won't they, Kimmy?"

His eyes darted between Kimmy and me. He licked his lips, which were badly chapped. "Well, then they'll have to keep on looking."

We sat in silence for a few minutes. Sampson whimpered and looked questioningly at me, her brown eyes full of pain, wondering what was happening to her and why I wasn't helping her. Then she gave one big sigh and closed her eyes. Kimmy stroked Jason's hair rhythmically and spoke to him in a gentle, soothing voice. Aileen watched Kyle.

"I knew your dad in school. Mrs. Michaels did too," I said, trying to open some sort of a channel of communication. "Did your dad tell you that we dated for a while?"

"Yeah," Kyle sneered. "He said you were hot for it all the time. A real bitch in heat. And now you've come back and actin' all hoity-toity like you're better than us Hope River folks." He looked at me down the barrel of his gun and eyed my casual sweats and muddy socks. And the trace of a bruise still darkening my cheekbone. "You don't look like such a stuck-up rich bitch to me."

No one said anything else for a good bit of time.

But of course, I had to talk again. "My father will be looking for us soon. When he can't find Jason he'll call the police right away." Actually, once Dad realized that both Jason and I were not in the house, he would assume that I'd taken the boy to visit Aileen and go off for his afternoon nap. Calling the police would be the last thing he'd think of doing if he assumed his great-grandson was with me. I could only hope that he wouldn't decide to join us.

"Well if no one makes a sound then the cops will think that no one's here, won't they? And then they'll go away." Kyle pointed the gun at each of us in turn. "And no one will make a sound, will they?"

If someone came to the door, Sampson might well bark. If she could. Her eyes were closed and she lay still, but she was breathing, thank God. It was hard to tell from where I sat, but the flow of blood seemed to have stopped. But stopped or not, there was a lot of it on the floor, and I was terrified for her. How would I be able to cope if I lost her? Tears welled up in my eyes, and I fought to push them away. Time enough to cry when all this was over.

Outside, the rain continued to fall, coming down harder than ever, if that were possible. The windows and doors rattled and the roof shivered. Kyle jerked at every sound. If we were really lucky his heart would simply give out under the strain. Best not to count on that. More likely he would shoot one of us in panic if a window clattered behind our heads.

"You." Kyle waved the gun at Aileen. "Get me a beer."

"What?"

"You heard me, lady, get me a beer."

Aileen gripped my hand once, released it and stood up.

"And no funny stuff, like running out the door for help. Remember that I have your friends here. Pass me that phone, I'll listen in, make sure you aren't calling the cops from the kitchen."

Aileen handed him the cordless phone and walked into the kitchen. Until she stood behind him, her eyes never left Kyle Taylor's face.

"Help me out here, Kyle," I said, trying to be conversational. "I don't understand what you want with us. Jimmy isn't here and we can't sit here until he comes back. He sometimes goes off for days at a time, doesn't tell anyone. Heads to Toronto or Buffalo looking for some fun."

Aileen handed Kyle a can of beer, making sure that her fingers didn't come any closer to his than was necessary. He exchanged the handset for the drink, and she replaced the phone in the cradle. He tossed most of the beer back in one swallow and wiped his mouth with the back of his gun hand. Too bad he didn't accidentally shoot himself in the head.

"So what about it?" I said. "Suppose Jimmy doesn't come back?"

Kyle shook his big, ugly, stupid head. He had stopped sweating and the shakes were under a degree of control. If he had been calmer I would have been much less worried. He was like a huge, fat bomb with a big clock attached, the numbers ticking relentlessly down to 00:00.

"He's not going nowhere," Kyle said. Mentally I corrected the double negative. "My dad told me that he's under police orders not to leave Hope River."

"Does your dad also know who killed Jennifer?" I asked.

He finished the rest of the can, not bothered by my question. Not that I expected he would be. Kyle knew who killed his sister, guaranteed. He wouldn't have gone to these lengths otherwise. The only question was whether he had been alone or if the murder was a family affair. If he'd shown up here all set on avenging his sister's murder he would have told us, in great detail, all about the justice of his noble cause. His silence spoke volumes.

"It was an accident," he said.

Aileen gasped. Kimmy continued to murmur sweet nothings to Jason. The boy was curled up in her lap, but his wide eyes were fixed on me.

"Of course," I said, "I understand. Accidents happen."

"Damn right, they do."

"Everyone will understand. So why don't we call the police and you can tell them all about it. They seem to be quite understanding, don't they?"

"Do you think the cops will believe me, lady?"

"Of course," I purred. "Everyone gets caught up in the heat of the moment."

Kyle nodded.

"People understand that things happen as we might not necessarily want them to." And I might well choke on my own garbage.

Kyle's head dropped forward. I almost had him. "It was an accident," he said, and he began to cry, noisily and messily. The tension in his right hand collapsed and the gun slumped down, to point harmlessly at the floor.

Fear, booze, braggadocio, and, hopefully, a touch of guilt, all combined to turn Kyle Taylor into a bubbling brew of emotion. The time to get to him was now; if he swung back to anger we might all be finished. I stood up and took a step forward, my hand outstretched, not daring to breathe. Deep in my pants' pocket my cell phone rang. The William Tell Overture, a stupid ring that I'd once thought so clever.

Kyle jumped straight out of his chair, as if he heard the army arriving in a fleet of helicopters. "What the fuck is that?" he screamed. The gun came back up, I could see down its tiny black barrel all the way to the gates of hell. I lifted my arms out to my sides, as I had seen them do in so many movies. "Calm down, it's my phone. That's all."

"Give it here." Not totally out of control, he maintained enough sense to keep some distance. "Throw it here, now!"

I did as he asked. The William Tell Overture played on. There isn't a young person in the world who can ignore the siren call of a cell phone. Kyle pressed a button and held the phone to his ear. He kept the gun trained directly on my stomach. The Overture stopped and Kyle grunted once.

"She's busy," he shouted.

Then, after listening for a moment, he screamed, "I said she's busy, bitch!" and threw the phone across the room. It bounced off the wall and the battery casing fell off as it hit the hardwood floor. "Who the fuck was that?" he screamed at me. Sampson shifted on the floor; she moaned and flicked her eyelids.

"I don't know. You didn't let me talk to them." It was probably Jenny, calling to begin the pre-arranged conference call with my boss and the executive team. Something else I'd forgotten today.

"Sit down."

Sampson whimpered. Jason pulled himself out from the depths of Kimmy's comfortable bosom.

"Please, mister," he said, "the dog's hurt. She's scared. Can I sit with her?"

Kyle looked at Sampson. The newspaper reports on his family mentioned that the Taylors had two dogs.

"I guess it won't hurt. You can sit there, but no funny stuff, understand?"

"I have to go to the bathroom. Please, is that okay, mister?"

"Yeah. But come right back. You go anywhere else and I'll shoot the dog."

Kimmy tried to hold him to her, but Jason wriggled out of her arms and off the couch.

The toilet didn't flush and water didn't run and my great-nephew came back in record time, cradling an armful of thick yellow bath towels.

Kyle didn't look at the boy as he slipped back into the room, staying close to the walls. Jason dropped to his knees beside Sampson and gently lifted her big head to tuck a towel under her. He covered her with another towel and folded it around her body. My heart cracked in two. The bright, cheerful yellow towel gulped red liquid with the thirst of the man who had swallowed the sea.

Kyle gestured to Aileen. "You, get me another beer."

Aileen did as she was told. When she returned from the kitchen one hand held a can of beer, the other rested at her hip. Her eyes darted between Kyle and Kimmy and me. Kyle wasn't watching her. She looked into my eyes and pulled her sweater back a fraction. She'd slipped a kitchen knife, one of the fabulously expensive, top-of-the-line, sharp as a sword Henckels, into the waistband of her colorful skirt. The sweater fell back into place, and Aileen walked into Kyle's line of vision to hand him his beer.

"Do you want to tell me how it happened, Kyle?" Kimmy said. It was the first time she'd spoken, except to whisper to Jason, since she sat down.

"How what happened?"

"How the accident happened? How Jennifer died?"

"No."

"You'll feel better if you tell someone, Kyle. Really you will. And I'd like to hear about it."

"She was a whore, a common whore. My dad said so. Hanging around with the likes of Jim McKenzie, wanting to do a man's job."

Kimmy sucked air through her teeth; Aileen lifted a hand to her chest. Jason stroked Samson's head gently, murmuring softly to the big dog, exactly like Kimmy had held and comforted him.

Children copy adults. It's how they learn.

What had Kyle Taylor learned?

"If your dad felt that way why did he let her work for Jim?" Kimmy asked, her voice so calm she might have been asking a question at the church women's group.

"He didn't like it, but Jennifer made a big fuss and said she'd quit school if Dad wouldn't let her learn to be a carpenter, and Mom said it would be all right long as Ry or me was around."

"Sounds like a good plan," Kimmy said. "What went wrong?"

"Ry didn't want to go back this year. It's a fuckin' boring job and hard work too. Can't imagine why Jenny likes it. Stupid girl. Good money, though. But if Ry isn't gonna be there this summer then I don't wanna be hanging around babysitting." Now he sounded like a petulant child, whining because he couldn't have a second piece of chocolate cake or stay up past bedtime. A petulant child Kyle might be, but he was still a petulant child waving a loaded gun in our faces.

"That must have been tough," Kimmy said. "But I don't quite see how she managed to get herself killed."

My hackles bristled at the wording. Jennifer didn't "get herself killed." Her brother killed her, perhaps with the collusion of their father. But I guessed where Kimmy was heading, and I kept my mouth shut and my eyes on the barrel of the gun.

"They had a big fight. Jennifer and Dad. When Ry told him that he wasn't going to work for Jim this year, and I said that I wasn't neither. So Dad said that she would have to quit too, and she said she wasn't going to. She said Jim was a nice man and he was teaching her to be a carpenter. Dad got all mad and said she was acting like a common tramp."

"What did your mother say?"

"Oh, Mom pretty well goes along with whatever Dad says. But this time she stood up for Jennifer. Said she was a good girl and wouldn't get herself into trouble. Dad didn't say nothin', but we all knew that he wouldn't be able to stop her doing what she wanted. Not any more."

Aileen fingered the rich wool of her sweater, feeling the edges of the cold, hard knife stuck into her waistband. I widened my eyes and jerked my head toward Kyle, hoping to send Aileen a signal. I didn't really give a rat's ass why Kyle murdered his sister, and I didn't know why he was here, lying in wait for my brother, who he didn't seem to know had been arrested for the murder. I certainly didn't care how stupid Kyle was, nor did I want to hear the sordid details of his troubled childhood. I wanted to bash him over the head with the fireplace poker while Aileen got him with her lovely sharp knife. I wanted to get my dog to the vet and Jason to his mother.

I looked at Kimmy. She read my face and blinked once. A nod. "But why did she die, Kyle?" she asked, sounding as if she cared.

I stretched and shifted in my seat.

"Dad said she was no better than a whore."

"And I'm sure she wasn't," Kimmy said, her voice oozing with sympathy.

"But she wouldn't let me do her."

Kimmy sucked in a lungful of air. "Oh, God," she whispered and the pretence of sympathetic listener cracked.

I stood up and walked with great care toward Jason and Sampson. Toward the big stone fireplace.

Kyle didn't appear to see me move. His eyes were fixed on the image locked inside his own head. "She laughed at me, the bitch. So I shut her up, good."

Kimmy sobbed and buried her face in her hands. The spell was broken. Kyle's head jerked back and he saw me, creeping across the room. But he was too late; I wasn't going to stop now.

Chapter 48

Outside a car pulled up with a loud squeal of tires on wet gravel and brakes applied at the last minute. I instinctively glanced toward the window, although with the curtains pulled shut there was nothing to see. Kyle leapt off his chair, grabbed my arm and threw me off balance. "Where the hell are you going, bitch? You sit back down. Now."

A rap at the door. Loud, decisive. Kyle turned the gun on Jason. But his empty eyes were fixed on me.

"Police, Mrs. McKenzie."

Silence. Sampson was too far out of it even to whimper. But still her chest rose and fell under the red-soaked yellow towel.

"Police, Mrs. McKenzie. We'd like to talk to you for a moment, please."

Kyle pointed at me. *Get rid of them,* his lips moved.

The police knocked again. "We're looking for Rebecca McKenzie. Her father said she was here."

I opened the door. Constable Rosemary Rigoloni stood in the doorway, Dave LeBlanc behind her and slightly to one side. The rain fell in a steady torrent. Visibility was so limited, the edges of their patrol car blurred into the rain and mist. The lake and road had disappeared completely.

"Good afternoon, Ms. McKenzie."

"Here I am," I said, rolling my eyes like a mad woman at an orgy and drawing the edge of my hand across my throat. "What's up?" I pointed to my chest, tucked three fingers into my palm, held my index finger out straight, and made the hand-jerking movement with thumb held perpendicular that everyone knows as imitating the firing of a gun. Could Kyle possibly be so stupid he wouldn't expect that I would try to warn them?

Rigoloni stiffened, every muscle in her body coming to attention. Her hand went to her gun belt.

I shook my head. "I'm here with my nephew Jason, Aileen and Kimmy Wright, I mean Michaels." I made the shooting gun gesture once again, this time pointing at Rigoloni. "We're sitting in the living room having a nice chat."

"Just checking, Ms. McKenzie. Glad everything's fine."

Behind me Kyle hissed, telling me to hurry up.

"Have a nice afternoon. Please give the Taylor family my regards."

Rigoloni's eyebrows twitched at that and a question creased her forehead. With her face full on me, I closed my eyes and shut the door.

We listened to the heavy tread of police boots tromping down the steps, LeBlanc's murmured question and Rigoloni's light laughter. The engine roared to life and their car pulled away.

"Well done," Kyle said. "You get to live a bit longer."

Aileen fingered the buttons of her sweater and Kimmy moaned. I returned to my seat.

"Shit," Kyle exploded. "I have to go to the can." He looked at us, three middle-aged women sitting in a line on the living room couch and one little boy comforting a gravely wounded dog. "Kid, come here."

Jason hesitated.

"I said come here." Kyle crossed the room in two steps and jerked the boy to his feet. Sampson's head hit the floor with a thud as the support of Jason's arm was pulled out from underneath it. The dog groaned and her eyes flicked open. Kyle held the gun to Jason's temple. "I'm gonna have a leak. One of you bitches so much as breathes too heavy and I'll plug the kid. Understand?"

"We understand," Aileen said.

Kyle stood in front of the fireplace, unzipped his pants and pulled his penis out. The gun remained firmly planted against Jason's head. The scene was so ridiculous that I almost laughed. But if I did, Kyle would shoot Jason.

Never laugh at the penis of a man who is threatening you with a gun.

If I live through this I will publish that bit of wisdom.

Had Rigoloni understood my wild gestures? Was I too confident about my own ability to communicate without words? Why did she laugh as they walked away? Was she laughing at me?

Sampson heard it first. Her ears twitched and she tried to lift her head, but the effort was too much and with a grunt she collapsed back onto the towel. Soon we could all hear it—tires crunching on gravel, doors slamming, men scurrying for cover, a whispered shout.

The cavalry.

Kyle ran to the window and ripped the curtains to one side. "Fuck it," he screamed. Once again he jerked Jason up off the floor. "Get rid of them, kid."

Jason yelped and Sampson growled, as much of a growl as she could manage.

"You can't get rid of them, Kyle," I said. "They obviously know something's happening here."

He wrapped his forearm across Jason's chest and lifted so that the boy's toes weren't touching the ground. "What did you say to them, you bitch?"

"Me? I didn't say anything. You didn't hear me say anything, did you? They must have had someone creeping around the back while we were talking at the door. They're so sneaky."

Jason's eyes were wide with terror. His fingers, small, chubby, and streaked with my dog's red blood, scratched at the muscular arm squeezing his chest. His oversized running shoes waved in the air, seeking solid ground.

"Let the boy down, Kyle," Kimmy said. "You're hurting him."

Kyle loosened his hold and Jason's feet reached the floor. He slipped out of Kyle's grip, took a deep breath and returned to Sampson's side.

The phone on the table beside Kimmy rang. Wide-eyed she passed it to me.

"Rebecca McKenzie speaking."

"Ms. McKenzie, this is Inspector Eriksson. Are you in some danger there?"

"Yes."

Kyle ripped the phone out of my hand. "Who the hell are you?" he growled into the receiver. Kyle listened for a moment and then slammed the phone down.

It rang again.

He picked it up.

"I want Jim McKenzie here," he said. "You find him and tell him I have his wife and sister and I'll kill the loud-mouthed sister in half an hour, if he isn't outside."

A tinny echo as Eriksson shouted into the phone. Kyle slammed his end down.

"Hear that?" he said, waving the barrel of his gun at me. "Time to get this show on the road."

"That wasn't much of a threat," I said. "Jimmy McKenzie wouldn't cross the street to pick me out of the gutter if I had anything less than a hundred dollar bill lying underneath me. You must have heard what they say about us around here, Kyle. Why do you think I haven't set foot in this town in more years than you've been alive?"

He had enough sense to look confused. No doubt he had heard all about my family history. From the sound of things, his dad, the bastard, would have been happy to educate him.

"Then I'll kill her, the wife, next."

"You're running low on hostages. The cops will be in here at the sound of a shot. You don't think the police in this town care much what happens to the McKenzie family, do you? Probably be glad to get rid of us all."

"Aunt Rebecca, you're wrong," Jason squealed. "My dad's friend, Mr. LeBlanc, is a police officer. He'll help us."

How could I not smile?

The phone rang again. Kyle knocked it out of the cradle.

"You have to stop and think, Kyle," Kimmy said. She had regained her composure and her voice sounded soft yet strong, with the considerable authority of motherhood behind it. "Of what you want to happen now. The police are outside. I don't know where Jim is; they might not be able to find him. He might have run away." Aileen and I exchanged glances. "You decide what you want to do, Kyle, and I'll help you."

"What about Sampson?" Jason cried. "She's bleeding again. You have to help Sampson."

"What harm can it do?" Kimmy said. "Let the dog go. The phone's still working. Tell them I'll carry her out. And then I'll come back."

I stared at her.

"You won't come back," Kyle said.

"I will. I promise. I'll take her to the bottom of the steps and then I'll come back to the house. I promise. Can I make the call?"

She didn't wait for his reply, but picked up the phone. There was no need to dial. They were listening.

"We have a dog in here," Kimmy said, not bothering to identify herself. "Seriously wounded. I'm bringing her out. She's big so I might have trouble carrying her. Please don't interfere. I'll put her at the bottom of the steps and then come back into the house. You can send one officer to get her. I've given my word on this."

Kyle slammed his hand down onto the cradle.

Kimmy handed me the receiver and crossed the room. "Help me pick her up, Jason," she said. "Sampson seems to trust you."

Sampson was unconscious again. She twitched as the fat woman and the boy struggled to lift her. I moved to help them, but with a growl Kyle told me to remain where I was. Kimmy staggered under the weight. Bright red blood had soaked into the hardwood floor. So much blood. How much could the dog have left inside her? Aileen slipped an arm around my shoulders. Jason held the door open and stepped back. Kimmy staggered under the weight of her burden. I could see what was happening; Kyle'd left the curtains open. The rain had slowed to a steady drizzle, and the mist thinned enough so that we could see cruisers lining the road, black hats and rifle barrels poking up from behind cars. One officer broke away from the rest and moved forward. LeBlanc. He was dressed in a flak jacket and his hand rested on his gun belt. From where I sat I momentarily couldn't see Kimmy for the porch supports.

LeBlanc broke into a run, although his movements were more of a lope. He crossed the lawn like a wolf that has caught the scent of the hunt, his body bent low, his head moving from side to side.

Kimmy slipped back into the house, true to her word. As instructed, Jason slammed the door behind her. She was breathing heavily and gripped a bookcase for support. Her stockings were torn, she'd lost one shoe, and the front of her dress was stained red from the collar to the hem. I looked back outside. LeBlanc staggered under the weight of a bundle wrapped in yellow towels. He reached a patrol car and slipped into the back. The driver waited with the engine running, and they pulled away under full lights and sirens.

I burst into tears. Aileen gathered me into her arms and murmured words of comfort. I sobbed for Sampson as I had cried for Ray. I imagined them reuniting in the afterlife, together, happy, not needing me, and wept buckets of self-pity.

The phone rang. Kyle snatched it up. His hand shook badly and the copious sweating had resumed. To my considerable surprise he had let the dog go, but I wouldn't assume that he would be as compassionate to the humans he held under his thumb.

"Twenty minutes," he said, and hung up. He looked at Aileen. "Get me another beer."

She complied.

"Time to think things through, Kyle." I blew my nose on a scrap of tissue I'd found in my pocket and wiped the tears from my face. I wanted to sound calm and reasonable, although I was sweating as heavily inside as Kyle was on the outside. Until now we had been in more danger of being hit by a wild, frightened shot than a deliberate attempt to wound. Or kill. But the boy was changing. He could see out the big front window as well as the rest of us. With the arrival of the police the game had shifted. They were sure to be coming around the back of the house as well as waiting out front. All of them well-armed and well-trained. Fear, indecision, determination, and sheer pigheadedness traveled across Kyle's wide-open face like a one-man silent performance of all the plays of Shakespeare. He simply didn't know what to do.

"They won't let Jimmy through, you know, even if he does come. The cops like to handle things like this themselves."

A mistake. Rage contorted his ugly face, and Kyle pounded his fist into the wall so hard he smashed through the drywall. Too bad it wasn't solid brick. Aileen froze in the doorway, the can of beer clenched in her hand. He crossed the room in two giant steps, grabbed the drink, and hit Aileen full across the face. She fell to the hardwood floor with a cry.

Kimmy and I half rose, but the gun had already swung back around toward us.

"Sit down," Kyle said.

We sat.

Aileen staggered to her feet, holding her hand to her face. She took it away and looked at her blood-spotted fingers. He'd split her lip.

"I'm in charge here," he screamed. "You understand that, you bitches?" His eyes bulged and saliva dribbled out of the corner of his mouth. Jason scurried across the room heading for Kimmy's wide, comfortable lap. Kyle grabbed him by the collar and almost yanked him off his feet. "You sit back down there on the floor, kid, and don't move again." He shoved Jason with enough force to propel the boy halfway across the room. Jason crumpled onto the floor and began to cry.

"That make you feel like a big strong man?"

Aileen gasped. "No, Rebecca. Don't make him angry."

"Why do you want to speak to Jim McKenzie anyway?" Kimmy asked. I was gaining a new respect for Kimmy with every minute that passed. She was one amazingly strong woman under pressure. Whereas if I didn't keep my mouth under control I might well get us all killed.

"People in town think he killed Jennifer. I planted a handful of her hair in his truck. I've seen on TV that the cops can find most anything these days. Strands of hair, drops of blood, and then they call tell whose it is. So I put some of her hair in the truck."

"That was clever," Kimmy said.

He smiled at her and puffed up his chest. "Yeah. But I guess they ain't as smart here as the cops in the States. Where they look for blood and hair and stuff. So then I thought I'd put this." He dug around in his pocket and pulled out a single mitten. "In the garbage out back. Then I'd call the cops with a fake voice and say that I saw Jim taking out the trash and looking all suspicious like. They were bound to find it."

"Is that one of Jennifer's?"

"Yeah."

Aileen turned to me. "I saw him, out the kitchen window, sneaking around in the shed."

Kyle shook his head. "Fuckin' bitch. You had to interfere."

What a mess. Jimmy was already in jail and Kyle too stupid to realize that even in Hope River the police don't broadcast their every movement to the public. His chances of getting away were now absolutely nil and our chances of being killed were rising like the take at Casino Niagara on the Friday night of a long weekend.

The phone rang. This time we all jumped. Kyle grabbed it and started screaming before Eriksson had a chance to so much as draw breath.

He was making wild demands, a helicopter, a flight to Cuba. Money. Jim McKenzie.

Unexpectedly he handed the phone to me.

"Hello?"

"Inspector Eriksson here, Ms. McKenzie. Are you people all right?"

"For the time being."

Kyle snatched the phone out of my hands and threw it across the room. "Don't want to talk to her no more, anyway."

"But how will they tell you when your helicopter arrives?" Jason asked, his voice so small Kyle didn't even hear the question.

"The cop said my father's out there," Kyle said. "Do you see my dad?"

I looked. "No."

Kyle sat back down again. He checked his watch.

"Do you see your brother?"

I didn't know what to say.

"Do you see your brother?" A scream.

"No."

"Then it's time. Who wants to go first?" He pointed the gun at each of us in turn. Three terrified middle-aged women huddling together on the couch in a century-old farmhouse.

"No mister, don't," Jason cried out, his sweet little face convulsed with horror. He leapt to his feet and started across the room. Kyle turned his head at the sound, his gun arm followed automatically. Kimmy was closest and with a speed that mocked her considerable bulk, she flew across the room and shoved Jason to the floor.

A shot rang out. The air burned and our ears screamed in protest.

Kimmy's eyes opened wide. She looked down to watch a red stain spreading across her chest, the fresh blood mingling with that of my dog, already drying.

Aileen screamed and pulled the knife out from under her sweater. She charged Kyle like the mad woman she no doubt was at that moment. He was still sitting down, as stunned by the shooting as the rest of us. Aileen leapt on him and the chair fell backward, taking Kyle, Aileen, and the flashing knife with it.

"Run, Jason," I screamed. "Run. Don't look back." The struggling bodies lay between me and the fireplace. No chance to reach the poker. I scooped an ornate iron candelabrum off the side table without a thought. I heard the door opening, feet pounding on the wooden deck, Jason yelling, men shouting. Aileen and Kyle were spread across the floor, a tumble of twisting bodies amid the scraps of the broken chair. Aileen lay across his legs, her knife buried into his fleshy side. Painful but not likely to keep him immobilized. Her fists beat into his face, every blow echoing her relentless screams as she pounded her terror and rage and anger into his ugly mug. But he still clutched the gun, struggling to get his arm out from under Aileen and into firing position.

I lifted my arms high overhead, gathered all the strength of which I was capable, and brought the candelabrum down on his head. Kyle's face was twisted with hate, battered by the force of Aileen's rage, his nose pouring blood, the delicate skin around the right eye already swelling, but he still managed to release a stream of profanities at me. His right arm came free, the gun swung upward. I hit him again. He lay still. I held the candelabrum high overhead, waiting for another movement, convinced it was a trick.

Strong arms pulled Aileen off the limp body; a black uniform crouched beside me. "You can put that down, Ms. McKenzie. We'll take it from here." Rigoloni. I handed her the candelabrum.

My legs wouldn't work. I crawled across the room on my hands and knees. By the time I reached Kimmy the paramedics were there.

"Is she okay?" I whispered.

"We'll get her to the hospital right away, ma'am," a shiny-faced young man told me. His partner crouched over Kimmy, her competent fingers opening a big bag at her side.

"Come, Rebecca. Let them do their work." Rigoloni lifted me to my feet. "Let's get out of their way."

My legs buckled, and the constable supported me. The room was suddenly full, and in all the confusion I couldn't quite make out what was happening. Police officers were piling into the room, some carrying guns and rifles; people shouted code words into radios; paramedics worked hard over Kimmy's still body. They looked so young that I hoped they knew how to do their jobs. Eriksson and Reynolds brushed past us, shouting orders.

Rigoloni led me outside. The rain had stopped and a weak spring sun was trying to come out. I turned my face up to feel the caress of its gentle rays.

"Jason? Where's Jason?"

"He's fine. Look over there, to your right. See, there he is."

I couldn't quite see Jason, but it was easy to figure out where he was. His parents formed a tight circle around him, while Shirley and Al made a second circle around them. Everyone was crying, sobbing uncontrollably.

Jimmy stepped in front of me. Chrissie from Aileen's store gripped his arm so tightly that her fingers were turning white. Without much thought Aileen had invited her assistant to come for lunch. But she arrived late—lucky Chrissie, luckier than Kimmy, who arrived on time for a simple lunch date, the offer extended grudgingly.

"Becky, where's Aileen?" Jimmy's voice brimmed with panic; his gaze darted back and forth. Then, like the sun coming out after a month of Vancouver rain, they cleared, and I looked behind me. Two men were supporting Aileen, half-carrying her out of the house. Streaks of red blood covered her dress; her hair had fallen out of its pins to tumble around her shoulders like an abandoned bird's nest after a winter storm. Jimmy rushed forward and gathered her into his arms. The police stepped back. Chrissie burst into tears.

"Thank God." My father stood beside me. "Thank God. You gave us a few bad minutes there, my girl."

"I'll make sure it doesn't happen again, Dad. Let's find out where they've taken Sampson and then I need to lie down."

"Not quite yet, Ms. McKenzie," Rigoloni said with an apologetic smile. A hostage-taking, charging the culprit, guiding the victims to safety. Yet her hair remained immaculate. Not a strand escaped from the long French braid. "They're waiting for you at the hospital."

"I'm fine, thank you. I need to go and find my dog now."

"The doctors would like to check you out first. You've had quite a shock."

Another smiling young man in a blue paramedic's uniform stepped up and lightly touched my arm. "Come this way please, ma'am."

I pulled back. "No. I want my dog."

"You go to the hospital, Becky," Dad said. "I'll check on Sampson."

"I'll help your father, Rebecca," Chrissie said. "We'll make sure she's looked after. You go along now."

"Okay." It was easier to agree than to argue. I allowed the young man to lead me to an ambulance. I wanted to sit in the front, I wasn't hurt, no need to go in the back. But, as he explained with a shrug of his shoulders, those were the rules. He opened the doors and I started to clamber up.

The atmosphere around me changed, nothing definite, nothing I could put my finger on, but everyone shifted, their attention diverted. We watched as a stretcher was carried out of the farmhouse, a paramedic and a police officer at either end. A body lay on it, perfectly still. The female paramedic walked beside, holding an IV line high. They moved quickly, their movements smooth and efficient, not wasting a second. The stretcher was loaded into the back of another ambulance. The paramedic with the IV clambered in, and the doors slammed shut. The police officer pounded on the side and the ambulance pulled away, lights flashing, sirens blaring. A police car preceded it, cutting a path through the crowds of the hard-working and the merely curious.

"Is that Kimmy?"

"I don't know, ma'am."

"Will she be okay?"

"I don't know, ma'am. They'll tell you more at the hospital."

"I hate it when people call me ma'am."

"Yes ma'am."

Chapter 49

They said that this was the biggest funeral held in Hope River in living memory. People came from all over the district and some a great deal further than that. They packed the tiny church to the rafters and beyond. Outside, there was standing room only on the neatly trimmed emerald green lawn, in the warm spring sunshine, among the blooming crocuses and white and yellow daffodils and the emerging tulips. My family sat close to the front, directly behind the family. All except for me. I had a special place right at the back. Sampson had been invited on the condition that she be taken outside immediately if she presented a problem. She wouldn't. She looked rather odd, shaved all down one hip, exposing the jagged scar that ran across her right haunch to disappear under her belly. Her head was wrapped in a giant plastic cone to stop her from ripping out the stitches. I sat by the aisle and she sat beside me, her soft, warm body a solid, comforting presence against my leg.

Everyone was seated, and the minister stood at the lectern. But before he could open his mouth a murmur started outside and spread up the aisle, like an ice-choked river cracking apart at break-up. Wrapped in heavy black, a remnant of another age, Mrs. Taylor walked down the aisle, her head held high and her son at her side. Ryan gripped his mother's arm, but his own head drooped self-consciously. His suit hung in loose folds on his lean frame; clearly it belonged to someone else. The packed crowd of mourners murmured their approval and shifted in their seats. Two more places were found.

My father sat at the front, his only son and eldest daughter on either side of him and then their spouses, children and grand-children. Jason's shoulders, confined in the funeral suit that had recently seen too much wear, shook with steady sobs. The rip in the trousers had been hastily repaired. His grandmother, my sister, wrapped an arm around him and held him close.

The minister took his place. "Friends," he said, his voice as deep and solemn as his office, and the occasion, warranted. "We are gathered here today to celebrate the life of Kimberly Wright Michaels."

~~~

They served tea in the church hall after the interment. Kimmy's children wandered about the big room, lost and confused, while the entire district pressed sandwiches and tea and heartfelt con-dolences on them. Mrs. Wright, close to the age of my own late mother, sat at the front of the hall, under the basketball net, on an uncomfortable fold-away auditorium chair. She was in a state of such profound shock that it was unlikely she felt the hard seat under her scrawny bottom or tasted the overly sweet tea in her cup. She had made a brief, near heroic, attempt to organize the funeral reception but collapsed under the weight of her grief. The women of the church calmly stepped in, guided Mrs. Wright to one side, and took over.

I ate a tuna sandwich, beautifully prepared on thin, snow-white bread with the crusts cut off, without tasting a thing. Sampson was out in Aileen's car, hopefully napping. She'd been an angel throughout the service, but the presence of food would certainly be her undoing. It had been Kimmy's son, the rebel-lious Clint, who insisted on the dog being allowed to attend the service.

Driven by nothing but curiosity, Clint had gathered on the hill, among the rest of the sensation seekers, with a pair of pow-erful binoculars to watch the goings on down at the big house. He had taken a swallow of beer and tossed a joke to his friends when he saw his mother walk out of the house, covered with blood, stumbling under the weight of the big dog whose life she was in the process of saving. And then, to his unbelieving horror, she went back inside, as she had promised. Clint visited Sampson in the animal hospital every day, and he fought against convention like the grief-maddened thing he was to ensure that the big dog came to his mother's funeral.

"Ms. McKenzie." Inspector Eriksson greeted me. She was dressed in a different, but almost identical suit to the one she wore when we first met: lifeless brown but well cut out of good wool. Perhaps she had them tailored ugly, especially for her.

"Inspector. Nice of you to attend. But don't you people only come to funerals when the murderer has yet to be found? Hoping he will return to the scene of the crime, so to speak?"

"Mrs. Michaels was a lovely woman. I know her mother and am here in my private capacity."

I flushed. "My apologies. That was insensitive of me."

"Don't apologize, please. The more I hear of what went on in that house, the more impressed I am with all of you. And young Jason there…" We stopped talking to watch him rush by, a wicked smile on his face as he chased his squealing cousin Jessica past the refreshment table. His father reached out one hand and collared him. Jessica stuck out her tongue and disappeared into the crowd. "…not least of all."

"I'm glad Mrs. Taylor came. And Ryan with her. It was brave of the both of them."

"It was. You may not have heard, but Mr. Taylor has vacated the matrimonial home. Until the strain of the trial is over. Or so he says publicly."

To no one's surprise Mrs. Taylor and Ryan didn't attend the reception. Kyle was being held without bail, charged with the murders of Jennifer Taylor and Kimberley Michaels. No one had seen Mr. Taylor since the arrest of his son.

"Afternoon, Inspector. Ready to go, Becky?" Jimmy appeared at my side.

"I've probably drunk all the tea and eaten all the tasteless sandwiches I can handle for one day. Nice talking to you, Inspector. Please don't take this the wrong way, but I hope I never see you again."

Eriksson burst into shouts of laughter. She had a deep, rolling laugh that had me grinning along, although my comment wasn't all that funny.

Conversation paused and heads turned toward us. I glanced around, and for the first time I noticed that Jack Jackson was here, standing in a dark corner by himself tossing back the delicate sandwiches and beautiful pastries by the handful, and not watching me. No sign of his buddy Pete.

Jimmy collected Dad and we made our way to the door. Aileen hadn't come. She was resting at home under her doctor's orders, attended by Maggie so that Jimmy could come to the funeral.

I almost made it out the door before being cornered by Norma Fitzgerald "what was." The high-school acquaintance I'd last seen tagging along in Kimmy's wake at my mother's funeral. Norma threw her arms around me and wept copious tears into my shoulder. I managed to disengage myself, murmuring about needing to take my father home to rest. Norma swore that we must keep in touch, sobbing all the while into a shred of tissue so thin it might flutter into the winds at any moment.

I climbed into the back of the car beside Sampson and gathered her onto my lap. The cone made the hug awkward, and she glared at me in reproach. But a rub of the tummy and all was forgiven.

Twilight was falling into what promised to be a lovely night.

"Feel like coming for a stroll down to the lake after dark?" I asked, scratching at Sampson's favorite spot. She waved one leg in contentment. "One last chance to look at the stars in all their glory."

"What, you don't get stars in Vancouver?" Jimmy chuckled as he switched on the engine.

"Sure we do. Lots of them. But they're hidden by the city lights, that's all. We know they're there."

"Nine o'clock late enough?"

"Sounds good to me."

Dad and I piled out of the car, and I helped Sampson jump down.

Jimmy continued on up the road, with a wave and a promise to meet me at the lake at nine.

"I have a few last-minute things to pack up, Dad," I said. "Then I'll join you in a drink, if you like."

"Sounds good." He pulled off his shoes and settled in front of the TV. Sampson curled up at his feet, trying to rest her head despite the invader-from-outer-space getup in which she was trapped. She wasn't well enough to travel, the vet had told me. Flying was exceedingly stressful for dogs at the best of times, and in her condition… She left me to fill in the rest of the sentence. My boss had been wonderful about all the time I'd missed—and now another week tacked on for Kimmy's funeral—but he'd reach the end of his sympathy mighty quick if I told him I had to stay in Ontario a bit longer because my dog wasn't well enough to fly. So Sampson would remain behind with Dad for a month, then I would come back for her. It would be a tough month for us both. Me most of all.

Chapter 50

The Diary of Janet McKenzie. July 19, 1990

Reverend and Mrs. Wyatt invited me for tea today. She's a bit of a stuck-up old cow, but he's a perfect dear.

While Mrs. Wyatt was refreshing the teapot, her husband asked me oh so casually if I had heard of Al Anon. I have heard, of course, about AA—Alcoholics Anonymous. But I didn't know that there is a support group for the families of alcoholics. I took the little card with the phone number out of his hand and slipped it into the pocket of my cardigan as Mrs. Wyatt bustled back into the room with another plate of her perfectly dreadful fruitcake.

October 4, 1990

I have been attending Al Anon for several months now. Somehow, without even asking if I needed help in getting there, Reverend Wyatt arrived at the front door that first night to pick me up. He sits in the back of the hall while I attend the meeting and then drops me back at home. On the Tuesday nights that he can't make it, Mrs. Wyatt has taken to coming to collect me. She sits beside me at the meeting. She doesn't seem like such a cow any more.

Tonight, I had gathered my coat and handbag, and I was sitting in the living room, watching for the lights of their car turning into the road. Bob walked in, his hands in his pockets. "Going out?" he asked. All of a sudden I was feeling so bold. After all these years, what did I have to lose? "I am going to a meeting with Reverend

Wyatt," I said. "A meeting of a group called Al-Anon. Have you heard of them?"

He shook his head.

"They're a support group to help people who are dealing with alcoholism in their family," I said, holding my breath.

Car lights turned into our driveway and flashed once. Mr. Wyatt always comes to the door, but Mrs. Wyatt remains in the car and flicks the lights to tell me she is here.

"I don't have anything much to do tonight," Bob said, "Can I come with you, Janet?"

I held out my hand and my husband lifted me off the sofa.

Chapter 51

I went down to the cellar and checked the seals on the tea chests. All nice and secure. Earlier I had fastened the crates and prepared big labels with my name and address and flight information. Satisfied, I returned to my room, took off my Armani funeral suit and packed it into my suitcase. I slipped on the pair of worn jeans and an old sweater that I planned to wear on the plane. The only things remaining to be packed were my pajamas and toiletry bag. It would be nice to be home, to see the mountains and smell the sea and sleep in my own bed once again. And it would be wonderful to be back at work.

From what I had heard, my secretary, Jenny, was having the time of her young life, dining out all over town on the thrilling story of her quick-witted rescue of her endangered boss. I planned to give her a big hug, a sincere thanks, and then order her back to work.

When she'd called my cell phone to hook me into the conference call and heard the confusing and inappropriate response from Kyle, Jenny immediately called back. That I failed to answer worried her, so she phoned Dad at the house. He'd been napping but recovered consciousness enough to tell her that I was at the big house. Jenny's nerves screamed that something was wrong. She knew that I would never give my cell phone to someone else, nor disconnect it after asking her to call me for something as important as a call from my boss. She made Dad get up from his nap and insisted that he call the police and ask them to drop by. Which, of course, they did.

If Rigoloni and LeBlanc hadn't given me the chance to alert them as to what was going on, I have no doubt that Aileen and I, along with Jason and Sampson, would be resting in the church-yard beside poor Kimmy. Kyle's hysteria had been mounting. Fast. Nothing would have brought it back down.

But what do I know? I'm an investment banker, not a psy-chiatrist. And it was long past time I got back to banking.

Jimmy was sitting on the rocks looking out over the water when I arrived. Sampson found him first, of course, and rushed to his side to offer herself up for a tummy scratch.

"Don't worry about your dog, Becky. Dad will look after her, and Aileen and I'll pop in regularly."

"To check on Dad or Sampson?"

"Both."

He shifted to one side to make a place for me on the rock. The good solid rock of the Pre-Cambrian Canadian Shield. Almost as tough as some of the families living up here in the Near-North. We sat in silence for a long while. It was a clear night with a big, round, full moon. The moon cast a luminous streak of white light to run across the dark lake waters up to our rock. The promised stars were largely invisible under the searchlight strength of the moon. The air lay still and quiet, the wonderful silence broken only by the sounds made by Sampson as she scrambled up the rocks to dig at something rustling in the undergrowth.

"Do you remember the time you went for a swim in April?"

"Oh, yes," Jimmy groaned. "God, that was so awful."

"Awful! It seemed to me that you positively loved it."

"I loved the attention, sure. The adoring crowds and all that crap. But the swim itself? You can't imagine, Becky, how much that water hurt. Like a thousand little knives digging into my skin. At the time I thought it was worth it. I would have done anything for Grandpa's approval. Absolutely anything."

"And now?"

"Now?"

"What would you do now?"

"I'd do anything for my wife, and almost anything for my father. I hated him when we were kids."

Together we looked up at the heavens. In the sky far from the bright moonlight a tiny meteor crossed the horizon and disappeared in a heartbeat.

"Geez, did you see that? A shooting star."

"Lovely."

"I hated Dad. I considered him weak, spineless. Not a *real man*." His voice filled with bitter echoes as his tongue spat out the final two words. "It took a lot of hard years and a bit of hard time. And most of all the proverbial love of a good woman to teach me that a man isn't a man because he can fight all comers, terrify a child, and abuse a frightened woman."

"Don't blame yourself too much. Dad's drinking didn't help any of us respect him."

"Yeah. But I know now that he wouldn't have drunk so much if he had a bit of approval from his own father. And my contempt certainly didn't help his self-respect any."

A slash of yellow headlights broke into our perfect world. Sampson gave one sharp bark and then trotted off to greet the intruder. It was someone she knew.

"What on earth are you two doing sitting down there," Shirley's voice pierced the night. "I wouldn't have even noticed you, if that dog hadn't dashed out of nowhere."

Pebbles scattered and twigs snapped as she clambered down the bank. "I remember that rock. Before we were married, Al and I would sit out here for hours, doing nothing but watching the water and the stars."

We wiggled over and made room.

Shirley picked up a pebble, small, washed smooth, perfectly oval. "Do you know, I haven't stepped foot on this beach since the day I found out I was expecting Jackie. I came down here and threw rocks into the water and wondered what on earth I was going to do. Grandpa found me. He asked if I was waiting for customers and told me to get back up to the house and pretend I was a decent girl. I didn't even know what he meant." She tossed the rock from one hand to the other.

"We were talking about Grandpa," Jimmy said. "How many lives do you imagine he ruined?"

In the moonlight I could see surprise dart across my sister's face. "I thought you liked Grandpa," Shirley said.

"I worshiped the ground he walked on. When I was in jail for the first time, what kept me going was the knowledge that my grandpa would've taken care of any bastard who dared mess with him. So I looked after myself and I survived. That first time and all the others. But it would have been better if I hadn't been in jail in the first place, wouldn't it?"

Shirley and I mumbled our agreement, and then the three of us settled into the silence. In the city it is never silent. There's always something going on in the background, the cacophony of what a neighbor's teenage son calls music, police sirens, cars honking, a party breaking up, or a restaurant shutting down. But here, sitting by the lake in the soft moonlight, the silence was more than the absence of noise. It had a physical presence all its own that I could breathe in deeply and swirl around my tongue like fine brandy.

"What brings you out this late, Shirl?" Jimmy asked.

"Came to say bye to Rebecca. You're off home tomorrow, right?"

"Yup."

"I wanted to make sure that the arrangements are all set with Maggie."

That could easily have been accomplished over the phone. I leaned over and hugged my sister's bony frame. She stiffened slightly but made an effort to relax.

"Jackie told me that you invited Jason to go skiing next winter," she said.

"Jessica and Melissa as well. They're welcome anytime. I can take vacation when I like."

"They're rather a handful, at that age. Need watching every minute."

Time I learned to be an aunt. "They can help me by looking out for each other. We've decided that Dad's coming out in July for a month. It's hard to believe that he's never been on an airplane."

"Neither have I," Shirley said, her voice low, as if it were something to be ashamed of.

"Then you'll have to come with him. Keep Dad company. Flying is a perfectly horrible experience, not in the least bit glamorous or adventurous, but you can endure it for Dad's sake."

"For Dad then." We watched the stars, which were struggling to be visible against the all-powerful glare of the moon. The solitary cry of a loon echoed across the lake. Sampson plopped down at our feet and sighed deeply.

"I've been wondering about one thing," Shirley said after the loon's call died away.

"Yes?"

"It doesn't make me an expert, but I read police novels all the time. Their search dogs are supposed to be good. How come they couldn't find Jennifer's body, but Sampson did?"

"Because she wasn't there when they searched," Jimmy said. "Kyle isn't exactly a rocket scientist; he would have been caught pretty soon. Reading between the lines, and going by something Rosemary Rigoloni told me, Eriksson stepped out of the office for a bit just as the lab report came in. She came back to find the posse heading out to arrest me. They gave her a precis of the lab report and so she came along for the bust. The local cops—no names of course—got a mite excited at the idea of solving the murder all by themselves. I gather Eriksson just about hit the roof when she actually read the lab report: The evidence had obviously been planted. She was in the process of not-quite apologizing to me when they got the call about the hostage taking at the house. Anyway, Kyle originally stashed Jennifer's body somewhere else. Then when the police searched the swamp after Sampson found the scarf, he got the bright idea of planting her nearer to me. So he waited until the cops finished the search and left and then he dumped her."

"Idiot," Shirley mumbled.

"Digging her up again must have been rather unsettling," I said. "To say the least."

"For sure," Jimmy said. "Kyle isn't exactly a hardened criminal. Not yet, anyway. That's still to come."

"The experience probably pushed him over the edge, made him take a chance on doing something so stupid as to march up to your house in broad daylight to plant evidence."

"He just wanted it to be over," Jimmy said, his voice soft in the velvet darkness. "But screw him, he'll get nothing but what he deserves. I keep thinking of poor Jennifer. She was a great kid, full of dreams, full of life." His voice broke. "She reminded me a lot of you, Becky, when you were that age. A single-minded determination to get away from the rotten family that fate had given her. Maybe that's why I liked her so much."

I slipped my arm around his waist, and pulled my brother close.

"Their poor mother." With a heavy groan, Shirley pushed herself off the edge of the rock. "Daughter dead, son responsible, husband run off.

"I'll pop up to the house and say 'night to Dad. Won't see you tomorrow, Rebecca. Have a good flight."

"Thanks. I'll be back in a month for Sampson. And I expect to see you and Dad in July. The two of you on your own if you like or as many of those grandchildren as seems appropriate."

"I've always wanted to see British Columbia. I've heard it's nice. 'Night, Jimmy. 'Night, Rebecca."

"Good night." We listened as she clambered back over the rocks, huffing and puffing the entire way.

"How's Aileen?" I asked.

"Good. Doing good. She's back with her therapist and making progress."

"I'm glad. She fought like a demon, you know. Against Kyle."

The silence stretched on. The rock reached cold probing tentacles into my bottom. A wisp of cloud covered the moon.

"I'd better be going in. Long day tomorrow." I struggled to my feet, trying not to groan as my sister had.

"He was my father, you know."

I sat down with so much force the shock traveled up my spine into the back of my head.

"Who was what?"

"Grandpa. May he rot in hell. He was my biological father."

"How do you know?"

"I note, sister dear, that you don't clutch your hand to your maidenly heart and cry, *What nonsense is this*? No confusion, no misunderstanding. You know more than you've ever said."

"I've never been cursed with a maidenly heart."

"True. But that's no answer."

It was also no answer that he didn't tell me how he knew. But I decided not to press it. "It's late, Jimmy. I have a long day ahead of me. But I have something to give you. Come by tomorrow, after I've left, bring the truck. There are three old-fashioned wooden tea chests in the cellar. Take them home. Open them. Then read the contents."

I stood up again. Sampson pulled herself awake, stretched luxuriously and scratched the hated plastic cone against the rock. Unfortunately, for her, it didn't come off.

"I'll be back in a month, to get Sampson. I've told Aileen that I don't use my chalet in Whistler much; it's empty most of the year. You open those crates, and then, if you want, we'll talk."

I followed my husband's dog across the rocks, over the crumbling lip of the embankment, across the road, over the wild patch of half-cultivated lawn to my father's house. The moon sulked behind its cloud, and the braver and brighter of the stars came out in the western sky, over the lake. Bright, shining stars, the reflection of life long past and of worlds so far away they lay beyond my imagination. Shirley's car was gone and a single naked bulb shone over the doorway.

One light, guiding me home.